Aamina Ahmad was born and raised in London. A graduate of the Iowa Writers' Workshop, she has received a Stegner Fellowship from Stanford University, a Pushcart Prize, and a Rona Jaffe Writers' Award. Her short fiction has appeared in *One Story*, the *Southern Review*, *Ecotone* and elsewhere; she is also the author of a play, *The Dishonoured*. She teaches creative writing at the University of Minnesota.

'Stunning, not only on account of the author's talent, of which there is clearly plenty, but also in its humanity, in how a book this unflinching in its depiction of class and institutional injustice can still feel so tender . . . The fullness of the characters and their intersecting lives make this far more than a murder mystery . . . Ahmad's compassion, her deep care for the psychological and emotional nuances of her characters, never wavers . . . It extends through generations and transformations of place, all the way to a devastating final chapter, fully human, fully engaged with what makes us human'
Omar El Akkad, *New York Times Book Review*

'Extraordinarily accomplished . . . This is a great novel, rich in setting, shocking in its depiction of brute, inexorable power, but unexpectedly sweet in conclusion'
Katherine A. Powers, *Washington Post*

'Ahmad moves across borders and through decades to create a mesmerizing portrayal of crimes and coverups in the walled-off world of Lahore's red-light district. That a novel so epic in scope can remain so intimate at heart is nothing short of astonishing'
Anthony Marra

'Heralds the arrival of a strikingly accomplished and mature talent. Aamina Ahmad has managed to meld fast-paced, intelligent noir with a devastating portrait of the true costs of ambition and desire'
Maaza Mengiste

'A masterpiece. An intricately woven, deeply affecting labyrinth of history, hope, and longing that fulfils its every great ambition. I'm stunned by the gentle grace and spellbinding storytelling of Aamina, a writer I will return to for years to come'
Fatima Farheen Mirza

'A riveting exploration of the dangers of patriarchy, politics and power'
Monocle

'Aamina Ahmad has done the impossible: made her literary debut with an enduring classic. Essential and compelling'
Adam Johnson

'It has everything a reader could ask for: a sizzling, noirlike plot; political intrigue juxtaposed with a rich intergenerational family saga; capacious, conflicted characters, including women who may be marginalized by society but are masters of their own narratives; and sublime sentences. A debut novelist, Ahmad manages this complexity seamlessly. A feat of storytelling not to be missed'
Kirkus

'Dark and compelling, this debut novel is one of secrets, murder and loyalty. It's one that will stay with you'
Ms Magazine

The RETURN of FARAZ ALI

Aamina Ahmad

sceptre

First published in Great Britain in 2022 by Sceptre
An imprint of Hodder & Stoughton
An Hachette UK company

This paperback edition published in 2023

1

Grateful acknowledgment is made for permission to reprint the following:
"The Advisor" by Habib Jalib, used with permission of Tahira Habib Jalib.
English-language translation by Rukhansa Ahmad used by permission.
"Let me lay my life down in your streets" by Faiz Ahmed Faiz. Copyright
© Faiz Foundation Trust. Used by permission of the Faiz Foundation Trust.
English-language translation by Rukhansa Ahmad used by permission.

A CIP catalogue record for this title is available from the British Library

Paperback ISBN 9781529356038
eBook ISBN 9781529356052

Printed and bound in Great Britain by Clays Ltd, Elcograf S.p.A.

Hodder & Stoughton policy is to use papers that are natural, renewable
and recyclable products and made from wood grown in sustainable
forests. The logging and manufacturing processes are expected to conform
to the environmental regulations of the country of origin.

Hodder & Stoughton Ltd
Carmelite House
50 Victoria Embankment
London EC4Y 0DZ

www.sceptrebooks.co.uk

For my husband,

OMAR,

and for

AYESHA,

forever the heart of our family

You were my birth, daughter
And your birth, your daughter will be

SARA SHAGUFTA,
"To Daughter, Sheely"

Prologue

LAHORE, FEBRUARY 1943

It was said, or so he had been told: Fatima, beloved daughter of the Prophet, had not felt the heat of the fire as she stirred a pot of simmering halva with her hand. She didn't feel the burning sugar climbing her arm, darkening to the color of her skin, such was her grief. He didn't know the rest of the story. No one had remembered to tell him what sorrow had made Fatima more powerful than the fire, but he thought of her when his mother held up her hand to stop the men who came for him.

She pushed him through the doorway behind her and called up to his sister, who knew exactly what to do. Rozina pulled him up the steep staircase to the roof; then she let go of his hand to jump across the narrow gap between their roof and their neighbor's. The terraces stretched behind her into the distance. She turned to him: *Jump, jump*, she said. How many times had he watched his sister and her friends hop from roof to roof, till they disappeared? He wasn't sure he could do it, he was only five years old. Rozina made it look so easy but he struggled to keep up with her—she was stronger, faster, always faster than him. *Don't look down, just step across*, she said. She held out her hand. Down below he heard his mother screeching.

A crowd of women had gathered around her. Others leaned over their balconies, they yelled at the men to leave her alone, they called out to God because God sees everything and there had to come a time, his mother always said, that God would give you what you needed, if you just kept asking. Voices rose around him, others fell away: *God hears you, sister. God hears you.*

His mother looked up; she was searching for him. The strangers looked up too. He heard them push open the door below. *Jump, jump!* Rozina said. *Go on, Baba, go on*, a voice called from a terrace somewhere. The terraces, the balconies, were dotted with people now. The women had abandoned their washing, the boys their kites, the girls climbed onto their charpoys for a better view. Some stared, but mostly they shouted, their hands beckoning to him: *Jump, jump, they're coming.* Their voices were sharp in the cold air. Rozina held out her hand: *Faraz! Now, now!* And he thought of the amulets that decorated the whole of the Mohalla, its walls and shops and doorways, delicate, silver hands; Fatima's hand. A hand that feared nothing. Not even fire. *Take it*, Rozina said. And so he did. The boys whistled and the women praised God, their fingers pointing to the sky, as Rozina dragged him from roof to roof, and the men who had come for him could do nothing but watch because the whole of the Mohalla had come out to protect him, and nothing was bigger than the Mohalla.

Six months later, they came back, the same men. And this time his mother invited them in and gave them tea, and then told him to sit with them. The men didn't say much, but when they got up to leave, she told him he had to go with them, that he would be back soon. It didn't seem possible that his amma would lie to him, that she would not want him back, so he let one of the men carry him downstairs to the tonga waiting around the corner. This time, no one came out to watch. An old woman stared at them from a balcony but she said nothing. He smelled smoke and iron in the air, and the musky scent of the man who held him. He waited for his mother and his sister, who had followed them downstairs, to wave good-bye, but they didn't. His mother went back inside the kotha and called for Rozina to follow her. She didn't watch as he disappeared around the corner. He knew then they would not bring him back, just as he knew his amma's sorrow had not made her powerful.

It had not, he realized, made her remarkable in any way at all.

PART ONE

Here is what I said to him
You are God's own heavenly light
You are Wisdom itself and Cognition
They follow you, this entire nation
In your being lives
This country's salvation
You are the rising sun of our new morn
Behind you lurks only the night
The few who venture to speak out
Are troublemakers, one and all!
Pull their tongues right out
Strangle them by their throats

HABIB JALIB, "The Advisor"

One

Faraz stared into the fog, sensing the movement of men, their animals. As the mist shifted and stretched, he glimpsed only fragments: the horns of a bull, the eyes of shawled men on a street corner, the blue flicker of gas cookers. But he heard everything. The whine of the wooden carts, the strike of a match, the snuffling of beasts.

He wasn't sure where he and his men were. They had been led by the officers from Anarkali Police Station through winding streets and now they were somewhere near Mochi Gate, one of the twelve doorways to the walled city, but that was all he knew. The sound of the riot was distant, like the static of radio. The street vendors who'd lingered longer than they should have were nervous now; they dropped their wares as they packed up their things, clipped their animals and their apprentices about the ears, berating them for being too slow. He sensed the nerves of his officers, too, as they lined up next to him. He was jittery himself. This wasn't their beat; he and his men were just reinforcements driven in from Ichra, a place known only for its bazaar crammed with cheap goods, far from the elegance of Mall Road, from Lahore's gardens and the walled city's alleys.

"Closer," he said to the men on either side of him, and so they pressed in, their shoulders touching his. They could not afford to get separated or lost. He felt the men lined up behind him pushing. They were panting; the air, the city, was panting. Or perhaps it was him, perhaps he was panting. He couldn't see much so he tried to still himself to hear better. The trouble-makers couldn't be far; they had gathered just outside Mochi Gate to wait for Bhutto, who was just as impatient for battle with President Ayub as they were, who was, they said, bringing a revolution with him. They didn't know police orders were to stop Bhutto from getting to Lahore, but it didn't matter. Bhutto or no Bhutto, everyone knew there would be trouble. The gardens could only be a few hundred yards away but just now he couldn't hear them, couldn't hear anything anymore. Closer, he thought, and his men pressed in again, though he had not spoken out loud. He was still lis-tening when a minute later, or perhaps just seconds later, a dog trotted out of the fog. It looked around, tongue hanging out in the cool air. It took a few steps one way, then the other, skittish, sensing danger. Thick black letters had been painted on the dog's brown fur: AYUB, they spelled. The officer next to Faraz gasped, incredulous at this smear on the president's good name. A rifle somewhere in the line was cocked, an officer poised to shoot, to obliterate this insult, but before that could happen, the air cleared and there they finally were: the rioters.

He squinted. They were boys—just boys. They waved their arms, they chanted; he saw their mouths, their white teeth in the dim light. They took a step toward the lines of armed police but then stopped, uncertain. Faraz waited, willed the boys to disappear back into the fog. But a moment later the ground shook. The boys barreled toward him, his men. And because he was surprised, he was late with the order to charge, and later he would wonder if he actually said it at all. Someone said it, or he did, or no one did, but their bodies knew what to do, or did what they had to, and they charged; a roar, and he was inside it.

When he brought down the lathi the first time, he hit air, then the ground. The second time he heard a crack. Maybe a shoulder, a skull; bone.

The clink of a tear gas can as it rolled on the ground. A hiss. The smoke caught in his throat, his nostrils, his eyes stung with it. He brought down his lathi again and again. His eyes were closed but streaming, the only sound his breath. When he paused, he realized he was exhausted, as if he had been doing this forever. The line of officers was gone. His men were scattered, some tearing after the boys, others scrambling from them. Plumes of white smoke hung in the air. The street emptied, the noise of the riot became a hum somewhere else—everything slowed—and the thought flickered, like an unexpected memory: What is this for again?

That was when they slammed into him. He fell forward, bodies on top of his. But these boys were light. Their thin arms circled his waist, his chest; they clambered on him like children in play. He shook them off and they landed on their backs. There were two of them. One scrambled to his feet and ran. The other boy lay there, breath gone. His eyes were closed— he was playing dead—but Faraz pulled him up and the boy opened his eyes. Faraz didn't think about how fragile the bones in a face are, how he might feel them with the pads of his fingertips if he pressed hard. He thought instead about how he didn't want to be here, that he must get back to Ichra, to the safety of its empty streets. He yanked the boy closer and brought his fist down on the boy's face, again and again. There was relief in the way the boy's face opened up to him, its contours, its ridges caving in so easily, as if he wanted nothing more than this, as if he were being freed. The boy gasped, heaved, before slumping from Faraz's arms to the ground.

Then, the sound of a cry. Behind him, a girl in a doorway was squatting on the floor, a baby in her arms. She shushed the baby, squeezed him to her chest. Faraz took a step toward her, to tell her to get inside, get back where it was safe, but he couldn't speak. He was all breath. She didn't move. He lifted up the boy and dragged him to the doorway. He sat on the steps and held him. He gestured to the girl to go. She disappeared for a moment but then came back down the stairs with a cloth and handed it to him. He held the rag to the boy's broken face and then leaned down over him, his ear to the boy's mouth, listening for a sound.

Two

It was after midnight when Faraz returned to the station with his men, the van loaded with a handful of rioters whom his men continued to beat in the holding cell. They didn't need to, because the boys were afraid and compliant, but as Inspector Karim, his old station house officer, used to say: *Best to let them get it out of their systems, and, besides, with all the desk work the sisterfuckers need the exercise.* At three a.m., when he felt the boys could take no more, he told his men that was enough and most of them left the station, their bodies still thrumming, to find something to bring them down—a smoke, a fuck, anything. But he didn't leave. He walked the court-yard listening to the boys in the cell whimper and call for their mothers. *Shh,* he thought as he paced, *shh.* He looked down at his hands; it hurt to make a fist.

He lay down on the sagging charpoy in his office, a portrait of President Ayub Khan in his field marshal's dress uniform above him, the line of gleaming medals across his chest almost as dazzling as his smile. Was the president smiling now? Had they done a good enough job of shutting these boys up with their whining about freedom and elections and the price of flour? He thought of unmoving clouds of tear gas, smashed faces, his thuggery—he turned to his side.

He'd just fallen asleep when the phone woke him. He should have ignored it, but that was impossible; as always, its ring induced panic; he might be needed; it could be Mussarat, something might be wrong with the baby, or perhaps someone was looking for him—not for an inspector, but for *him*. Though it was never any of those things.

Still groggy, it took him a moment to recognize Wajid's voice, which was gravelly, as if he, too, had just woken up. "Are you all right?" Wajid asked. Faraz, disoriented, nodded instead of speaking. "Faraz?" Wajid said again.

"Yes, I'm fine. Are you?" It had been at least six months since they had spoken. Wajid had called to say he'd heard that Faraz was now living in Lahore, that he would come to see the baby. Faraz had not expected to hear from him again and he hadn't until now, but truthfully he had been disappointed; the baby was Wajid's first grandchild, and he had hoped it might mean something to him even though really he knew better.

"I was worried you might have been caught up in this mess on the streets last night."

Faraz paused; Wajid had never expressed worry about anything before, least of all about him. "We got back a while ago. Things seem under control out there now," he said. He wished for a moment he'd been hurt, that he might perform the kind of stoicism that would impress Wajid, but instead, to his surprise, he said: "I hurt some boy. I don't know who." Wajid was silent and then he cleared his throat, and Faraz knew he'd said too much, made the old man uncomfortable; he was pleased. "I left to get him help. He was gone by the time I came back."

"Most likely dusted himself off and went home, lesson learned."

"I don't know. He was in bad shape."

"Well. Needs must. I'm sure you were just doing your duty. That's all anyone can ask of you," Wajid said. Faraz was shamed, knowing that this was exactly what he wanted to hear, that he wanted absolution of some kind, that too from Wajid. "I mean, really, these boys are asking for it when you think about it." Faraz felt a loathing then for both Wajid and himself.

Yesterday in Rawalpindi, police had killed a young man at a student rally. The students had gathered to hear Bhutto speak, and police orders had been to make sure that Bhutto with his *roti, kapra, aur makaan* nonsense should not speak. No one was *supposed* to get killed, but when the boy was shot, Faraz's bosses had said the same thing: *He asked for it.* Faraz stretched his fingers wide; had the boy he'd beaten last night asked for it? Yes, he had. Wajid had said so, and so would everyone else.

"The thing is," Wajid said, "I'm actually calling because I need help with something. I hate to ask when I know Bhutto Saab is intent on dragging you all into his circus act."

"That's fine," Faraz said. He wanted to sound poised because his father had never asked him for anything before.

"The superintendent from City Division is going to call you shortly. He'll tell you you've been posted to Tibbi Station in the walled city."

"The walled city?"

The old man was silent again. "Yes, I'm afraid so. Shahi Mohalla." A pause.

"I don't understand," Faraz said.

"Something's happened. And I need some help, I need someone I can trust."

Faraz leaned back. Wajid was trusting *him* with something.

"You're the last person I would send there, but I . . . I think you're the only person I can rely on . . . in this situation." Faraz could hardly imagine the kind of crisis in which Wajid would trust him above any of his many other lackeys and connections. "I know you're smart enough not to go wandering into . . . matters from the past. I mean, *your* people are all gone from there, I think. But we don't want your connection to the Mohalla announced. It'll be all over town if anyone gets hold of it." He waited. "That wouldn't be good for anyone, would it?"

A breeze, and the stack of papers on Faraz's desk fluttered, awakened. "What is it you need?"

Wajid sighed, as if exasperated by all he had to do. "There was an accident in the Mohalla tonight. All a bit of a mess. And there were some people present, witnesses, who really can't get embroiled in something like this. You understand what I mean?"

"What happened? What kind of accident?"

"I don't know. Some kind of drunken brawl, that's all I know." Wajid sounded irritated.

"Who are these people? These friends of yours?"

"That's irrelevant," Wajid said. Irrelevant meant that they were important, and not only to Wajid. "They have nothing to do with this. They were just in the wrong place at the wrong time. Terribly unlucky. When you get there, you should find the officers at Tibbi amenable to your instructions. But I need to be sure that they'll clean this up properly. No records, no paperwork. Official channels are not open on this."

"So the local officers know, but no one upstairs?"

"I believe not. And I'd like to make sure it's kept under wraps, so I need someone in charge whom I trust." Trust. There it was again. "You've seen the mess on the streets. We don't want to add to the drama by giving the newspapers a story that might inflame people."

Faraz thought of the boys on the street; what kind of accident and whose involvement would inflame them further?

"It's a plum job too, Tibbi, lots of opportunities there," Wajid said, sweetening the request, blurring the lines of who was really doing a favor for whom. "Faraz?" Wajid sounded subdued, almost anxious—the very idea of that impossible—as he waited for a response. "I wouldn't ever send you there if I had a choice . . . and I wouldn't ask, but . . ." A silence that said, But given everything I've done for you, it's the least you could do. "Well? Can you take care of it?" But it wasn't really a request.

A cleanup wasn't difficult; Faraz had followed orders like this before, given them when he had to. He looked up, his eyes coming to rest where the corner of the wall met the ceiling, holding it up, pinning it into place.

Three

The superintendent of police, City Division, didn't sound tired when he called an hour later. He would have been awakened if they'd lost an officer, but no one would have bothered him about the injured protesters. "Good news," the SP said, sounding less than pleased, before announcing that Faraz was being posted to Tibbi Station, in the walled city, as the new station house officer, effective immediately. "They're sending a man for you. Be ready," he said.

It was an act of insubordination to ask why, and pointless, given that Faraz knew, but he asked anyway. The SP masked what sounded like uncertainty with irritation. Are you complaining? What had Wajid said? *Official channels are not open on this.* The chief secretary had called the SP with the order in the middle of the night, with little explanation. Who knew what he'd had to do to reassign the existing SHO. But no one was about to question the most senior bureaucrat in the province; Wajid could do as he pleased. Never mind that the assignment could only make Faraz look suspect, given that jobs at Tibbi Station were known to go to those who paid hefty fees or boasted powerful connections. "It's quite a piece of luck, this falling right into your lap like this," the SP said. His voice carried a current of resentment at Faraz's good fortune, which he had not been the one to bestow; how had such a nobody managed to lobby the chief secretary for this job? Who *was* he?

"Sir," Faraz said.

A boy pounded against the cell door. "I'm dying," he cried.

Faraz wanted to say, I'm not ready, I can't, the things he didn't dare say to Wajid. Perhaps he could say, What about my men here? But the SP wouldn't care, and he himself wasn't supposed to, and he knew his men didn't. So he thanked the SP for this unexpected opportunity and promised not to let him down.

He stepped out of the station into the white of the morning sky. He'd only been in Ichra six months, policing traveling peddlers and vagrants. But he'd found the post—which was dull and quiet—soothing. He checked his watch; it was too early to call Mussarat to tell her the news. Although she often pleaded ignorance of such things, she might have an inkling of what it meant; she would know that Tibbi Station's officers were responsible for policing Shahi Mohalla, the city's red-light district, and she would swallow her distaste at the thought. What she might not know was that the kind of wealth generated from taking bribes from the pimps and whores in Shahi Mohalla could set up an officer for life. She wouldn't know that Tibbi Station divided officers—those desperate for a job there from those who recoiled at the thought because they valued their reputations, their honor. And what kind of honor was there in squeezing old whores and their punters for every paisa you could get? What kind of officer was *he*? Faraz wouldn't have chosen Tibbi, but not because his honor mattered. He knew he had none.

The reason to refuse a position in Tibbi was—how had Wajid put it?— because of *matters from the past*. Wajid's turn of phrase—so elegant, so evasive. That was, of course, why Faraz had never vied for a chance to go back to Shahi Mohalla: because of these *matters*, and because Wajid had spent a lifetime telling him never to return. He hadn't even wanted Faraz to take the posting in Ichra when it came through six months ago. Rawalpindi, he'd said. Such a lovely city for a young family. Why not Rawalpindi? I could arrange that. Mussarat wants to be closer to her parents, Faraz told him firmly. I need to be in Lahore. Of course, of course, as you wish, Wajid had said.

And now Wajid, who had the power to have him posted anywhere, was sending him to Tibbi Station, despite everything he had repeated to Faraz over a lifetime: Wajid had rescued him, a Kanjar from Shahi Mohalla, from the curse of a grim ancestry and an even grimmer future. Kanjari women were born to entertain men, and Kanjar men, if they did anything at all, did the selling. It had always been that way. And it would have been the same for Faraz were it not for Wajid. Of course he had been brought up by Wajid's poorer relatives, because he wasn't respectable enough to be seen with his powerful father. But he had been saved, nevertheless. He knew he was supposed to be grateful, and he *had* been grateful for the mild interest Wajid took in him as a boy—he had felt that he belonged to *someone*—until Wajid had his own family, his real children. Wajid's visits dwindled then, and though he was still generous with money, favors, opportunities, his distaste when they spoke was palpable. Look at you now, would anyone believe it, he liked to say, as if he could hardly believe what he had made of this Kanjar boy. And then he would warn: Imagine if people knew; imagine if Mussarat ever found out. Do you think a woman with any kind of reputation would stay with a man she discovered was a Kanjar? You would lose everything, all of this, he said, by which he meant the life he had given Faraz.

But the truth was, since the arrival of his daughter, Faraz had thought constantly of going back. Nazia was of him now; who else was? He longed for the family he scarcely remembered, his mother and sister, to know Nazia, who ought to be known, and to understand the legacy—however poor—he'd given her. But he'd remained suspended in Ichra, held back by Wajid's warnings and by other fears he could not name.

He went to collect his things from his desk, bare except for a pile of paperwork and a small Pakistani desk flag. Although he'd been at the station six months, he had almost nothing there to take with him except for a binder in which he'd stored a few photographs of his daughter, a slim volume of Faiz's verse, and maps of the cities in which he'd served. Mussarat had not called the station to see if he had gotten caught up in the night's events, or even to check whether he had returned. Of course she hadn't. He was too tired to feel dismay. He waited awhile and then phoned her. She dutifully echoed what he had told her: what a good opportunity this would be for them. It was, as always, an excellent and sincere performance. He was relieved when she put the handset up to the baby. He heard nothing, not his daughter's breath, not her babbling, but he felt her somehow in the silence, in the huge, empty opening between his ribs, when he said softly into the phone: "Nazia, hello, meri jaan, hello, meri jaan."

⊰

LATER, HE WASHED HIS HANDS, pressing the cuts on his swollen knuckles for as long as he could stand the pain, and then he went to the holding cell. The station was a shack in the middle of nowhere, manned by just a few of them. A constable dozing in a chair outside the holding cell woke, stood up, said, "Sir," apologetically. When Faraz told him to let the boys out, he squinted uncertainly—the orders from on high were that they were supposed to charge as many of the hooligans as possible—but then he obeyed, as Faraz knew he would; an order was an order. Together they opened the door, banging on the cage, telling the boys to get up, get out. Faraz watched the young men drift out of the station in a huddle, then they stopped and looked back at him as one. Perhaps they would always do everything together now, as they had last night.

"Where are we?" one of them asked him.

"Far from where we found you," Faraz said.

"How do we get home?" one of them said. The boy looked dazed, and Faraz wondered if he looked the same.

Four

Rozina had angled the crystal ashtrays several times, plumped the embroidered cushions on the sofa, and now stopped to rearrange her collection of glass animals, delicately perched on lace doilies on the sideboard; every adjustment, if repeated just enough, methodically, comforted her. "Try the radio again," she said to Bobby, who was sprawled out on the sofa. He twirled the dial: static, filmi songs, a religious sermon, more static but no news.

"They're not going to cover it," Bobby said. "They're going to pretend nothing's happening. It's what our president does best." She went to sit next to him; he reeked of cigarettes and stale cologne. She inhaled; this also soothed her. "Smoke?" he said, lighting the cigarette hanging from his lips and passing it to her. He plucked another from behind his ear, hidden by his hair, graying, unkempt. You need a haircut, she thought, but neglected to say so out loud because she was preoccupied with Najam's whereabouts. After the chaos in Rawalpindi last night—the killing of some college boy at Bhutto's rally—everyone knew trouble would come to Lahore too. Students, laborers everywhere were ready to blow; they had been for months. But there was no dissuading Najam from going to receive Bhutto at the station, along with his Pakistan People's Party cronies. He'd spent the last year droning on about the man—Bhutto this, Bhutto that—eyes wistful, lips puckered with longing over that final small o. It was strange to see a man fall in love with another man in this way, but that was the best way she could describe the unexpected change in her lover, from exacting ad man to party idealist.

As boring and pointless as she found Najam's new preoccupation, she'd done her best to show an interest in whatever he now wanted to be, to do, and he'd decided he wanted to change Pakistan. So she'd told him to bring his PPP friends home tonight, and had gone to great efforts to track down some authentic Black Label and those French cigars they liked for them to enjoy as they honed their plan to wrench Pakistan from President Ayub's hands. But no one had come. No one except for Bobby, of course. But Bobby was her friend, not Najam's, as they both liked to remind her.

She considered opening the Black Label and having a decent drink instead of the cheap stuff she'd served herself and Bobby, but the whole effect would be ruined if Najam came in now; it would look as though she had put all this together for herself, when in truth, nothing she did in this house was for herself.

"You think Amma and Mina will be okay?" she said.

"The protest will be around Mochi Gate, your mother and Mina are far from there."

"That girl likes to wander. Amma doesn't keep close enough tabs on her," she said.

"Firdous won't let her out, not tonight," Bobby said. "Your mother knows how to keep her safe."

Rozina tried not to bristle. He was trying to be reassuring, but she didn't like to be reassured when it came to Mina; suffering was easier. "Let's have a drink." She nudged him, but he didn't move. He was staring up at the painting—the oil portrait of her that Najam had commissioned from one of his National College of Arts friends years before (a highly collectible artist now, she'd heard). It was a long, narrow panel and she had loved the drama of its length when she first saw it. She was barely twenty-two when it was painted, and the artist had made her a good fifteen pounds lighter than she was even then, giving her an implausibly small waist and leaner limbs, but what surprised her now when she looked at the picture, drawn at the height of her fame and wealth, was how well he had captured her satisfaction with all that she was. She had been a movie star then, and the painting glowed with it.

Bobby's eyes didn't shift. She fidgeted; what was he seeing? The weight? The matronly squareness of her shape now? She sat up straighter. "That smile," Bobby said. She was pleased for a moment; the symmetry of her features hadn't changed, the dramatic arch of her brows, the flecks of hazel in her green eyes, but he wasn't admiring her. He sounded—exasperated, irritated. There *was* something smug about the figure's expression, and that depressed her too. She seemed so far from that woman now. Though really the painting, like everything else, had been a performance; it wasn't her—it was Heer, "Diamond," a stage name that alluded to the luster of her eyes but also served to remind her what she needed to be: cold, hard like a rock.

"Najam always liked that piece," she said defensively.

"He would," Bobby said. She could hear that he was on the verge of one of his rants, the kind of tirade that made her throat feel tight. "Take this People's Party nonsense." Here it came. "A feudal like Bhutto has suddenly become a man of the people, and Najam Rao, who sells washing powder and Coca-Cola to the masses, is shouting about socialism. As if *they're* going to be the ones that save us from Ayub, from martial law."

"Wanting elections isn't a bad thing."

"We all want that. But what's the difference between Bhutto and the generals? Bhutto was working *for* Ayub five minutes ago. And Najam hasn't suddenly seen the light, either. He's seen an opportunity. They're not thinking about the people; they just want Ayub out so they can have their turn. I know you know it," he said. "Just like you know it isn't you in that painting. Fifteen years I've been coming here, and every time I do, I have to sit here and look up at *her* and wonder, where the hell is Rozina?" He was making her anxious, more anxious than she usually was. "Why would he not want a picture of *you*?"

"Stop it. Stop being such a chutiya." She'd asked him to come because she'd feared that once again Najam would not show, but perhaps being alone was better than being around Bobby in one of his moods, churning with some frustration he wouldn't name.

"A chutiya?" He stood. "You know what, I have to go." He waited, probably for her to plead with him. Instead she took a swig of her drink, held the whiskey in her mouth, planning to savor the burn as it slid down her throat. She might want to beg, but she wouldn't. She turned her back to him as he put on his jacket, her eyes on the collection of tiny glass animals: pink-eyed deer, horses, dogs. "Just because I won't be here to stop you, I'm going to say it now," he said. "Don't call his wife to see where he is."

"I wasn't going to."

"In another hour, you'll want to. Don't."

She looked away, sulkily, disliking how predictable she was. "*I'm* his wife," she said to herself.

He stopped. "What?"

"Sisterfucker," she said. "Is this because he won't hire you for a commercial? Is that what this is?"

He looked at her, his large eyes shiny now. "I don't want to direct some mindless cigarette ad. I'm a filmmaker."

"You *were*," she said, pleased by her cruelty.

"I still am," he said, disappointment in his voice.

Neither of them had worked in years, and no one believed either of them was anything much anymore. Whenever Bobby cycled up on his ancient, beloved bike, the one he'd kept through the good times and refused to be shamed by now that he relied on it, Najam rolled his eyes; *he could at least take a tonga*. But even if Bobby refused to be embarrassed by his reduced circumstances, she knew he struggled to hold on to the idea of what he had once been.

He had only her—his oldest friend in the business—to whom he could still say: *I am an artist.* He turned, eyes down, and she flushed, shamed.

At the door, he stopped. "No one else is going to tell you, but you need to know: I don't know where Najam is tonight. Maybe he got arrested or he's holed up with Bhutto somewhere. But the other nights when he's not here, he's not always at home with Shaheen and the kids, like he says. He's got someone else. Someone new."

She blinked. She folded her arms. She tried her best to slow her breathing. "What? Since when?"

He shrugged. "I just found out. I don't know any more than that."

"You're lying. Who is it?"

"Does it matter?"

"You're angry with him, that's why you're saying this. You're always bad-mouthing him."

"He's an idiot, but I'm not telling you this because I can't stand him, which I can't. I'm telling you because you're my friend and you need to plan. I want you to be able to plan."

She screamed at him then. "You chutiya, you liar!" He held out his hands in a gesture that said calm down. "Get out, get out, sisterfucker," she yelled. When he left, she stood for a time staring at the door, at the walls of the house, as if they might collapse on her, breathing hard, although it felt as if she could not breathe at all, before she began to sob.

⬦

IT WAS FOUR A.M. when she awoke, head banging, her face strangely numb. She'd opened the Black Label after Bobby left, willing it to warm her up, and at first it did. Then it seemed to make the despair she felt infinitely more real, filling the room like a thing she might touch or that would certainly, soon, touch her. *Someone else, someone else.* From the Mohalla? A younger version of her? Or, worse, some woman from outside. Some young party activist? One of the bored, perfumed wives in the colony? It didn't matter, not really. It wasn't as if she felt the loss of Najam himself; she had grown somewhat fond of him over the years despite his bombast, his extravagant sense of his own importance, his belligerence with anyone who didn't recognize it—all the things Bobby despised about him. But what had she done it all for? He'd flattered her, courted her lavishly, and how she'd lapped it up. *You are black with beauty, I could fall into you and die*, he'd said when they met. She was still living in the Mohalla then, an up-and-coming star, making films, dancing privately for VVIPs still, but for sums she had once only dreamed of. When Najam, head of a thriving new ad agency, arrived, flush with cash and contacts, he'd offered her something different. The women in the Mohalla called all the men they entertained their husbands, and some stuck around for a while, but Najam's proposal was real. He couldn't divorce Shaheen, his cousin, but he promised her a home outside the Mohalla, that she would be his wife in all but name. That was why she'd done it: a life outside, no more dancing, on screen or off, a husband of sorts. Wasn't that as respectable an existence as she could have? Moreover, it gave her the chance to make sure Mina's life would be different. Yes, it had meant leaving her, just months old, with Firdous—Najam wasn't about to have some tamash been's child here—and somehow over time Mina had *become* Firdous's. But Rozina had been able to buy them an apartment in the Mohalla, take care of their expenses, and, above all, guarantee that her daughter would never have to work as she had. But *she* still lived in Najam's house, as his guest. She could take it all with her, each small item she'd collected—the coasters, the ornaments—but if she had to return to the Mohalla after all these years, a kanjari still, and an aging one without work at that, what did she really have?

The phone rang, she didn't want to answer it. "Who is it?" she said.

"It's me, jaaneman," Najam said. He puffed, excited, as if he'd been running. "I know it's late but I thought you'd be worried. It was madness out there tonight, the city was in flames."

It was a struggle to speak. Come on, Rozina, she told herself, come on. "Are you okay? Are you safe?" she said, sounding as concerned as she could.

"Oh, jaaneman, there's a revolution happening. Everything's changing," he said.

She wanted to say she couldn't care less, the revolution had nothing to do with her, but she fawned, sounded suitably astonished as he spoke. Don't you miss the work? Bobby had asked her when she stopped performing. Don't you want to be on set again? What he meant was: How do you stand this, how do you stand *him*? How did she? I'm still working, Bobby, she said, and this is the role of my life. She hadn't thought at the start that she'd get fifteen years out of Najam; when did that ever happen? But she'd become complacent, hadn't she? Comfortable. She'd believed this was all hers. She should have taken better care of herself, planned for every contingency, put more away. How long did she have till he asked her to leave or had her thrown out so she might be replaced?

She looked up at the painting, not once asking where he was calling from or when he would come home. Instead, she calculated what she could sell, what was in the safe-deposit box at the bank, the jewelry he had given her over the years, its quality, its weight. Bobby was right, the satisfied young woman on the canvas looked nothing like Rozina, not then, not now; that woman hadn't needed a plan, she was so sure everything was going to work out perfectly. Najam chattered on, sounding high, drunk. "After this, nothing will ever be the same," he panted. Sisterfucker.

If she couldn't sell the chutiya painting, she'd burn it.

Five

The driver from Tibbi was a shabby-looking sergeant called George, his gap-toothed smile making him seem even shabbier. Faraz could smell the trace of alcohol on his breath when he got into the car and George leaned toward him and said, "We have to make a stop at the Mohalla first, sir. I'm not sure if they told you? About the woman?"

"What woman?" Faraz said.

George looked sheepish. "The dead one?" he asked hopefully.

"She was in some kind of accident?" Faraz said.

The man tilted his head. "Accident? You might say that, I suppose."

An accident, a *brawl*, Wajid had said. Faraz had assumed someone had gotten a pounding, that they needed scaring off. He'd spent his career doing whatever the higher-ups wanted done; *that's the job, following orders— and what kind of mule of a man can't follow an order?* Inspector Karim used to say, but he felt now the uncomfortable weight of all that he hadn't been told. "What would *you* call it?"

George shrugged apologetically. "I don't know much, sir. I believe the sub-inspector is waiting to brief you at the scene." George was sharp, he realized, because he said no more and put on the radio: news of the planned inauguration of a school by the president's daughter, a resignation from the

Pakistan Cricket Board. Nothing about last night, no mention of riots, arrests. Officially, it had been a slow night.

⚜

THE MALL, CIRCULAR ROAD, still seemed deserted. It wasn't until they got close to the inner city that the streets became crowded with traffic: bullock carts laden with bulging sacks, donkeys braying as their drivers whipped them, a stream of men on bicycles vanishing into the morning fog. "Business as usual," George said as the car crept along behind a crowd of carts and tongas. "You're new to this part of the city, sir? The walled city?" Faraz nodded. "It's always slow heading toward Heera Mandi Chowk, even early," George said.

"It's all right. It's not as if this woman's going anywhere," Faraz said.

"In the Mohalla, sir, anything's possible," George said.

At Tarannum Chowk, by the cinema, a poster of the latest Shabnam-Waheed movie loomed; Waheed's eyes and Shabnam's pink lips just visible in the mist, like a broken face in the sky. When they turned into Heera Mandi Bazaar, he scoured the doorways, the open apartment windows above the stores, searching for something—anything—he might recognize, his body stiffening in anticipation. But the bazaar looked familiar only in that it looked like most others in the city. He tried to temper his disappointment; he'd always known he'd need another way to find his people—his memories, which were vague, fragments at best, wouldn't lead him to them. They passed a line of shops that sold handmade instruments, dholkis, tablas, sitars, and then a stretch of function rooms where audiences came for dance, song, and, Faraz knew, the other things you could buy here. "This is where everything happens," George said, "the heart of Shahi Mohalla." Faraz scoffed. "*This* is the 'Royal Neighborhood,'" he said. George glanced at him. "I know it doesn't look like much, sir, but it has a long history. Some of the artists who work here, their families go back generations, back to the time of the emperors."

"Artists," Faraz said. "You mean kanjaris."

"They prefer to call themselves tawaifs, courtesans, sir."

"What do *you* think they are, George?"

George paused. "I think," he said, smiling cautiously, "they give a lot for whatever it is they get in return, sir." He gestured at the window. "Over in that direction is Tibbi Gali, where the station is. Tibbi is where, let's just say, the working women don't know as much about music and dance as some of the kanjaris here. They sell one thing only."

The buildings on either side of the road, four stories high, cast shadows over the narrow street. An ancient, ornate wooden door gaped, forlorn. The balcony of one house, lined with elegant arches worked into the stone, was shattered in places, its walls thick with grime. A banner hung from one side of the street to the other. On it was a picture of a heavy man, his expression severe, and the words CONGRATULATIONS TO PRESIDENT AYUB AND PAKISTAN ON A DECADE OF DEVELOPMENT! PROUD OF PAKISTAN!

George gestured to a doorway where a constable stood smoking a cigarette. "There, that's it." He parked by a butcher's stall. The mist drifted past the constable and in through the open windows of the building, and Faraz imagined it streaming through the rooms, circling the dead woman. Then, from somewhere, he remembered: a street corner, a pile of bricks. Strings of sehras hanging from a stall, golden and glittering, then a sehra around his neck, tickling his chin. His sister, Rozina. She was dressing him up as a groom, marrying him to a goat.

"Shall we go, sir?" George asked. "The sub-inspector's already here."

Faraz didn't move; the memory had come so suddenly, so distinctly— not a shadow of a memory like most of them, and he was desperate not to let it evaporate. He had to concentrate to hold it in his mind's eye.

"You're probably tired, sir. We'll be very quick," George said, coming around to open the door for him. "You know what the dead are like." He smiled a little more broadly. "They wait for no one."

"George, did you even offer Inspector saab some breakfast?" A uniformed man pulled himself away from a cluster of men in front of a shuttered stall nearby and sauntered over, adjusting his cap.

"Sub-Inspector?" Faraz said.

"Shauka, sir," he said, as if Faraz ought to have heard of him.

"I expect you didn't get much warning about my arrival." The man shrugged. *Official channels are not open on this*, Wajid had said, but the local police will be *amenable*. "They're up early," Faraz said, nodding at the pimps at the stall.

Shauka grinned. "Hardworking men, sir," he said. "I don't think they've been to bed yet." He jammed his hands into his pockets. "I'm sorry we had to get you here so early, sir. We were all hoping for a little break after last night." Somehow, the sub-inspector had found time to shave. Faintly, on the right side of his face, Faraz could make out a darker patch of skin. A bruise. The work of one of the rioters? "But the kanjaris around here'll get themselves into trouble no matter who's in charge of the government."

"Shall we?" Faraz said.

"Sir." Shauka nodded. He looked up at one of the windows. "Third floor."

The constable moved aside to let Faraz by, and there it was again: a familiarity, in the way he readied himself to duck inside the doorway, in his reach for the wall, already knowing there would be no handrail. He drew back, slowing himself down. He looked around for the others. George was trotting back toward the car, which could not be left unattended here, and the constable was whispering something into Shauka's ear, Shauka's face impassive until he realized Faraz was looking at him. Then he smiled. "Be right with you, sir."

The steps on the dark spiral staircase were so narrow, there was barely enough room for his boot. He climbed slowly, uncertain of his footing in the dark, passing the closed doors of other apartments. From above, someone thrust open a door and it hit the wall with a bang. Light leapt into the stairway.

"Finally you sisterfuckers decided to show up."

Faraz looked up into the light. He could just make out the outline of a woman, her long hair hanging loose around her face.

"Come on, then, Shauka, you sisterfucker, let's see you do it, come and get this cleaned up like you always do." Her voice was shrill, breaking.

A boy, a teenager, came to stand next to her. He leaned forward and looked down into the stairwell at Faraz; he opened his mouth to speak, then froze. "Inside, Amma, inside," he said, pulling the woman's arm back toward the open door.

"Get off me, you bastard."

Faraz hurried up, breathless. She stared at him, her face blotchy, her lip trembling. She looked about to speak, but then she slammed the door shut, leaving him with the boy. He was tall, thin, maybe fifteen years old. His hair was long, a choppy fringe falling into his eyes. He looked as if he hadn't slept, as if he never slept. "Up there," the boy said, gesturing to another flight of stairs.

THERE WAS A GREAT WASH of blood on the wall. It was thick and wide, like a gash you could step into, and, above it, bright splatters radiating outward. An accident, Wajid had said. She must have been standing against the wall when it happened. She was small. She had stumbled to the left before sliding down, leaving a column of blood on the white paint. The spray above it indicated a different wound; more than one shot had been fired. Perhaps more than one person had been injured? White sheets spread across the floor for the girls to dance on were marked with bloody footprints. And there were thick patches of blood on the sheets, which suggested the body had been dragged around or moved at intervals from place to place. The sheets were littered with five-rupee notes. A dholki lay against the far wall, tucked into a corner.

The boy had come up behind him.

"Who are you?" Faraz asked.

The boy mumbled something.

"What?"

"Irfan. I'm . . . her brother." He gestured to a door on the other side of the room.

"Wait here," Faraz said, crossing the room.

Inside was a carved double bed, too big for the room. In the middle lay the body, covered by a blood-soaked sheet. A child's body.

For so long there had been nothing to it, this work, just the spectacle of the scene. In the village where he'd been raised and later returned to work as a rural policeman, bones in dried-up wells, bodies blistered under the sun, had seemed as natural as the bloom on the fields. He'd learned quickly: Everything—everyone—had to die, one way or another. No one—no animal, no man—chose how or when. The whole world was a place of violence, of waste. But the arrival of the baby, the rhythm of Nazia's breath, so precious, had shifted things. Yes, everything had to die, but now he couldn't help but think: Not yet, not yet. He stood over the figure for a moment. You are much too small, he thought. His emotion shamed him, yet there was relief in feeling something, too. He lifted the sheet.

She was about twelve years old, thin, ninety pounds perhaps. The wound in her throat was smooth and deep, a circle the size of his fingertip. A delicate silver chain circled her neck. He lifted the locket in his fingers. It was shaped like a book, and he didn't have to open it to know it was a taveez, and that inside it was probably a pir's prayers written on fragments of paper. Prayers for a long life or perhaps for protection from the evil eye. A second shot had hit her in the chest, leaving a star-shaped stain. She looked as the dead always did to him now, frailer and somehow older than she was. Her makeup had faded, but her cheeks were still dusted with glitter. The film of creamy pink lining her lips was just visible under the rust-colored stains around her mouth and chin. She had spluttered blood, which someone had tried to dab clean. Her skin was smooth, a childlike plumpness to her cheeks. It would tighten and shrink. She was dressed in a bright orange satin outfit, heavily embroidered with gold-colored thread. She looked like the dolls Mussarat bought from the local craft store for the servants' children at Eid—cheap rag dolls dressed like village brides. When he reached down to close her eyes, he felt the stiffness settling in the lids. After all these years, he was still struck by the stillness of death as he noted the flutter of his eyelashes, the rise and fall of his chest. He reached for her arms and turned them over; no marks or wounds. How delicate her wrist was in his fingers. He patted her hand, as if to comfort her. And he did want to comfort her somehow, because she was just a child and she must have been terrified.

Shauka stood in the doorway, holding two cups of tea. He held one out to Faraz. "Sir?" Faraz put the girl's hand gently down by her side. "I don't want anything right now," he said. Shauka put the cup on the floor and took a long slurp from his own.

"What do we know?" Faraz said.

"Sonia Begum. Fifteen. Her family are local."

"Fifteen?"

Shauka shrugged. "That's what I was told."

"Kanjars?"

"Most people around here are, sir."

"Is this where they found her?"

"The family didn't want her left out there. In that mess," Shauka said. "We moved her. The boy helped."

"The family live here?"

"Usually. The apartment below is vacant, so we asked them to wait down there."

"Where were they when this happened?"

"They were calling on friends by Bhati Gate. She was alone here."

"You know him, the boy?" Faraz said.

"I've seen him around, sir. When you've been here in the Mohalla as long as I have—"

"You're from here?"

"Not *from* here, sir." He looked put out. "My people are Gujjar," he said, making a point to distance himself from the Kanjars and their trade. "But I've worked in Tibbi for a while."

"You knew the girl, then, too?"

"Not really, sir," Shauka said, firmly and too quickly, keeping his gaze on Faraz. "The girls don't come out much." He hadn't come farther inside the room to look at the body or studied the apartment with any special interest.

Faraz opened the drawers of the dresser, which were filled with a clutter of old tins, half-used tubes of cream and makeup, and costume jewelry. At the back of one drawer he caught sight of a small red notebook, a picture of a movie star taped to its cover.

"It looks like she was dancing here for someone."

"Practicing, maybe. Family say she was on her own, had no appointments or anything. She hadn't started working yet. The boy says they left her in the evening for a condolence visit. They got back in the early hours. Found her like this."

"Why didn't she go with them?"

"She wasn't feeling well. Headache."

Faraz flicked through the book. There were countless pages filled with her name, Sonia, surrounded by carefully drawn hearts or garlands of flowers. On one page were a few lines, he guessed, from a filmi song, many of the words spelled incorrectly, written in a childish hand, and on another a list of things she wanted to buy: nail polish, English Rose soap, gold high heels, face bleach, and a deck of playing cards. On the upper right-hand corner of each page she had painstakingly drawn a small smiling face. What the hell had Wajid asked him to do?

"Anything in it, sir?" Shauka asked.

"No." Faraz dropped the notebook back in the drawer, feigning indifference, feeling the need to protect it from this man's gaze. He rummaged through the cheap bits of jewelry, picking up a pair of plastic earrings, fake diamonds. He held them up; they looked like tiny fragments of glass in his hand. For a moment you might think they were worth having, worth taking. He pocketed them clumsily, and when he turned, he caught a glimmer of a smile on Shauka's lips. The sub-inspector had seen him. *Good*, he thought, *good*.

"No witnesses, no weapon, family are accounted for. As you can see, sir, there really isn't much to go on here."

Faraz nodded. A few filmi postcards of actresses hung next to a heart-shaped mirror by the dresser: Heer, Tara, Gulshan. "Beauties," Shauka said, nodding at the pictures. "I've met some of them," he said, picking his teeth, "before they were famous." These were the women who'd made it out, the most talented and beautiful. Still paid to dance and gyrate, but in the movies, not here.

Sunlight was coming in through the gaps in the shutters now, falling in strips across the sheets. Shauka retreated into the living room. He found the dholki in the far corner of the room and kicked its head with his boot. He did it again and then again, a racket more than a rhythm; at once the sound of the riot came flooding back to Faraz: blood rushing in his ears, boots on the street. Shauka had stopped, but the banging in Faraz's head went on. The fluttering of sehras, the bleat of a goat. He was shaking. He placed his hand on his service pistol, felt its weight against his waist, thought of its smooth ridges, the cool metal, and willed his body to still itself.

"If you're satisfied with things, should we go ahead and get the place tidied up, sir?" Shauka said. *The local police would be amenable.* The sub-inspector was waiting for Faraz to sign off. He was in the know, but Faraz couldn't believe a man of his rank had been instructed by Wajid. So, how? At whose behest was he working?

"I mean, as you can see, we don't have enough to file an FIR," Shauka said. It was up to the police to file a first information report, and without one, nothing would happen; there would be no investigation. Not filing an FIR was the simplest and most efficient way to make a crime disappear. *This,* Inspector Karim used to say, *is how illiterate men like ourselves write history, and sometimes rewrite it.* When Faraz did not respond, Shauka added tentatively, "Suicide is a possibility." Faraz looked at him. "An unusual pattern of gunshot wounds for suicide." Shauka sighed; he knew it was ridiculous, too. "In that case it could only be . . . a mishap with the gun. An accident."

"We think she *accidentally* shot herself? Twice?" Faraz said, lengthening each word. Perhaps if Shauka had just said: No leads, a confounding mystery, sir. If he had said anything that didn't make the loathsomeness of what they were doing so obvious, Faraz would have kept quiet. Shauka crossed his arms, as if to say, Well, what do we say, then, if not an accident?

The dead girl's brother had edged back into the room. "You're not filing an FIR, sir?" he said, his voice strangled. Shauka turned to glare at him. "Eavesdropping on official police business?" He turned back to Faraz. "The other scenario, sir, is that there may be some family dispute that we don't know about. They say they have alibis, but Irfan here was last to see the girl alive. Maybe the family know more than they're telling." He turned back to the boy. "How do we know that you or your mother don't have anything to do with this?"

The boy's Adam's apple bounced. Faraz had seen this tactic used before when officers didn't want to file an FIR; implicating the victim or their family in the alleged crime was a guaranteed way to make their complaint disappear. But he had never seen it happen like this; a child threatened as another child lay in a room, shot. The boy's mouth hung open. Shauka looked at Faraz, eyebrows raised in an unspoken question: Well, does that scenario work better for you? It didn't. Whatever had to be done to clean this up, Faraz didn't want this boy involved, implicated—they didn't have to make things worse for the family.

Faraz turned to the boy. "You shouldn't even be in here right now."

"Exactly right," Shauka said. "Go on, you heard the inspector." The boy looked from one to the other. "I said, *go on*," Shauka bellowed. His clothes and chappals still splattered with his sister's blood, the boy backed out of the door, as if afraid to turn his back on them.

When he was out of sight, Faraz nodded at Shauka. "I think you're right, Sub-Inspector, not enough to go on right now. No need for an FIR."

Shauka sighed, satisfied. Fifteen minutes and they were done. He could release the body to the family straightaway; a quick burial would be good for everyone, and once the body was gone, they just had to hose the place down.

"It would be a great help if you and the constables made it known to the neighbors what exactly has happened. That whatever they might have heard, there has been no crime, just an accident, and no FIR is being filed. It deters the busybodies from spreading rumors," Faraz said.

Shauka chewed his lip, uncomfortable perhaps about being dispatched from the crime scene to run an errand meant for a lackey. "Send up that constable. I'll leave him with some instructions on how I want this tidied up," Faraz said. Now, that was a job for a lackey. "And I'll talk to the family, explain things to them."

"Sir." Shauka nodded, easier.

When he was gone, Faraz went back and stood in the doorway of the bedroom.

Of course the girl, Sonia, had not been alone. She had been dressed up because she had been dancing here for someone. There had been more than one man, and they had moved her bleeding body around the room. He'd been asked to oversee a simple job, and once it was wrapped up, he could get straight to reaping the vast potential of this new appointment. He could go home, call Wajid, say: It is done. His father would be pleased with him. Finally.

But why was Wajid so interested in protecting these men, whoever they were? And if he didn't do as he'd been told, what would Wajid do? Post him somewhere else? Demote him? Cut him off altogether? He glanced at the bloodied sheets. *This is the job. Just get it done,* he thought as he felt in his pockets for the earrings, turning them over in his hands, their sharp points stabbing the pads of his fingertips.

❖

THE GIRL'S MOTHER WAS SITTING on the terrace of the apartment below the one in which they had found the body. There were two watercoolers on the small terrace, and a broken dresser. She sat on a charpoy, a shawl wrapped around her. Her hair hung loose, as it had when he had seen her on the stairs. She was slight, like the girl. Her makeup was caked in powdery clumps in the lines around her eyes and mouth and there were black smears under her eyes where the kohl had run.

"Get out of here, you chutiya."

"That's the inspector, Amma," her son said from the corner of the terrace, his face strangely stripped, skull-like.

"Did I ask you, sisterfucker, did I?" she said. On the terrace facing them, a group of teenage boys were listening to filmi music on the radio, some dancing, some flying kites. It was still early, but it looked as if they had been drinking; they whooped as a green-and-red kite inched its way up toward a bigger yellow kite from another terrace, calling for the flyer to *take it down, take it down.*

"Didn't you hear me?" said the woman. "I said, get out. Finish and go. I don't want to talk to any of you." Her voice rose to a screech.

"I'm not here to upset you, bibi," Faraz said.

An expression of disgust crossed her face and she mumbled another insult. Then she was silent, and her mouth went slack. Faraz moved closer. The boy turned. He seemed more focused. Here he had someone to protect. She didn't turn to look at Faraz as he sat down next to her but stared blankly into the distance.

"My condolences, bibi."

She said nothing but her eyes welled. "Why are you here, what do you want?"

If he said it out loud, there would be no going back. "I want to help."

She looked furious, as if she were about to spit at him—*liar, liar!*—but she was silent. Sometimes he felt ashamed when he lied. But he wasn't sure he was lying now. "Can you tell me what happened? What did you see?"

"What did I see," she said.

"Amma," the boy said, approaching her.

"You shut up, you bastard," she said to him.

"Does it look like an accident to you?" Faraz said.

"Well, that's what the brilliant police of Tibbi Station say, sisterfucker," she said. The boy folded his arms across his chest, defiant now. "If we file an FIR, you both get brought into the investigation. *You'll* be suspects," Faraz said. "That's worse."

"Why don't you just go?" she said.

"I can still look into it. I could investigate quietly without an FIR." The boy glanced at his mother. She sat back. The boy might be naive enough to want an FIR or even an investigation on the quiet, but she knew better. Even if they were not implicated in the investigation, they put themselves at risk if there was one, if they talked or said anything now.

"Why was she dressed up?" Faraz said. He wanted to hear her say it. Out loud.

"Why do you think?" She looked at Faraz and held his gaze. He swallowed. No respectable woman would hold a man's eye like that. A kanjari could, only a kanjari.

"Don't you look at me like that, you sisterfucker," she said. "What, you think you're so much better than us? My family have been in the Mohalla hundreds of years. We're not from the gutter. We don't sell ourselves around here for nothing." Her voice was breaking.

"Why don't you just tell him," the boy said.

"You shut up, you bastard. This is your fault. You were supposed to look after her."

"Amma," he said.

"Get out of my sight," she said, throwing her bag at him, then her metal paan daan, and then a plastic plate. The boy cowered. "How am I going to feed you now? He brings nothing in ... I'll have to go work in Tibbi like the old whores, sell myself for five rupees a time to feed you, you useless sisterfucker." She picked up a cup to throw, but Faraz held her wrist back; he felt the needlelike point of the narrow bone.

"Get your hands off me," she said, pushing him away. Her pupils were black and wide. She looked terrified, as if she were on the brink of realizing that this was all real, that her child was really gone, that she was not.

The boy crept back to the far side of the terrace. He put his arms down on the balcony and buried his head in them. He was supposed to look after the girl. Had he been there the entire time, seen everything? Did he freeze when he saw the gun? Or was he outside, too afraid to do anything at all? He wouldn't say anything without the woman's consent, that was clear.

"Leave us alone," she said. She sounded tired now.

"Okay," Faraz said, but he didn't move. "She was very pretty," he said. "A very pretty little girl." He meant it. The woman tried to swallow a sob but her face crumpled, her shoulders slumped. "My Sonia was an angel, a gift from God." The girls *were* a gift, their bodies kept everyone, whole families, fed and warm and sheltered.

The boys on the other terrace were shouting. The yellow kite was theirs.

"My mother started me early. But I wanted to wait with her. I paid extra to get her the best dance masters, best singing masters around here. So she could be the best. A director wanted to meet her for the films," she said. "I know girls who've done it, they're famous now. They have big houses, jewelry, servants. They travel on airplanes. Some have cars, they go to Gymkhana club, Faletti's. They eat at tables right next to the tamash been while they sit with their wives and children." Her eyes flickered with something: pleasure. "I thought Sonia could have all that, too, one day. The best life. But the offers for her nath kept coming. I said no so many times."

Faraz felt the inevitability of it all. "In the end you have to say yes. To someone."

She closed her eyes. "Yes."

"Who?"

"Amma, please, tell him," the boy said.

"What difference does it make? Especially when nothing's going to happen to any of them. We get ourselves into more trouble for nothing." She stared at him, daring him to contradict her. And then she was silent, and there was just the sound of the wind scampering across the terraces.

There was a dull pain behind his eyes. She was right. There was no disrupting the order of things. But if everyone stuck together, they could all do well out of it, and the woman and the boy would be safer if they kept their mouths shut. Her expression darkened and she started talking again, her speech confused, incoherent, interspersed with insults directed at the boy, the police, her neighbors—everyone.

He got up and walked to the balcony, where the boy was crouching. Faraz scoured the terraces in the distance, a prickling in his chest, in the palms of his hands; they might be here, too, mightn't they? His mother, his sister, waiting for him still. Could they have found a way out? Like the lucky few who slipped into new lives outside the Mohalla? Or was his mother working in Tibbi for the price of a few rotis, maybe even begging somewhere if the tamash been were no longer willing to pay? He drew back, reining in the agitation, the fear he'd suppressed for so long—that no one was waiting for him at all.

The boys on the opposite terrace were calling out to a transvestite below, harassing her. She yelled back, insulted them. He heard Shauka's voice from the street, scolding the boys. The transvestite made a big show of thanking him and Shauka cackled. A teenager shoved another boy playfully, but the boy, embarrassed, spun around to hit him. A moment later they were wrestling, the other boys trying to pull them apart, the joke curdling. Wajid had always said the Mohalla was an ugly place, one he ought to forget. What could be uglier than this—coercing the family into silence, colluding to erase the truth of a little girl's death, her short life?

The woman lay down on the charpoy, the boy didn't move as the racket on the terrace continued. None of them seemed to notice a kid tugging at a kite the older boys had forgotten, caught between the electrical wires that ran between the houses, desperately trying to turn it loose.

Six

Rozina wore her plainest shalwar kameez, cream-colored, a faint butterfly-like print on the borders of the kameez and the dupatta. The last time she'd worn it, Bobby said that every time she moved, the butterflies seemed to flutter. But even if she'd picked the outfit to minimize attention, she knew she was still too visible. She hadn't worn her burka in years, but wondered if she should today; women in the Mohalla still wore them. Only there was no trace of hers anywhere, so she settled on a cream-colored shawl. Tasteful, mindful of the occasion, and it still matched.

She should have left for the Mohalla by now, but somehow she couldn't bring herself to go. She smoked a cigarette alone on the veranda, grateful that she could have it to herself without Bobby stealing it from her: Just one puff, he liked to say, and then *poufft*, it was gone. She knew she ought to call him to apologize, but she couldn't bear to; that would be admitting that her days here really were numbered, which in one way or another he'd been hinting at for years, hadn't he. Though this morning, incredibly, Najam seemed the least of her problems. She went to light another cigarette. Her hands quivered. She shook them as if she might shake the tremble away, but since her mother's phone call her whole body had been jittering.

"Sonia's dead," Firdous had said, her breath ragged on the crackling line.

Rozina had to think for a moment. She'd been dazed when her mother called; after a night of fitful sleep, her anxiety had wormed its way into dreams of drowning—the same she'd had as a child—where she flailed in the murky waters of the Ravi, lungs filling, gasping. "What? What do you mean?" she'd said to Firdous, feeling in the darkness for the solidity of the bed, the pillows, the nightstand.

"What do *you* mean?" Firdous shrieked. "What don't you understand? She's dead."

What Rozina had meant was, Who is Sonia?

"Mehru's girl," Firdous said, as if she'd heard Rozina's thoughts.

"Oh, God," Rozina said. Poor Mehru. It was terrible news, yet she couldn't help the thought that slipped through: Thank God it wasn't my girl.

"How? What happened?"

"Shot. She was shot."

Rozina brought her hand to her chest, where she felt the jolt of it—shot. Mehru's girl had been shot. Then a flutter of panic. Children died not infrequently in the Mohalla, of typhoid, of malaria, in pointless, avoidable accidents, but not like this. Mehru's girl, Mehru's girl. For a moment she couldn't quite recall the child's face; she thought instead of Mehru's face when they were children: angular, thin, pretty. She closed her eyes. And then she saw the girl. A smile with too many teeth, which Mehru must have told her to cover up, because every time she grinned, she covered her mouth with her long brown fingers.

Never before, in all these years, had Firdous called Rozina and said take your daughter back. Mina had been hers to raise, to love, to protect. But that was what she said now: Take her, please take her. Rozina imagined the pointed displeasure in Najam's eyes if she told him she would be bringing Mina here, but what did that matter now? She didn't care if Najam liked it or not; the real difficulty was telling her mother she wasn't sure how long she could offer them protection outside the Mohalla. Nothing would terrify Firdous more than the thought that Rozina's position with Najam was at risk.

When Salima came out to tidy up the tea things, she said, "I need you to come with me on an errand. In the walled city. Put on your shawl." Salima, whose distracting overbite always made her look as if she were openmouthed in bewilderment, drew her lips down over her teeth in protest, but she didn't have the nerve to say anything. She reappeared, wrapped in a dreary brown shawl that covered her hair entirely; a bid to make it clear that she was not to be confused with the women of the Mohalla, or even a woman like Rozina.

They took a cab as far as Taxali Gate. Rozina put on her dark glasses. She worried they might draw more attention, not less, but it also seemed easier to look at the Mohalla through them, especially today. She breathed deeply; the streets in the Mohalla took you round in circles, landed you in dead ends; to find your way out you had to know where the twelve gates were—twelve gates and a mori, she couldn't forget the mori, a gap, a chink—through which you might escape. She still knew where they all were, even though many—destroyed in fires or riots or by invaders or by time—now existed only as names, invisible doorways that separated the inhabitants of the inner city from the rest of Lahore.

She started toward the Mohalla, memory guiding her through the alleys, Salima trailing her like a child, pulling her shawl over her head. Salima's eyes shifted from the balconies to the stores to the kothas and then to Rozina, scanning the windows for the things she knew went on here, that might be going on right this minute. Every now and then her eye caught something—a dupatta drying on a half-open shutter, children calling to one another from the balconies—and she looked up, her mouth hanging open, as if this were evidence of the degradation she expected.

Abdul Rahim, who usually provided security for the music shop downstairs—a front for an illegal gambling outfit—wasn't outside the doorway to Firdous's kotha. Perhaps he and the local pimps were keeping a low profile until the police left. She looked up. Mina was staring down from the roof in that beady-eyed way of hers. When Rozina raised her hand, Mina stepped back, disappearing. Rozina wondered for a moment whether Mina might come down and bring her inside, but no, the girl would never do that. She pointed Salima toward an alleyway to the side of the building. "Through there is a courtyard. Go and find a seat. I'll come and get you soon." Salima didn't move, her eyes darting around fearfully.

"Go," Rozina hissed. Slowly Salima started walking, glancing back at Rozina, who waved her on impatiently. She sensed the drop in Salima's estimation of her. Tomorrow the girl would resist orders, smirk when asked to clean up. It didn't matter, there were so many more Salimas, just as here there were so many more Rozinas. Tomorrow, the girl would be gone. She'd fire her as soon as they got home.

❧

FIRDOUS PEERED OUT AT ROZINA from the door to her rooms; her cataracts must have worsened. "Amma," Rozina said, bowing her head for her mother's touch, but Firdous had already turned away. Rozina stiffened.

"Thank God you came. I've packed a bag for Mina. I want you to just take her. There are police still around Mehru's, Tasneem told me. Best get her out before they come around here asking questions."

"But what's happened? What does she have to do with this?"

"She's been up to no good."

"What's that supposed to mean?"

"She's got something going with that boy, Sonia's brother. Irfan's his name."

Rozina crossed her arms, tense. How and when in God's name had Mina gotten involved with a boy? She was fifteen. Maybe that wasn't so young; Rozina had started work when she was thirteen. Still, this wasn't supposed to happen, not with some local kanjar. "Like you and that Mirasi boy when you were her age," Firdous said. Rozina was thrown for a moment. She didn't know what her mother meant. But then she saw him: Imran. Her master-ji's assistant. It had been shocking and extraordinary what she had felt for Imran, who had been so beautiful, his features delicate, his long hair like a mane. She'd hardly known him but was sure that without him she'd die. And yet she couldn't remember very much about

43

him now. What she did remember was how she'd felt her body discovering new longings, an ache that was painful, tantalizing. She'd done little more than exchange looks and a few handwritten love notes with him before Firdous put a stop to it by firing her master and giving Rozina a good beating. A judge, a balding man in his fifties, was ready to pay a fortune for her nath, and she couldn't stupidly jeopardize that for some boy in the Mohalla. Imagine if it got out! Firdous was shaking her head in disgust at Mina, just as she had then at Rozina: to sully your name and worth, for nothing! After Imran, Rozina could not remember feeling that excruciating longing again. She eventually learned to perform being in love for the men who came to see her, and then later on screen—it didn't seem worthwhile to really feel it, to feel anything at all.

"I don't know what will happen to him, or even to Mehru."

"How could this have happened? Who brokered the deal?"

"Who do you think?"

"Izzat Raheem?" Rozina said.

"Who else? Everyone's panicking. No one will want to work with Izzat if he's going to get girls killed, and he knows that. And he'll have to protect this big shot he brought in, whoever he was. Izzat will be panicking, too, and you know what he's like in that state." Rozina didn't like to think of Izzat, unpredictable at the best of times, in the midst of a crisis. "Until they've decided how to tie this up, who they want to arrest, I don't think Irfan is safe, which means neither is Mina."

"What about you?"

"I have to stay. I'm not leaving this place."

"Amma."

"What do you mean, 'Amma'? You think I'm some kind of idiot. If I'm gone even a few days, someone will come in and squat here, you know what they're like here."

"I have papers for this place. It's mine. Ours. No one can do that."

"You think papers will stop this lot? They'll come and we'll never get them out."

"We'll lock it up. Pay Abdul Rahim to keep an eye on it."

"He'll be the first to lay claim to it. No. I'm not leaving, just take the girl with you."

Rozina sat down on the bed. There was little point arguing with Firdous, she knew that well enough. It was true, it took little to lose a property here. And then there was her mother's unspoken, irrational hope that the boy—the son lost years ago—might magically appear one day; how could he possibly find her if she left? It startled her now when she was reminded of him, this—brother. He was a wound she'd carried for so long as a child, but then so many other more pressing wounds had taken his place. Like Mina.

Firdous wiped her face with her dupatta. It had only been a few months since Rozina had seen her mother, but Firdous looked more haggard, shrunken. Rozina recoiled a little at the sight of her mother's chipped front teeth, the way her shoulders rolled forward, making her seem hunched and small. Her amma had been a beauty once, famous once, her skills as a dancer legendary. Now look at her. It was after Faraz that the decline set in. They'd had more money than ever, and Firdous hired the Mohalla's best masters for Rozina, even secured her first bit parts. And yet she stopped caring about her craft, about herself entirely. Until Mina was born.

"I don't know if she'll come with me," Rozina said, by which she meant: without you.

"Of course she will." Was that a glimmer of a smile on Firdous's face? Probably. Because she knew Mina would never leave her alone here. Was that why Firdous had called her? So that Rozina would have to beg Mina to come, and then watch Mina choose Firdous? They had fought endlessly over the girl for years. How many times had she, overwhelmed by longing, threatened to bring Mina home with her, ignoring Najam's distaste? Fine, Firdous would say, take her, but then you tell her the truth: tell her she's yours, not mine. Go on, she goaded, go on, tell her, a spitefulness hovering at the corner of her mouth, because she knew Rozina would never do it. The truth is, Firdous said, you want to be a mother without doing the work of a mother. What *is* the work of a mother? Rozina would scream. Preparing her for the life she was born into, Firdous said, as though Rozina were an idiot. She had hated Firdous then. She nursed her bitterness still.

There was a thud as Mina jumped from the balcony of the apartment above onto theirs and stepped inside in that lithe way of hers. "The police are still there. I saw from Tasneem's roof. Tasneem says they've even brought in some new SHO," she panted.

"Isn't she a bit old to be doing that?" Rozina said. "Climbing buildings like a jungli?"

Firdous pursed her lips, sat down on the bed. "You think she listens to me?"

"Such an honor to have you come see us, Rozina," Mina said.

"You speak to your sister properly," Firdous said. Mina looked down; she didn't like to be told off by Firdous. "Sorry, Rozina Baji." She sat down by Firdous and leaned into her, picking up her hand and stroking it; an apology Firdous accepted by patting the girl's hand in turn.

Rozina recalled the affection with which Firdous had once treated her; when Faraz disappeared, so had her amma's touch. She remembered how irritated she had been when Mina clawed at her: Get lost, stop bothering me, you're ruining my face, my clothes, she'd scolded, clicking her tongue, probably making the girl feel as bothersome to her as the heat. She had not expected to feel so bereft when the girl no longer reached for her.

"So, do you want to explain how you've gotten mixed up in this mess? What's been going on with you and this boy? What have you been doing?"

Mina's stare was hard and flat.

"And what's he got to do with this murder?" Rozina said.

"He has nothing to do with it," Mina said, outraged. "He must be . . . I haven't seen him, but Sonia's dead. She's dead." The girl's jagged rage made itself known in the deep creases in her brow, around her mouth, making her look like an old woman. Rozina blinked. She had never found much of herself in the girl's features, apart from the one green eye. The other was brown, and her face, thin and plain, was made strangely asymmetrical by those eyes. This unfamiliar expression seemed another reminder that the girl was not—would never be—hers. "I don't expect you to care," Mina said bitterly. "I don't even know why Amma called you."

"She called me to get you. Your lover has put himself and you in danger."

"He didn't do anything. Something terrible has happened to *them*. I don't know why you're blaming him. Don't you care? Don't you care about Sonia? About Mehru Baji?"

"I'm here, aren't I?" Rozina didn't want to think about Mehru.

"Are you even going to see her?"

Rozina knew she should. If she didn't, and anyone saw her in the Mohalla, she would sully them all. But she had planned to slip away as soon as she had Mina in her grasp. She felt for the woman but she didn't want Mina connected with Mehru or her son now, and in all honesty who wanted to be around that kind of grief?

"You should see Mehru," Firdous said. "It looks bad if you don't."

Rozina sighed. "This is hardly ideal for me," she said to Mina. "But because you've been going around behaving like a randi, we all have to do what we can to help you."

"I don't need your help. And I'm not going anywhere with you."

When Mina glared at her like that, with such hatred, Rozina sometimes wondered if she knew. "You don't have a choice," she said. "And neither do I."

"Amma, tell her to get lost."

"I asked her to come. She's right. You have to go. And that's it. You come back when they've arrested someone. When that's all fixed, it will be easier. Right now, while they're deciding who's to blame, no one's safe. Who knows what Izzat Raheem might do."

"I'm not leaving Irfan."

Firdous spat onto the balcony behind her. "One girl's already dead. Isn't that enough?"

"This wouldn't have happened if you had kept her at school," Rozina said.

"It's not my fault if she won't go, if she wants to wander the Mohalla instead."

"And now she's starting up love affairs with the local losers, quite a kanjari you've turned her into, Amma."

"I'm no kanjari," Mina said pointedly.

"Thanks to me," Rozina said. "And if it weren't for me, *she'd* have you working."

Firdous looked as if she might spit at Rozina now. "There is no shame in our work. The shame you carry is all yours."

"I never hear you turn down the money I send. The money that lets you stay in the Mohalla, live here without having to work for it."

"We don't need anything from you," Mina said.

Firdous looked at Mina nervously. A fight between the girls was one thing, but Rozina knew Firdous wouldn't want money to come into it. Rozina had never questioned her duty to support her mother in her old age, and her daughter, but shouldn't that command some kind of respect? If she lived here, they would know exactly what she had to do to feed them.

"Don't speak like that to your sister," Firdous said. She looked at Rozina apologetically, as if to say, She doesn't understand, but I do.

Rozina bit the inside of her lip as hard as she could. "It's fine, Amma. You seem better off without my help."

Firdous's eyes darted from Rozina to the girl. "Mina," she hissed, "apologize to your sister."

Sister, sister, sister. It was as if she, too, had forgotten, as if by denying her the girl all these years, she could just erase the truth.

Firdous slammed her hand on Mina's back, hard. "I said, apologize."

But Mina wouldn't say anything.

"Fine." Rozina shrugged, but it wasn't fine. She had planned to walk out of here with Mina, and instead she was leaving the girl. Worse, the girl was leaving her. Rozina stood up and took a step toward the door. A real mother would forgive her child, would turn around and let it go, pretend nothing hurtful was ever said, but she couldn't. She had never been able to do that with Mina. She paused at the door, giving the girl another chance, but all she heard was Firdous, now pleading with Mina.

Rozina started down the stairs. She had failed at everything, even at protecting the girl in a moment of crisis. Then she heard footsteps behind her, and she slowed. It was not too late after all. The girl was here, she had come to apologize. But Mina came pounding down the stairs, slamming into her side as she passed her. Tears pricked Rozina's eyes—the humiliation of it all, the pain, the excruciating pain of it: "Haramzadi, bitch," Rozina yelled after her. "She's ruined you. Go on, then, go to your donkey of a yaar. Get him and yourself killed. You brainless kanjari. You deserve it."

Rozina's words made her feel sick as soon as she had said them, but they were gone, trailing Mina. And even after Mina had disappeared into the streets, Rozina stood on the threshold of the kotha, shaking, her words hanging in the air around her like a terrible curse.

Seven

The air had cleared, but even so, when Faraz stepped into the street, the glassy, unlit bulbs of the fairy lights strung along balconies and above doorways underlined the miserliness of the daylight. A dhaba across the road was open now, the cooks preparing for lunchtime: Pans clattered, oil crackled in anticipation; chickens, crammed into cages, squawked as if they understood what was coming.

Shauka stood by the car, waiting for him. "It was getting quite lively up there, sir," he said, nodding at the constables he'd sent upstairs to quiet the boys on the terrace. He didn't ask about the family, what they'd said. "Everyone's assembled at the station, sir. But perhaps you'd like to get some rest first."

"I've been thinking, Sub-Inspector saab, about this accident." He'd had only minutes to come up with some kind of ruse to buy time to investigate, and he wasn't sure what it would sound like until he said it out loud. Shauka squinted at him, already not liking the sound of it. It didn't have to be watertight, but it had to sound reasonable. "As you know from last night, these are difficult times on the street. I'm concerned that if word gets out about this incident, despite our attempts to keep it quiet, things could get complicated."

"Sir?"

"There are no witnesses, the family have an alibi. There's nothing to go on. But *if* anyone asks—and who knows, with everything that's happening out there, in a few months we might end up with new people in charge . . . Bhutto Saab, for example. You don't think his people might take an interest in a case like this?"

Shauka put his hands on his hips. "I'm not sure I understand, sir. Are you wanting to file an FIR?"

Faraz got into the car. George was behind the wheel, finishing a cigarette. "Of course not. But these are volatile times. We need to be prepared to protect our investigation, no matter who we answer to. If we end up with new saabs upstairs, we should be able to say we left no stone unturned. Our processes should look flawless. Yes?" Faraz looked at Shauka intently, hoping to convey that he had a special understanding of the big picture, of what the higher-ups needed. That's why he'd been sent here, after all.

Shauka chewed his lower lip, glanced at George. But George was looking out the window of the driver's side, surveying the posters plastered on the wall.

"So? No FIR, but—"

"Let's get the legal medical officer to take a look at her, do the usual checks, time of death, see if anyone touched her. Just for the paper trail. We can say we covered everything before we determined no FIR was necessary. Keep me up to date, okay?"

Shauka managed a half smile, uncertain but nodding in a way that implied a respect for the higher concerns of Faraz's strategy. He tapped the top of the car and leaned in to talk to George. "Take Inspector saab wherever he wants," he said, and they pulled away.

"Home, sir?" George said. Faraz hesitated. He had had enough of bloodied bodies—more than enough—but he was gripped by an irrational fear that as soon as he left, the Mohalla would disappear, and with it the chance to find *them*. And besides, what was there to go home to? He thought of the small, loveless house where his wife would be sitting by the radio, listening to the hour of ghazals they played at about this time.

"I could take you to the station of, course," George said. "Tibbi is just a few minutes away. But if you'd like to call it a day, it should still be standing tomorrow." He smiled. "God willing."

Faraz nodded; his memories might have faded, but the place hadn't gone anywhere. Now he was back, and he had time to do this properly, carefully. "You're right, George. Home."

⟡

HEERA MANDI BAZAAR was in midmorning swing. They weaved their way amid shoppers and traders pushing carts. Hawkers leaned close to the car, tapping on the window as they held up newspaper cones filled with spicy roasted channa and baskets brimming with freshly baked kulcha; George waved each one away. "When you're settled, sir, we'll bring you back to eat. This place does the best goat testicles in the city, and over there the best siri paye. The girls in the Mohalla recommend it to all their . . . guests. They swear by it."

A cleanup always left a sour taste, but Faraz had grown accustomed to them over the years; he'd had to. Sometimes the higher-ups claimed they were for the greater good; if a landlord's run-in with a tenant farmer turned up as a body in the fields, what good did it really do the other tenants, all of whom were dependent on the landlord, if he was jailed? Their justifications were false, but he understood them: This is the job, find a way to live with it, they meant. He wasn't sure why this one was troubling him so much. Children died all the time. Sometimes they were killed violently; this was not new to him. And yet he knew that the callousness with which they had treated her body, her brother, was because she was less to them than other children: a Kanjari child. And if being a Kanjar was in your blood, then his daughter, born to a Kanjar like him, was also a Kanjari. And if this Kanjari's life didn't matter, then what would Nazia's life matter to anyone? Was that why Wajid hadn't even bothered to tell him what he was being sent to do? Had he wanted Faraz to know how little this Kanjari's death meant to him? He had not doubted that Faraz would help—he'd been certain of the weight of Faraz's loyalty, or his debt. Or perhaps he understood something about Faraz as an officer, as a man, that Faraz himself had not. For that matter, how well did he know Wajid, really? Did he know just what his father might be capable of in certain circumstances? Unthinkable as it was—could Wajid have done this? He'd have heard it in Wajid's voice, wouldn't he? But was that why Faraz's help alone would do? Who else could you ask for help but your blood in such circumstances?

"You know the family? The girl's family?"

"Not well, sir."

"The sub-inspector thinks she was on her own practicing and somehow got herself shot." Faraz paused a moment to allow the preposterousness of Shauka's scenario to sit with them. "An accident." George leaned closer to the steering column but said nothing.

"Do you know who else lives in the building?"

"There's a low-level pimp—a junkie, really—on the ground floor. Khwaja," George said.

"He might have seen something?"

George shrugged. "He's a heavy smoker. He spends half his days outside Shahi Masjid getting high. I wouldn't set that much store by what he might have seen." Faraz couldn't work out if George was telling him the man would make a poor witness, or that they needn't worry about him mouthing off about what he might have seen.

"With no witnesses, we should be able to get everything tied up quickly. They'll be able to bury her soon," Faraz said, looking at his watch. "Then they can be done with it, the family."

"I doubt the family will ever be done with such a thing." George's eyes narrowed, and Faraz followed his gaze. It was the boy, Irfan. He stood at the mouth of an alley so narrow it was only wide enough for one person to walk through. A girl about his age stood by him, her hand on his arm, unconcerned by the impropriety of such a public display. Faraz gestured for

George to stop the car, which he did, although he was still shaking his head, his face a picture of concern as Faraz got out.

The girl was the one to look up at his approach. She stepped forward. "I heard what you said to him," she said defiantly. He was taken aback a moment, a young girl daring to speak to an SHO like that, but her fear was apparent in the way her voice broke, the way she swallowed as she spoke. "What's that, bibi?" he said.

There was something lopsided about her narrow face, one eye brown, one green; the red streaks down her face and blotchy nose made her seem younger than she likely was, despite the hostility of her stance. He felt the urge to crouch down by her and the boy as he might by small children.

"You know he had nothing to do with this. But your men threatened him instead of filing an FIR," she said.

"I can only investigate if I have more information." The girl glanced at Irfan, waiting for him to say something, but he'd gone limp. Faraz turned his attention to him. "There were important men in the room last night. Men you might recognize from the newspapers." Not a question. A question he could deny or choose not to answer. "I know the kinds of men there."

Irfan looked at Faraz. "Everything is going to go on. They'll all just go on. Look." He gestured at the street, the bazaar. It was a marvel, the world's insistence on the irrelevance of your loss. Faraz tensed. It wasn't wise to speak to the boy so long here.

"Where were you last night? When was she alone?"

"They told me to leave, to go downstairs. It had been quiet all night, no problems. I didn't think anything would go wrong after I left."

"How many of them?"

"She seemed fine when I was there. She was quiet. At one point she laughed and I thought, She's okay. It's not as bad as we thought it would be. I didn't think anything like this . . ."

"Of course you didn't. How many men, Irfan?"

"I don't know. Four, maybe five."

"Give me a name."

"Amma's right. I should have stayed upstairs. I don't know what I was—why I did that. I shouldn't have gone down. I just . . . I just didn't want to hear it all."

The girl made a hushing noise. "It's not your fault," she said. He shook his head: No, it is, it is my fault.

"I heard these bangs. I thought it was firecrackers at first, from the riots. Then I ran up to see what was going on and they wouldn't let me back in."

"Who was there? Did you know them? Had you seen any of them before?" Faraz said. The boy was silent now. "What did they look like?"

"Irfan," the girl said, "tell him, just tell him."

"Who was there?" Faraz said. The boy looked at him, his eyes alarmingly bloodshot.

"I didn't recognize any of them. Except for *him*." The boy pointed up.

Faraz, feeling the street watching, stopped himself from following the line of the boy's finger. But he had a good idea he knew which poster Irfan was pointing at, one of many plastered along the walls of the kothas. "That man, that man in the picture was there? Last night?"

The girl's eyes darted the street. "We have to go now," she said. But the boy didn't move. "Come on, Irfan. Please. We need to go now." She pulled at him, but he dragged his feet, immobilized.

"Don't say anything, not to anyone," Faraz said. "To no one from Tibbi Station, either. Talk only to me." The boy didn't move. "She's right. Go now," he said. "Go on, son."

Back inside the car, Faraz dared a glance at the poster. It was the one he'd remembered, for a local councilman, Salim Mushtaq, fat and grave-looking, presiding over a slogan that read: CONGRATULATIONS TO PRESIDENT AYUB AND PAKISTAN! PROUD OF PAKISTAN! George started the car, asked nothing. Faraz exhaled. He would certainly report this back to Shauka; Faraz needed to give the man something. And yet, given how little time he suspected he had—Wajid would be calling, and Shauka, answering to some other authority, would suspect him soon enough—he needed someone's help. He indicated the poster with his chin. "What do you know about him, the man in the picture?"

"Local councillor, does a lot for the people around here. Well liked."

"The boy says that man was one of the men there last night."

George sighed. "I believe he likes to bring guests here. Lives in Gulberg," he said, as if he knew that this would be their next stop.

"Let's go see him."

"To make sure there isn't another accident, sir?"

The man was sharp. "For the paper trail, that's all," Faraz said.

George kept his eyes on the road ahead. "I've been here a long time, sir, longer than Shauka Saab. People around here don't care much for paper trails when they want something done. If they've asked, they expect it to get done." He paused. "And if they don't, sometimes they take things into their own hands."

"I suppose I'm the same, George. Sometimes I like to take things into my own hands."

"So it would appear, sir," said George, with the air of a man who had done his part. And then he added, quietly, "Sometimes that's a good thing, taking things in hand."

By morning, Shauka would know that Faraz had talked to the boy at length, though Faraz was now certain that it would not be George who told him. But someone in the Mohalla would pass it on, and the boy, his mother, or this girl, whoever she was, might become targets. Faraz had to move quickly. When he looked back, the boy and the girl had disappeared, like the alley, into a forlorn darkness.

⬦

THEY'D STOPPED AT FARAZ'S HOUSE so that he could get some rest, but later, as they drove into the smoky gloom of the night, he felt his sense of recovery dissipate. Gulberg, still in the midst of development, was desolate, save for a handful of newly constructed houses sitting beside vacant plots.

He turned to George and asked, "How much do people pay these days, for a girl's nath?"

George swallowed as he answered. "I don't know, sir." He paused. "I've heard if she's been checked by a doctor, untouched, pretty . . . maybe three or four thousand. But it could be more. Maybe even five. They say a girl like that makes them . . . virile, that they'll live longer. For that, some will pay anything."

"I heard the Mohalla was on its way out, falling out of fashion."

"It's not what it was in its heyday, sir. But people still come. People with money to spend. There are the gangsters but also the VIPs. And outsiders, people who are passing through from Karachi, Islamabad as well. The Mohalla still has a reputation."

Faraz knew the cherished stories of the Mohalla, of refined tawaifs from films, like anyone else: the romance of beautiful courtesans who danced and sang of love. But he'd policed plenty of red-light districts in his time and what he'd seen was this: girls, their faces rigid with makeup, their ghungroos jangling as they crossed and uncrossed their legs, nervously awaiting the tamash been. The Kanjar might claim to take pride in their history as descendants of royal courtesans, but there wasn't anything regal about the men who loitered outside the function rooms. He had a dim memory of watching his mother prepare for work, and the thought plagued him now that his sister had done the same, and that somewhere in the Mohalla she, too, might be readying her own daughters, that they were right now putting on their makeup, dressing in their bright gowns.

"So a man might have paid five thousand, only to kill her," Faraz said. "She made him—them—angry. She did something."

"Sometimes the broker will say a girl's untouched and she isn't. It might not be the first time they've sold her nath, maybe not even the second. Men don't like to be conned. They want what they paid for." George held a matchstick between his teeth, then chewed it. "Or she panicked, couldn't manage it. When they're so young . . . especially if it's the first time. And the buyers, they don't like that, for them a deal's a deal." It was a reasonable explanation: booze, drugs, an unruly party, the girl doesn't comply. The gangsters all carried guns, so did the security guards for the VIPs. It wouldn't take much for a man with money to feel cheated if the girl resisted, for him to lose his temper.

"This councillor, Salim Mushtaq, he has that kind of money?" Faraz said. George shrugged: probably. George pulled up by the wall outside a rambling bungalow; they had arrived. Faraz turned to look at him. "And Sub-Inspector Shauka, does he take care of you? On cases like this?" It was a risk to ask George so openly and so soon, but somehow Faraz felt he could trust him.

George flushed. "Flour is fifteen rupees a sack, sir. We all have children to feed." He hadn't lied about it. He hadn't smirked or evaded or shrugged or said, "Everyone does it." He was ashamed. Here that made him an honest man.

Outside the councillor's house, the sounds of an intimate party reached them. Faraz sent George to walk the block to see what the neighbors—the kind who talked, or who could be made to talk—knew, but he didn't expect him to come back with much. Words hid more readily at night than during the day, and an officer had to learn to hear the things that disappeared in the dark.

He leaned against the car, closing his eyes so that he could hear the men above the sounds of the night, which clicked and squawked around him. But he could not make out what they were saying, their voices a hum except for the occasional chuckle or the sound of someone slapping his hands together, the tinkling of ice in the glasses. From the languor of their voices, he pictured them sprawled out on lawn chairs, bellies hanging over loosened belts, their bare toes curling around the cool grass. They were enjoying themselves. Friendship was a strange thing, but then he thought that likely it wasn't a strange thing to most men. How many of the men he knew could he count as a friend? He suspected he ought to see this as a failing, the inability to make friends, to find people whom he could trust, who would trust him, but he didn't. It all seemed so burdensome, weighed down by unspoken obligations and expectations.

He opened his eyes. Where was George? The drinking party could go on all night, and the longer they waited, the harder it would be to glean anything from the men.

There he was now, trotting toward him. "Sorry, sir. Old woman, a maid, wouldn't shut up. You know how they are."

"Anything?"

"Just that Mushtaq Saab likes to help his neighbors. He's always doing something or other for the colony. He's talking about building a little playground here. Knows how to look after people. Entertains lots of VIPs and invites the locals, too. They've met all sorts: politicians, generals, cricketers. They think he's very impressive, very generous. He's good to the help, too. The old woman was a big fan."

"Anyone know anything about where he was last night?"

"Said she wouldn't tell me even if she did, said the chutiya police ought to leave a decent man like Mushtaq Saab alone."

"A man with all kinds of friends, then." Faraz turned back to the bungalow. Even in the darkness he could detect the relative freshness of the paint, the smell of a garden watered daily. A well-maintained home. And then there was the outside. No one in the city much bothered to take care of the land that lay outside the gates of their homes; the land might be yours, but if you had to share the pleasure your planting might bring with passersby, then it wouldn't really feel like it was yours anymore, would it? But it seemed Salim Mushtaq had the capacity for a kind of generosity, or at least wanted to give that impression, because he'd had bougainvillea planted on either side of the gates.

Faraz nodded a *go ahead* and George rapped on the gate, hard. The voices within fell quiet. "Police," George called. And then all they could hear was the sound of mice and lizards scurrying near the walls of the house. It was a minute before a servant, an elderly man, his face as pale as his white hair, opened the gate. He said nothing but let them in and locked the gate behind them, as if he intended to keep them there.

Salim Mushtaq, spilling out of his chair, was larger than Faraz had expected; a mound of a man, bigger and more threatening than he had seemed in his posters in the Mohalla. Although from where he stood Faraz couldn't make out Mushtaq's features clearly, the sheen on the man's face was clear.

He rose to greet them, as did the other men, clasping their hands behind their backs or sticking them in their pockets, looking stiff and awkward. Salim Mushtaq approached them, holding out his hand and affecting an air of deep appreciation when George introduced Inspector Faraz Ali as Tibbi's latest SHO. "Wonderful news, wonderful news," he said, too quickly, with much too broad a smile.

"We wondered if we might have a word?" Faraz said. Salim Mushtaq glanced at the house behind him but seemed divided on whether he should take them inside. From the veranda came the sound of women's voices. Faraz could just make out a couple of figures, the tips of their cigarettes glowing. Mushtaq glanced over at his guests.

"What trouble did you get yourself into this time, Salim?" one of the men joked.

"Very funny, hazoor," he said amiably. He looked around; there was nowhere to take them. "Why don't you join us, Inspector saab?" one of the men on the lawn said. They were all curious. Mushtaq ordered the servant to bring over extra chairs, his voice a touch shrill, and they all had a seat.

Salim Mushtaq introduced the other men: two businessmen who were setting up a newspaper together and Khawar Sattar, of the great landowning family in southern Punjab. Sattar bowed his head in a gesture that seemed servile in a man so rich. Mushtaq said nothing of the women on the veranda. He continued to smile and glance at his friends every time someone spoke, as if to say: *See, I am very calm right now, nothing is wrong.* That itself was striking. Over the years, Faraz had turned up at the houses of many important men, and the usual reaction was one of indignation: *Who the hell do you think you are, do you know what time it is, I'll be having a word with your superiors about this.* But Salim Mushtaq had the servant bring them drinks, made them welcome. The guests were exceedingly polite, exemplary citizens; they asked about the riots, the feeling among the officers, what could be done to help the police at this time? At Faraz's behest, it was George who responded, shyly but politely. It was to his own advantage, he knew, not to seem too personable.

"You didn't get caught out in them, did you, sir? The riots?" Faraz said to Salim Mushtaq.

"I made a point of staying well clear, Inspector. But don't tell anyone, I've a reputation to uphold, man of the people and all that," he said with a big laugh, which his friends echoed even more loudly.

"I don't know," Sattar said. "If anything's missing from that langar on Lakshmi Chowk, a big degh of nihari or chicken tikka, you might have the right man, Inspector."

"You do spend a fair amount of time in Shahi Mohalla, I understand?" Faraz said.

"I go there all the time. As you know, I'm a councillor. I take my work of looking after those people very seriously. Isn't that right, George? I've done a lot for that community, ask anyone. George will tell you."

"They very much appreciated your renovation of the public taps, sir," George said reassuringly.

"But last night—you were home? Sir?" Faraz said.

A flicker of irritation on the man's face. "Yes. With my family. We were listening to the radio. My daughters were hoping for news reports but there was nothing on at all. We decided to play a game of rummy in the end." He grinned. "Of course, I lost. Never play with women."

The men tittered. Faraz waited. From the veranda, one of the women stepped down onto the lawn. Faraz could see her better in the moonlight; she was young, made up. Perhaps she was Mushtaq's daughter. The lights were on inside the house. It was late for the whole family to be up.

"Khawar," she called, "who's your friend?" She was drunk. Sattar looked at Faraz, embarrassed. "My . . . wife," he said to Faraz, in a way that indicated she was not his wife. A second later, the other woman called from the veranda, her voice a high whine: "Why don't you ever introduce us to your friends?"

"Also my wife," Sattar said, smirking now. "You know how it is, one is never enough." He grinned, daring Faraz not to laugh.

"What are your wives called?"

Sattar slapped his hands together in delight, as if to say, This inspector is a riot.

"Get inside, will you?" Sattar shouted to the women. "What will the inspector think? You'll get me arrested." The women laughed, and then the men laughed. The screen door clanged shut as the women went inside. George was looking at the ground, trying, Faraz suspected, to make himself invisible.

"There was, sadly, an incident last night. In the Mohalla." Faraz paused, waited for: What kind of incident, what happened? But no one spoke.

"I think a lot of things happened all over the city last night," Mushtaq said, his grin a grimace now.

"A young girl was killed. Very young. Shot dead."

Salim Mushtaq took a swig of his drink. The other men looked down, or up, or at their watches as if they might like to leave now. "That's terrible. Just terrible. Ya Allah," Salim Mushtaq said. Another big, long gulp. "Who was she?"

"Daughter of a woman who goes by Mehrunisa Bibi. The girl who was killed was a kanjari—a prostitute."

Salim Mushtaq drained his glass. "Another," he said to the servant who was standing at the edge of the circle of men.

Faraz considered how much further he could take this—the pressure of an audience might force a slip. He glanced at George; he imagined the man was thinking a public drama would not be of much help to anyone. But he hated to squander the opportunity now that they were here. Something benign, the gentlest of prods might be all that was needed: "I believe you entertain guests there from time to time. Sir. In the Mohalla."

Salim Mushtaq's eyelids fluttered, he licked his lips nervously. "What has that got to do with anything?"

He ought to say, Nothing at all, sir, just background, sir, but he was silent, letting the question hang in the air, gathering darkness and implication. He waited another moment, then: "Nothing at all, sir, just background, sir." Casual enough but also just late enough to sow discomfort.

Mushtaq's face shone in the moonlight. Sattar cleared his throat. "Many of us visit the Mohalla, Inspector." He smiled but he didn't look happy. "There's nothing wrong with supporting our great artists, our singers, our dancers. I speak not for the mullahs." He laughed, but there was an edge to it.

Salim Mushtaq was still, silent, but the other men leaned forward now. "Indeed," one of the newspaper publishers said with irritation. "And I'm not quite sure where you've come from, but making inquiries of a man of Salim's position at home, at this hour." He paused. "Whatever the circumstances, all of this seems . . . really quite irregular to me," he said, looking to the others for agreement.

Salim Mushtaq breathed out. His friends were doing for him what all men in their position did—stick together. It wasn't a surprise when Sattar said, "Perhaps the rebellion on the streets has extended to the rank and file." He smiled. "I'm wondering how our senior officers would feel about that."

At that, Salim Mushtaq sat up, as if he'd just been reminded of the powers that could be exercised in a swift phone call to just about anyone above Faraz's rank. He risked a small smile. "I think the inspector's working out the lay of the land. Shahi Mohalla's a unique place. It takes time for outsiders to understand it." He was going for benevolence, but Faraz heard a new firmness in his tone. There should be consequences for this kind of intrusion, for the tawdry insinuations; his friends had said as much. And Faraz knew there would be. Who, he wondered, would Salim Mushtaq call? Wajid?

"I thank you officers for trying to do something for this family even as this tamasha plays out on the streets. What can I do? How can I help them?" Salim Mushtaq pressed on, newly energized.

"I'm sure they'd appreciate a visit, sir," George said, stepping in. He glanced at Faraz in warning: You've gone as far as you can, further than you should have.

Faraz knew he was right. "We're sorry to have interrupted your evening, sir. Having heard about everything you've done for the neighborhood, your concern for the people there, we thought you'd want to be informed at the earliest."

Mushtaq nodded, somewhat placated: of course, of course. Faraz lowered his eyes, reassuring them that all was fine, that he understood his place.

"Thank you for informing me, Inspector. We are both here to serve these creatures. Poor as they are, we are all they have." Salim Mushtaq looked as if he meant it, and the other men fell into a thoughtful silence, their drinks for the moment untouched.

"Nauzubillah," Sattar said with a deep sigh; how exhausting it was to think of them, the creatures of the Mohalla.

The servant saw them out, bolting the metal gate behind them. In the car, they were silent for a moment. Then George looked at him, weary, because he knew that there was no going back now.

"The servant will know, his driver too, that he was there," Faraz said.

"I doubt they'll talk, sir. Not to us. And Mushtaq Saab would get wind quickly."

"Someone in the bazaar might. Everyone will know his car, his staff. We'll start there, in the Mohalla. Quietly. See if anyone recognized others in his party."

The windows were down, the night warm for November. The men had not started talking again, but Faraz stopped George when he went to start the engine. Not yet, not yet, he gestured, and so for a time they sat there in the silence, and they listened to the men listening, waiting for them to leave.

Eight

Wajid's message was simple: *Find me at the office tomorrow after three.* Faraz had risen early and seen the note Mussarat had left for him. Wajid must have telephoned late. *Uncle Wajid*, Mussarat had written on the note. *Uncle.* He tried to imagine their conversation. They didn't know each other well, but his wife understood the important part gratitude, or its performance, played in Faraz's relationship with Wajid. He could hear Mussarat's deference, Wajid's benevolent inquiries after all of them, after the baby. Faraz had looked to Wajid when he'd wanted to marry Mussarat. He'd glimpsed her at a wedding when he was posted in Faisalabad. She was attractive but not striking, her cheeks broad, her nose a little too wide, her eyes a little small, but there was something open, even about her expression, a sincerity in the way she spoke, listened. He decided he wanted her, and when he discovered that she loved an engineering student, a classmate at Punjab University, that the lovers were waiting for the boy to get a job so he could approach the family, Faraz did not want her any less. Perhaps he wanted her more.

He told Wajid he needed his help quickly, before the boyfriend took a proposal to the house. Mussarat's father was an NCO who'd eventually been commissioned, making it to the rank of captain, so the family were stupefied when Wajid Sultan, chief secretary in the provincial government, arrived with a proposal on behalf of Faraz, a distant cousin's son. Promising career, only steps from success. Yes, yes, they said, marveling at their daughter's good fortune. Far better than some would-be engineer with no connections. Mussarat had complied. She was astute, pragmatic, and there was something reassuringly straightforward about the arrangement: He had known she did not and would not love him, but also that she could live with it.

He folded the message up into the smallest of squares, disappearing it into his palm. The bag Mussarat kept for the baby, packed with spare clothes and bottles and toys, was sitting outside the bedroom door. She'd probably go to her mother's today. Now that she didn't have to accommodate him, the day was hers. When she woke, he ate breakfast with her, and as usual, she put the radio on as they ate, imagining, he supposed, that it masked the absence of conversation beyond their commentary about the baby, the exchange of information about their planned whereabouts. Wajid was likely still asleep, Faraz thought. Soon he would rise, dress, have breakfast with his family. He tried to imagine the scene, and somehow he knew, without having seen it, that breakfast at his father's house was a festive din.

After Mussarat and the baby left, it was still hours too early to show up at Wajid's office, but he could not stand waiting, so he decided to slowly wend his way to the meeting. The streets were quiet, vendors slow to start work on a holiday, but he found himself shrinking from the open space, walking close to the buildings, the stalls. Hadn't he learned as a policeman to make himself larger? Take longer strides, occupy more space, claim the street as your own. But he wasn't in his uniform today. He still remembered how he'd felt when he first put it on; the power of this new skin. Even now he understood that every gesture he made in it conveyed something more to those watching. Without it, what was he? As anxious as a boy at the prospect of meeting an important man. Was this his true self?

To his surprise, Faraz found himself not at the chief secretary's office but at his official residence. But he knew that when he was afraid of something, he could do little to stop himself from going toward it. This was also his true self, wasn't it?

As he had not been expected, the guards asked to see his identity papers, then relayed the news of his arrival inside, waiting for the okay before they let him go any farther. Faraz walked up the driveway, pleased now by his disobedience. So this was it: Wajid's home. A gardener watered the trees, his assistant crouched in the beds, weeding. There was a badminton net on the lawn. Chairs, books, and magazines littered the grass. The bungalow was large, the huge pillars before it seeming to stand guard. Faraz waited on the veranda until an old woman came out and asked what he would drink. She disappeared inside, and shortly an orderly emerged with a glass of skanjbeen for him. From somewhere inside, he heard the sound of a record being played.

It was several minutes before Wajid emerged, smiling. "There you are," he said as if he had been looking for Faraz all this time. When they shook hands, Wajid placed his left hand on Faraz's shoulder. "I thought we were meeting later at the office—"

"I have to get to Tibbi urgently, but it seemed important to talk," he lied. A flicker of worry around Wajid's eyes.

"Well, a wonderful surprise."

Faraz nodded, surprised at his disappointment that he was not going to be punished for his transgression.

The study that Wajid led him into was on the other side of the veranda, with a separate entrance. "Forgive the noise," Wajid said as he offered Faraz a seat. "It's the girls and that bloody gramophone." Girls, Faraz thought. *Sisters.* Wajid asked him a stream of questions about Mussarat, the baby, but he could barely answer, distracted as he was, his mind now ranging through the other rooms of the house to which he had not been admitted, and all that they held.

"I'm so glad things are going so well," Wajid said, as if he had arranged them to be so. He offered Faraz a cigarette.

Faraz shook his head. Wajid had gained weight since they last met—and, tall as he was, he dominated the room. Then there was that voice of his—a bellow, really. Next to him, Faraz struggled to feel a sense of his own size. On Wajid's chin was a large beauty spot. His hair was still thick and set in waves; his pomade smelled like cherries. He looked like a 1940s movie idol even now. Faraz was impressed by the man's control. Anyone else would have asked about the case by now. Not Wajid. Wajid would perform every social nicety first; after all, he was not the kind of person who needed anything from anyone, least of all Faraz.

"And how are you finding our beautiful city?" Wajid said.

Faraz wasn't sure how to answer. In Jhelum, he had always been struck by what his chacha said was God's work, visible in the river's width, the dark gold of the wheat fields. Lahore, for all its greenery, was a city of red sandstone buildings, of ornamental gardens, of paths and roads; a city made by men, men unlike him, men like Wajid.

"Lahore is Lahore," Faraz said, quoting Lahoris' favorite saying about the city. A safe response, and Wajid clapped his hands together.

"I knew we'd make a Lahori of you," he said.

The room was crowded with books, framed photographs, and vases, and the floor was lined with rugs. "You like it?" Wajid said. Faraz was confused until he realized that his eyes had, without his realizing it, come to rest on a painting on the wall, and that Wajid had followed his gaze.

"Come and have a look," Wajid said, inviting him behind the desk. "Sadequain. I don't know much about this sort of thing, but Safia tells me this is good. And a good investment."

Faraz stared at the painting, confused. Swirls of fawn, of dull blues and grays, a face, the curve of a body, something that looked like a branch growing from just below the woman's breast. He wasn't sure what it was but he couldn't look away from it.

"He's a talented man. Safia says he speaks the truth."

"About what?"

"God knows. That's a question for Safia. I am but a simple man. But I like it, still. He's not afraid of what's ugly. I suspect he rather likes it, in fact." Wajid stared at the painting a moment. Faraz had never been in a home where people hung paintings on the walls. He felt just then that he should not have come.

"Really, though, books are my weakness," Wajid said, gesturing to the cluttered shelves. "I spend far too much money on books." Faraz wondered how many other weaknesses Wajid had. Women? At some point women had been a weakness, his mother had been a weakness.

"They kept me going during the war," Wajid said. He nodded toward a couple of old photographs on the shelf. Faraz indicated he'd like to take a look. Of course, of course, Wajid gestured. "I was in better shape then," he said as Faraz picked up a photograph of Wajid in uniform, young, handsome, a ship in the background. "Like you," he thought he heard Wajid say. But before he could turn to look at Wajid, the door opened and a woman came in; she was small, stout, and pretty, middle-aged but youthful in her movements.

"Ah, Safia," Wajid said. "My wife."

"Do forgive me," she said, smiling. Her eyes were large and slanted, her cheeks and nose round and soft. She greeted Faraz with charm, her manners precise. The only wild thing about her was her hair, which was thick and frizzy, and she ran her hands through it again and again. Her poise, her entirely unselfconscious manner, struck him, discomfited him.

"They didn't tell me you had company," she said, waiting for Wajid to introduce Faraz. Wajid paused, and for the first time since he'd known him, Faraz saw a moment of hesitation, of uncertainty, flit across Wajid's face.

"Inspector Faraz Ali, the new SHO at Tibbi Station," Wajid said.

The old woman who'd opened the door to Faraz was standing behind Safia. "Is he staying for lunch?" she said gruffly.

Safia blinked, taken off guard. "Oh, yes, you must stay, Inspector," she said, not quite masking that the old woman's blunder had compelled the invitation. Faraz couldn't imagine that a man of his rank had ever graced their table. Still, she smiled, trapped, waiting, he was sure, for him to decline. "Amma-ji over here has made her biryani, which is a rare treat." He was struck by how casually, how easily she could accommodate a guest without the subtle flicker of calculation he was used to seeing cross Mussarat's face: Was there enough, was it good enough to offer a guest?

The old woman looked at Faraz again. "The girls will be out," she said. Safia shared a conspiratorial smile with him, an indication that this servant held a privileged position but was old, so not to mind her. "But Chota Saab will be here," she went on. "That's fine," Safia said. She smiled at the old woman, then shared a slight roll of her eyes with the men as the old woman shuffled out. Privileged or not, she was still a servant.

Safia looked at him expectantly, awaiting a response. Wajid stared at Faraz, his lips pressed together, his eyes still. Faraz imagined this was how Wajid might have looked at him had he grown up in this household, whenever he disappointed or displeased his father; a look of faint contempt.

"Thank you, but I can't stay. I'm expected at Tibbi," Faraz said to Safia.

"Of course. Given the situation on the streets . . . I understand," Wajid said.

Safia's smile thinned; if an invitation, even one reluctantly issued, was to be refused, a great deal more formal push and pull ought to precede it. But she was clearly expert in reading her husband's cues, and certainly relieved. "Yes, thank goodness for the work you do, Inspector. We shall expect you when you are less busy."

The sound of a male voice, of rapid speech, in the next room. Safia excused herself. Was that him, Chota Saab? They both waited for the voices in the corridor to quiet.

"I'll have to be going soon, so we should catch up . . . though I hadn't really wanted to talk here," Wajid said. Faraz waited. He wanted Wajid to ask him outright. "Is it *done?*" Wajid said at last.

"The accident wasn't an accident," Faraz said.

"I don't know the details, and I don't need to," Wajid said, his expression neutral. "I just need to know if it's done."

"Everything's being handled."

Wajid's eyes didn't move, and Faraz was struck by the strangeness of his demeanor, of all of this. "I was concerned, because I heard a postmortem's being done when I was quite clear I really just need the whole thing to disappear as quickly as possible." So news had gotten back to him at the speed Faraz had expected. Shauka? "And then this morning I get a call from some councillor I've never heard of. What's going on? I've gone to some trouble to keep nosy parkers out of this, the SP, the police higher-ups. They've all been told to back off. But that will become impossible if more bystanders are dragged in."

"The visit to the councillor was nothing, a protocol visit to keep him informed."

"There's no need for protocol. What I need is for this to go away."

"No FIR has been issued. I'm just trying to take account of the situation on the street right now—"

"I don't really see what that has to do with anything. Listen"—Wajid leaned forward—"people aren't going to be happy." His eyes narrowed. "Heads will roll." Wajid threw him a wan smile, but he held Faraz's eye, and Faraz understood: not Wajid's head, but his. Would he be banished to another station, like the previous SHO? Or worse? And was Wajid worried for him—or threatening him?

He understood that if he wasn't convincing, Wajid would get rid of him now, before he'd had a chance to uncover anything, and then he'd never know. "I understand, but this isn't easy to hide. It has to be handled carefully. If this gets out, if Bhutto's people get wind, or if they come into power anytime soon, they'll be quick to ask why this wasn't investigated, to implicate people connected to this government"—he gestured at Wajid—"in covering this up. So we conduct a 'thorough investigation'"—he waved his hand to convey its sham character—"and if anyone asks, we have a story. We investigated, found nothing. We can't do an amateurish job, or they'll call it what it is: the cover-up of a dead girl."

Wajid glanced at the closed door.

"If things stay as they are, there's nothing to worry about. It's a plan to keep in reserve. For a little extra protection." Faraz had delivered all this with a casualness and authority designed to impress on Wajid that this—cleaning up murders—was his domain, and that entailed thinking of all eventualities, the kind of work a Kanjar was born to do. Would Wajid buy it, as the sub-inspector had? Faraz leaned back in his chair.

"That makes . . . sense, I suppose," Wajid said. "You might rather have a knack for politics, Faraz." He smiled, although his voice conveyed displeasure. It was a plan that was perhaps too well thought-out, making him wary of the man who'd thought of it. "I'm just glad to have someone there who I can trust. You know, people in my circle, they get jumpy. No one wants to be seen out having a good time in Shahi Mohalla when the city's ablaze. And then get caught out in something like this. They're worrying."

"They were just out having a good time? The people involved in this?"

"They weren't involved, as I said. They were nearby when the accident happened." Wajid was speaking slowly, deliberately.

"Have *you* been there recently? To the Mohalla?" Faraz said.

"Good Lord, no. Not in years. Decades. Not since . . ." He trailed off. *Not since.*

Faraz tried to picture it: Wajid in the Mohalla, gun in hand, the little girl. It was an impossible picture. But how sanguine he seemed, how easily he had just said it again: *accident.*

"If there is anyone you'd like me to make sure doesn't get caught up in this . . ." It was a ridiculously transparent attempt at probing, and Wajid was much too clever for it. Faraz stared earnestly at his father, hoping the way he had arranged his face, eyes wide, brow furrowed with concern, would express loyalty. Wajid stared a moment and then broke out in a wide smile, as if he were amused at how easily he might have fallen for the ploy.

"That is good to know. You just look after yourself out there. It's not an easy job. And it can be a dangerous place. I'm glad to have someone with real smarts on this, someone who's thinking through all the potential complications."

"Thank you for making this opportunity possible. Once this is done, I'm sure I'll get a lot from it."

"You certainly will," Wajid said, patting him on the back. "Wonderful to see you. Bring the family next time." He walked Faraz to the door. "Keep me posted. It's helpful to have early warning when there are any developments," he said, staring out at the garden distractedly. The phone on the desk rang, and Faraz had just enough time to catch Wajid's glance at the photograph of his younger self in his soldiering days before he turned to say good-bye, his relief evident, and shut the door.

Faraz stood for a moment on the veranda. Wajid had always been generous with things, money, jobs. But he always managed to hold something back. This time it was what he didn't want Faraz to know.

He heard voices inside, people gathering for lunch. How complacent Wajid was, how little he feared him. He did not think for a moment that Faraz might dare walk into the dining room and upset the conversation, that he might reveal who he was and why he was here. He wondered just then if he wouldn't quite like to burn the place down.

The old woman came outside. "You sound just like him," she said. "For a second there, I thought he was talking to himself." She held his gaze, and for the briefest moment he felt himself made visible. Then she crossed her arms and went back inside.

He made his way back to the street, leaving behind the shade of the garden, the blooming potted plants, the soothing sound of the water on the lawn. It made sense that people who never had to look at what was ugly might like to have paintings of it on their walls; they could look at it whenever they wanted, and then turn away.

⟡

WITHOUT THE PROTECTION of his uniform, or the car, or his constables, he was freer. He could move through the Mohalla more easily, and maybe without all the accessories that conferred power, people would fear him less and talk more. The place felt deserted at this hour. Through the open windows of a kotha he heard the sound of a tabla, and behind the jute curtains of another he made out the shape of a woman walking back and forth. But the stalls were mostly shuttered, except for a lone trader selling charred sweet potatoes, and a pack of stray dogs nosing the street corners. It was when he looked up that he saw it: the entirety of the sky above the inner city dotted with kites, hundreds of them. He took a step into the street and threw his head back; boys, young men, old men were on the terraces, the roofs, their kites fluttering above, colors rippling across the sky. No one was looking down. No one would notice him here today. The thought lifted him; he could walk the lanes, scour buildings, corners he might recognize. But first he had to see her, the little girl's mother. Only she could tell him what he most needed to know.

When he rapped on the door of the apartment this time, the girl he'd seen with Irfan answered. She looked at him a long moment. "I need to speak to the bibi about something," he said. The girl looked uneasy. "I need her help to find Sonia's killer. Isn't that what you want me to do?"

The girl rested her head on the door, defeated, then let him in. She gestured at the charpoy behind her. "We've told people she's away for a few days, till the burial. So many people were coming to condole and she . . . couldn't."

He craned his neck; the woman was slumped on the bed while the boy sat by her on the floor, his back to the wall. Faraz approached. It was quiet; just the low crackle of fire in the hearth, the kites outside, lashing at the air. He crouched beside her, peered at her. "Has she taken something?"

No one answered, but the boy pushed in front of Faraz and patted her arm. "Amma, Amma, wake up."

She looked at him. "What is it? Did you find her?" she said groggily.

"Amma. It's him, the inspector. He's back."

She pushed the boy away weakly. "Chutiya, tell that bastard to get lost."

"I'll be quick," he said. "I just have a few questions." She turned to stare at Faraz, unblinking, and he shuddered, though he wasn't sure why. "Please," he said.

She hauled herself up to a seated position, puffing. She rummaged on the table next to her, which was covered in dirty cups and plates, and retrieved a small hand mirror. "You'll forgive my appearance, won't you," she said, caustic. She pressed her cheeks and she looked suddenly ancient, the bones of her face astonishingly pronounced. The light in the room flickered on and off. They all looked at the single bulb above the bed.

"It's the kites," the girl said. "It happens all day on Sunday when they fly."

"You need to get yourself home, girl," the woman said. "I told you not to come around here right now. Your mother will be looking for you."

"Mehru Baji," the girl pleaded.

"I told you to go home," Mehru said. The girl crossed her arms a moment, then turned to Irfan, waiting for him to intervene, but he nodded at her to go.

"I can help, Mehru Baji," she said, irritated with the boy.

"You can't help with anything," the woman yelled. "Why won't you listen?"

The girl started, then her eyes welled and her cheeks flushed. She hurried to the window and hauled herself up onto the balcony ledge, readying herself to hop onto the one next door.

When she had gone, the woman turned to him. "My girl should have been buried by now, and no one's told us anything about the body."

"You'll get her back soon."

She scoffed, perhaps at the clumsiness of his words. "They said it's because of you. Because she has to be examined."

"I wanted to know if they touched her." The woman turned away to look at the wall.

"It doesn't matter. She's dead now. Nothing can be done now."

"I know Councillor Mushtaq was there. I need to know who else was," Faraz said.

The woman pursed her lips. The boy got up and moved to the small kitchen area, where a portable kerosene stove stood on the floor, unlit. "I know you would have met them. You did the deal. You were Sonia's naika."

She turned to him, her eyes red. "I was her *mother*," she shouted. A moment later she began to sob. "I was her mother." She looked at him, defiant. "You think I deserve this."

"No," he said, suddenly chastened. "No." The boy was staring at him. "No one deserves this."

"It's what we are. The life that was fated for us." She leaned forward; sunlight from the open shutter fell across her skin, ashy, clammy. "There is no shame in it. The shame is theirs—yours." Slowly she bit down on her lower lip, something deliberate, salacious even, about the gesture. He felt his cheeks flush as he caught the derision about her lips: His discomfort pleased her. "And we don't need some inspector coming here taking a *special interest*, trying to save us. We work hard, all we want is for you people to respect it, given how you need us." She turned her face to the wall. "We honor God, just like you. We still have honor," she said, but now she sounded exhausted, her energy spent.

He didn't want to do this to the woman, already crushed, but he pushed on. "Do you know who the chief secretary is? Of Punjab?" She was silent. "Well, do you?" She shrugged a maybe. "Was he here? Was he with the men who came that night?" He looked over at the boy. "Was he here? I need to know."

The boy looked at his mother. "What do you want us to say?" she said.

"What do you mean?"

"It sounds like you want us to say he was here." Faraz was taken aback. "Mushtaq came briefly, but he's—" She waved her hand, as if to say *no one*. "I don't know who else was there. Mushtaq would know."

"You didn't stay."

"They paid me not to. I left Irfan to keep an eye. Turns out he wasn't up to it." She looked over at the boy, whose eyes were downcast, and waved her hand at him, wanting something brought to her. He understood and crouched down on the kitchen floor, where he pulled out cigarette paper and began to roll a cigarette lined with charas. The lights flickered.

"Is she eating?" Faraz said to the boy. The boy shook his head. "Here," he said, reaching into his pockets for change and pulling out what he had. "Go get some food for both of you. She needs to eat."

"Why are you here? What is it you want?" she said.

She held her hand out for the cigarette, but Faraz blocked the boy. "Why don't you eat something first?"

"Don't come here and tell me what to do. Who do you think you are?" She was furious again. "We haven't said anything, we've kept quiet, so why do you keep coming here, harassing us?"

"Who told you not to talk? Who did you make the deal with?"

She slammed her hand down. "Who *are* you? Why are you here? What do you want?" she screamed. Truthfully, he wasn't sure anymore. Everyone was doing their part, except him. No explanation he could give her would make sense. But he had to give her something, or she would never talk.

"I'm not like them, like . . ." Like the others, he meant: Shauka, the VIPs, the tamash been who came here, used them, and then condemned them for giving them what they wanted. But he'd spent so long trying to pretend he was like them, he wasn't sure what was true anymore. "My family are from the Mohalla," he said. "A long time ago, my people were here."

Mother and son were silent; they glanced at each other, unsure. He wouldn't win their trust so easily; who would believe an officer from Tibbi? Tibbi police were the kind who could be bought, who lied, who came in to cover up murders.

Faraz took a step back. He'd thought it would be a relief to say it out loud, to people from here, but it wasn't. He felt more alone than ever. He had wanted to feel as if he belonged to some place. But now that he'd said it, he also wanted to say, Keep this quiet, no one can know, even as he hated himself for thinking it.

He looked at the boy. "Make sure you both eat today, something hot." His face burned; he had to get away from this place, from what he'd said. The last thing he saw before he closed the door was the woman leaning back against the wall, the boy lighting her cigarette for her, before she turned to stare out of the window, he and his secret meaningless to them, forgotten already in the midst of their grief, the lights still flickering on and off.

Nine

Wajid tasted sand in his mouth. He crunched it against his molars, swirled it around his mouth. He could eat anything now. Sand, air. His belly was full of both. A snatch of a song came to him just as his stomach cramped, but he couldn't remember the words. He thought he heard birds calling, but that was impossible. The sky was baffling in its emptiness; what was the point of so much sky when every living thing seemed to want nothing to do with it? He stuck his hands in his pockets, hoping to find something he could busy them with, but there was, as always, only the sand; in his pockets, his hair, clinging to the crevices around his groin, his nostrils, between his toes. He had, in this last year, come to know his body, its joints, its soft hollows, in a new way, thanks to the bloody sand.

They'd been offloaded from a truck a half mile back, two squadrons, to save on petrol, he guessed, but the Jerries didn't seem to mind marching with them. "Not far," said the one who spoke some English. His face was long and thin, his eyes so pale they seemed colorless. He looked worn-out, too. All the Jerries did. "Could you be more precise, old chap?" he said. Being obnoxious, he'd learned from the British officers, didn't change much, but it did make you feel better. The German, not much younger than him, opened his mouth to speak but then said nothing, his mouth hanging open like an empty black cave. Poor bastard, Wajid thought, then he chided himself, as Sam Rustomji would have, for feeling sorry for a German. "Walk," the Jerry said, "walk."

He saw nothing ahead, nothing behind, just the rocks, the stones, the dust flying up around them. No sign of the fort to which they were headed. He tried to recall the birds of Lahore, their calls, but of course he'd never paid attention to such things. Why, *why* hadn't he learned their names, or the names of the trees of the Punjab, or those pink, papery flowers in the garden? It didn't seem important then, but what if this was just the start? What if soon he would no longer be able to recall any of the things that mattered to him? His home, his life, who he had been before all this? Bastard desert. Bastard war. Bastard Jerries, bastard all of it.

He said her name under his breath—it had become the easiest way to find any kind of serenity here. He said it again, and there she was: the long nose, her lipstick smeared where he had kissed her. Wajid ran his tongue over his lips, soothed. Wet. Soft. The taste of a breeze as he opened his mouth. He thought of her skin, her sweat in his mouth. She didn't know, but he'd brought her picture with him. The others had fiancées, wives; he had Firdous. If she'd known that he kept her picture tucked inside his shirt pocket, her eyes would have narrowed with satisfaction; it bothered him that she still had, even after all this time, a claim on him. He didn't love her as the others loved the women whose pictures they glanced at coyly before sleeping. It had never been that. He worried more about dying and the picture being sent home to his family with his personal effects; his mother being aghast that he carried a picture of a dancing girl right by his heart.

One of the sepoys marching behind him murmured something incomprehensible. Water, he must want water. The Germans had given each of them less than a half pint since yesterday. The chaps had been careful with the water, but a half pint, in the bloody desert, in bloody June? That morning, his men, tired, starved, had slurred tearfully in his direction, as if he could help them, a kind of grating hum that the Germans would surely silence with a few rounds if they didn't shut up. Eyes forward, do as you're told, maintain order, Wajid said to them. They were pathetic and it was almost impossible to feel anything but contempt for them. "Quite frankly," he said, "I'll have Havildar Singh shoot you myself if you carry on like this," though Havildar Singh looked as if he might not even require an order to do it; the sound of frightened men was one that could drive a man mad.

Havildar Singh marched a step behind him. He had a tendency to nod: a clip for hello–good-bye, a stern nod yes, a nod of contempt if you were a sisterfucker, but now the havildar nodded uncertainly up ahead. Wajid squinted. Just beyond the desolate hills there was movement: lines of tanks, trucks. Plumes of black smoke. A fire, the smell of petrol, the jagged angles of the fort rising toward the sky. And then he stopped, as the desert in the distance rose, then shrank, snaking its way among the guns and jeeps as if it were alive. Stay sane, he told himself. When he looked again, he saw that the desert wasn't moving, but up ahead, men, tens of thousands of them, were disappearing into the horizon. Havildar Singh nodded again, his shoulders slumping. They would disappear into these columns of men, and he had the sense he might never reemerge. He had not imagined this— capture, disgrace. Death, lost limbs, he had thought a great deal about those possibilities, but this? What did it mean? And what would the bastards do to them now? Now that he had been saved from fighting, he didn't want to die not fighting. He scanned the horizon, but there was no escape. The sepoy rasped behind him. Don't look down, he thought, don't look at it and you won't want to dig at it with your hands, hoping to scoop out a little bed, a comfortable little hole for what's left of you. "Eyes forward," he said out loud to the men behind him.

There were thousands of soldiers in front of him. They stood in long columns, a disorderly mass stretching from the fort somewhere toward the Mediterranean, which he could not see. The Italians called out to one another from the edges of the crowd as they trudged up and down the lines of men, just as disorderly and confused and overwhelmed as the prisoners. The Germans handed them off by the fort and then turned back toward the desert. He raised his hand to the Jerry. "Auf Wiedersehen." The Jerry looked back, his face rigid as if he were expecting a smirk, not the anxiety Wajid knew was crossing his lips, his eyes. The Germans had not killed them, and here, where all that was unknown was shadowed with the possibility of death, he wished that the Jerry would stay with him. The German soldier nodded, gesturing at him to keep walking, as a mother might encourage her child on his first day of school: Go on, go on, you'll be fine.

"You," an Italian sergeant said to him. "Go, go," the man said, shoving Wajid to one side, separating him from his troop.

Wajid fumbled for his French, and the Italian, unshaven, his breath dry and foul, shoved him again. Wajid was spent when it came to heroics but his men were watching. "I say," he said, "I want to speak to an officer of my rank. These are my men. They are in my care." He was struck by the strangeness of the word: *care*, as if he were their nursemaid. The Itie wasn't listening, looking just past him. Wajid tried to stand taller, to impress on the man his importance, but then he felt a jolt in his side and he was down on his knees. He was confused, unsure what had happened till he felt the pain, dull and hard. His hand went up to his kidney. The butt of a rifle, an Itie behind him grown impatient. He held his side, tears pricking his eyes. He grimaced, thinking he couldn't afford to lose any more water. When he looked up, his men were being led away. He was relieved; now he could cry. He just made out Havildar Singh's anxious expression; the havildar was considering whether he should come to him. But Wajid nodded at him to go on, just as the young German had nodded at Wajid: Don't worry, I'm fine, you'll be fine, too. Havildar Singh nodded, defiant. As the men disappeared, Wajid flopped onto his knees, arms around his middle. "Alzati," an Itie yelled. The thud of a boot in his back. He was on all fours now, like a dog. Amma, he thought. His mother was the only word, the only thought left as pain radiated through him. He thought he felt her arms around him, holding him as she had when he was a boy.

"I thought you'd be dead by now," a voice said.

These were not his mother's arms. Wajid strained to hold back the tears he could still feel sitting in his eyes, because he knew this voice, and crying in front of a man like Ghazi Ashraf was unthinkable. Goddamn Ghazi: sisterfucker. Although he hadn't seen him in the chaos that was Gazala, they had been billeted together in Cairo, months ago. Wajid and Sam Rustomji had spent their time in Cairo smoking and visiting big-breasted Egyptian girls—whores, if you please, Sam liked to say—their nipples a beautiful black mouthful in dark, sweaty rooms where they drank the malty homemade beer you could get on the cheap. In Cairo, Wajid's heart banged away, calling attention to itself: You, Wajid, are alive! Here! So close to the war! And this gave him the illusion of invincibility that had served him well out here. Ghazi, on the other hand, lurked in the camp, cleaned his gun, stared at maps. "You trained with him, didn't you?" Sam had said. "What the hell's wrong with him? Doesn't he like to have a night off of being a miserable bastard?"

"He doesn't know how," Wajid had quipped back. But he sensed that Ghazi didn't need to forget his misery; this was the happiest he had ever been. How to explain that to Sam?

Wajid felt Ghazi crouching over him, the man's frame lithe, ready even now, thriving while the rest of them disintegrated in the heat, their bodies turning to sand. A ring of pain circled his waist still, but it was only a steady, dull throbbing now.

"Ashraf Saab," Wajid said. He scanned the area around them. Men huddled in groups as the Italians haphazardly pulled them out of the lines or shoved them back in. He had to find other people, he had to find other people to stand with. He had to get away somehow from Ghazi, who brought nothing but trouble, terror at times. "I better get myself in line before that Itie comes back this way," Wajid said. He tried to stand, but another jag of pain came on. He felt Ghazi steadying him. He mustered a smile—I'm fine—but Ghazi sensed something, perhaps the distaste Wajid was trying to mask, and held up his arms in a gesture of: Fine, please yourself. The man wasn't stupid.

Wajid hobbled toward a group of white men, more red than brown from the sun, in the line up ahead; gunners, probably. They didn't make space for him. They did not acknowledge his rank. "That's a King's Commissioned Officer behind you." He looked around. "Eleventh Cavalry." Ghazi Ashraf again. Wajid threw him a thin smile. Thanks, but I don't need help, he meant. The white men glanced at Ghazi and then at Wajid. It seemed to make no sense that all of them—these men from all parts of the world, from India's villages, from hamlets on the Thames, the bush of South Africa, strangers all—had been prepared to die for one another a few days ago; it seemed nothing short of absurd as he stood among them now.

"Sorry, sir," one of the white men said, his tone caustic. He stepped back to make room for Wajid, and the other white men tittered.

Wajid laughed. Always best to join in. "Much obliged, Lance Corporal," he said, miming tipping a cap. The men laughed again and he sensed he could find his way among them, as he always did; he would have to endure some snickering, some ribbing, but he could do that. It couldn't be worse than Eton, than Sandhurst, or even the officers' mess. He caught Ghazi's eye before Ghazi turned away to head farther back into the line.

"I'm glad you made it," Ghazi said. "I saw you at Gazala. I didn't think you would."

Gazala, Gazala. Bastard battle. What no one had told Wajid at Sandhurst or even in Thall, where he'd trained, was how confusing battle was; the impossibility in the midst of it to know what to do now: Fire? Run? Go east, but where's east? Where's Sam, where's everyone? Is there anyone left? The officers made sure they were the only ones who knew how to do the planning, the ordering, perfecting the art of talking over, talking down to the other men—he was quite the expert himself. But once there were no officers left to explain why their strategy had not come to pass, he didn't know what to do. The only option left then was to die fighting, but that seemed like a terribly wasteful thing to do. So Wajid threw down his gun and surrendered to the Jerries. Surrendering with a gun was dishonorable, of course, fine for a private perhaps, but unacceptable for an officer of the Empire, who should fire down to the last bullet. But the truth was, he'd fought hard for the last year, in a state of perpetual fear, and now he was awfully tired. It didn't seem so terrible to want to save his own life, and maybe the lives of his men, not that he'd been thinking of them at that moment.

He looked back now and spotted Ghazi, and when Ghazi stared back at him, his eyes somehow darker in the sunlight of the Libyan desert, he realized that Ghazi had probably seen him throw down his gun at Gazala, that he knew the secret of Wajid's cowardice and was not, in the least, surprised by it.

Ten

Rozina awoke with Mina's name in her mouth, her breath sour with it. Her ragged sleep had felt like a prolonged gasp; it was Mina, all the terrible things that might now befall Mina. Her chest hurt with it. Najam stood by the dresser, banging through the drawers; he looked more drawn than usual—lack of sleep—though still impeccably neat, impressively compact. "I didn't wake you, jaaneman, did I?" he said, moving to kiss her on her forehead in his usual brisk fashion. "I can't find my silver cuff links anywhere. I've got to get over to Qaiser's place. Party meeting. Bhutto Saab is going to brief us on next steps. Ayub's under pressure. And we have to strike before he does," he said, looking through the trinkets and jewelry box on her dresser for his cuff links. He didn't seem to note that she'd almost emptied its compartments.

"Shall I get the girl to get you something to eat, some tea?"

"Ha! Panic makes men stupid," he said, holding up the cuff links, his smile ripe. Good line, he was thinking, good copy. Damn. She'd meant to pack those, too. "I'm going to shower and then I must run," he said. "Get the girl to put those in a bag for me." He pointed at a pile of things by the bed: packaged Austin Reed shirts he'd brought back from London, some ties, a few more boxes of cuff links.

It wasn't a promising sign, Najam taking his things with him, and she felt her eyes well. "How's Shaheen?" she called.

"What?" he said from the bathroom.

"I said, how's everything at home?" The shower's staccato rhythm pounded the tiles and he said nothing, though she was sure he'd heard her. He would never tell her; she would have to be the one to say she knew. It wasn't him, it wasn't even the house, really, but she'd left Mina for this life. The day it became clear Mina was going to stay with Firdous for good, Najam had shushed her as she sobbed; we'll have our own babies, you'll see. She had, guiltily, perked up: children, those with the honor of a real name. Only no other children came—perhaps it was those abortions the midwife in the Mohalla had done, who knew?—but the only baby she did have was lost to her. She plucked one of the shirts, pale pink, and put it in her wardrobe before bagging the other things for him; there was, at least, some comfort in stealing from him.

"You look terrible, jaaneman," he said as he came out, his shirt sticking to his back because he never had the patience to dry himself properly. His churning energy made her head ache: the flick of his tie, the slap of his aftershave, the way he deftly slid his feet into his shoes, all so innocuous before, now seemed like signs blaring his imminent departure from her life. She opened her mouth to speak. I do feel terrible, she wanted to say, you're a bigger sisterfucker than I could ever have imagined. Who is she, who is she, she wanted to scream, but she didn't. She was aware, instead, of her mouth hanging open. "You must get some sleep, darling," he said, tapping her cheek. "All those lines around your eyes. It's putting years on you," and he brushed past her.

⬦

IT WASN'T EVEN LUNCHTIME but there was already a string of bicycles parked outside Pak Tea House, their wheels tangled in a silent clatter. She hopped out of the taxi and stood for a moment in the searing midday sun, reluctant to go in. She didn't feel shame as often as she suspected she was supposed to, given all she had done, but she felt her face flush as she recalled what she had said to Bobby. It wasn't the first time she'd taken out a rage, a mood, on him, but each time she did, she wondered fearfully if this would be the time he would not forgive her.

Inside, the cool of the checkerboard tile seeped through her thin sandals, and even though the place was a blur of occupied tables and harried waiters, the café felt spacious and airy. Men in suits or kameez shalwars huddled at the tables, far too engrossed in their conversation to recognize her. Relief again. This is where the real revolutionaries meet, Bobby liked to say. Ordinary, thinking men. Men like Najam don't come there, but the real socialists do, the ones who want change for the poor, not just for themselves. Najam laughed at the Pak Tea House types; there's socialism, jaaneman, and then there's getting things done, really changing things, he said; you think these whingeing Pak Tea House intellectuals can do that, make deals, negotiate? They don't even want to win, just talk.

She recognized Habib Jalib, the poet, his dark hair flopping across his mournful eyes, surrounded by a throng as he stared into his tea. When he looked up and spoke, the men around him were quiet a moment before their conversation began again with a new ferocity. That was when she saw Bobby rise from the group, his hand briefly on Jalib's shoulder before he headed to the counter, where the waiters were gathered. He helped a struggling busboy with his loaded tray, saying something that made the boy smile, and she remembered the surprise on the faces of the runners on set when Bobby knew their names, something other directors never bothered with. He stopped to stand by a man at the counter whose head was down, scanning orders. Bobby's eyes were shadowed by dark circles and she thought for a moment of leaving, but then he saw her. The other man looked up too; Nasir, a producer they used to work with years before, heavier, drabber, and now managing the café part-time—but *still here*, his smile said. Bobby grinned and pulled a cigarette from behind his ear and held it out to her: a welcome, a gesture of forgiveness.

She hesitated to say it out loud to them—she knew that actresses, like tawaifs, became less desirable over time, but—*could* she get acting work again? Her days at Najam's were numbered—days, months, a year, she had no way to know how long, but she couldn't let him decide. She had to find work, enough to support Firdous, Mina, herself. Bobby looked uncertain, but Nasir clapped his hands together in a gesture of *of course*: "You're a star." Rozina scoffed. Truthfully, she still liked to hear it, but she hadn't been a star in years. She looked to Bobby, who smiled cautiously. "You're Heer. That still means something."

"Only to us." Rozina paused. "Only to *you*," she corrected; she wasn't sure if it had meant anything to her—becoming a star had been Firdous's dream for her. They all fell silent, and she realized she was reminding them of what they had once been, too; Bobby hadn't made a film in six years and was eking out a living writing articles for Urdu magazines, and Nasir looked as much at home managing waiters here as he had orchestrating a film shoot, perhaps more so. There'd been no dramatic exits, just a slow falling out of favor, out of fashion, the record of their work fading away. How could they help her when they couldn't do anything for themselves, when they met here to reminisce, hanging on to the edge of these circles by their finger-nails? She felt a sob from deep within her belly, hurtling up through her body, it was going to choke her, steal her breath, because if they couldn't help, that left only the pimps—men like Izzat Raheem, who'd somehow gotten a girl killed. Outside the Mohalla, in Najam's care, she hadn't had to think of Izzat and his prickly temper, of any of the brokers. Over the years, Izzat had called occasionally—but he could only ask now, not demand, and so he had offered to introduce her to special fans, VIPs. She'd laughed about the offers with Bobby, with Najam, even, from time to time; it seemed good for him to know that she was still in demand. But it had been years since she'd heard from any of the brokers; a kanjari of her age ought to be putting her daughters to work now, not looking for work herself.

Bobby reached for her hand, held it; he rarely touched her. "Let's remind the people who Heer is," he said. "It just takes one great part, right, Nasir?" She wasn't sure if it was only pity that made him say it, but she was grateful, and she flashed them her most dazzling smile, the kind she had reserved for publicity stills, knowing that before she could remind anyone else, she had to remind them and herself of who she had once been.

·✧·

ROZINA GLANCED UP at the sign for Prima Studios, extravagant, swirling, and then at Bobby, who looked as overwhelmed as she felt. He smiled: Don't worry, we look the part, but she didn't feel it as he frantically wiped his hands—blackened from fixing his bike chain—with a handkerchief. Nasir had befriended Shehzad Peracha, head of Prima Studios and the biggest producer in town, who liked to while away his evenings at Pak Tea House. Peracha said he came to look for talent, but Nasir thought that really he came to enjoy the attention of the crowd of young writers trying to impress him. Nasir always gave him a good table, held the hangers-on back when they got too much, and Peracha had a soft spot for him in turn, so when Nasir had called to ask for a pitch meeting, he said yes.

But now Nasir, who had said he would be there to make the introduction, was nowhere to be seen. Rozina felt ridiculous standing outside the studio walls; she hadn't worked in more than a decade, she sometimes went weeks without being recognized. Why had she thought this would work?

Once the security guard let them in, Rozina saw exactly what a string of silver jubilee films bought; Peracha had built an industrial production house. Signs in the lobby pointed to the color laboratory, the soundstages, the editing suites. She had only ever worked on rickety sets housed in ramshackle, mice-ridden warehouses. "It looks like the studios in Bombay," Bobby said, something flickering across his face. He had been a child when he came to Pakistan, but he'd often told her of his trips to the studios in Bombay, where his father had worked as a cameraman, how seeing the crew, the stars in a huddle under the lights, had felt like glimpsing a secret. In Pakistan, his father worked on lesser films, with lesser actors, lesser technicians, and thought that Bobby, working as a director in this newer, smaller industry, was also a lesser version of who he might have been in

India. But standing in a building that seemed to belong in Bombay, or Pinewood, or Hollywood, Rozina thought perhaps they had resigned themselves to their status as lesser too easily. This Peracha had dreamed of something more, and now here it was, standing in the heart of Lahore.

"Can I help you?" a smart-looking young man said, approaching them from a corridor lined with offices.

"We have a meeting with Peracha Saab," Bobby said.

"Today?" he said.

Bobby nodded. "I'm Bobby Sethi. Nasir Shah is our producer and this is—" But the young man was already looking at her, placing her. "Madam," he interrupted, recognizing her, "what a great honor. I'll let Peracha Saab know you are here. He's in a meeting with the publicity team, but I am certain he wouldn't want to keep you waiting." He hurried back toward the corridor.

"Where the hell is Nasir?" she whispered to Bobby.

"He must be having trouble getting off work. Don't worry, we just have to tell a story. What's so hard about that?"

Peracha was walking around the room when the door opened. Three men sat on the sofa by the wall. He was short, with a fleshy face, and his hair, as white and bright as his teeth, was stylishly slicked back. When he saw them at the door, he strode toward them; he reached for Bobby's hand, but it was Rozina on whom his gaze was focused. "Alhamdulillah, Alhamdulillah," he said, winking a little. "I could not have hoped for a better surprise, to meet in person one of our foremost heroines." He gestured toward the sofa. Instantly his associates scurried out, and the young man who'd brought them in closed the door and stood by it, as a security guard might.

"Nasir called and spoke so fondly of you, Sethi Saab," Peracha said graciously, but he was eyeing Bobby as if trying to recall him. There was a knock on the door: Nasir, frazzled, his shalwar kameez a stark, impressive white but reeking of fried onions. "Ah, the very man!" Peracha exclaimed.

"We are so grateful for the time you've made to see us, Peracha Saab. Please forgive my tardiness."

Peracha waved the apology away. "You're a hardworking man, Nasir. That's how we all begin, working our way up from those damn day jobs, yes? I was a news reporter once upon a time. It fed me!" He patted Nasir on the back.

Nasir smiled, they all smiled, ignoring the fact that Nasir was far from starting out. "Our star, you'll of course have recognized, and Bobby Sethi, director of *Mohabbat ka Waqt, Doh Rastain Ek Pyaar*, and many other . . . classics." They all knew *classics* suggested has-been, but what else could you say of a director who hadn't made a film in years, whom the biggest producer in town had likely not heard of?

"Such an honor," Peracha said, not sounding certain that it was, in fact, an honor.

"Bobby's working on an incredible new script."

Bobby swallowed. There had been a time when he stole the show during meetings, pacing, his patter brilliant, but now he sat tight-lipped, uncertain, making no move to speak of the script.

Nasir went on, "The story is, well, it's a very classical kind of story, only with a modern feel." He looked to Bobby. "Tragic," Nasir said. "A real weepy."

"But also, at the same time, a happy ending," Bobby said quietly, "the kind where the audience has to work hard for it. They have to earn that ending by working with the characters."

Peracha smiled. There was something warm in it, encouragement. Bobby took a breath in and leaned forward, as if leaning into his old self. "It's the story," he said, "of a tawaif, a courtesan." Rozina turned to look at him. "A woman who gives up her child, leaves her behind in a kotha to start a new life and then spends the rest of the movie searching for her child. Of course she finds the child eventually, on her deathbed, but by then it's too late. An incredible tragedy, of course, but also a heartfelt reunion."

Rozina had not even asked about the pitch, distracted as she'd been with her worry about Najam and Mina. Just get through it, she'd told herself.

"With Heer in the lead, I think we'll be looking at a performance that will have the audience weeping in their seats. A golden jubilee for sure," Nasir said, his arms crossed now. None of the men were looking at her, but she stared at Bobby, willing him to see her, waiting for him to answer for what he was doing.

"Hmm . . . I feel like I've seen it before, you know?" Peracha said. He looked to the assistant. "The thing that Rumi's working on, does this sound similar?"

"I think that's about a city woman who has an illegitimate child and abandons the baby in the country."

"I mean, the people want *drama*, emotion, excitement. Throw in a couple of good musical numbers with that kind of a story, one that gets them *here*"—Peracha put his hand on his heart—"and you have a hit. But you know, it still has to *feel* fresh."

"Didn't you say something about a murder?" Nasir said to Bobby quickly.

"Yes. This isn't just a tragic domestic story, but a thriller. Very complex, very knotty," Bobby said. He looked animated now, brought back to life by this discussion of story, by the certainty that in this room, at least, stories mattered. Rozina had never imagined she could hate him so much. Peracha nodded, and the other men nodded, too. She hated all of them.

"Interesting twist. That's why we've had such a terrific run, because we're surprising the audience. We're not afraid of giving them something to think about," Peracha said.

"And Heer is the actress of her generation. She's perfect for the part," Nasir said.

She looked at Bobby, but he wasn't looking at her, he was seeing the set, the film, and it didn't matter that it was her story. He was already making it his.

"Perfect to play a terrible mother who abandons her child?" Rozina said.

"This woman is not a terrible mother. She's a woman trapped by circumstances, by a society in which women have fewer opportunities," Bobby explained gently, and they all nodded kindly; they were forward-thinking men who understood the particular suffering of women. Peracha stared; there it was, just behind the lines around his mouth—assessing her: age, body, face. There would always be someone else if she wouldn't do it, or wouldn't do; someone newer, younger. Hadn't that always been the threat? There are many who will take your place, for less, for nothing. Not just in this, in everything. Wasn't that why she'd lost so many years to Najam, because she was lucky, lucky to be picked when there were so many others he could have chosen?

"It's a great story," she said, "but it's actually *my* story, my idea. I should tell it." Bobby seemed about to respond, but she stared at him, daring him to pretend he wasn't taking something of hers. The only thing that really was hers.

Bobby looked down, and Peracha glanced from one to the other, aware that something was up. Rozina knew how a man like Peracha would assess this moment: A director who cannot control his star is not a man who will deliver a film on time, or in budget. He did not want to get in the middle of this, whatever it was. "I don't think we can take this further today in terms of commissions and the like, but I'd be happy to look at the script."

Nasir slumped back in his chair, but Rozina sat up straighter. She wouldn't be made to feel she had destroyed this. It was Bobby. Bobby, who had, without a care, decided to use her life for his script without even asking her permission.

Peracha stood. He shook the men's hands warmly. "I'm sure we'll talk more at the Tea House about this fascinating story." As they left, he reached for her hand. "It was a special pleasure to see you, Heer-ji," he said. "I remember *Shama Aur Sitaray*. Even now. That death scene"—he put his hand to his heart. Rozina smiled. She wanted to get out, to go home, take the pins out of her hair, speak to her mother, track down Mina. "You know," he said, coming in closer to her, putting his arm around her waist as she walked toward the door, "a friend of mine is recording a radio play soon. I'm wondering if he might have something in it for you. Something small. Have you ever done anything for Radio Pakistan?"

⌖

IN THE PARKING LOT, Bobby and Nasir were leaning against a car, talking to a young, scraggly-looking runner. "I thought you were my friend," she said to Bobby, her eyes welling.

"What?" Bobby looked surprised. "It was just a pitch, Rozina. Come on."

"You've been writing that story, *my* story, without telling me." She crossed her arms.

He wouldn't say it now, but she knew what he thought: His art was a way to understand the world, a way to understand himself. She'd never thought about her acting as art, really. It was business—business with better perks and privileges than those she'd had when she danced in the Mohalla, to be sure, but it was still work crafted to please others. Surely when you made art, some part of it was for you? Nothing about what she did was for her, and she hated him for not seeing that.

"The point was to try and get you work," he said, but his cheeks were pink. She thought of Peracha taking her hand, his arm around her waist. Before they parted, he'd invited her to a party to talk more about the radio play, about other opportunities. She understood, she had never been stupid, she had never been naive. She would have to give more than a performance in order to get a job from him. That was the way it had always been. Where she had slipped was in believing she had a real friend.

"I think your point was to try and get *you* work," she said. "You're a sisterfucker, and deep down you know it, too." She heard Bobby calling after her as she walked away, but she didn't look back. Up ahead, the main road blurred as she tried to hold back angry tears; there was no limit to what people would take from her—especially those she loved.

Eleven

The morning light peeking through the gap between the curtains and the floor was cold, bluish, when Faraz heard the baby wake. He hadn't slept much, perhaps three or four hours. Both Mussarat and the baby had slept through the phone call that had come in early from Shauka. The sub-inspector's voice was wiry, nervy, as he reported that the journalist on *Dawn*'s crime desk had told them he was running a small news piece on the death of a woman in the Mohalla on the night of the disturbances in the inner city. There was speculation that she had been killed in the riots. Could Tibbi Station confirm, he'd asked. You denied everything, yes? he'd asked Shauka. Of course, sir, told him no such thing happened. But he was insistent he had a lead. Make sure no one speaks to him, Faraz said.

He hadn't been able to go back to sleep afterward; news coverage would generate panic. The pressure to shut the case down immediately would increase, the sham investigation he'd argued for wouldn't wash with Wajid, Shauka, anyone. Bury it, bury *her*, they'd say. Only then could everyone move on, forget. He shaved, dressed, and paced the house, waiting for George, glad for the distraction Nazia brought upon waking. She touched Mussarat's face, trying to wake her, and was cross when he plucked her from where she was nestled against her mother. I know, I know, you want your amma, he said, understanding her, feeling for her. He held her close, wondering if he could be enough, but also pleased, as she squirmed away from him, to know that he would never be enough. This was as it should be.

He carried her from their bedroom to the small living room and distracted her with the light switches on the wall, flicking them on and off, talking to her as he turned on the ceiling fan. Look, he said, pointing to the fan, studying her face to see her reaction, surprised at his own endless fascination with the way she looked at everything. How bewildering the world is, her face said. Yes, he wanted to say, it is. He wanted to explain to her the mechanics of the fan, the wires, the invisible movement of the electricity that made it whir, because, bewildering as it all was, there was no reason to be frightened, things could generally be explained. Even if he wasn't sure this was true, he wanted her to feel this way. But he actually didn't know how anything worked—he wasn't an educated man, something he hadn't cared about until Nazia was born. So he taught her what he knew: Touch it, try it, don't be afraid. She should never be afraid.

In the courtyard, the sunlight was warm, and he took off her soiled nappy so she could walk freely. He fed her a banana, which he held as he sat on a chowki. She came up and took a bite before waddling away from him, turning to check every now and then that he was still where she had left him. Did the girls in the Mohalla get to play? he wondered. Were their lives like Nazia's till the time came when they could no longer be girls? *It's what we are*, the woman had said. He hadn't been able to sleep, to dislodge the picture of them from his mind, the loneliness of the woman immobile on the bed, the boy wandering the corners of that gloomy room.

Inside, Mussarat opened the bedroom windows and the baby turned her head, alert to the clink of bottles on the dresser, the careful opening and closing of drawers. Mussarat attended to his things meticulously, his shirts, his underclothes painstakingly ironed, folded, and placed neatly one on top of the other in little ascending towers he was loath to disturb. He had noticed that in her own dresser, she stuffed her clothes into the drawers carelessly, her dupattas and underclothes balled and tucked into the corners wherever there might be space. She hid this from him, quickly slamming drawers when he came into the room, as if they contained shameful secrets. He waited to hear her lock the bedroom, the bolt at the top of the door squealing as she turned it. Then she would undress. He had felt her in the dark, but he had never seen her unclothed. He had felt the softening of her body since the baby, around her belly, her thighs. She always acquiesced when he reached for her, careful not to resist, but signaling in her restraint that this was compliance. But since the birth of the baby sometimes, every now and then, he felt that if he was patient, that if he moved carefully, she opened to him more easily than before—as if having seen what her body could do, she didn't need to worry over its care so much, as if she were now just curious about what it might feel. Perhaps it was just resignation.

When Mussarat stepped out into the courtyard, she put her hand up to her eyes, shielding her face from the sun. "I didn't hear you get up," she said. She knelt down and held her arms out, and the baby fell toward her. He looked at Mussarat as if to say, Look at her. Mussarat laughed, and he knew she was thinking: Yes, yes, you are right; she is perfect. Whatever Mussarat felt for him, which was little, she didn't deny him this joy. She had agreed to share in this with him, and he was grateful to her for that.

"Your baba fed you. Allah ka shukar," she said, lifting the baby's arm to the sky. "You stay with Baba and I'll bring you a bottle." The baby settled in his lap as Mussarat went back inside. The baby pressed her hands against his face, his mouth. He kissed her fingers. She yawned and then he did, too. He closed his eyes a moment, the tiredness hitting him. One, two, three, up! One, two, three, up! He blinked his eyes open: He saw them, his mother, Rozina, on either side of him, swinging him up as he walked with them, his feet just gliding above the dirt below. He didn't see their faces, but the color of their shalwars, green, pink; their dusty feet, toenails with chipped nail polish. And then a moment later he was unsure, as always, as to whether he'd uncovered a buried memory or conjured one from his imagination. Sometimes it seemed too good to be real.

Mussarat returned with a bottle in her hand, ready to take the baby, but he reached for the bottle.

"You didn't say anything about your visit," she said. "With the chief secretary?"

"It was fine. He sent his regards."

She looked as if she'd like to ask more, but didn't.

"He said we should visit with the baby sometime," he said, embarrassed actually by how little Wajid wanted to know Nazia, by yesterday's polite but crushing dismissal—but wanting somehow to give Mussarat something from the visit. Mussarat smiled, surprised, pleased as she returned to the kitchen. Perhaps, given Wajid's involvement in this case, it was for the best that he cared so little for Nazia. Better not to think of what he was to her. Better not to think about familial inheritance at all, to think Nazia would just be herself. But then was anyone just themselves? What parts did we carry of our parents, of long-dead ancestors? Didn't these traces seep out eventually, arriving stealthily in the pains of old age, in unexpected heart attacks? Or in beauty? The hazel-green flecks in his daughter's eyes— had his mother given those to her, or were they from somewhere else? Might she look just like his sister, his mother, when she grew up? He would never know.

Nazia fussed in his arms, pushing the bottle away. She wanted only Mussarat now. "Just a minute," Mussarat called from the kitchen. "I'm coming, maa sathke jaaey." Sathke jaaey, Mussarat always said: *Let me die for you, sacrifice my life for you.* That was what mothers said, what they *did.* Except for Kanjari mothers, who asked their daughters to sacrifice themselves. Like the woman who'd dressed up her daughter and had her dance for money. Like his own mother. *His* mother, who'd given him up so easily, who'd never come back for him. The tightness in his chest unspooled, springing through him, making it hard to catch his breath. He got up, and Nazia writhed in his arms. He was sure she had sensed the quickening of his heart, his arms weakening. He bent to kiss her hair. "Sorry, meri jaan, sorry," he said. "Amma's coming, she's coming."

He handed Nazia to Mussarat, who asked him if he was all right. I didn't sleep well, he said, jamming his trembling hands into his pockets. Again? she said. He hadn't slept properly since the move to Lahore. He said he'd rest before George came. But he didn't lie down. He paced the room, conscious that George was late, that in his absence the news story might have developed, the potential chaos of it unfolding the longer he was stuck here. Through the screen window he watched them: Mussarat sitting in the doorway to the courtyard, Nazia circled by her legs. Whatever disaster this case was about to bring, this, at least, was safe. But then again, what was he doing, thinking he had any right to this? That he could deserve them? Was Wajid right, would Mussarat disappear if she found out? Wouldn't he lose his mind if Nazia were taken from him? Was that what had happened to his mother, had she lost her mind? Was that why she never came for him? His fists were clenched and he felt pain, hot and quick, where his knuckles were bruised. Damn this. All of it.

It was a terrible mistake: coming back to Lahore, agreeing to help Wajid, seeing Wajid in his home. He could try as much as he wanted to outplay him, but he never would. Wajid always won. He should let Wajid have this. Shut the damn thing down. Ask for another posting. Leave Tibbi, leave Lahore—never think of the Mohalla again. Put a stop to whatever was happening to him, this—*unraveling*. And yet he knew that as soon as George came, as soon as he'd dealt with this journalist, as soon as he'd bought more time, he would find a way to track Wajid's movements on the night in question, where he was, with whom. He knew it of himself just as he knew that the picture outside his window, of Mussarat humming, Nazia banging a bucket with her hand, all of it so lovely, could never wholly be his.

✣

TIBBI STATION'S REDBRICK WALLS CONVEYED, from a distance, heft, important in a place like this, where you needed to convince the locals you could compete with the gangsters, the pimps who ran the place. But inside, it looked like all the other stations where Faraz had worked, a semi-derelict building abandoned by the British decades before, languishing in its infirmity. A plaque at the entrance listed the names of the district's previous senior superintendents: a roll call of strange-sounding British names from before '47, followed by more familiar names, the SSPs of an entirely new nation. Uniformed constables, sergeants, and staff in grimy kameez shalwars and sweaters had assembled in the courtyard—waiting by a sickly peepal tree, its trunk painted white—to greet him. A pair of sweepers watering the spindly plants in clay pots that dotted the veranda outside the offices stopped to watch, too. Those who did not know why he'd been posted would assume, as the SP had, that he had in some way bought this job, and it pricked that this new appointment had nothing to do with his policing.

None of these men cared. He wished it didn't matter to him. George called out the names of each man as he stepped forward, and each offered a firm salute, eyes fixed ahead, eager to show the new SHO respect—all but Shauka, who was missing from the lineup.

"Sub-Inspector Shauka?"

"Over at the newspaper offices," George said as he led him up a set of exterior stairs and onto a wraparound terrace overlooking the courtyard below. They passed the open doors of small, dark offices where men sat at desks next to windows covered in ragged floral curtains or beneath patches of exposed brickwork where the plaster had chipped; where it hadn't, it was speckled black with mold. "They kept calling, so Shauka Saab thought it might be better to pay a visit."

The SHO's office was large, its walls whitewashed; still, he smelled the scent of rotting leaves here. The heavy desk was covered with piles of paperwork and notebooks. On a hook on the wall were a couple of laundered shirts, the last traces of the previous SHO.

"Shall I go make inquiries in the bazaar, sir? About Mushtaq Saab?" asked George.

The councillor had already called Wajid once and would certainly make more noise if he discovered they were asking questions in his constituency. That could stall things. "Discreetly," Faraz said.

"I'll keep it friendly, sir."

Faraz imagined George excelled at this kind of investigation, his easy manner masking his probing. "He was there, but we need to know for how long. And who else was there, and his usual associates. For example, what's his relationship with the chief secretary?"

George took off his cap, scratched his head, but asked nothing more; he didn't want to know.

After George left, Faraz stared at a patch of damp on the wall, its tendrils stretching up toward the ceiling, as he drank the cups of sweet tea the constables kept bringing him. When he asked how they had sugar, they shrugged, looked coy; Mussarat had been complaining for days that she couldn't find any in the bazaar, even though the president's sugar rationing hadn't started yet. They said they'd keep some aside for his begum, smiled: perks.

He left the room and wandered the station, the men turning silent as he passed, then trying to look busy. He stood in the middle of the courtyard, listening to the quiet his presence had brought to the station. *One-two-three-up.* His mother, his sister, him gliding above the ground. The memory was startling, starker this time. He looked around, worried. Don't *unravel*. Not here. He went back to the office and closed the door. How could he do this, solve this, if he kept finding himself in this state?

He sat down and did what he should have done before. He picked up the phone. It was a long time before his call was answered. A familiar, harried voice said, "You son of a pig, you better have a good reason for not showing up this morning. It's madness here."

"It's me, Billa," Faraz said.

A pause. A splutter of laughter, pleasure, relief, too. "I thought it was that idiot Javed. He was supposed to be in an hour ago. He hasn't even called in sick." Then Billa called to his assistant and told him to manage the shop, to tell anyone who asked that he was busy. Billa puffed into the phone and Faraz sensed he was settling in for a talk. "Well, brother, where've you been?" There it was: brother.

"How's everyone?" Faraz said.

"We're fine. It's you we worry about, me and Baba and the girls. You know we don't like it when you disappear like this. You never call me back, and Baba keeps asking if I've heard from you." Faraz felt his throat fill, a lump that made it impossible to speak. Billa said nothing for a moment, then: "What's happened? Are Mussarat and Nazia okay?"

"They're fine. It's work. A case," he said.

Billa was silent, waiting for more. He would never believe a case alone would prompt a call. He waited. Faraz pictured Billa's face, which he knew so well: the carefully groomed mustache, his large eyes always steady in their gaze but interested in all they saw. He told Billa everything; the only person he could. "Wajid Chacha always was a sisterfucker." Faraz wished he could insult Wajid so freely. "You've waited a long time, brother. I told you, when God wants you to find them, you will. You want to look for them, it's your right to do it. You're your own man now."

"My own man. A lowlife Kanjar, fully grown."

Billa sighed: "Is that what you think, or what he thinks? As far as I see, there's only one person who's behaved like a lowlife all these years. A real chutiya. And it wasn't you. This is God's will."

When Faraz had first been brought to live in Billa's house and told that these strangers were his relatives, that this modest home surrounded by wheat fields was his new home, his terror had made him mute. Then, he screamed. Long, anguished cries for his amma till it became apparent it would not bring her to him, nor compel these strangers to return him to her. He hid—in corners, in the house, in the fields, eyes closed, willing her to appear. She didn't, but Billa did. Squatting next to him, a hand on his back, his head. Come on, little brother. Faraz kept waiting, eventually without hope, then he stopped waiting altogether. She never came.

"Will you call sooner next time, brother?" Billa said. Faraz nodded, and Billa, as if he had heard him, said, "Good boy, we'll be waiting."

God's will, Billa had said, and his own will. Faraz stepped outside his office. "Where's the muharar?" he said to a sergeant picking his teeth in the courtyard.

"Murtaza? He's over there, sir." The sergeant pointed to an overweight man in a woolen cap sitting at a table at the edge of the courtyard, his tan shalwar kameez immaculate, a mustache hanging over the sides of his mouth giving him the appearance of great sadness. He sat as the station record keeper always did, before reams of paper and diaries, documenting by hand every last thing that happened in the life of the station. Every FIR, every suspect detained and charged would be somewhere in the station's archive. Prostitution records, too. He wondered how far back they went, if they'd survived the disasters a station like this would have seen: fires, floods—Partition. A sheaf of papers slid to the floor, and the muharar scrabbled around, collecting them. It was a fragile system—this was how FIRs went missing, why police reports weren't filed in court on time, how crimes committed were erased, never prosecuted. But he might find their names there, mightn't he?

The muharar looked up from his work and caught Faraz's eye. He stood. "Sir? Did you need me?"

He could even ask this man, he might know. Or George. Any number of men in this station might know. He just had to say their names out loud. Firdous. His mother. Rozina, his sister. It wouldn't take long for him to find them if they were here. And then the muharar could add a new entry into the station's historical record—one he'd be careful not to preserve on paper, but one no one would forget: the story of the Kanjar SHO.

"I'll call for you shortly," he said.

He might find their names in the records, but they wouldn't tell him what he really wanted to know. He headed for the wide doorway that led outside the station to find the sergeant trailing him. "Do you need anything, sir?" Other officers looked up to watch. "Shall I call for a car?"

"No, I want a look at the area. I'll walk."

"I can escort you, sir," the sergeant said.

"I'm sure I won't come across anything I haven't seen before, Sergeant." He could feel the men's eyes on him as he stepped out of the courtyard.

Tibbi Gali was only steps away from the station, the alley crooked and winding. Small shacks lined both sides of the narrow passageway. It was quiet. There was a smell of rot: open drains, food spoiling, and shit. Rubbish had been piled up in corners and occasionally a rat slid from one heap to another. He walked past men lounging on charpoys who sat up to stare at him, and he glimpsed women in the rooms, wrapped in chadors, scurrying deeper into the darkness at the sight of his uniform. What was it the girl's mother, Mehru, had said? The women in Tibbi sold themselves for nothing; it was where the unlucky and the old ended up, eking out a living for their daily meal. The names in the station records would most likely be those of women picked up here—who worked without protections and connections, with no money to pay off police during a raid. His elderly mother might be in one of these rooms, working.

A man emerged from a room up ahead and then a thin woman came out after him to empty a bowl of dirty water. Although it was early, she was made up, the powder on her face heavy, her lipstick a shocking flash of pink. Unlike the tawaifs in the Mohalla, these women worked all hours of the day. She called out to a boy loitering on the other side of the street, telling him to come inside. Faraz turned back toward the station. What was here wasn't new to him or a surprise, but he'd needed to see it before he opened those records, to understand all the things the names, neatly recorded in a register, wouldn't tell him.

At the alley's mouth, he found Shauka coming toward him. "Sir?" He was out of breath. "They said you'd come this way."

"I wanted to see the place," he said, shrugging off Shauka's questioning look.

"Not very pretty, sir." Shauka sounded apologetic. "Back in '64, we had orders to clear the whole place out. Looked all right for about five minutes before they all came back." He smiled.

"What took so long?"

"The journalist was being a pain, sir, but I think I've convinced the editor to stall for a while."

"Stall? I wanted you to put this to bed."

"The thing is, sir, we got another lead." Shauka looked at him steadily. "A witness, a reliable witness, came forward and can put Khwaja at the scene."

"Khwaja?" Faraz said. "Who's he?"

"He lives in the apartment below the girl. Wannabe broker but he's not up to much."

"The junkie? What witness? One of the neighbors you spoke to?"

"Someone in the Mohalla, sir. He has it on reliable information that Khwaja was there that night." Shauka held his gaze.

"Who's the witness?"

"Izzat Raheem," Shauka said, putting his hands in his pockets as if he expected the name to mean something to him. "With this new information, we could register an FIR."

"So we're not dealing with an accident, after all?" Faraz said.

Shauka shrugged. "Perhaps not, sir. But that's not necessarily a setback. If we bring the suspect in, get it out of him, we can still get things tied up quickly, which I know would be desirable. For everyone."

Faraz stared at Shauka. This change of strategy couldn't have come from Wajid, who'd made it clear he wanted the case to disappear. Someone was panicking—the newspaper report. If the journalist and the editor weren't toeing the line and the whole thing was going to spill out, pinning the murder on someone, anyone, might be better insurance than a cover-up or the sham investigation he'd proposed. It gave them a more plausible story to work with: girl murdered, killer found, arrested, tried, hanged. Implicating the family might have been easier than framing someone else, but perhaps this someone didn't have the stomach for that, not Shauka, who clearly did.

"Shall I take care of it, sir?" Shauka waited, his mouth open just a fraction in anticipation.

Faraz didn't turn to look back down the alley, though the pull was strong. He could let this man pursue his new scheme, tie it all up with whatever story he had in mind, leaving Faraz free to pursue his own plans, to thump on every door here until he knew. But he didn't. He said, Yes, let's take care of it, imagining the story Shauka was concocting, the permanence of lies and half-truths that would be preserved forever in the station's records, their dismal stain.

Twelve

"A re you sure you want to be here, sir?" George asked as they passed the clanging workshops on Fort Road.

"I'm fine, it's good to get my feet wet," Faraz said. That was how he'd pitched it to Shauka: a getting-to-know-the-area exercise. He hoped they'd find Khwaja before Shauka did. It was their best hope. Most of what George had discovered from his inquiries in the bazaar was irrelevant to the case: complaints about thefts, anti-government neighbors whom the police should lock up, predictably rivals of the complainant. But a broker had confirmed seeing Salim Mushtaq's driver loitering by the one dhaba that was open, before being abruptly called away by another man. Any other case, Faraz would have had the driver hauled in, beaten—their best chance of making progress—but in this instance, that was not possible.

At Roshnai Gate, which led them out of the inner city, working men huddled in shabby roadside restaurants over steaming tea, charred kulcha, and pats of freshly made butter. A fakir begged for change in exchange for a blessing and George obliged. "Bismillah," the fakir said as they stepped through the gate, leaving the walled city behind and entering the gardens of Hazuri Bagh. Lahore Fort lay to their right and Shahi Masjid to the left, the city this side of the gate suddenly shockingly fat with might and Mughal grandeur.

"Minto," George said, pointing him toward a park that looked like scrubland in contrast with the manicured lawns of Hazuri. "The junkies usually look for shade," he said, scanning groups of men along the perimeter of the park. The men they passed didn't look interested in getting high; they sat in circles, leaned in close to one another, their discussion intense. These must be the students, the kinds of young men who'd been in the streets the other night. He'd forgotten them entirely.

"What are they up to?"

"Planning on getting themselves arrested, by the looks of it," George said. "And some of them look like they only just got out." Similar groups dotted the whole park, Faraz saw, and he and George, in their uniforms, were drawing their attention. "We're not going to meet many fans here," George said as he steered them to the eastern corner of the park.

The sound of a hiss as they trudged past another group. Faraz put his hand on his sidearm, but George shook his head: Ignore it, sir. Yes, the police had killed a boy, but this rage had been fermenting for months. The president had declared his tenure the "Decade of Development," a golden period for Pakistan, but it had been golden only for some. Even Faraz had been pricked by Bhutto's defiant *roti, kapra, aur makaan*. Bread, clothing, shelter—he hadn't thought of himself as having a right to anything before Bhutto voiced such demands; had anyone? Still, it had not occurred to him to go out and riot for them.

George jogged ahead to where a couple of men were reclining in the grass. Faraz observed the tightening of George's jaw as he crouched to speak with the man who lay with his head in the lap of the other; he was close to the catch. When Faraz reached them, George was saying, "Get up, Khwaja, we need you to come with us. Come on, son."

"Why's that, George Saab?"

"We need to talk to you about a few things. We'll bring you right back."

George's voice was reassuring but firm. Khwaja laughed as if he had never heard anything more incredible. "What things, saab?"

"Some things that happened in the Mohalla a few nights ago," George said.

"Things have been happening everywhere, saab," Khwaja said, gesturing at the young men around them. "But I haven't been anywhere near the Mohalla in weeks."

"You were seen," Faraz said.

Khwaja turned to look at him. "Who saw me, saab? What are they saying I did?"

"We'll talk at the station," Faraz said. Khwaja laughed nervously; his pupils were black and wide. "I don't know what's happening, saab, but Shauka Saab has had it in for me for a while. You know why," he said to George. He sat up. "He'll blame me for anything. A month ago, he said I was stealing from the fakirs at Data Saab's. Those sisterfuckers are always stealing from me. I'm not doing anything, I haven't done anything, unless enjoying a little charas in the sunshine is a crime—"

"It is," Faraz said.

"Come on, saab. *They're* the ones you want," Khwaja said, pointing to the young men sitting in their circles, staring at them. "They've been here all morning, who knows what they're planning." He whispered as if they might hear him. "They'd kill you if they could, saab," Khwaja said. "They hate you. They see you, they see the president." Khwaja's friend laughed.

"A dead girl's no laughing matter," Faraz said.

Khwaja blinked. "What?" He was still smiling, but his face was twitching now.

"A child," Faraz said.

"Who? Why? Why would I do that?"

"You live in the same building. You had easy access."

"What? I wouldn't hurt anyone, least of all a kid. Who? Who am I supposed to have killed?" He stared at them. "Mehru's girl?" He put his hand to his chest. "What happened? What's happened to her?" His reaction struck Faraz as the most human of them all, including his own. "Was it Izzat's people? I told Mehru she shouldn't deal with him. He's dirt."

"You can tell us whatever you know in your statement," George said.

"But I don't know anything."

"Then let's go to the station and get this cleared up quickly," George said. Now Khwaja looked somber, as did his friend. Things didn't get cleared up at the station, they got tied up, everyone knew that. His skin looked transparent in the bright light; Faraz felt he could see right through to the muscles and veins. Faraz put his bruised hands in his pockets. He remembered: bones, blood. It would probably take less than an hour to get a confession from Khwaja. But it would be a lie. This quivering boy couldn't wield a gun, aim for a child's chest. He was only a little older than the girl's brother. "I would come, saab, but Iqbal here needs my help with some work on a construction site this afternoon. I need the money. I'll come in straight after. On my mother's life." He fiddled with a bunch of threads tied around his wrist; Faraz felt the heat of the man's fear.

"I won't ask you again," George said. His voice was low, quiet now. Khwaja looked at him for a moment, and then up at Faraz. The man needed to be pushed.

"I think I've had enough," Faraz said.

"Come on, son, now, come on," George said, cajoling him. "Let's not get the inspector upset. He's new in Tibbi. Make it easy on yourself."

Khwaja looked defeated. "Okay. Whatever you say, saab. Actually I've been missing all those bastards at Tibbi. I ought to get down there and lift their spirits a little." His smile was much too wide now, his eyes disappearing.

He stood and stretched. He looked back down at his friend, raised a hand in good-bye, and began to walk. George picked up after him, and Faraz followed. Just ahead, a group of young men watched them approach, their eyes on Khwaja and the men in uniform. *Now,* Faraz thought, *now, do it now.*

Khwaja glanced at George and then lifted his hands in the air: "Roti, kapra, aur makaan," he called. Bhutto's slogan. The young men rose to their feet. He said it again, louder, like a man who believed in nothing more. Other groups, farther away, stood now, too; everyone in the park, it seemed, was on their feet. Then he yelled: "Ayub Khan, kutta!" Ayub Khan, dog. *Good boy*, Faraz thought, *good boy*. There was a moment of silence, and then the echo came: "Roti, kapra, aur makaan!" the young men called out. "Roti, kapra, aur makaan!" It came from all sides, from all around the park, and the men, all the young men, came toward them, running, because if Ayub Khan was a dog, then these men, doing Ayub's work, were dogs too. And the boys who might have been beaten by them under cover of night had nothing to fear in the sunlight.

"Sisterfucker, sisterfucker," said George, to no one in particular.

"Run!" a voice called. It was Khwaja's friend. "Now! Run!" And just as the mob of young men surged forward, Khwaja bolted, as Faraz had known he would.

Faces, hands, mouths yelling, there were too many coming at them for Faraz and George to push their way through. Faraz pulled out his gun, waved it. Those in the front stopped, and a few panicked and fell back, but some couldn't see the gun or saw it and didn't care. There was nothing left for them to fear. He would have to fire it. George shouted at them to get back, but their faces were set. George shook his head: Don't fire, retreat, his face said. And so, like cowed dogs, the two of them held up their hands in surrender and backed away, their heads down: Don't hurt us, don't hurt us. At first the boys seemed unable to believe it, then they cheered. On the other side of the park, Khwaja was shouting and whooping like a drunkard. The young men jumped up and down, they danced bhangra as if they had won something far greater than they could ever have imagined. And even as Faraz moved toward the din of traffic into the walled city, it was the jubilation of the boys, which had such heart, that rang loudest in his ears.

Thirteen

Wajid sometimes found himself looking for Ghazi, scouring the camp, dawdling past his tent in the hope of catching sight of him. The tents—really just groundsheets slung over poles the Ities had given them—were so low he had to crawl inside, and as he walked past he could see the men crowded together in them, lying next to one another, their limbs tangled as they slept. But Ghazi had tied what was left of his shirt to the front of his section of the tent, hiding the space he had claimed, as if he did not want to be seen, least of all as he slept. When a breeze came in from the sea, the rag would flap open, but Ghazi was never there. Sometimes he could be found by the palm trees that lined the sides and back of the camp—an open-air cage in a stone quarry.

They'd been waiting for transit for weeks or more—was it two months now? He was sure Tshepo would know. Tshepo liked to count things: the palms, the stones in the wadi, the Allied shells that fell on the harbor through the night. Oh, and days, of course. Each night he would say, To-night my daughter is 444 days old, tomorrow she will be 445 days old, and so on till he fell asleep, as if he were counting sheep. Wajid had met Tshepo in those early weeks in Tobruk, and here in Benghazi spent most of his time with him. He had tired of trying to find a perch with the whites; they eyed him suspiciously, turned to one another when he approached. There hadn't been time during the fighting for that sort of thing, but now that's all there was: endless time to spend, as meanly as they wanted. To the men from Wembley and Slough and Exeter, places he'd barely heard of, he was just another bastard darkie, officer or not, a toff to boot. The Blacks were different; they moved over, made space for him without thinking, it seemed, and then he found Tshepo: an optimist, a man who understood the importance of trying to smile through all this, like Sam Rustomji, like him.

"Indian man?" Tshepo had said that day at Tobruk as they waited for their rations inside the fort.

"African man?" Wajid said.

"*English* man." Handsome and broad, the Black man held his eye a moment and then he laughed.

"Me, too, as it happens," Wajid said. "Bloody king, as it happens." Then they both began to laugh, so hard that other men turned to look at them. "Where were you fighting?"

"Royal Pioneers. Sixty-Five Group. Humble carpenters. We built the roads for your tanks. Your Highness."

"You did rather well surviving all this without guns," Wajid said.

"Well, who knows what we might have done with them," the Black man said, leaning back, scanning the whites on the other side. And again, they laughed.

⚜

TOBRUK HAD BEEN a whirlpool of men. How vast the empire was. At school, when he had turned the globe around, its possessions were marked in red, and he had thought of all the land, the rivers and fields, that belonged to it. But now the empire revealed itself in a new way: in the bodies of men, their dark limbs, their white palms and soles, their foreign speech. There had to have been thousands of men in Tobruk, from everywhere you could think of, and the Italians didn't seem to know what to do with them, how to feed them, water them, so he got used to the gnawing in his stomach, the sense that everything inside him was drying out, the weakness that came with it. The mass of men splintered over weeks, marched or driven toward different makeshift camps across the desert. It seemed as if the lucky ones ended up sailing straight to Italy, lucky at least till they heard some of the ships had been sunk by Allied forces who had no idea their holds contained their own men, starving POWs. Or perhaps they did; who knew? Who would ever know? This war is a mystery, he said to Tshepo. What's mysterious about war? Tshepo said. You fight, you die, maybe you win. And what happens to the likes of us, if we win? Do we go on as before, or . . . ? Ah, Tshepo said, therein lies your mystery, a beautiful one at that.

As all the things he understood himself to be slipped away from him—his physical strength, his ability to see silver linings—he became Tshepo's responsibility. Tshepo, who wore leadership more easily than Wajid ever had. He made sure Wajid got his rations even when Wajid had decided he'd rather die than eat another mouthful of bully beef. He dug the dirt over Wajid's shit, endless streams of it, held him when the cramps from the dysentery made him cry, and taught him Setswana to give him something to do other than look out into the nothingness beyond their cages. I can teach you French in return, he'd said to Tshepo. Fuck French, Tshepo had said. Wajid wanted to laugh, but he couldn't anymore. Yes, fuck French.

He squatted down over the trench they'd dug along the far slope of the wadi—their latrines—to shit again, and had the sense that everything was being pulled from him, not just the water from his body but the will to go on. He was sure he would become as vacant as the desert. It was then, when he was at his lowest, that he always sought Ghazi. Is it true, Sam had asked him back in Cairo, what they say about Ghazi Ashraf? What do they say? That he's rich. No, Wajid said. Not rich. *Filthy rich*. A feudal. Acres and acres of wheat, whole villages of tenant farmers who do the family's bidding. It was a mystery why he would pick so risky a life for himself except that he liked it, he was good at it. Did he tell the CO he was a nationalist? Not in so many words. But had he suggested to Captain Macguire that he was curious about what a dead white man might look like? Maybe in the way he looked at them, sizing them up as they drank in the mess, never laughing, never joining in. And is it true that he killed an old tribesman on a mission in Thall? For nothing? No. Leered at their women—chronic issue, others had complained of it—and he had almost gotten the troop into a firefight, gotten himself a dressing-down. It was true that Ghazi would have died to save every man there but also that he wouldn't have given them a second thought if they died. That was Ghazi through and through. He cared nothing for the things other men cared about in the face of war, the things that helped them endure it: friendship, loyalty, love. Brotherhood. And that made them all uneasy. So in those moments when Wajid resented Tshepo for his kindness, for preserving something of himself out here in this emptiness, he looked for Ghazi, in whose company such miserliness of spirit was not shameful.

❧

"You seen Tshepo, old man?" He'd found Ghazi among the rocks below the palm trees at the back of the wadi, his eyes closed.

Now Ghazi opened his eyes wide and stared at him. "Why do you like the Blacks so much?"

Wajid smiled. "Why don't you like anyone?"

"I don't know," Ghazi said, as if he, too, were baffled.

Wajid sat down next to him. Men sat underneath the trees or lay in their makeshift huts, wherever there was some shade. It would be another twelve hours at least before they got their rations. He glanced at Ghazi's chest; the man's build had been stocky but muscular a few months ago, but now the ridges of his ribs were visible. Wajid put his hand on his own chest; he must have lost a good twenty pounds, too. Less they were, less in every sense. He looked up at the palm trees and remembered the shady veranda of home. He remembered Amma pouring tea; the clink of spoons, the creaking of the wicker chairs as they waited for Abba, for the sound of the tonga to stop outside the gate, for him to call Hullo! as he walked the curved drive toward them, briefcase in hand. The urge to speak of it, of the garden, of the gardener watering the potted plants as they drank their tea as dusk fell, of the colors of things that were alive, pulsed through him, its power rattling him.

"At home," Ghazi said, "the date palm trees on our land, in the wheat fields, they're shorter, far shorter than these."

Wajid stared at him. It was the most Ghazi had ever said about himself. It was, Wajid realized, an invitation, a gesture, and he took it. "My father was a lawyer. We grew up in the city. This very old house by Shimla Pahari," he said.

"Go on," Ghazi said, his eyes scanning the camp. "An old house."

"When I was a boy, the pillars on the veranda, I thought they were huge. When I came home many years later, they weren't much taller than me."

Ghazi looked at him now: "When you came back from England. *England-returned.*"

Wajid pressed his lips together. To be England-returned was a matter of prestige, of pride. Lawyers and doctors had it printed on their business cards, or on the ads they placed in magazines for their services, his relatives at weddings introduced themselves by way of it, but Ghazi made it sound— like what? What was it he meant?

"Now you will be Africa-returned, too," Ghazi said.

"I bloody hope so."

Ghazi squinted at him. "What's left of you."

"I'm doing all right, thanks."

"Looks to me like you might not be getting all your rations." There it was. "I know he's your . . . *friend.* But you have to look out for yourself here." This was what Ghazi did, rattled the ties that sheltered you, scouring the trust you had in those around you, that sustained you. Why had he come looking for him? Because the bastard desert had made him mean, and sometimes there was pleasure to be had in bitterness, even hatred. But now here it was, and the loneliness of it was so much worse than the pettiness of his own thoughts.

He turned to leave. "Of course the best thing you can do for yourself is get the hell out."

"Should happen soon enough." One way or another, they would all leave, and as the days went by, he cared less and less how it might come to pass. "Sooner, if I have my way." Ghazi put his hands in his pockets. He nodded up at the guards leaning against the fence above them. That was when Wajid knew what Ghazi was thinking. He felt himself recoil. He ought to leave now, before Ghazi said it out loud. "You see that one there, you see how sick he is," Ghazi said. An Itie guard, thin, gaunt, leaned against the wire fence above them as if he needed the fence to hold him up. The guards were starving, too, drinking the same filthy water, most suffering from dysentery like the POWs. "He's ripe for the taking."

Ripe. What an interesting word, Wajid thought. Ripe, here, where nothing grew. "You'll need something to buy him off, and they've taken everything off everyone, far as I can tell."

"I have things I can trade."

"Not unless you've been stealing off the men in here. And if you have, they'll kill you when they realize."

Ghazi picked at the skin around his nails. His hands were filthy but the new skin growing around his nails was white, pristine. "I have enough to get water, and a head start."

The man was mad. How far could you get without water in enemy territory? In a desert? "Well, good luck."

"I need another man." Wajid knew Ghazi's opinion of him, so if the man was asking for his help, he was desperate. "I can pay off only one of them. If another spots me, I won't get out of here, not without help. I'll need another man." Ghazi Ashraf in need of a friend, finally.

"Like I said: good luck."

"You like it in here."

"We won't be here that much longer. They'll send us to Italy soon enough."

"You'll still be a prisoner. Here or there."

"I'm planning to work on my Italian, read some Dante."

"It's your duty as an officer. To escape." Duty. To whom? Wajid wanted to say, but didn't quite dare. "What about your unit, your men, the regiment?"

"Do you expect me to believe you care about the bloody regiment, the king?" Wajid said.

Ghazi considered this. "You're right. I couldn't give much of a damn."

"You're a nationalist," Wajid said, "aren't you?"

"Aren't *you*?"

Wajid looked around the cage. "Of course I am," he said. He had never said it out loud to anyone. But who cared now? If he hadn't died in the fighting, he was dying now, dying without even really trying; he might as well admit to the truth of who he was now. It was a relief to say it. Ghazi looked at him and grinned, those small, sharp teeth of his yellow in the sunlight. It was the most treacherous thing they could admit to, and it pleased him. It pleased Wajid, too. India, a free India. Or even Pakistan. In this Pakistan place, he'd heard they'd rule like the Mughals once had, returned to the position that was their rightful inheritance. *They* would be the saabs again. That was a thing to smile about, wasn't it, Ghazi's grin seemed to say.

"Well, then, why risk getting yourself killed for them?" Wajid said. "Just wait it out, like the rest of us."

"If I'm going to die, I want it to be out there, not here." Ghazi ran his hands through the sand. "Fighting is better than this, this silence, of men dying." He looked at Wajid, disgusted; what he really meant was, giving up.

"Good Lord," Wajid said, laughing. "We'll have to agree to disagree on the merits of that, old chap."

Wajid had liked the army. He'd loved getting his commission, filled out his uniform nicely, if he did say so himself. Sandhurst had been ripping fun. He was a physical man, he liked being outdoors, and he had suspected that if he survived this, he might well spend the rest of his life behind a desk; so a little adventure before real life had seemed a wonderful plan. But he hadn't known how shabby the whole enterprise was going to be, that one day he'd be burying a young sepoy in the desert, that he and Sam Rustomji would desperately be looking for the man's leg to bury him whole, not because burying him whole mattered but because they knew if they didn't, they'd have to dig another pit for the leg when they found it, and that was unbearable. He didn't think he'd have to listen to Sam's screams as he burned in a gun carrier, he didn't think he'd forget every line of poetry he'd ever learned. He'd done more than enough, more than he thought he could, they all had.

He got up. He couldn't go back out into it, not ever. But he didn't say it, because even after all this, it was impossible to admit you were afraid. Not allowed, old man; shut the fuck up, old man.

"What about home?" Ghazi said. "Your family."

In the distance, a desert mole. A good hundred yards outside the enclosure. Wajid took a step toward the fence. He felt saliva collecting in his mouth. Tshepo had said they'd catch one one of these days. On nights when the men couldn't sleep, he'd tell them the story of how any day now they'd trap a mole or a desert dog. They'd kill it, cook it, feast on it.

"Don't you want to go home?"

Where the hell was home, really, he wondered. He was supposed to go back to the house by Shimla Pahari after the war; but he'd spent as much of his life in England as he had in India, he dreamed in English, he thought in it now, mostly. He liked the idea of this *Pakistan* people spoke of. India, so vast, still so much of it unknown to him, felt like a country he didn't know every time he left the small world of Lahore. Perhaps home could be somewhere new with none of the old, exhausting associations.

"What's wrong with you?" Ghazi said, moving close, his teeth gritted. "You want to die here, starving, shitting until then?"

"Your problem, Ghazi, is you don't really want to live."

Ghazi considered this. "I don't have anything to go back to. That I *want* to go back to. But you, you have a family, I know."

"I have a son." The words came out and Wajid was surprised by them. He hadn't told anyone about the boy.

"I didn't think you had a wife."

Wajid laughed. "I don't."

A flicker of something he couldn't read crossed Ghazi's face. Wajid reached for the photo he now kept in his boot, his shirt long gone. Slowly he unfolded it: Firdous's face was segmented by the creases in the paper, the deep white lines swallowing the detail of her eyes, her mouth. "She's a singer in the old city. A dancer," he said.

Ghazi stared at the photo. His eyes narrowed with understanding. "She's had your bastard. How do you know it's yours?"

"He's mine."

"Then what are you doing leaving it with her? If he's your son, you ought to get him out of there. Don't you want him to have some kind of life?"

Wajid looked at Ghazi; he hadn't thought at all of the boy having any kind of life; he had not until this moment acknowledged that the boy could have a life, a real life like his own. He felt ashamed for a moment, and then, to his surprise, impressed by Ghazi's compassion—was that what it was?—that let Ghazi see the boy in a way that he somehow could not.

"He's yours, isn't he? You should save him, take him. Get out of here alive and do right by him."

What would he do with a boy from the old city? His family wouldn't have it.

"You can't leave him with whores, with a kanjari," Ghazi said.

It was like being pricked—he did not think of Firdous as a whore, though that was what she was. She had made him feel things, she had been attentive and interesting and kind. She was a decent mother, of that he was sure. She had wanted things for the boy, as all mothers did. But he had let her know plainly that she ought not to expect anything from him. He would not provide for a kanjar. He had yet to marry, to have his own children, real children. But the thought of marriage, of real children, seemed remote now. His stomach cramped again. What if he died here?

"A son. You're lucky. A son is a fine thing, a great thing. Get out of here, then, for him. Go home to him."

Wajid got up. As he walked away, he heard Ghazi calling out again: "A son, a son. How lucky you are. Your name will live on." And Wajid kept walking away from Ghazi, away from the palms, as if couldn't hear a thing.

Fourteen

The main thing about Izzat Raheem," George had said, "is he's a very handsome man." The assembled constables had nodded, as though this were both true and a great problem. Now that he was standing face-to-face with Izzat, Faraz saw why this could be difficult for a man of his stature. Izzat was as pretty as a young girl, his eyes heavily lashed, a long, hooked nose, though large in profile, strangely delicate head-on. And then there were the lips, theatrically red, the small, heart-shaped mouth. Faraz imagined that such a face might never fade, even as the hair grayed and the body bent, as all bodies did eventually. For a man like Izzat Raheem, who George said ran the biggest deals through the Mohalla, a face like this might be a burden, something his enemies would long to smash, to scar somehow.

"We are so pleased to have you here, saab," Izzat said. His guard was up; as Faraz had expected, he'd been warned of the visit by Shauka. Shauka, whose eyes had flashed with irritation when Faraz told him to wait in the car with George while Faraz went in.

Izzat Raheem's apartment was off the main bazaar and better maintained than most in the Mohalla. The living room was adorned with expensive-looking mahogany furniture, the heavy armchairs and sofa upholstered in a cream-colored leaf-print fabric. A thick Persian carpet covered the floor. Other than a sheet of a newspaper with a picture of the national cricket team tacked to the wall and a red plastic clock, its face printed with the words NEW YORK, NEW YORK, the room was thoughtfully decorated, even elegant.

"I had it all made in Kharian," Izzat said, gesturing to the furniture, following Faraz's gaze. "There's a man with a workshop there and he makes it all by hand. I ordered the same design as the president. I waited months for it. This old baba, he gets orders from Italy, Germany. You won't find anything like this anywhere else in Lahore."

"My wife would love it," Faraz said. Izzat's eyes narrowed. "She has eyes above my station," Faraz added, with a note of apology in his voice that must have appeased Izzat, because he smiled generously and leaned forward.

"Not necessarily."

Faraz returned the smile; it was better to keep this on a friendly footing—at this stage, at least.

"You didn't bring Shauka Saab with you."

He recalled Inspector Karim's long-ago advice: *Flattery is the key to the hearts of all small-minded men. Take you, for example—how you beamed when I said you had the makings of an inspector!* "I like to get to know the important men in my district myself."

Izzat smiled again. He called a servant. "Bring something cold for the SHO saab." The man disappeared and emerged a moment later with a tray bearing glasses and a bottle of whiskey. "What's this?" Izzat stared at him. The servant looked down, tucking in his large body, as if he might need to protect it from Izzat's anger. "Bring the inspector some juice, some skanjbeen. For God's sake."

Faraz demurred but acquiesced when Izzat insisted, and Izzat seemed pleased to have overpowered his guest on an issue of courtesy. "Get a juice from Akbar's, the freshest," he called after the servant as he slipped out the front door, then turned back to Faraz. "Best in the city." Izzat tapped the pocket of his kameez, looking for something—a small pink comb. He ran it through his slick black hair as he spoke. "I'm glad you've come by, saab. I was thinking of coming to see you, actually."

Faraz waited.

"I was very affected by the news of this death in the Mohalla. A sad start to your tenure here."

"Yes, the girl," Faraz said pointedly. "Sonia."

"I've known the family for years," Izzat continued, still combing his hair. "We're all like family around here."

The man had something he wanted to say, a manner in which he wanted to direct the conversation, and Faraz waited to see where he might go.

"I don't know if you know, but I'm no newcomer around here. I'm from the Mohalla, and I have a number of business interests around here."

"Business interests."

Izzat smiled; he shrugged: What's a man to do? Faraz smiled back: I understand.

"The thing is, I know everyone, and people, well, they come and tell me things," he said. "They come to me because they say I am a man who gets things done."

"Yes, I imagine you do," Faraz said, looking around the room.

"And that's why I wanted to come and see you. But in the end, I asked Shauka Saab, only because I've known him longer, and I passed on some information that could be useful to you."

"I would welcome anything you have to share."

"I already told Shauka. The junkie from across the way was responsible for the girl's death. He lived in the same building. Fancies himself a pimp, but . . . he's no one. He was interested in developing her, she wasn't."

"Khwaja."

"I know they say he's just a petty criminal, but the truth is much worse."

He leaned forward. "He has some strange proclivities, some of the girls have told me." Izzat stared at him steadily, waiting for this to sink in.

"How do you know he's responsible? You were there?"

"Tauba, no. He told someone who told someone. You know these kinds of men, they can't keep a thing to themselves. Eventually everything gets back to me."

Just as Wajid would have had no dealings with Shauka, there was no way he would have anything to do with a Shahi Mohalla pimp. But if this man had brokered the deal in which a girl was murdered, he would have as much reason as Wajid for wanting the case to be filed away. They must in some way be working in parallel, if not in tandem. Just as Faraz was supposed to be looking after Wajid's interests, it seemed Shauka had been looking after Izzat's.

"I heard he weaseled his way out of your hands, but when you find him, saab, he'll crack quickly," Izzat said. "You'll have your man."

Pinning the murder on someone before the story grew further was a smart move. The pimps of the Mohalla could hardly trust the important men who used their services; they had far too much to lose. Best for Izzat to name a culprit rather than risk being named himself, and Khwaja was as good a suspect as any. At least they weren't implicating the family this way. Everyone won.

"In fact, my associates in the Mohalla have said they'll keep an eye out," Izzat continued. "We'll find him for you."

Izzat was waiting for Faraz to thank him. Instead he said, "What is it you *do* in the Mohalla?"

"I get by, saab, like everyone else."

"A bit of this, a bit of that?"

Izzat shrugged, a faint smile on his face.

"You're a pimp," Faraz said slowly, lengthening the word, the insult of it. It was only just perceptible: the tightening of Izzat's jaw, although he kept smiling.

"I am a businessman, saab. I make deals. I make deals with everyone around here. And everyone around here does the same. Even the officers at Tibbi."

"Who do you bring to the Mohalla?"

"I don't bring people. They come to me," Izzat said irritably.

"Who comes to you? Councillor Salim Mushtaq? He comes with his friends?"

"I don't see what this has to do with—"

"You arranged the event that night. Who did you bring to the party that night where the girl was killed?"

"I really don't know what you're talking about, saab."

"Important men come to you," Faraz said, and Izzat couldn't keep the pleasure of hearing this from touching the corners of his lips. He sighed as if to say, Yes, it's true, they do, but he held himself back from the temptation of confirming it.

"I don't know anything about that night."

"But you know that Khwaja did it?"

"Yes."

"Who saw him? That's what I want to know. I can't try him without witnesses. Someone told someone, everyone knows, and so you claim you know—but all this means nothing. Any prosecutor worth his salt will want more evidence."

"Confessions go down well with all lawyers, in my experience." Izzat pursed his lips. "And I think you'll find he will confess with a little persuading." The SHO was creating all manner of unnecessary obstacles to what should have been a sad but conclusive end to this business; what a bore.

"Who was there? Someone must have seen him there."

"Anyone you need to see him saw him," Izzat said slowly, as if Faraz were stupid. He crossed his legs. He had given the SHO exactly what he needed, without asking for anything in return.

"It's not enough as evidence," Faraz said obstinately.

Izzat's man came back into the apartment and set a glass of dark red pomegranate juice down before Faraz. Izzat stood and walked toward the

window, opening the shutters a fraction. "I hear you join us from the out-
skirts, saab. Perhaps you don't know how things work here yet. But we like
to collaborate in this community. All of us gain when everyone is looked
after."

"That girl wasn't looked after."

Izzat paused. "We're ordinary men, saab. We can't save everyone. But
we take pride in how we look after each other. There isn't a richer culture
than the one here in the Mohalla. But we have our share of difficulties,
tragedies. This little girl, of course. She's not the first unfortunate. There
was that accountant who worked for the councillor, the one they found
wrapped in a plastic sheet, George will remember him. The constable at
Tibbi whose poor brother took a terrible beating, he hasn't been right in the
head since. They'll all remember that one. All kinds of things happen here."
He stared at Faraz. "Terrible things sometimes happen here, just like anywhere else." He was spelling it out for Faraz: You could die, maybe also
those you love. Others have. "And even those of us with some say in the
Mohalla are unable to stop them happening."

Do as you're told; *that's the job.* In how many meetings with important
men had he watched the senior officers acquiesce? Even when they couldn't
quite bear to, they worked around the higher-ups to do a decent job, never
refusing, never defying. He'd also seen what happened when you shot your
mouth off, when you had the audacity to talk back to the men in charge.
How many people, how many truths had been discarded to please such
men? And it was always in these kinds of beautifully furnished rooms that
you were told how it should all turn out.

Izzat had his hands on his hips, waiting for an answer.

"I'm sorry," Faraz, said without a note of apology in his voice. "I need
more evidence."

Izzat's face clenched like a fist, and although Faraz understood the risk
he was inviting, for the first time he also felt the power that came with
making himself free. It was so much easier than he'd imagined, saying no. To
make sure Izzat would always remember his ingratitude, his intransigence,

he reached for the glass of juice and drained it, taking and giving the man nothing back. A look of disgust crossed Izzat's face, followed by a smirk. Faraz nodded in acknowledgment of this, pleased to have insulted his host, to have him recognize it. And then they stared at each other in silence like the cheap kanjars they were, in a room far too good for the likes of men like them.

Fifteen

He left Izzat's cautiously, wondering if his defiance would somehow be immediately punished, but outside, nothing seemed off-kilter. George and Shauka stood by a drinks stall, both of them sipping on bottles of bright green Pakola. Shauka handed his bottle to the vendor and said something to him. The old man waved at Faraz and called, "How did you like the juice, Inspector saab?" and Faraz saw that he had no front teeth.

"It was very refreshing," Faraz said, and the man beamed, looking around at the neighboring vendors, as if to say, *See, see,* and they nodded, impressed: *Yes, we see.* "I have the best, the cleanest stand in the inner city. And if you come back, sir," he said to Faraz more quietly, "I have special vials from the hakim. Keeps all the begums very happy. Usually expensive, but for our friends at Tibbi, I do sale price. Ask Shauka Saab, he knows."

"That's right," Shauka said. "And your miracle juice has blessed me with four daughters."

Akbar ignored him. "All the important men in Lahore come to me, saab."

Faraz laughed. Here was a man who knew how to sell to men.

"Good meeting, sir?" George asked.

"Excellent," Faraz said. "Couldn't have gone better."

Shauka didn't ask for details. He didn't need to; Izzat Raheem would surely convey directly what he thought of the new SHO.

Akbar turned to shout at his assistant, who instead of collecting bottles was watching a group of children playing some sort of game in the street. One of the kids called out to him, "Come on, come on, yaar, come play." The boy shook his head.

"Djinn Baba," a heavy kid called as he ran past the stand, a half-dozen others running after him, the dust flying as their screams and laughter filled the street.

"What game is this? Hide-and-seek?" Faraz asked Akbar's assistant. The boy shook his head. "It's called Djinn Baba. The djinn steals a boy and then he sleeps. The others have to rescue the boy before the djinn wakes up and catches them."

"Who's the djinn?"

An older boy sauntered around the corner, smoking a cigarette. He gave an exaggerated yawn, then he bellowed, "Get out of here, I'm going back to sleep!" From afar, the younger kids shrieked with laughter.

"You shouldn't be playing here," Akbar scolded. "We have customers."

"They're just playing," George said. "And there's nowhere much for them to play."

"They're here for hours," Akbar grumbled. "You'd think they'd tire of it."

"Must be a good game," Faraz said to the assistant, who sat by the stand, forlorn.

"It is. And it's a true story. It's real."

"That's what they love about it," Akbar said, "because *really* it's a very stupid game."

"What do you mean it's real?" Faraz said. "You think there are real djinns?"

The boy shrugged.

Akbar explained. "Years ago, a boy went missing from the Mohalla. Just a little thing, he was. One of the old kanjaris sold him. He never came back. When my own children wouldn't do as they were told, my wife used to threaten, 'I'll call the Djinn Baba to come and take you away as well.' All the mothers said it. After a time, the kids in the Mohalla started playing this game."

Faraz stared at him. "I don't understand."

"What's to understand, saab?"

"The true story. Who was the boy? The one they took?"

"Oh, I don't remember his name. This was from a long time ago, before Partition. Some said he was taken to India, others to England. Who knows? The old woman gets cross if she hears them playing near her, so they come here."

"The old woman?"

"The kanjari. The one who sold the boy."

Faraz watched as the band of kids crept back toward where Djinn Baba was pretending to sleep by the boy he'd captured. As they inched closer, in a bid to rescue their friend, the djinn jumped up and roared at them, sending them scrambling again. Another flurry of dust; he felt light-headed.

"Where? Where in the Mohalla?" he asked, trying to steady his voice. "Where does the old woman live?"

"I heard she has a nice place," said Akbar. He turned to his assistant. "Where's the old woman live, the Djinn Baba woman?"

"Above the music shop," said the boy. "Where the old cinema used to be."

Faraz reached for the stall, for something to hold on to.

"Saab, don't look so worried." Akbar laughed. "They always save the boy in the end."

Faraz turned and walked slowly to the car, then sat down heavily in the backseat.

Shauka turned to look at him, his brow furrowed. "Are you all right, sir?"

Faraz nodded with difficulty. He couldn't breathe, everything was coming away from him.

"That juice. That Akbar is a chutiya, he keeps it sitting out in the sun half the day."

George was looking at him anxiously in the rearview mirror. "Did anything happen with Izzat, sir?"

Faraz opened his mouth to speak, but nothing came out.

"Don't be ridiculous," Shauka said. "Izzat's not stupid. He's not going to do anything to the SHO." He reached for Faraz's wrist, felt his pulse. "He's okay, he's okay. It must have been the drink, that's all. And it's hot for November."

Faraz nodded. He placed his hand on his stomach.

"Let's get him back to the station," Shauka said to George. "Call the medical officer just to be safe." He spoke gently to Faraz. "Don't worry, sir. We'll look after you." He kept looking back at him as they pulled away. "You'll perk up, sir, when we get some tea in you." He ventured a smile. "You better, or the SP will be asking us what we did."

Faraz acknowledged their concern mutely, surprised at how liberated he felt, freed from having to speak, from trying to appear strong. As they made their way slowly back to Tibbi, the radio off, he tried to concentrate on what he could see out of the window, but everything seemed to turn gray, as if it were going to slip away forever. He did not want to remember, and he fought it. He focused on anything his eyes fell on: the black flags flying from the rooftops, the clothes billowing on the washing lines, the poster of Salim Mushtaq, his smile torn where the poster had ripped. The panjan, the silver hands of Fatima that peeked out from the windows of the neighborhood. But even as he tried to fix his attention on these things, real things, the memory came back, bold, insistent. He was inside it, the memory: the image of his home growing smaller and smaller as he was carried away from it, the weight of the arms of the heavyset man, the djinn who held him, the smell of his cologne, his sweat.

Sixteen

When Peracha's assistant called to invite her to a party Prima Studios was hosting in honor of Madam, Noor Jehan herself, at the Punjab Club, Rozina considered not going. She knew what Peracha was offering, and the rewards were less certain than they would be if she just went to a broker—at least then you knew your cut, and you were fairly sure to get it. The best bet was to tell Firdous everything, then sell the place in the Mohalla and get out for good. This might be an opportunity for them all. But when she called Firdous, her mother was overwrought. Izzat Raheem was furious with the police at Tibbi. He was keeping Irfan close, presumably to impress on the boy the importance of staying quiet. What Rozina should be worrying about, Firdous said, was Mina, who, when she wasn't making a nuisance of herself at Mehru's, had been following Irfan into places she shouldn't go. If Izzat Raheem got his claws into that Irfan, he'd soon have Irfan putting Mina to work. What then? They'd be making money off her. *Not us*, was what Firdous didn't say, but Rozina knew she meant. So now Irfan, too, had become her problem. Given all that, how could Rozina tell her mother that everything beyond the Mohalla was also going awry, and that she might have to return there herself? Money. Money was what fixed problems—bought favors, bought freedom, both in the Mohalla and outside it. She called Peracha's assistant back: What time?

⸙

THE AIR WAS CLEARER and cooler on the Mall than in Gulberg, which smelled of the smoke from meat grilling in the bazaar and trash burning in the encampment just outside the colony. She had called on Nasir to accompany her, because to go to this without a man by her side signaled far too obviously that she was fair game. He arrived in a beautiful pale blue Mercedes he'd borrowed from a friend. We should look the part, he said. The trees on the Mall swayed gently and there were no bicycles or buses, just the occasional car, sleek in the dark. Punjab Club gleamed in the darkness. A valet took the car to park. Behind them, a line of foreign cars waited. "Wah!" Nasir exclaimed. "Now I know what the president means by the 'Decade of Development.'"

Rozina scoffed. "Well, he must not know the price of flour and sugar."

"I don't think anyone here does, Heer-ji."

Diyas lit the gravel path to the club, directing them to the lawn at the back, where a small crowd was drinking, mingling. The air was thick with the scent of hyacinth and cologne, the atmosphere sedate. Rozina felt Nasir tense a little; there was no crowd of artists at this party, even if it was in honor of one. These were bureaucrats and waderas and industrialists. VIPs liked to be around artists and film people if they were successful, but no one could argue that Rozina was anymore—and no one had recognized her yet. She stood tall; looking important, she knew, was as important as actually being important.

When Peracha arrived, she was relieved to see somebody she knew, someone who seemed thrilled to see her. He put his arm around her shoulder and squeezed her, and in the moonlight the skin of his hands was coppery against hers. "I see Sethi Saab also made it," he said. She masked her surprise. "I thought it would be good to talk more, all of us together, about this script of his, yours"—he shrugged—"whomever's. This is a collaborative medium, after all. And there are so many people I want you to meet tonight. Future partners!" She felt the dry skin of his hand rub her arm, up and down. "There he is," Peracha said, waving with his free hand at Bobby, deep in the crowd. Only when Bobby approached and held out his hand did the producer let go of Rozina, to shake it. When Peracha moved off to talk to someone else, Bobby said, "I thought you were looking for work, not for a new sponsor."

"I don't think it's anything to do with you, unless you're looking for more inspiration for your script," Rozina said.

Bobby looked contrite. "Look, Rozina. I—" But she held up a hand to stop him and turned to Nasir. "Find out if Noor Jehan's here yet, I'd like to say hello." She was careful to keep her back straight and her shoulders back as she walked away, as if to cast him off.

By ten, every inch of the club and its garden was crowded with people. Rozina had not been drinking—she wanted to keep her wits about her— but everything sounded louder than before, the laughter more raucous. She found a chair by the pool, where it seemed quieter. Noor Jehan had yet to make an appearance, but her absence hadn't dampened the party. People were dancing now, the band was playing English music. Peracha, for all his initial attention, had only waved at her in passing now and again and had said nothing more about the radio play, nor had he introduced her to anyone useful. Rozina felt the dreadful weight of her responsibility, all she had come to do, and all she was failing to do as she watched the revelers, feeling entirely apart from this world of pleasure, of excess.

A hand on her shoulder. Peracha. "I was talking to Sethi Saab, telling him how thrilled I am to have been reintroduced to your work. I very much hope we will get to do something together." He was slurring a little. Rozina tried to smile, but despair was climbing up her throat—she needed something real, something concrete, a promise, and the man didn't look all there. By the pool, a couple of girls were pulling up their saris, dipping their feet, yelping at the cold. The tone of the party was shifting: boozier, brasher. A heavyset older man was taking off his socks, his drink on the ground.

"Actually, Peracha Saab," she said on an impulse, "I've been thinking about some projects I'd like to get off the ground myself." She didn't entirely know what she was saying, but why couldn't she generate the work herself instead of waiting for whatever scraps this man might throw her? Peracha nodded but he was swaying, his eyes on the women by the pool.

"Heer has some wonderful ideas, Peracha Saab," Bobby chimed in. He had come up next to them. "I've often thought she'd make a great director, in fact." Rozina glanced at him, but there was nothing mocking in his eyes. "She could probably do what we all do, but better," he said.

Peracha looked at Rozina for a long moment. "I am sure there are many things Heer-ji can do better than most men," he said.

She could feel Bobby waiting for her response, a retort of some kind. He would never know what it was not to have a choice in this; you smiled, you tittered; even if the joke was at your expense, you concentrated on looking lovely, that's what you were there for.

A splash. The man by the pool had either fallen in or jumped in with his clothes on. The women screamed. Peracha laughed, a few people started to clap. The night was really getting going now. Peracha loosened his tie. "Too cold for a swim. But how about a drink by the water? What do you think, Heer-ji?" He walked toward the pool, beckoning her. Bobby looked despondently at her, then raised his glass as he walked away.

Now Nasir was beside her. "Listen, Peracha told Bobby you were too old to cast in anything, you've put on too much weight. He said you could never open a picture now." She turned to look at him. "Don't stay, there's nothing here for you, Heer-ji. Nothing will come of it. He just wants you to think it might." It wasn't a surprise once she heard Nasir say it out loud. She wished she could laugh at herself for going to all this trouble. But it wasn't funny, none of it. She followed Nasir back out to the front of the club, and there was Bobby, standing by the blue Mercedes.

"Apparently I'm too old and fat for your picture," she said.

"I never said that. I never wanted to make that picture. It was something I was writing for you."

"Heer-ji," Nasir interjected. "I think Bobby meant—"

"Who asked you?" she said.

He held up his hands and went to open the car door.

She pushed past Bobby to climb in, then looked up at him. "What is that even supposed to mean, writing it *for* me?" she said.

Bobby ran his hands through his hair, pained. "I wanted you to know that I, that *someone* understands what it's like for you."

"Understand, understand! I don't need anyone to understand anything! Chutiya. Sisterfucker. Why? Why would you think even think that?" She slammed the car door and hit her purse against the closed window, breathless with rage. Bobby walked away into the darkness.

"Why do you think, Heer-ji?" Nasir said, looking at her. "Why do you think he's spent years pedaling from one end of the city to the other on that old bike to visit you at Najam's house, when he can't stand being there, can't stand Najam, when Najam's made it clear he isn't welcome. Why is it he comes to Pak Tea House and talks about your life, your suffering, what you deserve, more than he ever speaks of himself? And God knows there's plenty to say about the state of his life."

No, she thought, no, realizing what he meant. No, because it was terrible. Because she could not believe in such things, not if she wanted to survive.

"All these years, you haven't realized, haven't noticed—"

She held up her hand to quiet him: Don't say it, don't say it out loud. There was no room in her life for such thoughts. She wouldn't allow it.

✧

NASIR OFFERED TO TAKE ROZINA to Faletti's for a drink, maybe it would make her feel better. But she told him to take her to the Mohalla. At Taxali Gate she got off, despite his protests, and took a tonga to Firdous's apartment. The revelry in the Mohalla was only just beginning, the crowds cruising the streets, and she slipped into the building quickly to get away from the crush. She had resolved to tell Firdous what was going on but she didn't go directly to the apartment as she had planned.

She climbed up to the terrace. The wind whipped at her face. It was cold, and the terraces were mostly empty except for the glow of a cigarette here and there. She remembered sitting up here as a girl, with Amma and Mehru and the other women, lowering a basket to the hawkers in the street to buy packets of crispy namak paray or cool drinks of sherbet in the afternoon, as they talked about the men who came to the Mohalla, the men who took too long, the men who asked if you had ever seen the thing they had growing down there on anyone else, the ones who only wanted to fondle your feet or braid your hair. They laughed at them and their laughter sustained them, helped them through the work. They argued with one another, too. Sometimes they didn't know why, but it seemed to ease something in Rozina to call Mehru a bitch, a randi, over some small thing and then just forget it as if it had never happened, knowing she would be forgiven, that she would do the same in return. She had left all that behind when she left the Mohalla. The only person who still knew something of her old life was Bobby, and he had come to seem like the only person who still knew *her*, not Heer. Had she sometimes quivered when he brushed past her, when his fingers touched hers as he reached for a drink? Impossible, she chided herself each time it happened, too much to lose. No one was supposed to see, to notice, least of all him. She wrapped her arms around herself, cold. This was her fault; she should have done a better job of convincing him, herself, even Najam that she loved Najam; she had left a gap for herself, only the smallest sliver, but in it, things she wasn't allowed to have had slipped in.

A voice on the next terrace. A boy. She couldn't make out who, but then a voice she knew. "Mina," she called.

There was silence, then Mina stepped forward. "What are you doing here?"

"I came to see Amma, obviously," Rozina said.

"Well, she's not up here, obviously. Why aren't you inside?"

"What's it to you? Why're you wandering the Mohalla in the middle of the night like some randi? What do you think everyone must say?"

Irfan came up behind Mina. Rozina would have liked to yell at him too; what the hell was this loser doing, trapping her girl, traipsing around the Mohalla with her. But she couldn't say anything—his pupils were wide and black, his face a picture of the bleakest grief. Rozina swallowed, unsure what to say. "I'm sorry, Irfan."

"Heer Baji," he said, "please get her out of here." Mina objected, protested. "Please," he said to Rozina, "she's making everything harder."

"Mehru Baji needs me," Mina said.

"No one needs you, no one!" he yelled. Mina breathed heavily. "Izzat won't let me out of his sight till he's happy things are the way he wants them. I can't worry about you, too, now. Can't you understand?" Mina clamped her lips together, trying not to cry. Irfan looked at Rozina. "Please," he said again. Then he turned and hopped across the terraces into the darkness.

Mina jumped onto the terrace and stood before Rozina. She folded her arms haughtily as if she couldn't care less, but it was clear she felt humiliated, rejected. Rozina wanted to do what she usually did—curse him, curse her for wanting him, for ruining her life. But perhaps her own excruciating longing made her feel more tenderly, because she said: "He's trying to keep you safe." And then, "He loves you."

Tears streamed down Mina's face—perhaps it had not seemed real because of their disapproval, because who knew what love was around here, but now, with it acknowledged by Rozina as love—real love—she relaxed. She could believe it, trust in it. And so, although she still cried when Rozina told her to go downstairs and pack her things, and to tell Firdous to do the same, she went. And Rozina thought how much she would have liked to tell Bobby, the only person she wanted to tell, that Mina—foolish though she was—had grasped for something Rozina had never had the courage to do herself.

Seventeen

The evening had felt long; Mussarat had wanted to watch a television play after she put the baby to sleep—it was something comic and she laughed and laughed. He couldn't concentrate, not on anything. After having him checked by the police doctor, Shauka had insisted he go home to rest. He hadn't been in a state to argue. He'd wandered the house, getting in Mussarat's way, willing her to see, to guide him, to tell him what to do, but she had only been irritated by his intrusion into her time alone, by his failure to explain why he was there. Now that they were sitting in front of the TV together, he realized it was making her self-conscious that he wasn't laughing with her. He went into the dining room, where he sat and looked at a book, but she grew still quieter as the canned laughter blasted from the television. She came in and stood in the doorway.

"Is the television bothering you? I can turn it off," she said tentatively.

"Of course not, please watch. I'm just not . . . I'm tired today."

She didn't go as he expected, but sat at the table. "What are you reading?" she said.

He looked down at the book of poetry that was in his hands. Over the years, he had amassed a stack of poetry books. He couldn't say why he had started buying them except that on a particularly bad day he had found himself looking for something to help him forget. It was better than drinking with colleagues—because that meant being around others. This—a book—was an easy excuse to be by himself, one that kept those same colleagues away. Mussarat had looked through the collection when they first married, as if it might tell her something about him, but the books seemed to leave her bewildered; he knew there was no pattern to them, he picked up almost anything, read everything, never sure what he was reading, what it meant, and only after years had he started to think about what he liked, to feel as if he could have a preference. He still wasn't sure if he liked what he should like, but some of the poems he read again and again, and sometimes he couldn't turn the page, as if he couldn't bear to leave the poem behind, no way to move forward unless he learned these words, memorized them.

He handed her the book. She flicked through it. He saw her yawn a little; old-fashioned, she was thinking. She scrunched up her face as if trying to think of something to say.

"You're missing your show," he said.

She shrugged as if to say she didn't mind, but he knew she did.

"I might go lie down," he said. He stood up and went to the bedroom. He heard her go back to the living room. She turned down the volume but laughed freely now, and when it was over, she phoned her mother and they talked about the program, and she laughed again as she talked. He kept his eyes closed when she came in, although he wasn't asleep; the ease with which she sighed as she changed into her nightclothes, the gentle sounds of her opening her pots of creams and lotions. He imagined she'd been waiting till she thought he was asleep before she came in to lie down, so that she could finally relax.

⊹

HE HAD BEEN LISTENING to Mussarat and the baby in the darkness, their breathing steady and soothing, but at some point he must have dozed off; it was eleven thirty now and Nazia had clambered onto Mussarat's chest, spread herself, starlike, on top of her mother. For a moment, he thought about going back to sleep. This room seemed to him the safest place, this moment the safest he had ever known as he listened to them; he would sleep the sleep of the dead here, he knew it, but he had to get up. He'd been waiting all night to get back to the Mohalla.

The lethargy of the Mohalla in the daytime had been replaced with something raucous, dangerous, at night. The alleys teemed with men, reeked of their scent. The dhabas were crowded: Metal spatulas clacked against griddles to make kata kat, innards sizzled in butter, trotters simmered in oily, sticky broth, all promising you would leave this place satiated. In the darkness, the crumbling buildings were seductive, the lights glimmering from the kothas suggesting that at this hour they housed tantalizing secrets instead of their usual dolefulness. The brokers stood on corners whispering their wares as he walked past: girls, booze, something to smoke, other things, boys maybe, anything you want, they said. He thought of the dead girl, Sonia; this was the world into which she was being inducted that night. How many years had she watched from one of these terraces? Had she dreaded it? Or had she shrugged it off, accepting that this was the world to which she belonged? He moved briskly, glad for the crowds, that few could possibly recognize him here. The old cinema, Akbar had said, the music shop. After he'd crossed a series of lanes, he thought he might have found it. A wide, clean lane, a boarded-up cinema on the corner, a smart music shop nearby. Outside the music shop sat a fat man on a stool, his hair long and greasy, his fingers stained orange with mehndi. The store behind him was lit up, smoky and busy—not with musicians but with men huddled around carrom boards. Faraz and Billa had played the game as children, but this wasn't child's play; this was high stakes.

"You here for a game?" said the man. Security, he guessed.

"I'm here to see my aunt. She lives upstairs."

"Firdous Baji's gone. They just left."

There it was: her name. "Where did they go?"

The man shrugged.

"Are they coming back?"

"They packed up their things and went."

"I don't understand. What do you mean, *went?*"

"They packed a big case and took a tonga out of here. My guess is they've gone for a while." The man looked at him, interested now. "Were they expecting you, brother? How's she your aunt? I've not heard mention of a nephew before."

Too many questions, Faraz had asked too many questions too quickly. "I'm from Jhelum. She has people there."

The man folded his arms. "I've never heard her say that, and she's been here a long while." He was suspicious now.

"We've not met for a long time. I'll try again tomorrow."

"I told you they won't be here for a while. If you want to leave your name, I'll let them know you came."

"I'll try again another time." He moved off, conscious of the man's gaze. The man didn't know him yet, but it wouldn't be long before everyone in the Mohalla recognized the new SHO. He ducked into an alley and found himself in a small courtyard, buildings all around it. A charpoy had been abandoned there and a tap dripped in the corner. He heard the sound of a flag whipping the air above. He looked up but he couldn't see the flag in the darkness; he was certain it was black, like most of the flags in the Mohalla. A marker to remember Ali, Hussayn, Hassan. He remembered—perhaps—that in his mother's home there had been pictures the size of playing cards of the Prophet's descendants, bought or gifted in secret, because they were locked away in a trunk. *Shh,* Rozina said when she snuck them out, these came from far away, she gestured, somewhere beyond the Mohalla. Where else was there besides the Mohalla, he'd wondered, not knowing how to ask. Then she lined them up: Ali, Hussayn, Hassan, moved them around. Sometimes they acted out the stories they knew about them, sometimes they gathered precious things they'd found—an anna, a cinema ticket—and placed them before the bearded men like offerings. Shameful, idolatrous, his aunt who raised him in Jhelum would have said; she said the same whenever she saw a roadside shrine. It hadn't seemed idolatrous to him, to crave the company of your dead, your saints, or God, so much so that you had to make a place for them wherever you were: by a taxi stand or in the middle of a roundabout or on a rooftop. Had *she* made a place for him? Was there somewhere in that home where she thought of him? Had she thought of finding him, had she tried? He understood he was gone to her, but he wanted to know that she had wanted him, that she had ached for him, that she had felt his loss like a death. He wanted to know she had prayed for his return. He wondered if she still held those cards in her hands, seeking comfort in the example of the martyrs, and he thought of their pictures, their beards faded from being held and handled, their smiles worn away by fingers that had touched their blessed faces again and again.

❖

HE COULDN'T HELP but be pleased with himself for having no trouble finding the kotha in the darkness, as if it proved he had some claim to this place. When Mehru finally opened the door, he saw that she was heavily made up. He guessed she had not done it as carefully as usual, but he imagined a woman like Mehru thought only women with the meanest sense of themselves wouldn't bother to care for themselves, even in mourning. This made him admire her. She looked at him strangely, as if she were trying to place him. He didn't want to say: It's me, but truthfully, he wanted her to recognize him. After a moment all she said was, "Why did you come?"

"They want to arrest this man Khwaja, but I know they've set him up."

She shrugged as if it didn't matter, and he saw that her shrug was a lie, that everything about her was a lie. He touched his face, glanced down at his civvies before taking her in; looking at her was like looking at himself; he was a lie. He had always been a lie. Even coming here was a lie. He hadn't come about the case at all, not really. "Where's Irfan?"

"Trying to make some money, somehow. Izzat Raheem seems to have recruited him, which suits us, suits everyone." Was Izzat Raheem looking after them, making it up to them, or paying them to keep quiet?

"Can I come in?"

She stared at him. Her mouth was open and her teeth looked yellow, waxy. She turned and left the door ajar. The condition of the room was worse than before, the floor littered with mounds of dirty clothes and shredded newspapers. A pile of bedclothes had been pulled from the bed and lay in a corner.

"Why don't I make some tea?" he said.

"Well, look at that, I don't even need that useless Irfan, do I. I have you."

He went to the small kitchen and turned on the kerosene cooker.

She followed him. He opened boxes and drawers, looking for the tea leaves, for powdered milk. She watched him, looking all the while as if she might like to throw something at him, the rage tight at the corners of her mouth. He took out two cups, one yellow and chipped, the other white, covered with roses, faded from age and washing.

"This house had people in it just a few days ago. Now it's just me."

"He will be back. He hasn't left you."

"She won't. Not ever."

He turned to look at her. The rage was gone. Her face seemed suddenly blank. She gestured to a small metal tin on the shelf and left the room. When he emerged, she was sitting in the corner among the bedclothes, by the window. She had opened the shutter a fraction. He brought her the tea, but she didn't take it. She reached for a small bottle next to her. She offered it to him. "Irfan got it for me." It was a cough syrup, and the outside of the bottle was streaked with sticky red threads of the hardened liquid. "I haven't got any charas left," she said when he declined. "You don't have anything to drink, do you? This goes down better with a drink," she said, putting the bottle to her lips. She didn't care what he thought, and not only because of her grief, he suspected. She knew who she was, what she was, and she didn't seem to see the point in trying to be anything else. He touched his face, wishing he could pull off the same thing. When she brought the bottle down, the red syrup had marked her lips in a circle. She stared at him. "You know, I used to say to my mother that I must have been cursed, to have children like mine. I used to complain about them. I thought all the other women around here had better children, nicer, better-looking, smarter. You have children?"

He nodded.

"You would never think that about yours, would you? But then you're the kind of people who *have* better children. My mother used to say to me, stop, you'll draw bad luck thinking that. I didn't really believe in all that"— she waved her hands—"nazr and black magic. Nonsense, all of it. So I never gave quite enough to the fakirs, to the pirs—something, because you have to, but always as little as I could—and now I am being punished. Cursed."

"There's no such thing as a curse."

"What do you call this, then?"

"You didn't do this. The man who did this, he's responsible. Just him." He looked at her, willing her to tell him what else she might know, but he didn't ask. If he did, he would have to tell her he could keep her and her son safe, and he wasn't sure that was true. He didn't want to lie to her.

"And now I really am cursed because I have no daughter, and what is a kanjari without a daughter? A woman without a pension, a future." She stared at him, daring him, it seemed, to tell her how cold, how terrible she was, but he said nothing. Her face seemed to dissolve. "My girl's dead," she said, looking at him. And then she clamped her mouth shut and looked out the window again.

"What was she like? Sonia?"

She laid her hand on the window. "Sharp," she said, "in that way, she was like me. I think she was like me. Though I keep having moments when I'm not quite sure. She loved the cats. All the Mohalla's filthy cats." She rolled her eyes. "Such a stupid girl. Always slipping off to feed them. They still wait by the door for her."

"And Irfan?"

She squinted as if trying to recall the boy. "Years ago, I took the kids out to this parade when that American woman, Jacqueline Kennedy, came. We went to see her on the Mall. Everyone said it was a very special occasion, so

I took them with Sonia's father. He still used to come and see me then. The crowds were terrible. So terrible. And for a short while I lost the children. I was screaming, panicked, and no one would help. A whole hour I couldn't find them and the crowd kept pushing me farther and farther from where I'd been. When it finally thinned out and I could get back, Irfan was still there with Sonia, holding her hand. He was only eight. He stuck to that spot even with those crowds. He didn't move." She turned to look at him. "What is it you want? Why do you keep coming here?"

"I need your help."

"I've told you. I don't know anything."

"It's something else, not the case. I'm not asking you as police." She scoffed; of course he wasn't here for this, for her. He flushed, shamed, as she sighed, impatient. He swallowed. "There are people I'm looking for from here, from the Mohalla," he said. "A woman. A tawaif. Firdous. She lived here a long time ago. She may still live here, by the old cinema near the music shop. And her daughter, Rozina."

Her eyes narrowed; she seemed more alert. "Why? What do you want with them?"

He opened his mouth to voice reasons he knew were rational: to know his family, to understand his history, but, truthfully, there was nothing reasonable or rational about this yearning. How to explain that he was here because it lived in his body, wildly, terrifyingly, and that he knew without this need—whatever it was—satisfied, he would only ever feel want in all the ways you could feel want. She clicked her fingernails against her teeth, waiting.

"I knew them once, I want to know them again," he said, and something yielded in him, because he was so unused to speaking the truth out loud; he felt the power of revealing himself to someone, someone like her, who might understand who he was. She was staring at him, searching his face, and he didn't veil his eyes with the distance he was so accustomed to performing: imposing police officer, remote husband. He let her look at him, feeling what it was to be unhidden for once. Her eyes moved across his face, his neck, his chest, and he felt himself made raw, his body thrumming with a new want, just as terrifying—he felt it in his mouth, his belly, his groin. Outside, he heard the laughter of men, the sound of a tabla, its circling rhythm, women calling out to others across the terraces.

"Who are you?" she said.

I am trash, he thought. I'm like the men outside trying to get a better deal on a fuck, like men everywhere. But she knew that—he could tell she knew as he looked into the dark brown of her eyes, shadowed by sleeplessness, deep crow's-feet at their corners, brown spots around her lids. He wanted to remember one of those lines in the poems in his books—those instances when the poets found words for what baffled them, compelled them—but he could recall nothing. He could think of no words, only that he wanted to run his fingers along the deep lines around her mouth.

She crawled toward him. Her mouth was open and he could just see the tip of her tongue. He was afraid of her coming any nearer, afraid also that she would stop, that she would recoil from him, leave him; so afraid, he squeezed his eyes shut. Then she climbed into his lap, put her head on his chest. He could feel her breath on his skin. He ought to go now. Go back to the empty hole in which he lived, but he could not move. How could he, when he sensed she understood this gaping emptiness in him, that she didn't pity him for it.

She lifted his arms and placed them around herself. She had decided he would hold her. He pressed his arms around her, felt the warmth of her body against his, inhaled the scent of her unwashed skin. "My sin is I wished for better children. But the truth is that if you offered me other children, the clever, beautiful ones, those ones that are no trouble, I would never have taken them, not really. But I wished it, and that was like wishing them away."

She sat up, touched his face, and he opened his eyes; she locked her gaze on him, insisting he see her, insistent he show himself: *What is your sin?* Then she took his hand and put it on her breast. "I can't sleep anymore. Not since that night. Or maybe I do sleep but I can't tell anymore, because all of it feels like a dream." She stood and lowered her shalwar. "Maybe I'll be able to sleep after." She pulled at his clothes, straddled him.

He wanted to brush back the hair that was falling into her eyes, to put his hands up to her face, but he understood it wasn't his place to want tenderness, or to ask her things, to want to know her, which he did. She would not give him anything of herself. Just this, and still it was more than he deserved, so he held himself tight until he felt the warmth of her, the grip of her hands around his shoulders, her wet mouth sliding across his, until he tasted her lips, sweet and sticky from the cough syrup. It was then he finally moved his hands to her hips, so he could feel her desperate need for relief from her suffering, so she could feel his.

⟡

AFTER, HE WAS FILLED with sadness. She had stared at him throughout, and when she had decided it was over, she crept back into her corner, falling asleep straightaway. He sat where he was and thought of his wife and child asleep in their bed, its sheets clean and starched, his side of the bed empty. He needed to go, to leave this half-dead woman. But he didn't want to, so he watched as Mehru twitched in her sleep, dozing off himself until her sobbing woke him. She was crying in her sleep and he held her as she spoke a stream of words he couldn't understand. He stroked her hair till she slept again and then he lay down with her in the corner of the room. When he woke a little while later, she wasn't next to him. She was sitting on the bed, smoking. He stood; he had to leave but didn't want to. He should want to run away, he should want to leave behind what he had done, as if there weren't enough to be ashamed of already, but for now he couldn't find it, couldn't quite retrieve the shame that was his constant state.

"You slept?" he said.

"I slept."

"I can make you something to eat," he said.

"Shouldn't you go home? Don't you have a wife and children? It's almost four."

There it was: He *was* trash; here he was like the tamash been, making their way home now. Although he hadn't come for the same thing—or had he? He was struck by the coolness of her gaze, so unlike the pant of longing he still felt. He opened his wallet and handed her money. Is this what Wajid had done? What had it been like for him? Wajid had never felt anything for Firdous, had he; certainly he had never expressed any interest in her. One of those things that happens, one of those things that you do, he'd implied, something half sheepish, half satisfied about his expression. It's for you, Faraz wanted to say, it's not for *that*. She stuck the notes in her bra, which meant: Yes, it is for *that*, it is always for that. He wanted to stay, but he knew he should leave. What was wrong with him? It would be light soon and he had to escape this place before then—then, he reasoned, it might be all right.

"Izzat brokered the deal," she said. "For Sonia. Mushtaq the councillor asked him to arrange it. Izzat told me they were important people and it had to be kept quiet. They paid extra so I wouldn't ask. But one of the cars was different. It had a green plate."

"The license plate?"

She nodded.

He stepped into his shoes, his hands faltering as he tried to buckle them. A green license plate was a Punjab government plate for civilian staff cars. It wasn't much, but a start. He had to move quickly on this. But just as he reached the door, she said, "Firdous."

He stopped.

"Why do you want her?" Mehru said.

"Do you know where they are?" he said. She shrugged, maybe, maybe not. "I've been looking for her. I need to get a message to her." She waited. "My name's Faraz."

He saw her eye twitch a moment, as if in recognition. "They know you?" she said. He nodded. She was silent for a long moment. "How will they know you are who you say you are?"

He wanted to say, If she is my mother, she will know, from my eyes, from my scent, she will recognize me as soon as she sees me. But this was as absurd as the thought that flickered whenever he passed an old woman, that if he ever found her, he would know it. Mehru was staring at him, assessing him; she wouldn't want to bring a man to Firdous who might hurt her, a man who, like the tamash been, was after something; hadn't he shown himself to be just like them?

"Because I won't look for them. They can find me, if they want to."

"And if they don't?"

Tears sprang to his eyes. He hadn't cried in years, in decades, but they felt so comfortable there. "I'll never bother them again." He felt relief, freedom as he said this—the knowledge that soon it would be over; this was it. "Can you get a message to them?" She shrugged again, noncommittal.

She tucked her knees under her chin and looked out the window. He wanted to go to her, to touch her face, so pale, so lonely, and then she glanced at him and in her eyes he saw her recognize his desire. She looked away, disappointed somehow, it seemed. He was worse than Wajid; he was the clichéd portrait of every film in which a man fell for a tawaif, the exceptional, rare tawaif, the kind who transcended her profession, who deserved salvation. Only this woman wasn't behaving as though she needed saving; she was impatient for him to leave so that she could get on with saving herself, as, he guessed, she always had. If only he were as sure he could do the same for himself.

It was quiet as he left, but the picture of her in the early-morning light kept coming back to him as he walked through the alleys of the Mohalla. The tawaifs in the films always died because there was no escape from their world really, no future, no prospect of real love for women who did this work; but there was tragedy, and in the tragedy of their deaths somehow their honor was restored. In the films it was the only kind of honor due a kanjari. He knew Mehru hadn't even turned to look at the door that had closed behind him. She was not thinking of him now as he thought of her, but instead only of her children, and he thought how wrong those stories were; the real honor was in Mehru's surviving, and how he wanted her to, he thought, as he returned home to Mussarat and his child.

Eighteen

The cards the Italians handed out were in different colors—blue, pink, and white—and they fit into the men's palms. Wajid blinked whenever he saw them, as if they were gems; much too bright for his eyes. The men who were given cards guarded them fiercely, and then a day or two later they lined up to leave the camp for somewhere else, no one really knew where, probably a boat for Europe. They looked back only once. Their eyes did not say: *Sorry to leave you, chaps,* or *We'll meet again, don't know where, don't know when.* They said: *Poor bastards, poor bastards, you poor fucking bastards.* The men marched out, but they, the ones left behind, had to imagine the rest; the path to the harbor, the days on the boat, the swell in the men's chests as the freighter made its way across the Mediterranean, that first sighting of European land, the sense they must have that soon they would be free. They would be, wouldn't they? There was no way to know, of course, but they had to be closer to it if they got out of here, because no place could hate life or the living as much as the desert.

Tshepo didn't think they were going anywhere better; he laughed when the men left. Enjoy the next shithole, he cried out, maybe you'll have a better view. I'll take Africa, I'll take the desert over where they're going, he said to Wajid. At least this is *my* shithole. Is it? Wajid said, thinking of those globes at school, their maps blocked out in imperial red as far as the eye could see.

Ghazi had not mentioned his plan again; he wasn't stupid. He must have decided Wajid wasn't a good bet; why risk saying more when Wajid wasn't willing to risk anything? Wajid had done his best to avoid Ghazi, but somehow found himself looking for him more often since he'd told Ghazi about the boy. He was still troubled by the slip, he hadn't even told Tshepo, Tshepo, whom he trusted more than anyone here, but the terrible thing about a secret was that once some part of it was lost to you, the impulse to rid yourself of all of it grew and grew. What was the secret anyway? That he had a son? That he'd visited whores? Or that he had started to wonder if home was the place he had left behind, or if it was, in fact, a woman, or a child, or a future in which you grew old, for any and all of these felt like they might be home now. And then he would take out the picture he'd kept of Firdous and he would fold and unfold it again and again, worrying it in his hands, afraid to look down at the white gashes the folds had made across her face, making it severe. He did not want to say more to Ghazi; he had already said more than he should have.

"They're sending us out to the docks, my friend." Tshepo winked at Wajid. The Ities often sent out the pioneers to the harbor to work. Although as POWs they weren't supposed to work, a day on the docks was not to be sniffed at; the Allies kept bombing their supplies, and so less and less food came their way, and a day at the docks meant Tshepo would pilfer what he could, and every stolen mouthful bought them extra time. "You look like you need some cheering up. Tell me: What shall I bring back for you today?"

"How about a nice rich brandy, the kind that burns a fire in your stomach," Wajid said. "And a coffee. A really smoky, thick Turkish coffee."

"Oh, yes. Coffee," Tshepo said, "with milk for me. A creamy, buttery, milky coffee. Maybe a piece of chocolate on the side."

It surprised him how well they remembered the flavors, the textures of foods they'd eaten, things they had hardly noticed before being here. After a year of swallowing grit and tinned sludge, you might think they wouldn't remember anything, but it was as though their senses had been sharpened by their longing; they just had to find the language for it now, and when they found the words, their mouths watered.

"Chocolate. Bitter, like soil," Tshepo said.

"Like the woman you left," Wajid said. Tshepo laughed a little. Then they sat in silence, waiting for the Ities to call the men wanted for work. When they did, Tshepo stood and held out his hand, and Wajid, as always, shook it. He looked at Tshepo, but Tshepo was already looking at the other pioneers lining up at the gate, the guards waving their rifles at them, yelling. He dreaded Tshepo's departure, even for a few hours—he was bereft without the succor of Tshepo's steady voice, the weight of his hand on Wajid's shoulder each time he passed, reminding him he wasn't alone, not really, that even here, where the loneliness of the desert was at its fiercest, there was a reason to get up, to protect your rations, to wait for a better end. He knew it would be worse for Tshepo, working in the heat without extra rations or water, that what would get him through the stifling heat would be the picture of the water, turquoise blue in the light, its waves a promise. He would focus on stealing a couple extra cans, because they were all depending on him to do that, and later, when he shared it with them, he would, as always, tell them about the sea, because he knew they needed the nourishment the image gave them as much as they needed the bully beef in those cans.

When Tshepo and the other pioneers didn't come back that night, or the next day, or the day after, or even a week later, when Wajid felt the atmosphere around him thin, as if he were at high altitude, his head light—when, as the days passed alone in the wadi and he felt close to a new kind of madness, he decided to imagine that Tshepo had stolen not a few cans of beef but instead a boat, and that on that boat he had found a way to sail those turquoise-blue waves, waves that turned black at night, back to Bechuanaland, back to his daughter, back to his life. Then Wajid would hold his hand up in a wave good-bye right there in the desert, his fingers, his nails edged with sand.

Nineteen

The water was cold. They were still asleep when he returned, but he knew that Mussarat would have woken to give Nazia a bottle, that she would have noted his absence. He sat on the cold chowki in the darkness, trying to wash away all that he had done, all that he was. Was this what Wajid had done? After? He guessed not. Faraz's mother had danced for him, and they had, if the legends of the Mohalla were anything to go by, enjoyed elegant conversations about poetry, about the higher things that a tawaif could teach a man like Wajid. What had happened between him and this woman? There was nothing romantic about it, but it had felt real to him. For all Wajid's cavalier talk, had it ever been hard for him to leave Firdous? Had he felt *anything* for her? Could you love a kanjari? Could a kanjari ever really love a man? Wasn't the truth that it was easier to fuck a kanjari in some dark room than to be a husband? That the kanjari didn't require you to give her anything, and in this was comfort? But it was the question that had plagued him for the entirety of his life, the one bleeding into everything since his return to Lahore: Could anyone love a Kanjar— like him? He looked at what he could see of himself in the mirror in the darkness; the moonlight fell in pieces across his face. Faraz considered his face; wide like Wajid's, the same heavily lashed eyes. Yes, he looked like Wajid, he always had. But Wajid had thought him less—and he had thought himself less also, but different in the ways that mattered. He would never indulge in the kind of lasciviousness Wajid had—he was, he thought, more upright. And yet he had now spent the night in Heera Mandi with a kanjari. Whatever certainty he'd possessed as to who he was or who he wasn't seemed to be falling away from him.

When he dressed and walked into the living room, ready for George, he found Mussarat awake, sitting at the dining table, a glass of water before her. "You went out?" she said.

He had not told her who he was, he had not told her the truth about Wajid being his father, and yet faced now with having to lie about where he had been, he couldn't bear to go through it. It wouldn't be the first lie, and yet it felt as if it would be; he had hidden his past, but he had not yet had to hide the truth of who he was as a man. "Yes," he said.

"Where were you? Was it work?"

Yes, he should say. That was what Wajid would say, what he would do. But he didn't. He looked down, glad not to be voicing another lie.

Her expression tightened. "You're not telling me where you were? Why?"

"It's better if I don't."

She sat back in her chair. He saw scenarios flash across her face, a stream of possibilities, nefarious activities a man, a policeman, might engage in: women, drink, gambling, killing. She couldn't reassure herself that he was not the type, that her husband would never do that kind of thing, because she did not know him. Distaste hovered at the corners of her mouth, and when she asked no more, he knew her disgust was not just for him, but because she wasn't going to pursue it, because her position in this household did not allow her to do so, because even if she called her mother to voice her suspicions, her mother would tell her to keep quiet, that it was not her place to question him. A woman in such a situation, her situation, had to be strategic, and it was strategic to let it go—but with that came a revulsion, for all of it. The only comfort he had now was knowing that Mussarat would never say the same thing to their daughter. You don't have to put up with this, you're the important one in this, she would say, even if no one had ever said it to her.

"I tried to read your book last night." She gestured to the volume of poetry he'd left on the table. "When I woke up and you weren't here, I was worried," she said, as if this had surprised her, "so I read." He felt shamed at this but also moved, that somehow she had wanted to know something of him; something seemed to open in him.

"What did you think? Of the book?"

She leaned back in the chair. "I thought," she said slowly, "that it was boring. It helped me get back to sleep." She pursed her lips, and he saw all the unhappiness she imagined ahead of them etched into the lines on her forehead, around her mouth, unhappiness to which she was resigned as her life's condition.

The sound of an engine outside. "Your car," she said.

George looked surprised; the door had opened before he'd had the chance to lift his hand to it. "In a hurry today, sir?" he said. George peered behind him into the courtyard. From the doorway, Mussarat raised a hand politely. He stepped inside to greet her and she just about managed a smile.

"Let's get going," Faraz said brusquely. George was just reaching for the door when there was a loud thump on it. A boy stood outside, a disheveled street kid. "There's a man in the bazaar asking for the inspector."

"At this hour?" George said. "Who is it? About what?"

The boy shrugged. "The man from the mithai place. He just asked me to call the inspector. Said it's very urgent."

George looked at the boy, astounded. "Just because the inspector lives here doesn't make him the neighborhood's personal police force." He looked at Faraz. "They need a talking-to, sir." He patted the boy on his shoulder. "Go on, off with you, kid," he said, and then he turned back to Faraz. "I can head down that way and have a word with them, sir. Won't take a minute."

"Leave it, George."

"It's fine, sir. Give you a moment to get your things together." George looked at him as he stepped out the door; the sharpest police officer at Tibbi had taken only a moment to determine the inspector was in some strife at home and ought to deal with it before heading for work.

Faraz turned to Mussarat. "I'll try to come home early today." She shrugged: Do as you please. And it was at that moment, the moment her shoulders lifted, that they heard the bang. Puzzled, Mussarat turned in the direction of the bazaar, as if it had come from there, but Faraz knew it was just outside the door. He ran into the street, chasing the taillights of a car disappearing into the darkness, past the police car, past George lying in the street, past the little boy standing over him, making deep, painful sounds as he cried, bewildered.

"Don't come out here," he screamed, running back toward the house. "Mussarat, don't open the door." He knelt by George, who lay with his face in the dirt, and gently turned him over. There was a bullet wound just under the left eye. He crouched close to George's mouth to listen for the sound of breath, but he knew the man was dead. Still, he kept his ear there. George's lips were just parted, his gap-tooth just visible, as if he might speak. Come on, come on, he jostled him, *please*. Faraz sat back, looked at him. Lights were popping on in a couple of the neighboring houses, people would wander out to see what had happened, traipse all over the scene when he needed time to think, to understand. The boy stood immobile, shocked, and Faraz grabbed him by the arm and dragged him to the house, shoving open the door where Mussarat stood, her face pale. "Don't let him out of your sight," he said, shoving the boy toward her. She nodded mutely. "Call the station."

"Tibbi?" she said.

"No, no, no, not Tibbi. Call the local station, now." He slammed the door shut, yelling at his neighbors peering from their doorway to stay inside. He squatted by George, trying to think but finding his head blank, thoughts dissolving to nothing as he attempted to fix the sequence in his head, the only certain, solid thing George's body next to him, still warm.

⸙

HE WASN'T SURE HOW LONG he'd been waiting when the police arrived from the local station. The inspector, the sub-inspector, three constables. A parade. A show of support for a fellow officer. The inspector—Inspector Bashir, heavy and imposing—shook his hand, commiserated, spoke gently. Faraz had met the man once before and remembered him as terse, but here, now, as daylight fell on George's body, his demeanor was attentive, sympathetic. "They asked for me," Faraz said. "They wanted *me*."

Inspector Bashir patted his arm kindly. "You always feel responsible when one of yours goes down."

Faraz told them he was investigating something highly sensitive, there'd been threats, but he was unable to say more. The main thing was to keep Tibbi Station out of this till they knew more, to contain this locally till he could put things together. Bashir nodded; Faraz sensed he was babbling, not making himself clear. "Why don't you go inside, we'll take care of things, Faraz-ji," the man said, but Faraz insisted on staying and the inspector clapped him on the back as if to say: *Good man, good boss.*

The local officers walked around George's body respectfully, checked the car; a constable went to talk to the boy. When after a few moments he saw the constable bringing the boy out of the house and telling him he could be on his way, Faraz said, "What are you doing?"

"He really doesn't know anything, sir. A man gave him twenty rupees to pass on the message. He's just a street kid, he's upset. No point keeping him." The boy looked at him, eyes large and terrified.

"He gave you a description?" The constable nodded. "He did, but we have a pretty good idea anyway."

"What do you mean? How?" He looked to the inspector, who was having a cigarette by the police car. He'd come because protocol required it, because another inspector, another station needed assistance, but the man was not supervising his men. "What do you know?" Faraz said to the constable.

"We've had some information, sir. And Tibbi—"

"Tibbi? You called Tibbi?"

Inspector Bashir approached, stubbing out his cigarette. "Of course, Faraz-ji. An officer from Tibbi down in our jurisdiction, we had to. And you're here, their SHO. You could have been a target. We called them as soon as the call came in. Before we arrived." Izzat Raheem's threat had come good and now Shauka, all of Tibbi, would understand it. They would know that this meant another cleanup, but this time they would have to mop up the murder of their colleague, their friend.

"What did they say?"

"Of course they were very distressed, but they were very helpful. They told us about some ongoing issues Sergeant George was having over an old case, some bootleggers he'd upset considerably. They'd been sending him threats for a while. It sounds like the boy has confirmed that?" He turned to the constable, who nodded.

"They asked for me, not George," Faraz said.

"Any ruse to get you both out would have worked. But it was George they wanted. They sent the boy in only after George had arrived with the car."

Faraz felt himself coming undone. Everything was being tied up around him at breathless speed, he could see, with little embarrassment over its obviousness or shoddiness. Inspector Bashir was better at this than him; he understood how to clean up, that what mattered was finishing, not fixating on details.

"If I were you, I would get some rest, Faraz-ji. You'll need to report to the SP and the others." He waved his hand to indicate the higher-ups.

"The SP knows already?"

"You know the protocol. Officer killed, higher-ups are all over this from

the SP to the inspector general and beyond." Beyond meant province officials, the chief secretary—Wajid. "It's all in hand, Faraz-ji." An ambulance
was pulling up to take George's body away. "See the inspector inside,"
Bashir said to his sub-inspector, as if Faraz—fragile and distressed—
needed help, as if removing Faraz from the crime scene had nothing to do
with the efficiency they intended to demonstrate to the city's bureaucracy.

✧

INSIDE, MUSSARAT APPROACHED HIM GINGERLY. She kept glancing at
Nazia, who was playing in the courtyard. "They asked for you," she said.
She'd understood, and he contemplated telling her everything then; she
was intelligent, astute, she would see it perhaps better than him, but he
couldn't do that to her.

"It was George. Some old grudge. They've verified the story."

She clattered the tea things; she looked at him bluntly; she didn't believe
him. "They asked for *you*." She was angry now.

"Pack a bag and go to your mother's."

"You said this was a good job, a good opportunity."

"I'll arrange for someone to take you there."

"What is it you've done? Why is this happening? Can't you make it
stop?"

"Just get packed," he yelled.

He went into the courtyard, where Nazia sat, a jumble of pots, pans,
and toys around her. He crouched down beside her. He knew nothing of
George, really, his family, his life. But he knew the man would be mourned,
a family would find themselves suddenly altered, diminished, perhaps im-
poverished, while he was still here beside his daughter. It was wrong to feel
saved—lucky—but he did. It was right to feel shame, which he did, for
everything. How stupidly he'd thought: It's just a matter of standing up to
them. What had made him think he could? *Can't you make it stop,* Mussarat
had said. He couldn't, it seemed. Instead he had managed to make everything worse—a man was dead, they knew where he and his family lived. He

could not say that he had not been warned. He could not say he didn't know these kinds of things happened to men who did not do as they'd been told.

Mussarat came in with a bottle for Nazia, her eyes ranging around the house, assessing him; none of it satisfactory, none of it the source of comfort and protection she'd been promised from a home, a husband. Nazia offered him a plastic wind-up toy, a train. He wound the little red train for her and all three of them watched as it zipped around the courtyard. When it came to a sudden halt, he felt as if his own heart had stopped.

⬦

ON THE VERANDA, Safia sat on a divan, a table covered in breakfast things, all china and silver, before her. She wore a shawl around her shoulders to counter the early-morning chill. An electric heater, its bars red, sat by the half-open door. A girl of about fifteen or sixteen was sitting next to her, reading. A big, heavy English book. They both looked up at Faraz as he approached. "Inspector!" Safia said, friendly, curious rather than alarmed.

"I'm sorry to interrupt. I was hoping to catch the chief secretary before work."

"It must be urgent." She looked at him quizzically; this was not usual. He smiled a little to reassure her. After sending Mussarat and Nazia away, he had considered his options; there were none. He had been asked to shut the case down, and because he hadn't, it was being done for him.

"Well, I hope he hasn't gotten himself into any kind of trouble." She laughed. "He went to the club for a swim. He'll be back very soon. Samina, did you say salaam?"

The girl had returned to her book. She sighed, compelled as she was to greet him, and offered him a clipped salaam before she cast her eyes down again. Her mother looked at her with mild irritation and then back at Faraz, an expression of mock exasperation on her face. The girl would have stood up for someone who mattered; he was just another member of a huge staff, the people who traipsed in to do things for them or to ask things of them, and Safia knew such courtesy was nice but not necessary. She smiled

163

again. "Tea?" He was about to decline, as was expected, but then he looked down at their breakfast things: a delicate silver toast rack, a china butter dish, silver cutlery glinting. He nodded and Safia blinked, surprised. He took a step up onto the veranda, and now the girl, Samina, raised her eyes to look at him.

Safia poured him a cup of tea, and in the chill its steam curled upward. Samina sat up and drank from her own cup. The girl didn't look much like Wajid, nor did she look very much like Safia except for her eyes, which were quick. Safia said nothing for a moment and he drank his tea, wondering if they felt the discomfort he hoped they did, but when he glanced at Safia, she said: "Do you see that tree, Inspector? We planted it not long ago. Doesn't it look wonderful in the light at this time of day?" He turned to look at the tree and thought, *George is dead*, as Safia kept talking, with the poise of an experienced hostess. She asked if he had visited Lawrence Gardens recently, if he had noticed the wonderful shisham tree outside Wajid's office. She watched him carefully, listened attentively when he spoke, and he felt acutely all that he lacked; he imagined Wajid mining that frothy charm of his, sharing some delightful detail about a tree he had climbed as a boy. Men like Wajid always seemed to have such stories. Faraz had no stories; he couldn't imagine he had any story worth telling here.

The girl seemed to have decided he was not going to do anything else as interesting as when he'd agreed to stay, and she returned to her book, her mouth open a little, as if she were hanging on every word she was reading. "Books, Inspector," Safia said, noticing. "Samina's addiction! She's become impossible to talk to for the last two weeks. She reads at the dinner table, in the car, it makes her father furious." Samina looked at her, appalled. "Not just any book, Mummy. *Middlemarch*."

"I never read it," said Safia. "I must admit I'm not a big reader, though I did like *Gone with the Wind*." Samina raised her eyebrows. "Samina is, however, a book snob," Safia said pointedly.

"I don't like romance novels, that's all."

"Every book's a romance, darling," Safia said. "Isn't that one?"

Samina looked irritated. "It's more than that."

"Do you read, Inspector?"

"Not really," he said.

The veranda door opened, and a boy—a young man—stepped out, another girl behind him. They stopped, mid-conversation, when they noticed there was company. The girl was in her late teens, and he seemed a bit older. They were both tall like Wajid, the girl awkwardly so, and slender. They looked more like each other than like the girl, Samina. Large eyes, prominent noses, but there was something more closed about the girl's expression, a shyness in the way she looked down after she greeted them. The boy, on the other hand, smiled easily and, Faraz guessed, often. Safia introduced him proudly: Fasih—Chota Saab—and his sister, Tazeen. Tazeen perched on the divan as if she were waiting for Faraz to leave so that she could get comfortable, but Fasih sat back in a chair and signaled to his mother he'd like a cup of tea. He looked at Faraz over his teacup as Safia continued to talk. Faraz sensed she was tiring; she would probably quite like him to make an excuse to leave now. They would quite like to get back to their family breakfast, to relax, to talk as they always did. It would be easy to say he would wait elsewhere, out back with the staff, but he didn't feel as if any of them, himself included, had a right to that kind of comfort just now.

The boy was still looking at him. "Were you in the riots, Inspector saab?"

Faraz nodded.

The boy grinned. "I thought I recognized you."

"What?" Safia exclaimed. "You were not there. And don't let your father catch you saying that."

"I was there!" he said. "But I don't recognize you from there, Inspector saab. I was joking about that."

"Why were you there?" Faraz said.

The boy licked his lips. "Will I get into trouble?"

Faraz said nothing. The boy wouldn't get into trouble. Boys like him didn't get into trouble.

"I went with some friends, just to watch. We went to the railway station to see if they would let Bhutto Saab in. I'm a big fan. I think what he says is right. We should have a voice. Or"—he appeared to correct himself—"the people should have a voice."

"I don't think Mr. Bhutto thinks *you* need a voice," Samina said, caustic.

"That's why I said *the people*." He narrowed his eyes at her, and she made a face in return.

"You have no idea what you're talking about, bewacoof," Safia said. "He loves to do this to his father, too, Inspector saab. Some days he comes in talking about Marx and communism. And all kinds of nonsense about workers and unions, saying terrible things about the army. It makes his father crazy."

The boy looked pleased at this, at the idea of being a troublemaker.

"*Vive la révolution*," Tazeen said good-naturedly. Samina laughed.

"One, two, three, four, we don't want your stupid war," Samina said.

"*Roti, kapra, aur makaan*," Tazeen said.

Safia blushed, and the boy, who had put his feet up on the divan, mimed kicking them both.

"All right, that's enough, children. What will the inspector think?" But they ignored her; either they were having too much fun to stop, or having an audience had made it more interesting. He thought the latter when the girl, Tazeen, glanced at him, before saying:

Arise! Awaken the poorest of the world from their slumber.
Pull down their palaces, smash the doors of their oppressors.

It was poetry; a couplet. He knew it: Iqbal. The boy looked at her a moment, scrunching up his face in thought, and then responded with another:

The day I thought was the most successful day
Of my life, turned out to be my darkest day.

Samina looked unimpressed. She leaned forward:

My pining heart quibbles and protests, refusing to listen to me.
How shall I reason with it, when the argument makes no sense to me?

This one he recognized from a ghazal. Her older brother and sister laughed and she sat back, satisfied, as Fasih said: *Wah!* It was a game. And she had won. Safia rolled her eyes at them. "Wajid's doing. He always says English medium school or not, we read Urdu shayari in this house. When he's here, they can spend a whole evening doing this."

So much time for play, for games. Faraz had had enough, he was ready to leave.

"You take the last letter of the couplet and quote another couplet that begins with that letter," Fasih said. He felt the young man's eyes on him, trying to hold his interest.

Faraz pictured them here, Wajid with them, whiling away the afternoons. No, that's not right, Samina would say about her father's couplet, you've remembered it wrong. They would squabble till Wajid said, "Someone go get my copy of Faiz from the study. We'll settle this right now."

"I'll go, I'll go," Samina would say, jumping to her feet, sticking her tongue out at Fasih before running to get it. And while they waited for Samina to return, Fasih and Wajid would talk about the Test match, and Tazeen would tuck her knees under her chin, and stare out at the trees in the garden.

Faraz looked at Fasih. He spoke quietly:

This is exactly how humanity has always resisted tyranny
Nothing new about our rituals, nothing new in their armory

This is exactly how we turned flames into roses,
Nothing new about their defeat, nothing new in our victory.

All of them looked at him, surprised. Fasih grinned, amused. "That's *two* couplets," Samina said. She crossed her arms, perhaps displeased she wasn't getting the last word, after all.

"Faiz," Tazeen said. She looked at him with suspicion, as if he had stolen something.

"Oh, God, not another one," Safia said, exasperated.

Faraz stood up; it was better for him to move away from them now, but as he rose, Wajid's car drove up. Wajid stepped out, glancing at Faraz before he looked past him to beam at his wife and children.

"Wajid, the inspector's been waiting. How was your swim?"

"Very good, refreshing," he said, holding out his hand for Faraz to shake. "The guards told me you were waiting. Sorry to have kept you." He stepped up onto the veranda and surveyed the breakfast things. Fasih got up to offer him a seat. He put his hand on Fasih's back and patted him. Safia had already started to pour a cup of tea for him, and Samina was speaking rapidly, asking about Faiz, when he held up his hand gently to quiet her. "In a minute, jaaneman. It looks like I may have some things to see to," he said, gesturing at Faraz. The girl looked at Faraz again; her eyes twitched with irritation as she leaned back against the pillows behind her.

"I hope you've had something to eat and drink, Inspector."

Faraz nodded. "Thank you, Chief Secretary."

"Let's move to the study," Wajid said coolly. "I don't have a lot of time."

Faraz followed Wajid into the study and sat down in the chair Wajid pointed to. Wajid didn't say anything for a moment, listening to his family on the veranda. Faraz listened, too: the clatter of the tea things, someone heading back inside the house, the girls' laughter. Faraz could sit here all day listening to them: his sisters, his brother. He focused on their faces, remembering all that he could, committing the pictures of them to some place in his mind from where they might not be dislodged. He knew that memories, like smoke, liked to drift away, and he knew the vast terror of facing the blank space they left behind. When he looked up, he saw Wajid's face; Wajid wanted him to forget. Just as he had wanted him to forget the Mohalla.

"This is the second time you've come here unannounced. Once, I can let slide. But a second time. Is there something you want?"

"I am here on official business."

"Official business should take place in official places."

Faraz faltered. "I thought, given the seriousness of the matter, it would be more discreet if I came here."

"Driving up in a police car, sitting with my family, is discreet?"

Faraz was silent for a moment. "Yes, you're right. I could have been more discreet." He let it hang there between them, the truth that he hadn't wanted to be careful, that he wasn't much interested in protecting Wajid or his reputation. He shrugged a little and felt the sharp quality of his own petulance. "I came because one of my men has been killed."

Wajid crossed his arms. He didn't look surprised. "I'm sorry to hear that. But I have no idea what that has to do with me."

"I need you to tell me the truth about what happened and what your involvement is in this case."

"I sent you to Tibbi so you would shut down questions about this case, not come here asking more, trying to implicate—" Wajid took out a cigarette from a case and lit it. "I had asked you for a favor." His words were clipped, as if they were distasteful to utter.

"A young girl was killed that night. You said it was an accident."

"It was."

"And now a man is dead."

"I have no idea what that has to do with—"

"It was meant for me, they were trying to kill me."

Wajid looked confused. "I don't know what things you've got yourself mixed up in down there. I thought you would fit right in, but clearly you're starting fires everywhere."

"Did you know they were coming for me?"

"Don't be ridiculous."

"Who was it?"

"I didn't invest this much time and energy in you to organize a *hit* on you. You really are . . . unbelievable." Wajid leaned forward, his eyes blazing. "I understand what you're doing. I see it and I think you should stop right now. That uniform you look so good in, like everything you have, is because I gave it to you."

"Were you there? That night?" Faraz said. He paused and then he said it: "Was it you?"

Wajid sat back in his chair and stared at him, disgusted. "Is all this because you *want* it to be me?"

Faraz hesitated. Perhaps he did. Perhaps everything would be easier if Wajid were a full-fledged villain. That might free him from this benefactor, this never-ending debt.

"You know who was there," he said. "You know who it was, and I'd like you to tell me."

"So you can arrest them."

"I'll arrest them whether you tell me or not."

Wajid shook his head. He looked indignant for a moment, but then his expression changed; his brow furrowed. "I can imagine it must be difficult for you, I can understand you might want things from me that I can't give you."

Faraz swallowed. "That's not what this is." He felt the throb of Wajid's pity and was humiliated, as Wajid had meant him to be.

"But I think you should remember what I have done for you. The life you have now, the fact that you are sitting here, a guest of the chief secretary, is because of what I have done. For you. It is more than a man of your origins could have hoped for in his wildest dreams." There it was, as always, Wajid's demand for gratitude. And he was grateful; he had Mussarat, Nazia because of Wajid. But in just a few days he'd discovered how much he'd lost. Wajid would never see that he'd taken as much as he'd given, perhaps more. That he'd left Faraz with no clear understanding of who he was, beyond the loathing he felt for himself. Faraz felt a new fury flowering in him.

"What about the girl? There is a dead girl."

Wajid stood, exasperated. "I have to go and have a shower and get to work. I have a province to run. Please don't come to the house again. You know why. I'm sorry if that's difficult for you, but that's how it must be. I am happy for you to come to the office. And if you need anything, I am always . . ." His voice trailed off. He stared at Faraz, daring him to make a scene, waiting for the Kanjar to have a tantrum.

Whatever you feel, act the professional, Inspector Karim had taught him: *Whatever the suspect's status, he will never be able to call you a chutiya then—not in public, at least.* Faraz stood. "A little girl is dead. I'm sure you don't think that's nothing."

"Of course I don't."

"Then you will understand I have a duty to find out what happened to her."

"We all know what happened. What good will dragging this out do anyone?"

What good would it do? None, that was certain, for anyone. But it still mattered. "Someone is responsible. I have a duty to find out the truth." Wajid looked at him, puzzled. Truth? And Faraz, too, was surprised by what he'd said, about how much he realized the truth meant to him, how much he wanted it to mean. The truths that really mattered seemed impossible to uncover but this—perhaps this was one that could be exposed.

Wajid smiled, his expression bitter but perhaps also sad. Then he led Faraz to the door, but not the one to the veranda. Instead, he opened the door that led into the house. He signaled to a bearer to show Faraz out. Faraz turned back, but Wajid had already closed the door. The bearer led him through a corridor from which he glimpsed large rooms, servants at work, a maid beating the upholstery, another on her haunches wiping the floor with a wet cloth. He caught sight of sideboards, paintings, cushions, trinkets. But the bearer kept going, past trunks, past a series of photographs on the wall: Wajid's children, his marriage, his army days, his time at Sandhurst. For a moment he thought he was being led deeper into Wajid's home, his life, and he was confused. But then they turned into a tiny kitchen, bustling with staff busy peeling and scraping vegetables, setting trays, a cook stirring a pot on the stove. They all turned to look at him. Wajid had not led him into anything, but out the back door, as behooved his status.

The old servant he'd seen the first time stood, held the door open for him. Everything in Wajid's home had been so carefully curated, every detail of his life. Anything for which there was no place was taken out the back: murdered children, bastard sons. He would always call it an *accident*— never horror, which is what it was. There was nothing here for Faraz; there was nothing Wajid had that he would allow himself to long for again.

She gestured that he should leave. When she closed the door behind him, the lines on the screen door crisscrossed her old face, another layer of etchings. She sighed, looked at him with pity. He stood on the threshold, not moving, looking back at her, determined to remember her face, all of it. Because he knew he would not see her again.

Twenty

BENGHAZI, SEPTEMBER 1942

Weeks went by and nothing changed; there were no orders to get them shipped out. There was no news of the war other than, no, they still hadn't won it. Since he'd come to realize that Tshepo was not coming back, hope had not dwindled, it was just gone, quick, like a light put out. To be here in this misery, waiting for some kind of ending, alone—he couldn't do it. The sharp sunlight of Libya turned into a darkness so whole and complete, he knew he would not emerge from it. There was a strange relief in this, in giving up. After that, it was a matter of days before he stopped getting up to get his rations. He spent most of his time in the makeshift tent, staring up at the slivers of sky visible where the fabric of the groundsheets didn't quite meet. He lay there now, not moving. How he had taken his body for granted before this, frustrated by its limits (if he were a bit quicker, then he wouldn't have dropped that catch!), but now as he felt life drain from it, he found a new appreciation of all it had done for him, all it continued to do. When he laid his hand on his stomach, he was sure he felt, just under the skin, the blood moving through him, the shape of his liver, his lungs, his heart behind the rib cage he could feel now. Still there, old man, still there. Why won't you die? How long is this supposed to take? I'm trying, his body seemed to say, as he felt everything slow—I'm doing my best for you, as always.

As he waited, he wrote letters in his head, to his mother, his father. They were blank after a while because he no longer had the energy to think of words but still he felt as if he were writing them—pleasant letters that asked after his siblings, his dear Afzal Chacha, the gardener. He wanted to ask his mother about the dinner parties she liked to throw: Were there still dinner parties in Lahore? Anywhere? Was there anywhere left in the world not scarred by the sound of munitions being fired, the whistle of falling bombs? Was anyone anywhere having fun? Were children still growing up? Was his son? As strange as it sounded to him, *son*, he was surprised to find himself relieved that his son was safe somewhere away from this, or so he hoped. Ridiculous that he was even thinking it. But the thought returned— he wanted his son to live. To be alive, to grow up, to become something. He wasn't sure where it had come from. But the fainter, the more distant everything around him grew, the more it persisted.

He sensed movement, someone at the threshold of his tent. He was much too tired to open his eyes, to ask who it might be, so he said nothing. He thought of ghosts, of djinns. Perhaps he was now being visited by spirits, and the thought didn't amuse him as it might have done once; instead it felt as if a yearning had been answered. You're here, he wanted to say, at last, at long last. Then he felt the breath of someone on his face. Still he couldn't open his eyes.

"Can you hear me?" a voice said.

"Amma?" he mouthed, but he was aware that no sound came from his mouth. How many days since he'd spoken? He felt a wet rag on his face. Drops of water squeezed from it into his mouth. He was dying, and God was showing him mercy, showing him heaven. The hands were tender on his face.

"You're an idiot."

Wajid winced. He thought of his dead grandmother, surely the only person he'd known who would speak to him like that. He looked up and there was no spirit, no sign of his grandmother. Only Ghazi Ashraf. He wanted to laugh, because surely if he and Ghazi were in the same place, then he hadn't made it to heaven.

"We haven't seen you for a couple of days."

Ghazi put something in his mouth. He couldn't move his mouth but Ghazi was insistent, shaking his jaw as if to wake it up, to make it move. Bully beef. The smallest taste of it. Then he was silent, and Wajid must have fallen asleep, because when he awoke, the slivers of sky were black and he could make out stars. His face was cool and moist and his lips were wet.

"Can you stand? Do you think you can stand?" Ghazi said.

"What for?" he wanted to say, but couldn't.

Ghazi lifted Wajdi's hand and opened his palm, placing something in it. "Look," he said, "look." It was a slip of pink paper, a delicate rose color, so pretty, much too pretty for the desert. "They're going to ship out a load of men tomorrow." Wajid was confused. "You need it more than I do," Ghazi said, putting it into his hand.

"No," Wajid said. He wasn't an idiot. He was dying. He lifted his hand: Take it, take it back.

"I'm going to get out of here on my own. I've spoken to some men, they'll help you out. They can lift you, walk you to the harbor, get you on the freighter. That's the most I can get them to do. I've given them some things and they'll probably take some of your rations on the boat. If you get to Italy, you'll have a better chance, the Red Cross will see to it."

Wajid shook his head no.

Ghazi leaned back, sighed. "You know the one about the man standing on the roof of his house when it's flooding?"

Wajid wanted to close his eyes again, drift off to the sound of a story, but Ghazi prodded him.

"He's a man of God and he's sure God will save him. So when his neighbors and friends come in boats and say they'll help, he refuses, saying he doesn't need them, God will save him. Three times he says no before he gets washed away. You know it, this one?"

Wajid remembered Afzal Chacha had roared at it in the teahouse years ago.

"So," Ghazi said, "he ends up in heaven and he's angry: 'God, why didn't you save me?' he says. 'I waited for you!'"

"God says, 'Fool!'" Wajid managed to say.

"Yes, that's it. 'Fool, I sent help three times and you're asking where I was,'" Ghazi said. "The moral of the story is, don't be a fool, a challenge for a man like you, I know."

That God would send Ghazi on an errand, or that God would want to save Wajid, was nothing short of amusing.

"I've a plan to get out. If you don't make it to Italy, I can take a letter back to your people, so they know what happened to you."

"You'll never make it," Wajid said hoarsely.

Ghazi looked displeased at this. "I can assure you my chances are better than yours. Even in the desert." The man was mad, he'd die here if Wajid took the slip of paper, either in this cage or trying to escape it.

"Why?" Wajid said.

Ghazi stared at him. "It's not because I like you. But you know that. It's my duty. You're the last man from my unit left here." Wajid shook his head, reached for Ghazi's arm.

"Look. I can't leave you here—to die. As much as you deserve it. The point is, the point of getting so far is to stay alive, it's the one thing that matters now. This is the only way you'll do it. Me, I'll do it. Out there, better than here." Ghazi held his eye. "It's what I do."

Ghazi left him his water and food rations but Wajid couldn't eat, his stomach cramping with pain at every bite, resisting, fighting the nourishment. His body was ready to die—he felt it—so why should a slip of paper compel him to change course now? What did staying alive mean? More suffering, that was all. Because if he didn't die here, he would die soon enough somewhere else, and here was better. Here, he knew what it would look like, at least. One night, in transit to the camp, they'd had to sleep in a cemetery in Derna; they'd lain on the graves. Tshepo had been reluctant, like many of the men, but to Wajid the desert had seemed a magnificent place to be dead, its black skies speckled with stars. A preview, he'd said to Tshepo, of what's to come. I won't be dying here, Tshepo had said, and neither will you. How hard Tshepo had tried to make sure that didn't happen, feeding him, caring for him. And now Ghazi. He wasn't sure he was worth the trouble. No, he was certain he wasn't worth the trouble. And yet, they persisted.

A gust of wind, and he felt the prickle of sand across his skin, in his eyes, rimming his lashes. Fucking sand. This would be it, his final memory, his final sensation of life: sand, scratching his cornea, the desert filling his mouth, his ears, burying him. Another whorl of sand; he squinted and there was a figure in his tent. Ghazi, returned, he thought for a moment, until the man crouched down, came close. Some man he didn't recognize, his face ravaged by sunburn. God, sending more help? But then the man's arm darted across him to grab the rations and Wajid's own hand came up instinctively to stop him. The man's wrist was thin, bony, but there was no power in Wajid's grip, it was an excuse for a grip. The man could have shaken him off, but he didn't. He sat back. "Sorry," he said, reproachful. "I thought you didn't need them." Fuck off, Wajid said, or thought, he wasn't sure. Then the man wiped his peeling, torn face; he looked disgusted; perhaps with himself, or with Wajid, or who knows what. Then he crawled out of the tent. They're still mine, Wajid called after him, mine, alarmed by the power of his own voice, the bellow he was still capable of making. He felt a quickening in his body, the kind that only a living man, a man who wanted to live, could feel, and it shook him, for he'd been so sure of his body's readiness to die.

⚜

WHEN GHAZI CAME BACK LATER, he'd managed to keep some water down, to hold a bite of the bully beef on his tongue without retching. He couldn't say that he would do anything to live, but he'd allowed himself to remember life: the clop of a tonga, garlands of fat, pearly motia, grass, buildings, books, lips, sticky gulab jamun, hands, mouths, rain, anything that wasn't sand. And he felt it: pleasure—abundant, throbbing. Was it possible he would see such things again, feel them? And if so, what would happen to all of this—the sand and bodies, the endless, grating sound of war? Where would he put all this? In stories, perhaps. Great stories: war stories, adventures, tales of derring-do. The kind fathers told their sons, teaching them how to last, not how to die. Wouldn't that be what he wanted his son to learn from his life, or even from his death? That he'd tried—at least—to last. Onward, upward. That's what he'd want him to know, to learn; to hang on until the end of the match. It was what had gotten Wajid through.

So when Ghazi explained his plan, Wajid nodded, grasped the magical pink slip in his hand. Miraculously, Ghazi had also found a pen to write with. Wajid told him he had nothing to write on, but then he remembered the picture of Firdous. There was so much to say, should the worst happen, he knew, but he could think only of one thing—the boy. He opened it out, and on the back Ghazi wrote his message for him:

> *Please find my son. Ask Afzal.*
> *Your loving son, Wajid.*

Ghazi stared at the message. "Good for you, old man," he said.

Wajid thought if it were anyone else saving his life, he could thank them, he could tell them how much this meant, that tonight he would pray for them although he hadn't prayed since he was a boy. And, well, it seemed that God had perhaps sent Ghazi. But it was Ghazi, and Ghazi wanted nothing from anyone. "I am forever in your debt, Second Lieutenant," was the most he thought he could say without offending the man.

"For what?" Ghazi said.

"For saving my life, for saving my son," he said with genuine gratitude.

And Ghazi smiled, sincerely, it seemed. "This must be what a good deed feels like," he said.

And then Wajid said: "Now give me your letter, in case you don't make it back."

For a moment Ghazi looked puzzled, as though wondering what he meant—and then his mouth went tight at the corners. "Fuck you, Mr. England-returned," he said. "I'll find you in Lahore when I get there." And he tucked the photograph into his boot.

Twenty-One

LAHORE, NOVEMBER 1968

It had taken all of Rozina's guile to convince Amma to stay inside the house rather than in the servants' quarters, so fearful was Firdous that their presence would offend Najam; he's away, he'll never know, Rozina said, and as another day went by without a call from him, this seemed entirely possible. He could be anywhere; he might never return. Still, Firdous crept around the edges of the rooms, while Mina lingered outside the kitchen door or traipsed the corners of the garden, trailing her hands along the undernourished shrubs. Such long, thin fingers, Rozina thought, as she watched the girl with a new kind of abandon. In the Mohalla, she'd always feared gazing at the girl too long, lest others who knew—and there, everybody did know—would notice, give it away. But now her gaze wheeled, scoured; what had she discovered? That Mina slept with her eyes half open; that her elbows, unlike any others she had ever seen, were pale and smooth; that when she cried, she looked exactly as she had as a little girl. Look at that, she wanted to say to Bobby each time she noticed something new, turning for a moment as if he might come up beside her, before she recalled there was no one to come up beside her.

Mina came to a stop by the newly planted neem tree and stood silent, sullen; Rozina knew the girl was thinking about the boy, about Mehru. "They're fine," she said, irritated. Mina made a face. "Mehru knows how to look after herself, as does . . ." and she gestured at the air to indicate the boy; she hated to say his name. Mina glanced at her, then turned her back. She hated it when Mina did that, sidelined her, looked away. "I suppose we could go and make an offering for them, to make sure," Rozina said, and there—Mina turned, and the girl's eyes were on her again.

It had been a year since Rozina had been to the shrine of Hazrat Bibi Ruqayya. She'd last brought Firdous, who liked to come on the Urs to pray for her mother, Mumtaz Bai, and for the boy. The story of the shrine—that here Bibi Ruqayya and her companions had been swallowed by the earth when they called for God's protection—had frightened her as a child; if you couldn't trust the ground beneath your feet, what could you trust? But over the years she had come to feel close to the women buried here; they had not died in the manner of other saints; the earth had opened to give them refuge, and so she imagined them as living presences, still here, really and truly listening.

This trip, to please Mina, she'd brought a degh of sweet, creamy kheer to donate at the shrine, which she worried, during the long, hot drive on the tonga, might curdle. Durand Road was especially slow, thronging with donkey carts and cycles and hawkers. Girls about Mina's age stood in groups outside the Convent of Jesus and Mary in pristine white kameez shalwars; Rozina couldn't help but stare—how starched and smart they looked—but Mina didn't look twice.

The driver pulled up at the opening of a narrow lane off Durand Road and Rozina paid a pair of boys on the corner to carry the degh up to the shrine's kitchen. The bazaar and the long path to the shrine were quiet for a change, and Rozina wanted to amble, to browse the stalls on both sides, brimming with framed calligraphy and silver cradles and standards and religious books embossed with gold. Everything glittered, giving the bazaar a strangely divine glow, suggesting the promise of miracles—and a miracle was what she felt she needed. But Mina, wanting to get back to Firdous—always thinking of Firdous—hurried ahead, and she had to trot to keep up.

In the shrine's courtyard, Mina stopped beneath the knotted trunk of a mighty waan tree, its coiled branches above forming a canopy over the scattered devotees and the shrine below. Mina looked tiny, childlike, by the tree's great trunk—but then it struck Rozina that she'd been about the same age when she first became pregnant. It was too soon to lose a year of work in the bazaar, Firdous had said, especially given her desperate hope that her lobbying at the film studios might turn into something—any day now, Rozina might get a break. Rozina didn't like to remember what the midwife had had to do, but she had been relieved. The first time, the second, too.

"Amma said that women who can't have children come here and eat the leaves from the trees so they can have babies," Mina said. The trees had grown where Bibi Ruqayya's camels had been buried in the earth. "Did you ever try it?" she said.

"No, I didn't," Rozina lied, making an effort to stand taller.

When she'd finally decided, or rather, when Firdous had decided it was time to have a baby—the birth of a child ought to align with Rozina's plans for retirement—she had found the experience entirely disappointing; she nursed the girl with pursed lips, squealing whenever the baby clamped her small mouth on Rozina's breast, wailing at the sight of her stomach hanging over her shalwar. She snapped every time Firdous shook her awake for a feed. "I hate this. When will it all stop?" Never, Firdous said, never. This is being a mother; your suffering is your love.

"Look," Mina said to her, pointing at a woman who was giving out threads in exchange for donations, threads you could tie around the grille on the covered graves for the wishes you wanted to make.

"Quickly," said Rozina. But Mina stood where she was; she looked up at the branches crisscrossing above them. "If you're thinking of eating those leaves, don't. You're too young." And then, to make up for the harshness of her tone, "One day. Insh'Allah." Mina, babies; she didn't know why she couldn't bear the thought.

"Would you pray for him, too, for Irfan?"

"My prayers don't do anything. I mean, here we are for Irfan, of all people."

Mina pursed her lips, angry, then moved off toward the woman who worked at the shrine. She took a thread from her and stood by the other devotees praying by the graves.

Rozina had felt nothing but relief when she first left with Najam; Mina was safe with Amma, and she was free. But later, when Mina squirmed in her arms, choosing Firdous, she'd felt resentful, then guilty; wasn't this the least she could give her mother? Hadn't Mina's arrival revived Firdous after all the years of pining for the missing boy? Hadn't it gone some way toward making the days easier for her mother? And yet her own had grown harder, year by year: Your suffering is your love.

Mina stretched out those long, thin fingers of hers to tie her thread on the grille, knotting her wish there. A breeze rustled the waan tree's branches, scattering leaves. After the birth, Firdous had told Rozina how lucky she was to have had a girl, to have secured their future, how blessed they were to have a profession, a legacy to pass down to this child. Maybe, but I want her to choose it, Rozina said. No one chooses anything in this life. It's all God's will, Firdous said. She couldn't argue with that. No one was free from what God had fated for them. It was at that moment that she'd known she couldn't do it—not any of it.

But Firdous had also always said that prayers could mitigate and appease, that God was generous and merciful and would hear you, that the women buried here were powerful intermediaries who would plead on your behalf, and miracles did happen, wild, impossible miracles happened. The earth could open up and hold you to its bosom if God commanded it, the leaves of a blessed tree could conjure a baby inside you. Mina's eyes were closed, her mouth moved silently, desperately. Her daughter had made a wish. For a boy, maybe for babies. And so she went and stood by her, brushing roughly at the tiny dried leaves and debris from the tree caught in Mina's hair, her dupatta, on her shoulders, chiding her, but asking God, under her breath, to grant her daughter's wish and her own, which was to keep the girl within reach, always close enough for her to touch.

⁂

WHEN THEY GOT HOME, they found Mehru sitting on the steps of the veranda, like a peddler come to sell them something. She wore a shawl over her hair, which was loosely braided, and heavy makeup; she looked flushed, her cheeks pink, as if she were drunk. Mina ran to her as if her prayers at the shrine had been answered, but Rozina walked slowly, dreading what she would say to her; what did you say to a woman who'd been through this? She put her arms around Mehru, surprised to find her warm, sweaty, although she wasn't sure why.

"You look . . . ," Rozina said, then paused, unsure how to finish.

"I didn't want to come here and embarrass you in front of your neighbors," Mehru said, touching her face.

"Don't say such things," she said. "Mehru . . . I don't know what to say."

Mehru gripped her arm, squeezed it hard, desperately: Don't say it, don't say anything, and so Rozina stopped. And she felt she understood then why she'd been surprised to feel Mehru's back damp, her skin warm; she'd expected Mehru's grief to be a kind of death, a stillness, but instead Mehru was trembling with it, as if her body were more sensitive to everything, more alive than ever before—one living being cruelly exchanged for another kind of being, one that was all pain, that she'd forever have to manage, to tame.

"Does Amma know you're here?" she said, and turned to Mina. "Go, call her."

Mehru shook her head. "No, not yet. I need to talk to you first, then we'll tell her."

"Tell her what?" Rozina said. Then Mehru took Rozina's hand in hers, knotting her fingers through Rozina's before taking in a breath to speak.

184

Twenty-Two

It had been early when they reached the Mall. The sweepers had come and gone, hosing down the tarmac so the black and yellow markings on the curb looked polished in the sunlight. The road was wide and empty, except for the occasional car and a lone bus. As they'd driven up from Tibbi, the pink sandstone, the solid, impenetrable lines of the General Post Office, the High Court, of Chief's College, which stood in the shade of ancient trees behind its gates, seemed fortified against disorder; designed to quell chaos, to civilize. Only the shadowy arches lining the balconies like cavernous eye sockets suggested that fear hid somewhere here in the Mall, as it did everywhere. Now, as he stood on the veranda outside the SP's offices, their graying marble steps stained red where men had mouthed and spat their paan, he thought of Wajid driving through here each day, the heads of the endless line of shisham trees on both sides of the Mall bowing to him as he traveled to the Civil Secretariat to sit in an office housed in its cool white marble cloisters.

Shauka and a constable were waiting for him in the car; he thought Shauka had seen him, but the sub-inspector made no move to get out of the car, to open the door for him. Faraz understood the insult, that Shauka had rightly guessed his only duty would be to escort the inspector home, that he would never have to see him again. Faraz hadn't realized it when he'd entered the SP's office an hour before, not really; a dressing-down he'd anticipated, but not this. He moved slowly—he would be angry later, he knew, but he couldn't reach for it yet; right now he felt bewildered—light-headed.

When he sat down in the car, Shauka waited—a last courtesy—for Faraz to speak, to give them the order. "Let's go," Faraz said.

"Sir?" Shauka said, intoning confusion, innocence; he wanted the inspector to say it. Faraz stared into the rearview mirror. "Home." The word felt ungainly in his mouth—he had no home, had never had one, and shortly he would have to tell Mussarat that she would have to leave hers. A killing outside her door a few hours earlier, now this.

At Tibbi that morning, Faraz had found the officers silent and seething at the news of George's death, but it wasn't until Shauka presented him with Khwaja in the holding cell, arrested for murder, that Faraz realized it was over. Khwaja knew it too, they all did—the man would have to hang, it was the only way out of this for everyone. And so Khwaja sobbed, nose streaming as he pleaded with them. Faraz stepped back from the cell. One officer was dead, and now another man might die. He couldn't undo any of it. All he could do was stop before anything else happened. "Let's get over to the SP's office," Faraz said, and Shauka had nodded with the nonchalance of a man who already knew he was no longer answerable to him.

Outside the station, as a constable held the car door open for him, Irfan came running up; the news of Khwaja's arrest everywhere now. "I know him," the boy said. "It wasn't him, Khwaja wasn't there." He said it again and again, knowing that if Khwaja was arrested, no one else ever would be.

Shauka pushed him back. "Go on, son, move along," Faraz said. Irfan stared at him; Faraz had promised to help, told them the truth mattered, claimed he cared about it. Faraz shook his head. I'm sorry, he meant; the boy's expression shifted from confusion to something harder. It turned out that the new SHO was just like all the other chutiyas at Tibbi. Faraz couldn't argue with that; the boy's lip curled with disgust, perhaps at Faraz's betrayal, or at himself for falling for the SHO's performance of decency. Or perhaps because the injustice of his sister's murder would now be forever sealed. "Let's go," Faraz said to Shauka; he wanted nothing more right now than to escape to the SP's office, to the Mall, all of it a world away from this place.

There'd been no escape here, though; just a new trap.

Now the Mall was a flurry of cars and buses and cycles; it would take time to get to Ichra. Shauka's arm dangled outside the open window, untroubled by the delay ahead; everything was settled now. Faraz tried to piece together a way to explain the SP's order to Mussarat, that they had to leave Lahore, her parents, that they would live out their future in the wilderness now that Wajid's favor was lost, that there was no future at all, in fact. That he'd been warned: Take it, the little now on offer, or lose everything. He imagined the cheerful resignation she'd so carefully cultivated finally dissolving, turning into something real, hard.

The Mall was beautiful, but Faraz remembered the shadows cast by the looming kothas in the Mohalla and thought how he preferred those gloomy, crumbling buildings to the bright facades here, behind which important men sat watching the rest of them, where he had to strain to sense the darkness he knew was there.

✧

ROZINA, IN A STATE OF PANIC, had yelled at the cab driver all the way to the Mohalla, so that once they got there, she found herself hoarse. From just outside Taxali Gate they sent word to Abdul Raheem, who in turn conveyed that his contacts at Tibbi said there'd been some kind of disaster, an officer killed, and the inspector had now left, perhaps posted, perhaps dismissed, no one knew yet.

She sat with Firdous, who was frozen with the shock of it all, stumped. On the way down, she'd been frantic but she had not, in truth, been thinking of the boy. Even when Mehru told them everything, said she thought this might really be him, she had not been thinking of him. She had instead thought of herself as a girl, of Firdous as a young mother, who they had been then, what they'd been like, how he might remember them. How she had longed for his return, how she had prayed for it day after day. But over the years, his memory became smeared, faded, like a half-remembered dream, a fiction from her childhood. And what was the boy now but that? He was a character in a game the Mohalla kids played, stolen in each telling of the story again and again and destined to be so forevermore. He had come, in that game, to belong more to the Mohalla than to them.

The cab driver shifted in his seat. "Where to now, baji?" he said. Rozina watched Firdous, pale, staring blankly at the street. How much was a woman supposed to endure? In the distance, Rozina heard the sound of the azhan. God hears you, the women had said, the day they came for Faraz. The day that she had saved him. But she had been unable to save him the next time the men had come. Firdous could not watch, so they had gone inside and listened to the sound of the men carrying him away. When they heard nothing else, Firdous said: He didn't cry. As if to say that now she knew he would be all right. The hardest part was done.

And then Rozina knew exactly where to find the boy. *He* had taken Faraz that time, and somehow she knew he had taken him again. She leaned forward. "Mall Road," she said.

When Wajid became chief secretary and was posted to Lahore, the news had prompted Firdous to make a visit to his office to ask after the boy. Rozina had taken her. He had made them wait for an afternoon in a corridor, eventually sending out an assistant who delivered a written message: The boy was, well, not a boy but a man now, who wanted his own life, a private life. That he hoped to marry into a respectable family. That Firdous should allow him the freedom to be like any other man in Pakistani society. If she cared for him, she would do this. Rozina had watched Firdous as she read the note. Of course, of course, she had nodded. She had made him free. She wanted nothing more for him. She gave up loving him to give him that, and this message delivered in Wajid's hurried hand told her she had done the right thing all those years ago; her son was a man now, not a kanjar.

Rozina wouldn't endure another lackey's message this time. She wanted an answer. And so she directed the driver to go to GOR by the Mall, where the chief secretary lived, and there they took their place alongside a handful of others just as desperate for an audience with him. Waiting outside in the dust, ignored by the guards and staff and cars going in and out, required a steeliness, an ability to subjugate yourself before people more powerful, to perform obsequiousness and to do so as if it were your reason for being. These were people who had cultivated the ability to wait endlessly. Rozina wasn't one of them. She did what she knew Najam would do, looked for the person who might like to be paid. A gardener told them the chief secretary usually came home for lunch at two, but they still had to wait, and Rozina knew she would have to make a scene to ensure Wajid stopped the car. They waited so long that the guards in the guardhouse brought a chair out for Firdous, and placed it in a warm patch of sunlight. When the car approached the gate a little after two, Rozina stood in front of it, gauche, loud, an embarrassment, and Wajid, as she expected, asked his driver to stop. He parked on the side of the road, and when Rozina escorted Firdous to his door, she saw his jaw tighten, though he smiled.

"How are you, Firdous?" he said. Rozina saw him assess her mother, taking in her slight frame, her hair streaked with mehndi. She knew that Firdous had been beautiful, it was why a man like Wajid had come to see her. And she knew that the years had been hard on her mother, as they were on all the women in the Mohalla, whose bodies went to work early. She spent whatever Rozina gave her on Mina, buying little for herself; what did an old woman like her need anyway? she liked to say. He seemed to look relieved as he surveyed her, as if he had escaped something rather sad. Firdous put her dupatta to her wet eyes and Rozina had to stop herself from yelling at her mother. She wanted to scream at her the things Firdous had always yelled at her: Never let the tamash been see what you feel. You control what you show them. That's the only thing you really control. But here was her mother, standing before the tamash been, crying.

"Faraz," Rozina said. "He came looking for Amma."

His face soured at this. He looked at Firdous for a moment, then shrugged in a gesture of: So what?

"Where is he? We want to see him. Amma wants to see him."

"I don't know. And I really don't appreciate your coming here. This is my home."

"Wajid," Firdous said. He winced at the sound of his name in her mouth. Her expression clouded at his look of distaste. They had waited to plead their case, to bow their heads before the chief secretary and ask a favor, but now her eyes narrowed and her jaw was set. "He was looking for me."

"He's gone."

Firdous hit the top of the car with her hand. "Did you do this? Did you send him away?"

Wajid's face was a mixture of alarm and bemusement. The driver got out of the car but Wajid waved him away. "Of course not. It's a posting. It's the life of a public servant. He has to go where he is told to go."

"Well, tell us where we can find him. We want to see him."

"See him? His wife will leave him if she finds out about him, about you, and she will take their child with her."

Firdous blinked at him. "He has a child?"

"He'll hate you for it, he'll never forgive you," Wajid said. "Is that really what you want?" He started to roll his window up.

Firdous's face was rigid like a mask. Rozina thumped the glass. "Sister-fucker."

Wajid sighed, sat back in the car, his eyes fixed ahead as the car slipped inside the compound.

"We'll find him on our own," Rozina said. "We can still find him."

"Did you hear? He has a baby. A family, a real family. What a blessing. What a blessing," Firdous said. She said it again and again, and when Rozina drew Firdous to her and felt her mother's body shaking, trembling as if it might never be still, she realized Firdous would never do anything that might risk her boy's losing his family. He might yet find them, but Firdous had decided she would not look again, and Rozina suspected that if he tried to find them, Firdous would now try to make sure he could not. Wajid had warned he would lose his family should the truth come out, and Firdous could not bear to be responsible for his losing his child, as she had lost him. Her body rattled, as if incubating a fever generated by her decision to endure another loss. The last one. A blessing, she said again. Yes, Rozina said to her mother, it is a blessing. It's thanks to you, Amma, thanks to you he has all that, you gave him all that, she said as people continued to gather outside the gate, all of them steeling themselves to ask for the things they could not get for themselves.

⬦

SAFIA INSISTED he drape a blanket over his legs when they lunched on the veranda, and quite honestly he didn't mind. He was rather reaching that age, feeling the cold a little more than he used to. The other winter ritual she'd instituted was a cup of bland yakhni before eating; low salt but lots of pepper, certain to stave off colds, heart attacks, and the like. Lunch at least was still the refuge it had always been, simple and comforting. Today, karele stuffed with keema and channa daal swirling in Amma-ji's tarka of browned onions and cumin. Of course his appetite wasn't up to much now; all morning on the phone dealing with this business Faraz had started, putting him behind on all kinds of other pressing issues. He ought to have worked through lunch, but he'd felt desperate to get out of the office, to get some respite from it all.

But then those women outside. The state they were in. He was fairly confident he'd gotten rid of them—for now. And as for Faraz; well, his hands had been tied there. He had to make this business go away and the boy had left him little choice; he'd never understand that it was for his own good. But a cooling-off period would help.

Damn Ghazi. He could kill the man for getting all this started. Bloody idiot, getting himself mixed up in *godknowswhat*, getting Wajid tangled up in it, too.

⋄

WHEN THEY'D MET two nights before at the officers' mess, Ghazi had been late—unusual for him, Wajid had noted, though after all that had transpired, he wasn't sure of anything much about the man anymore. Wajid had walked past the photographs of the army chiefs lined up on the wall of the mess lounge as he waited. Eventually he lit a cigarette and ordered a bearer to get him a soda water and let General Ashraf know he'd be outside waiting for him.

He took his drink out onto the lawn, where gardeners crouching in the grass were weeding. Every which way he looked there were staff. Was there nowhere to have a private word here? When Wajid had called, Ghazi had suggested he come to the house, but Wajid had thought that unwise. Here they might have just run into each other.

"Wajid." Wajid turned at the sound of his name. Ghazi walked toward him, his swagger stick under his arm, his aide-de-camp following. Wajid held out his hand, wondering what the bloody ADC was doing here.

"Thank you for finding some time to meet," Wajid said.

Ghazi waved the thanks away, his mouth tight, flashing that awkward, unnatural smile of his. Wajid paused, and Ghazi, understanding, gestured that the ADC could leave. Once he was out of earshot, Ghazi turned to Wajid and said, "You're calling more attention to the matter by insisting on meeting. Now, why all the fuss?"

"You said there'd been an accident." Ghazi nodded. "There are accidents, and there are young girls getting shot."

"Kanjari women," Ghazi corrected. "Look, it was a terrible shame, and I don't really know how it happened. I appreciate that when I called, you acted so quickly."

"I didn't know then what had happened."

"Yes. But you do now. Has anything changed?" Ghazi said.

Wajid stared at him. He was right: Nothing would change—he would go along with it still, and yet, after this, nothing could be the same.

"I've heard the man you sent in isn't getting this wrapped up as quickly as it might be."

"Who says?"

"I told you, I asked the broker, the one the councillor introduced me to, to make sure the local station would do what they could to help. Apparently your chap's delaying things."

"He's being thorough."

"Who is he? Local?"

"I brought him in from outside especially. I wanted someone excellent. And I trust him." Wajid took another mouthful of his soda, held the bitter liquid in his mouth. Sending Faraz had gone against his better instincts, yet he'd thought he could count on him above anyone else. Slowly, he told himself: Nothing must give away to Ghazi that there was anything about this officer worth knowing. If he thought that, he would be interested, curious, and who knew where that would lead. Ghazi twitched; he was on edge. Wajid would have to call the man's bluff to get him to back off. "I'll get his file sent over to you, but I think the less you're connected to anything to do with this, the better."

Ghazi considered this. "Quite right." He smiled. "I leave it in your capable hands. I know you'll take care of it." It sounded more like a warning than a show of confidence. The fairy lights strung along the mess switched on. "In other news, you might be interested to hear that some of my colleagues and I are keeping the lines of communication open with all parties in the midst of this . . . mayhem," Ghazi said.

Wajid looked at Ghazi; what did he mean?

"Bhutto."

"You're talking to Bhutto?" Wajid said.

"There's no harm in talking to everyone. The president and his opponents."

Wajid could have laughed. When they had started out, Ghazi had been so dreadful, so poor at politicking, at just getting along with people. Here he was now, keeping his options open. In the war, Wajid had learned, nothing mattered but getting out of it, away from it. Ghazi had learned that everything was war. That he could think like this, after whatever had happened a few nights ago, was remarkable.

"I'm just saying I have high hopes for the future, whichever way things turn, and I take those who have been loyal with me. I'll always look out for you, Wajid, you know."

Wajid felt a tightness across his chest; Ghazi's grip. It had been there from the moment he handed him Firdous's photo, with a message on the back. And although he could tell himself he had repaid his debt to the man now, he felt as if all he'd done was to indebt himself further. They weren't even; he was now forever Ghazi's. Somewhere in the city, the body of a child testified to this debt.

He looked over at the mess building. It looked rather lovely, magical even, from here—all the lights twinkling—like something out of a story. Not like an officers' mess, not like a place where generals met to calibrate their political plans. Generals weren't supposed to have political plans, only martial ones. But General Ghazi, who'd just killed someone—not in the field but right here in the city, a city that was Wajid's responsibility, whose people were his responsibility—was busy with his. There was only one way out.

"You saved my life, Ghazi. I would have had none of this if it weren't for you. My family, my work, which I love." Ghazi was waiting for more. "And my son, of course. But I think I'm more tired than I realized." Ghazi licked his lips, uncertainty about his eyes. Wajid knew this was a less predictable version of himself. His own bravery surprised him, too. "Thank you for thinking of me. But I think I've climbed the heights I intended. When I finish my term, no matter who ends up in charge, I'll happily hand over. Fresh blood's always a good thing, especially if there are new people at the top."

Ghazi held his gaze, displeased. A man who no longer depends on your favor is a man you might trust a little less. The only way to guarantee Wajid would be of no danger to him now would be to squash him to nothing. "Well, then," he said.

"Well, then," Wajid echoed. He smiled, accepted his lot; he would, once this administration was out, fade away. Rot in a dead-end job somewhere, forgotten, a nobody. People would remark how strange it was that he'd never made it to state secretary, the next logical step for a man in his position. Safia would comfort him, but she would be embarrassed, as would his children. They would wonder what he'd done wrong, whom he had displeased.

His glass was empty. The ice tinkled.

Ghazi sighed, held out his hand. Wajid took it. Ghazi would live with the risk; the man would even enjoy it. The breathlessness of danger.

But Wajid was finished with it all. As he walked back toward the car, he told himself not to look at the building, so pretty in the twilight. *Dead girls*, he said to himself. He imagined he would have to say it to himself every time he longed for this life, this world, again.

"Look at what Amma-ji forgot again," Safia said as she bustled out onto the veranda with some achar in a pretty glass bowl. "Lassoora ka achar," she said. "I told her saab can't eat his daal without it." She sat down next to him on the divan, wrapping her shawl around her, glancing at his plate. "It'll get cold," she prodded, and so to please her, he ate, holding the bitter taste of the karele in his mouth before swallowing, surprising himself at how easily he kept it all down.

PART TWO

We gather ourselves: souvenirs of bone.

TARFIA FAIZULLAH,
"Reading Celan at the Liberation War Museum"

Twenty-Three

DACCA, DECEMBER 1970

The man—dumped by the railway tracks near Karwan Bazaar—was half naked, his hairy belly ballooning upward. His death was likely a painful one. The marks on his bound wrists and feet suggested he'd struggled to wrench off the blue plastic bag tied around his neck. Its inky logo read AHMAD SHOES over an illustration of a woman's high-heeled pump and, positioned as it was, gave the impression it was stomping on his face. Faraz thought—as he did at every crime scene, even at this one—of the girl. He didn't say her name to himself anymore. Every moment in Dacca—alien in its humidity, its language, its profuse, shockingly beautiful flowers—was a reminder of everything he was not supposed to know, to suspect, to remember of that time. So how could he think of anything else when it lived in him now, like a breath he was just about to take?

Faraz straightened up, tired. There had been too much death here of late. Cyclone Bhola had smashed East Pakistan's coast the previous month, and the death toll was in the hundreds of thousands. The news had been full of clips of bodies and animals floating in the water, pictures of children half buried in black sand. How was it possible that so many could die in an instant? Despite the experts and their storm charts, the enormity of it made no sense. After weeks of such images, it had become easier not to feel anything.

A train pounded past the corpse. This, too, was a death they'd explain; someone was responsible, there would be a reason, banal as always, but a reason nevertheless, even if the violence of it made no sense.

Faraz's sub-inspector, Shamsuddin, crouched down by the man.

"He's definitely not local?" Faraz asked again.

"The men from the bazaar said they've never seen him there, and no one living along the tracks recognized him, either," Shamsuddin said, gesturing toward the nearby encampment. "The bag might be something we can look into." Faraz started to reach for the bag, but Shamsuddin stopped him. "Sir."

He was an interesting young man—Faraz had discovered that he'd dropped out of Dacca University, where he was studying chemistry, to support his younger siblings, but the scientific inclination persisted. He'd made himself the bane of the station with his insistence on modernizing protocols, irritating the underpaid constables and the old baba who'd been trained by the British to take fingerprints. Criminals here were still caught via informants and effective beatings, not note-taking at crime scenes.

"Does this look like Scotland Yard?" Faraz had said, gesturing at the leaking roof of the station. "What difference does it make how we collect evidence when no one knows how to look at it, or store it, or understand it?"

"Bengalis invented the Henry fingerprint classification system—we may not get credit for it but we are just as capable of understanding what we find," the sub-inspector had countered, "and if *we* treat the evidence like the sacred thing it is, the technicians will learn to do the same."

"'Sacred thing'? You sound like the mullahs in the masjid," Faraz had said, both piqued and impressed by the man's zealotry, his confidence in his own enlightenment.

"This knot, sir," Shamsuddin said now, lifting the string with the tip of his pen. "Is that how you'd tie a knot when you're in the midst of killing a man and he's struggling?"

Faraz shook his head.

"Only two sets of footprints," Shamsuddin said. "His and the killer's."

"Some kind of sailor's knot?" Faraz said. Shamsuddin nodded, waiting, Faraz sensed, for him to catch up. "Let's start with the men who work the passenger boats and cargo boats, speak to the captains, find out if anyone's missing, see if we can identify him."

"I'll take photographs of the footprints, measure them," Shamsuddin said with a faint smile. "We identify him, we should have a couple of suspects in hand quickly."

Faraz looked at him. "You've already done it, haven't you? Spoken to the captains."

"I made a start, sir."

When Faraz had first arrived and discovered he had a bright junior, he'd thought he ought to take him under his wing, pass on the knowledge he'd accumulated, his own intuitive knack for the work. But that soon came to seem ridiculous, given the man's talent. It was clear that one day they would all be led by men like Shamsuddin—who measured and documented, who developed processes built on reason rather than instinct, which was perhaps as it should be.

Faraz nodded a "Well done" and Shamsuddin shrugged—he was a man with a distaste for praise; he had done only what ought to be expected. How many more cases would a man like Shamsuddin solve, when his expectations were so much higher than anyone else's? Perhaps his immovable belief in the sanctity of the evidence would even restore the dignity of the naked man, undo the loneliness of his death.

⊹

AT THE STATION, he found messages from Mussarat waiting for him. She never used to call him at work in West Pakistan. Here it was different. The cyclone, the elections, just being here had her in a state of perpetual distress. "They blame us," she'd said during the previous night's newscast. "They blame us for everything, these Bengalis."

"Do you blame them?" he'd asked. "After the cyclone, American rescue helicopters arrived before West Pakistani ones. Now they win the elections and no one will let them run the country."

Mussarat pursed her lips at the notion of the Bengalis being in charge of East *and* West Pakistan. Since their arrival she'd worn the same glazed look on her face as everyone else in the cantonment whenever Bengali grievances came up—their complaints that they'd been sidelined, that West Pakistan lived off their labor, their jute. Faraz couldn't deny any of it now that he was here; he could see for himself the way West Pakistanis shrugged the place off, indifferent. It was the same contempt Wajid had shown for the world outside Lahore.

"Mussarat," he said when she picked up the phone, "all okay?"

"I've fired Sayeeda."

"Why?"

"I've told her so many times I don't want Nazia speaking Bengali. But as soon as I got home, there she was, just chattering away with the baby. The woman has no respect for my wishes. There's countless other things that bother me, and I've tolerated them, but this is so, so . . . brazen. I'm tired of it." She meant she was tired of being here. I want to be home, Mussarat would say as they walked through the bazaar, her eyes scanning the incomprehensible Bengali script on the storefronts, glancing at the women shopping for saris, bindis on their foreheads, all of it so foreign to her.

"It makes sense for Nazia to have some Bengali, when we live here. And she loves Sayeeda," he said, careful to keep his voice even.

"I specifically told her. I shouldn't have to tolerate this from a servant."

He didn't want to argue with her, not over this.

The day he had come home after being removed from Tibbi, when the SP told him he was being posted to East Pakistan effective immediately, Mussarat wept. Who gets posted twice in a week? East Pakistan was hundreds of miles away, another country, for God's sake. What did you do? What did you do? she had sobbed.

There had been rumblings around the investigation, the SP had acknowledged to him, some higher-ups were unhappy, but that wasn't why, he was careful to say. Nor was it the case itself, which had now been resolved. It wasn't even poor dead George—how was Faraz to know about some criminal who carried a grudge? No, there had been a complaint against *him*: He'd beaten a boy during the riots, so badly his eyesight was permanently damaged. The family had threatened to file an FIR, to go to the press. Bhutto's people would have a field day with it.

Faraz knew he couldn't be identified for what he'd done, or even be sure that this was what he'd done. Perhaps he had done worse. The only person who knew about the boy was Wajid. "The chief secretary wants me gone," he'd said to the SP. The SP said nothing. "I want to lodge a complaint," Faraz said.

"Look," the SP had said, "he wanted you to have the job, now he doesn't. I don't know what this is, but if you take this further, there's a good chance something worse will happen. You'll end up in Civil Lines; you'll have no posting, no station at all. That'll be the end." Faraz was silent. "I know what you're thinking, Inspector," the SP said. "Don't bother him, don't go and see him. And don't go poking around in Tibbi. You go either place, you will be arrested. Take the posting."

"I had no choice," Faraz had told Mussarat. Her face hardened; *she* was the one who had no choice, had never had any choice, would never have any choice, not in anything. She threw his book of ghazals across the room.

"You did the right thing, we'll find someone else," he said now, reassuring her that there were things she could still control, things that he would not take from her, even if it meant firing some poor Bengali woman for the crime of speaking in her own tongue.

⟡

SOME MONTHS AGO, Shamsuddin had taken him to a favorite teahouse in Gulistan, close to the cinema, and now he walked along Jinnah Avenue toward it, passing smart new shops and offices, wondering if the sub-inspector might be there. He ought to be at home, but Mussarat would be banging around the kitchen, snapping at him, enraged at the loss of a servant, the work to find her replacement, at him, at everything. The teahouse had been crammed with young men, some women, too. They'd joined Shamsuddin's brother-in-law, Amjad, and Amjad's friends—writers and students from Dacca University who liked to while away the time between classes talking poetry and politics, movies—and girls. Unlike Mussarat, he'd discovered a pleasure in his foreignness, in theirs—a curiosity about them, this country so entirely different from the dusty Punjab he'd known. "A jungle," Mussarat had said disparagingly when they first flew into the city; yes, he'd thought, looking out the airplane window, but rather marveling at the sumptuousness of the vegetation, a dark bottle green, and the rippling, jade-colored ponds. Perhaps Wajid's punishment could be turned into a gift of sorts; not exile, but freedom. Adventure.

It hadn't felt like that at first. Another humiliation, being turned out of Lahore the way he had been as a child. But you're not a child anymore, Billa had said over a crackling telephone line: *You know where your family are, write to them, tell them you will return.* He'd gone back once more to the apartment by the old cinema and the music shop before leaving, and found the apartment still empty. Then he wrote, they did not write back. He wrote again. Nothing. He'd gone through the reasons—the letters were lost, stolen, they didn't believe him, they wanted nothing to do with him. Okay, Billa said, you tried, you can be done with them now if you want. I'll never be done with them, he thought.

A young man bumped him as he clambered over a bench. He apologized, but his manner was impatient, abrupt. It was the elections—everyone was riled up. President Ayub might have gone and his successor might have finally delivered elections, but if East Pakistan was to be denied its fairly won right to govern itself, then this agitated energy in the teahouse was a precursor to strikes, to protests, ones that would be more bitter than those he'd policed in Lahore. Back then, young men and boys protested with hope for change, but here, he sensed, that was gone. He was conscious of intruding—this was no place for a West Pakistani right now—when he heard Shamsuddin's voice.

"Sir," he said, his hand extended for Faraz to shake. If he was surprised to see Faraz there, he didn't let on. "I have a list from the harbor master for every vessel that came in over the last forty-eight hours." The man was good police, his mind always on the case.

"When you're SP, no one will be able to get anything past you," Faraz said.

Shamsuddin looked at him askance. "I don't believe there's any danger of that happening, sir." He was right. No one, Faraz had come to understand, gave Bengalis those kinds of jobs.

Faraz glanced at the table where Shamsuddin had been sitting, his friends watching them now. "Maybe that will change," he said.

Shamsuddin pushed his glasses up his nose, tilted his head, assessing the scene—the bustle and movement—with that steady concentration of his. "Yes," he said, "I do believe *something* will change."

And Faraz was certain that, as usual, the sub-inspector could see things that other, less exacting men—men like Faraz—had missed.

Twenty-Four

Rozina had chosen a royal blue sari with a gold border. Her hair was up, piled high on her head. It was always difficult to do her hair on her own. She touched it: stable. It looked stable. Like you, she thought as she looked at her reflection, and then because she felt she might crack open at any moment, she lit a cigarette. She paced the room. There was still time before she was supposed to head down to the hotel nightclub where Aunty Kulsoom was going to meet her. *Aunty*, indeed. The woman was just another broker, a madam, even if her elegant, formal Urdu seemed to belie it.

Rozina felt too much like herself, and that troubled her. She had thought agreeing to come to Karachi would help, that distance would help to separate this from the rest of her life. But everything had happened much quicker than she'd thought it would. Her return to the Mohalla last summer—although Najam had been relatively gracious—had left her dazed. She'd paced the apartment, avoiding going outside for weeks, conscious her humiliating return was seen as a frightening reminder of what could happen to those who thought they could leave, but also, for some, as a source of satisfaction. When she wasn't bickering with Mina, who complained about the crystal vases and glass animals and other junk Rozina had cluttered their rooms with, she slept. She slept endlessly, weeks slipping away from her until at last Firdous told her they could no longer pay the electricity bill.

Only then had Rozina contacted Izzat Raheem, who'd promised a connection with a broker—a broker who handled only the most prestigious VIPs. Aunty Kulsoom called immediately, eager to work with her. A very special event was taking place in Karachi, very exclusive; would Heer join them? It would mean flying out tomorrow, and flying terrified Rozina, but from the silence on the other end of the line, she understood her commitment was being tested. Not a problem, she said.

Firdous, who had always negotiated for her when she was a girl, was in no condition to do so anymore. More frail and often despondent now, she snapped at anyone who spoke to her—Rozina, Mina, even the children playing outside. She could not be trusted to deal courteously with a broker. But negotiating the details for herself—the terms, when and how payment would be made, how travel would be organized—had overwhelmed Rozina, reducing her to tears after each call. She had to remind herself she had a daughter whom she needed to protect, to sustain, so that she would never *have* to do this. And doing this herself was surely better than having to broker a deal for her daughter.

She looked in the mirror again. Come on, she said to herself. Get into it. But the anxiety she felt was not the kind she liked, the kind that hovered when she got ready to perform, when she felt herself making room for another character in her body, a woman she would understand and who would also mystify her, in the same way that she understood and was a mystery to herself, a woman whom she would make real. She saw only Rozina in the mirror, not Heer; she looked like Heer, of course; the Heer of *Udaas Galiyan* and *Gagan Talay* and other hits and even like the later, more sophisticated Heer of Bobby Sethi's art house experiments. Aging, heavier, still lovely. A star. But how to dispel Rozina, who seemed to be seeping through now when she was least wanted? When in doubt, Firdous used to say, call on Ali, and if that doesn't help, apply more eyeliner. For once, the eyeliner seemed like good advice. She reached for the kohl and did what she could to hide from herself.

There was a live band playing, and the club was hazy and warm with bodies. In the darkness, the lamps on each table glowed while cigarette smoke swirled upward, and there was something dizzying about being there, although she had had nothing to drink. Small groups crowded the tables, their faces shining in the pools of light. "I'll get drinks," tall, austere-looking Abid—or was it Asif?—said; Aunty Kulsoom had sent him to collect her from the room and look after her till she arrived. He was terse, and so she'd suppressed her usual nervous chatter, looking as aloof as she supposed she ought to. He left her at a table before disappearing into the crowd at the bar. She felt eyes flicker in her direction, heads turn, checking: Is that—could it be—are you *sure?* She tried to enjoy it, though fear buzzed alongside the pleasure, the dread that her face had changed, was changing, that the changes brought disappointment to those gazing at her.

"There is nothing sweeter in heaven than the sound of your voice." Out of the corner of her eye she caught sight of a young man gazing at her earnestly, his hair falling into his eyes. It was a line from *Shama Aur Sitaray*, an oldie, before Bobby. She stared straight ahead. Then he broke into tipsy laughter, and the table of young men behind him started laughing too. She knew the type: young, wealthy, their surnames imprinted on the cutlery in restaurants, on the cottons and silks in the bazaar. This place, like all the best hotels and restaurants, was full of them, the children of the nation's rulers, passing the time till it was their turn. Bastards in waiting, Bobby called them. They sprawled in their chairs, thought nothing of shouting across the room to their friends or adding another round of drinks to their tab. We own this place, their laughter seemed to say. It's ours. She understood. Their place, and her own. She lit a cigarette and maintained a steady look of boredom until he wandered back toward his friends, who guffawed and patted him on the back.

She stood to leave—it had been a mistake to come—when Aunty Kulsoom's man reappeared. "Look," he said, pointing to a woman dressed in an elegant printed sari, who was approaching. Aunty Kulsoom was bulky and buxom, yet she moved with grace. Her hair was fashionably short, her nose long, and because she tilted her head to the side, there was the sense of a slant to her face. Her smile was demure and beautiful. "Heer, darling, your light is filling this room," she said, taking Rozina's hand in hers. "You have so many fans here, but me, I'm your greatest admirer." Rozina waited for the usual resentment to bubble up, the kind she reserved for pimps, for parasites, for the people who lived off her body and whatever talent she had, but it didn't come. "Aunty Kulsoom . . . you came," she found herself saying, as if she had been waiting for this moment all her life.

⌁

AUNTY KULSOOM INTRODUCED HER to all the people who mattered, explaining the geography of the room as they went. The mustaches, the paunches, they're the bureaucrats, Heer, darling, she said. The ones who stop at the door, look into the corners of the room first and then settle in at the back, they're the army men. That way they can see everything, no surprises. The bureaucrats, the politicians, they like to circulate, they can be moved. The army men, they don't change position. Aunty Kulsoom moved slowly and deliberately, looking every man she stopped to talk to in the eye. She laughed, she touched their shoulders, she was charming and attentive. When she introduced Rozina, she put her arm around her as a proud mother might. The men's eyes slid this way and that with the booze, but they all stood when the women came by, finding them chairs or vacating their own. She caught phrases in passing: *The Bingos have become insufferable . . . Sheikh Mujibur Rahman's the worst of the lot . . . Bhutto Saab's games . . . Bhutto always in the middle of things . . . Communism . . . What more do these people want? Tamasha, it's all tamasha, everything will be back to normal soon if we act quickly, nip this East Pakistan nonsense in the bud . . .* When she and Aunty Kulsoom approached, though, the talk stifled or shifted to snippets about Karachi, radio plays, and music, things they must have thought would be of greater interest to women. They seemed, to her surprise, not to be the oafs

Bobby always described them as, or the creeps Najam called friends; they were as good company as Bobby's Pak Tea House crowd. Better; they paid for the drinks. They didn't condescend to her or ignore her or talk over her. They complimented her, flattered her. They were old and overweight, and they seemed to think they were lucky to meet a woman as young, as beautiful as she was—a film star. One of them leaned forward. "I loved that film you did set in the Himalayas. Unusual. That chap who directed it . . . ?"

"Sethi, Bobby Sethi," someone else said.

"Yes! Whatever happened to him?"

"I thought he died," another man said. "Didn't he? He was the lefty one?"

She felt an unexpected panic at Bobby's name, and at the mention of death. Because the truth was, wasn't it, that something was gone forever between them. She would never be able to do this work, to tolerate it, if she had let herself love Bobby, and Bobby was in no position to provide for her, for Mina. Aunty Kulsoom looked at her steadily, interested in what she was going to say, if she was up to playing this new part she'd been cast in. Heer, Rozina thought, seeing herself for a moment as they saw her, not recognizing herself as herself. Sometimes it alarmed her when it was happening, when she let a character in, but yes, she could be Heer again. It was just a part. Just work.

She laughed. "Let's just say he's about as alive as socialism in Pakistan," she said, and the generals laughed with her.

⌖

IT WAS HUMID AND BRIGHT when Rozina spotted the three of them on Clifton Beach. The man's hair and beard were long, and the two women spoke loudly, unselfconsciously: Americans. She often saw them in Anarkali or on the Mall these days, their battered rucksacks adorned with souvenirs from shrines and temples. They were, all three, thin, their clothes hanging loosely about them, and although she had never seen the Arabian Sea before, it didn't hold her gaze the way those American women did, the way they lay back on their elbows, staring at the water, the ends of their hair trailing in the wet sand. They didn't care that their pale legs were exposed, that the hawkers setting up their grills on the promenade were staring at them, that the children begging on the beach turned every time they moved, because whenever they moved—upright, to the side, onto their fronts—you heard them: their beads, their ankle chains, their laughter, jangling.

Rozina put her dupatta over her head, bristling at the thought that to the women sprawled out so freely on the sand she must look like a middle-aged housewife. She slipped off her shoes and left the promenade for the sand, pulling the dupatta down onto her forehead. Better that the men on the beach stare at the white women than that she be recognized. Up ahead, the sea was restless and miserable-looking. She'd come here for some reason she couldn't quite discern. No, that wasn't really true, was it? She knew why she was here. Although she'd taken a pill to help her sleep after she'd returned to her room last night, she had woken up early, pictures from the night before flashing about her eyes: his mustachioed mouth, his smooth, bald head, his callused fingers on her breasts.

She had told Aunty Kulsoom that she wasn't available to keep anyone company in private yet; for a woman of her caliber, her stature, he would have to wait, to win her over if he was indeed serious. He's serious, Aunty Kulsoom said, but things are different these days, Heer; modern men don't have the time and patience for elaborate Mohalla games. He is willing to pay. Generously. Will you or won't you?

And so Aunty Kulsoom took her up to the room. "We've come for that nightcap," she said to the man. She seated Rozina on the sofa and mixed drinks, conversing all the while, making up for Rozina's reserve. Before she left, she asked Rozina if she needed something to help her relax. Of course not, Rozina said. But as soon as it began, she found herself at a loss as to how to get through it. She was a veteran, a skilled professional, but it had been years since she had done this, and she couldn't quite remember the tools she'd used to survive those nights—how to imagine she was somewhere else, that she was someone else. Look at the curtains, she'd told herself, look at the doorknob, the swirls on the carpet. Focus. But, try as she might to separate herself from her body, to leave the vital parts of herself elsewhere, she felt everything: the weight of his body, the pressure of his mouth, his sex.

When she woke, earlier than she'd expected, the pill having failed to help her sleep, she had come here. If she had not been able to transport herself somewhere else last night, at least she could now. The sea—the sea was vast, an expanse so much bigger than anything that could ever happen to her, which had made coming here seem like the best thing she could do. It would do what a shower could not. Feel the significance of it, she told herself, the power of God's work. Know that you are nothing, and if you are nothing, then nothing that happens to you matters, not really. But she watched the water numbly, feeling as blank as the sea before her. Bobby would like this, she thought; the romance, the drama of it—his heroine standing before the sea: "This, my jaan, is where the impossible happens: Pakistan ends," he would say. She wondered for a moment about what lay beyond—the lands you might find if you sailed a boat across, a thought that had always discomfited her. Better not to dwell on things you could not see. But now—perhaps beyond the water lay somewhere she might have another kind of life, where Mina might, too.

The hippies were standing now, wading where the water rippled across the sand. Then the man splashed the women, and they shrieked and splashed him back before running away. He chased them and the women ran like boys, their bodies athletic, strong. Rozina remembered what that felt like, the pumping of legs, of lungs. When had she last run? She must have been a girl. The man called out, and she wondered if white men liked tough, sinewy women like these. The shorter of the two women stopped and put her hands on her hips, panting. She had caught Rozina looking at her, and she smiled. Her hair and her eyes were the same color as the sand, but her cheeks were flushed with color. And then Rozina saw it happen, the way it did sometimes; the woman blinked at her, an uneasy smile about her lips. The man and the other woman were also looking at her now. They couldn't have recognized her, because how would they know? But Rozina knew when her face had startled those who looked at it. Sometimes it made people want to stare at her, other times she sensed they wanted to hide. This woman was one of the latter. She wiped her face, nervously tucked her hair behind her ears, worrying, probably, about her own very ordinary face. Rozina had always liked this moment; the sense of her own remoteness, of being inaccessible even as she stood before people close enough to touch her. But not today, she didn't want this today. She had come out here to disappear, not to be noticed.

The man laughed a little and said something to the women she could not understand.

"You look like Liz Taylor," he called out, and the women giggled.

They were laughing at her, these half-naked women and this scruffy man. She pursed her lips.

"You could be sisters," the woman with the sandy hair said. She smiled again.

Rozina stared at them.

"Liz Taylor's a movie star where we come from," the woman said. The woman took a step toward her, gingerly, as if approaching a wild creature. "She's very beautiful," she said. She was waiting for Rozina to say something: to thank her, perhaps to look bashful. She looked anxiously around at the others now, and said something Rozina couldn't catch. Then she looked at Rozina apologetically, as if she were worried that they had caused offense. Of course Rozina knew who Liz Taylor was. American stars were stars in a way she would never be.

"Diamonds," Rozina said. When Firdous had picked out Rozina's stage name, Heer, it had been because of the sparkle of her green eyes. They shine like diamonds, she'd said. And naming her for them could only draw riches, her grandmother had said. "Liz Taylor, diamonds," she said again.

"Yes, yes," the hippies said with excitement, delighted that she understood them, grateful for the universal language that was wealth.

"You like diamonds, like Liz?" The man laughed. He looked at her, his mouth open. It was a look, a pang she knew well. Your beauty is, the fat bureaucrat from last night had said to her, and then stalled, struggling to finish his sentence. Najam always knew what to say. Of course, Bobby rolled his eyes at Najam's fancy language; words are all a salesman has. What would Bobby say? How might he describe her? Anxious, high-strung, exhausting? Only with him could she be those things—herself. And he had not thought less of her for it. She didn't want to think about Bobby now. How trapped she had felt in that room last night, how trapped she felt now as she stood here, where there was nowhere farther to go. She looked at the women in their ragged cotton skirts, running on the beach like children, wandering the world like bums.

She pulled her dupatta off her head and let her hair fly up in the wind. She let the wind whip at her hair—hair that was thicker, glossier, and far more beautiful than their Liz Taylor's. She turned to the sea and threw her dupatta out toward the waves. There was a sharp intake of breath from the hippies. She turned around to face them, pleased at the theater of the gesture—the gesture of a star. One of the women took a step into the water as if to rescue it, if Rozina wanted. Rozina shrugged as it skipped away. There would be more rooms, more nights like last night when she would have to be Heer, but she could do it if she reminded herself what it was for, whom it was for. It was just a job. That was all.

Rozina turned to the Americans. "No Elizabeth Taylor," she said, deciding she would not be embarrassed by her broken English. She had seen a picture in the newspaper of a diamond ring Richard Burton had bought Elizabeth Taylor, the stone big and flashy and lush. "I buy my diamonds," she said, mustering as much pride as she could. "Me." With that, she walked away, knowing they would watch her till she disappeared, because, like any decent actress, she knew the way you closed a scene was what counted.

Twenty-Five

Dacca, 8th March 1971

The water was a dazzling green, reflecting the dense, leafy crowns of the trees nestling the lake. Faraz considered the possibility that Shamsuddin might not meet him as arranged. It seemed, in fact, as he walked in the new, startling silence around the lake in Ramna Park, ridiculous to think the man would come out. Faraz used to come here on Sundays with Mussarat and Nazia; they walked the park's paths as Nazia dripped ice cream on her clothes, her hands. The shady paths were the perfect retreat for lovers sharing discreet kisses, for children who wanted to play hide-and-seek, for those seeking the nourishment that only the smell of moist soil could provide.

The rustle of birds moving in the trees, but no song. He shouldn't have come. It wasn't wise to be out with curfews in place all over the city, but he didn't feel he had a choice, not really. His only comfort was that Mussarat and Nazia didn't have to see all this; it was he who'd suggested they leave for a trip home a few weeks ago, just to get some respite from the atmosphere in Dacca. Then the situation had deteriorated, and he'd told them to stay put. What few West Pakistanis remained were now scrambling to leave. They came from all over Dacca to the cantonment, pleading for help securing tickets home. *Home*. We must get home, they said, their faces pinched. Faraz watched, trying to mask his desperation to get out, too; just do your job, he told himself. You can go when it's done—but when *what* was done?

He passed three young men sitting on a bench. The soldiers who'd been coming in from West Pakistan on the same planes that were taking civilians home blocked roads, drove through the deserted streets in their jeeps. If they saw one of the flags flying for this new country—Bangladesh—they pulled it down. After the huge rally at the racecourse yesterday, the whole country had, on Sheikh Mujibur Rahman's orders, come to a grinding halt; enough was enough, he'd declared. In the cantonment, the West Pakistanis were overwrought: What do we do? Who is in charge? Is it still us? Best act as if we are, send out more soldiers; *show them*. These boys on the bench shouldn't be here. They were sure to be picked up for violating the curfew if spotted. He ought to warn them, but boys like them were, his colleagues said, also disappearing other boys, West Pakistani boys, Biharis. He was no boy but he was outnumbered here. They sat very still as he passed and he moved quickly, too; they had all become afraid of one another.

"Inspector," a voice said. He turned, and the boys on the bench did, too. It was Shamsuddin, in his civvies, looking pale, his shoulders hunched with fatigue. Faraz held out his hand, wondering if Shamsuddin would take it. Faraz had left the station two weeks ago, posted to security detail because the SP said it was no longer a good idea to have the Bengalis doing security for the VIPs—only West Pakistanis were VIPs here—and, well, who knew which of these Bengalis you could trust right now? Who among them might mutiny? Faraz had said good-bye to Shamsuddin at the station, told him he'd recommended him to be made acting SHO, but Shamsuddin shrugged. He wasn't interested in policing for East Pakistan anymore, not if they weren't free. He'd held out his hand, courteous as ever, but firm: We've tolerated too much already, it is time you left; our country belongs only to us.

Now here was Shamsuddin's hand once more. "I didn't think we'd be meeting again," he said.

"Nor I," said Faraz, glad for the feel of it in his, safer somehow for it. "Are you all right? Are the men okay?"

"The station's closed because of the strike. I left a few days ago," Shamsuddin said, then he looked at Faraz. "You're not leaving, going back?"

Faraz shook his head. Mussarat had wanted him to appeal to Wajid, but he would never ask Wajid for help again.

Shamsuddin looked at him, a little sorry for him perhaps. "I was surprised to hear from you."

Faraz glanced around. If caught, he could be in trouble for more than breaking curfew. He'd come here to pass on information; a betrayal, treason, his superiors might even say, but it didn't feel that way. As soon as he'd heard, he knew he had to track Shamsuddin down. "Security for one of the generals told me the army are gathering information on potential targets. Anyone with access to weapons, rifles. The police will be top of their list. I just wanted you to know, they're already thinking that far ahead."

Shamsuddin smiled. "Luckily, I took as many rifles as I could with me when I left." Two steps ahead, as always. But Faraz wondered if young men like Shamsuddin really understood the intent of the men in charge. Men like that didn't pause to reflect, to question. They were—Faraz had learned over the years—intransigent, ruthless when they thought they had to be, sometimes when they didn't have to be. Still, he'd come because there was no one else left for him to care about here.

At the sound of gunfire in the near distance, the boys on the bench looked around, panicked. Faraz froze. Shamsuddin pulled him into the trees off the path. The boys scrambled behind them. They waited. A gaping silence. One of the boys laughed nervously. Faraz swallowed. What if he died here? Another burst. He scanned the park—if this was it, how long would it be before Mussarat found out? Billa? Who else would even want to know? Wajid? His mother? He was annoyed at himself; why this pang still, why even now at the thought of her?

"Firecrackers," Shamsuddin said, grinning with relief. The boys grinned too. They all breathed out. We are still here. "Joi Bangla," the boys mouthed in the darkness, and he nodded: Yes, joi Bangla, joi firecrackers.

"I have to go," Shamsuddin said.

"Get out of Dacca, go where you'll be safe."

Shamsuddin looked bemused. "We'll never be safe anywhere if our country does not belong to us, when an army of occupation is on our streets."

Faraz bristled. Occupation? Was that what he was? An occupier? Like the whites who'd once been here? He started to shake it off, to protest—it was preposterous—and then he felt something else he couldn't quite name.

"If there's to be a new country, you should be alive to see it," he said. More than see it: Men like Shamsuddin would be needed to lead it, to build it.

Shamsuddin tilted his head to look at Faraz, the smallest nod to say he understood why Faraz was here, and although he appreciated it, he was resolved. "There will be a new country. And if I have to die for it, I will."

The boys were still crouching, cautious, and Shamsuddin left his side to join them. He surveyed the grounds and pointed them toward a path out of the park. He didn't look back, although Faraz had expected him to, hoped he would. He and the boys vanished into the darkening trees. Revulsion, that was it, that was what he'd felt on hearing what Shamsuddin thought people like him were, revulsion that he hadn't realized it all this time.

Faraz waited; he didn't have to worry as Shamsuddin and the boys did; if the soldiers stopped him, it would be for only a moment, to tell him to get back to the cantonment. He was just as safe out there as he was here in the lush quiet of the trees. He was one of them, after all.

Twenty-Six

Even though Muharram was a time of mourning in the Mohalla, it meant no work, so Rozina was content. She stood on the terrace, watching the procession below. Today was Ashura, and the Mohalla's inhabitants, hundreds of them, barefoot, filled the narrow streets for miles. The men bellowed prayers, sang laments, the sound of their loss and anguish rising to the rooftops. Rozina's face was bare of makeup, and each time a breeze skimmed her cheeks, she felt a sense of renewal. Perhaps it was just having a holiday from work, or perhaps it was because for years she had not marked Muharram. Najam would have rolled his eyes at her—you Shia are so theatrical, all that ranting and raving and *bleeding*—underneath the condescension, a current of distaste in his voice. Let us have our moment, she'd say, laughing it off, aware of how she had to diminish what mattered to her in his house, hoping God would understand.

The terraces were crowded with women and children, as many watching from above as walking below. Some of the women wept, and their children—for whom the story of the martyrs had yet to mean anything—wept, too, because seeing their mothers cry made them fearful. Much as Rozina had struggled with her return to the Mohalla, her return to work, she had also felt, with every marsiya she'd wept to, with every majlis she attended, every bowl of food she'd donated, a solemnity, a new purpose that made her life sacred, that revived her.

"Look, Amma," she said. The crowd surged forward to reach the taziya, hands stretched to touch its holy surface. They would do the same when the horse Zuljinah arrived in its finery, representing the Imam's loyal steed at Karbala, even as the horse, thronged by mourners, skittered and bucked through the city's narrow lanes. But Firdous, who used to wait with longing for Muharram each year, did not look down. She had come up to watch only because Rozina insisted. She seemed to take little interest in anything anymore. She sat outside in the courtyard for much of the day, inviting the sun to scorch the back of her neck, ignoring the children who came down with coverings for her head, sent by their mothers, who called down: Amma, Amma, come in now, it's too hot to be out there. They seemed concerned not just about the heat but about how little Firdous seemed to care about her own well-being.

It was the letters; it had all started with Faraz's letters.

Mina was peering down at a group of men in a circle below, their naked backs bleeding, cut by the knives and chains they carried. Rozina suspected she was looking for Irfan. She tried without success to stifle her irritation: "He won't be there, Mina. He'll be robbing some poor shopkeeper who's down there mourning the martyrs." She shook her head haughtily, both regretting what she'd said and feeling satisfied to have spoken truthfully; God would want that. Mina looked at her with hatred. "Shut up, you bitch." Rozina gave an exaggerated sigh of indifference. But this time she felt her sinfulness before God. For so long, she had yearned to live with her daughter, but being around the girl had proved to be the hardest part of her return.

Firdous looked up, as if she'd just been woken. "Is that any way to talk to your sister, today of all days? Have some shame." She tapped her chest, where she had folded the letters Faraz had written into two neat squares and hidden them in her brassiere. It had become a habit with her, putting her hand to her breast and tapping there, as if she were checking for them or referring to them for guidance or turning to them for reassurance.

"Why do you always take her side?" Mina said.

"This is Rozina's house," Firdous chided. "She can say what she likes." Since Rozina's return, Firdous had said this again and again—perhaps to make her feel welcome, or to acknowledge a truth they'd ignored before, or perhaps to get Mina to accept that Rozina would, in time, assume her rightful place as head of their household. Rozina wasn't sure, but she hated it, feeling each time that it made her more of a stranger in the Mohalla, to her mother, to Mina.

"You should be helping Rozina more," Firdous added. "You're old enough."

Mina looked back down into the crowd below, her jaw tight. These remarks had also become all the more frequent since Rozina's return. They were managing, but only just, on the work from Aunty Kulsoom, who still called but made it clear she'd prefer younger girls. Rozina had to make the case that the experience she brought had value. The harder truth was that in the Mohalla, your daughters worked so that you could retire, and they had no plan for their future unless Mina started working.

Mina was scanning the crowd, as if she thought Irfan might look up and see that she needed to be rescued from these women; it saddened Rozina that this boy, who worked for day wages at the bus station on good days and stole what he could on bad days, was her only hope. He does it so Mehru Baji won't have to work, so he doesn't have to pimp for Izzat, Mina liked to say of Irfan's thieving, as if this restored his honor. That's what all rotten people say, Rozina said: that their reasons for doing terrible things are good. Not that the boy was rotten, really, just lost, after what had happened to them, trapped, as they all were, too dim or just too blinkered to see a way out. Mina was different—fearlessly wandering the Mohalla, never minding that she didn't fit in with the other girls there—she was the kind of person who could imagine something else for herself, but she'd attached herself to this idiot. Forget him, leave him, you owe him nothing. Marry a man who will get you out of here, Rozina thought, but did not dare say again. She had said it once, when she'd first returned, and it had prompted their most vicious fight. Like who? Mina had screamed. *Like who?* Rozina had no answer to that.

"It's not too late, if you talk to the right people," Firdous said. "It's not too late for her."

"Is this any kind of time to bring this up, Amma?" Rozina's skin prickled with irritation.

But Firdous persisted. "I know what time it is. I know what day it is. That boy will have her working if we don't."

Mina's face hardened with rage. "Amma," she said. She looked as if she might break apart.

Rozina felt her own body go rigid, her heart frantic. The same thought had occurred to her but she hadn't dared say it out loud before. "This is your own fault," she said, angry at the girl for making herself vulnerable in this way.

"Are you talking to me?" said Mina.

"If you'd just done your matriculation, you could have been one of those PIA air hostesses or a secretary in an office or *something*." Rozina thought of the air hostesses on her Karachi flights, carrying their hard Samsonite makeup cases, their hair pinned up under their dupattas. Mina looked unimpressed.

"What?" Rozina said. "You could have gotten out of here at least."

Down below, a woman wailed, telling the story of the murdered baby, the son of Imam Hussayn killed in his father's lap by an arrow. Other women cried, calling the murdered baby's name, calling on Ali; if only they'd spared the baby. Firdous, sitting in a huddle on the charpoy, stiffened. Rozina knew her mother couldn't bear this part of the story. "Amma?" she said, but Firdous straightened, stood up, shook it off, as always.

"Talk to Kulsoom. What they want is young ones," Firdous said, looking at Mina. "Even if they aren't great beauties, youth is worth something."

"Just leave it for one day, Amma, will you," Rozina yelled, but Firdous had already disappeared inside. She put her head in her hands. How fragile comfort was here, gone in an instant. Mina stood where she was, not speaking, but, it seemed, waiting to say something. "Ya Allah, what is it?" Rozina said. "Can't I just remember the martyrs in peace? It's Muharram, for God's sake."

"I've found work as a maid," Mina said. "I didn't want to tell Amma just now."

Rozina blinked. She was asking for permission; asking Rozina, as head of the household. A maid. The girl was going to be little more than a choori.

"I won't have to dress up to serve people their tea and clean up after them, like your air hostesses. No one will look at me."

Rozina stared at her. Mina *had* imagined something else for herself. "Fine," she said reflexively. "Go pick up shit like some jamadarni, if that's what you want." She played up her shame as she would before Firdous later, but inwardly she was not shamed, not at all. The girl had made a decision, chosen something for herself. Well done, was what she wanted to say. Good for you. She couldn't imagine what it would be like to move invisibly through the world. If no one looked at a woman, would she exist at all?

"Can you tell Amma for me?" Mina said.

Rozina nodded, feeling the tingle of a secret shared. "Amma's got other things on her mind. Don't worry so much about her."

"I'm going to see Mehru Baji," Mina said, which Rozina knew meant she was going to Mehru's to wait for the boy.

She climbed up onto the ledge, ready to hop to the next terrace, and Rozina felt the brief moment between them dissolve away. She never knew how to make more of these slivers, these pauses; she wanted them to be something, but what?

Mina paused, balanced on the edge.

"I wish you wouldn't do that," Rozina said. "You make me nervous. Just jump across."

Mina spoke, her back still to Rozina. "People in the Mohalla," she said, so softly Rozina had to strain to hear her. "People say you're my mother."

Rozina stared at the gap between the terraces, wider, deeper in the evening light. "What?" she said, as if she had never heard anything more ridiculous. "Who says that?"

"Lots of people have said it, the kids used to say it to me, that everyone knows but me."

How rigid the girl's back was, straight like a line. Rozina had a sense that if she said the wrong thing, she would just fold in half, collapse like a paper fan into that dark gap.

"Jump to the other side, will you. I don't like you hovering there." Mina did not move and Rozina felt as if she might shatter. "Mina, cross it," she yelled, and then the girl did, in one wide bound.

She turned to face Rozina. "Is it true?"

Rozina glanced up at the sky, lit from the lights below, but starless. How often had she imagined this moment, even wished for it? She opened her mouth, but the words stuck in her throat. In the room below, her mother was fading away over what had been taken from her—what she had given up, and now she wrestled with her ancient guilt. She couldn't snatch Mina from her mother, not as she grieved Faraz's loss anew.

"Who raised you?" Rozina said.

"Amma," Mina said. Rozina shrugged, a there-you-have-it shrug.

Mina stared at her, her eyes conveying doubt. After a pause, she shrugged back an *okay*, and Rozina understood, too, that the girl wasn't going to argue, but still she did not move, as if waiting for something more.

What would happen if she just said it? *I am your mother.* Firdous had once said, You don't really want to do the work of a mother. It was true that she hadn't wanted to do the work of a kanjari mother. She didn't have Firdous's resolve. But then she hadn't been able to offer Mina any other kind of life either. She felt the prick of it, of falling short, of not deserving.

A flock of pigeons on a nearby terrace flew up, startled, and Mina turned, disappeared into the dim light in the distance. Rozina stood on the terrace a long while after. It is as it should be, as I meant it to be, she told herself as the mourners, hundreds of them, wept on the streets below.

Twenty-Seven

LAHORE, MAY 1937

It was his fat chacha, Afzal, a man with a hooked nose and the most pleasing manners, who'd introduced him to Firdous. Afzal was a Bombay man—beautiful English—but he liked Lahore for the quiet of its gardens and culture; this was where one came to be published, to sit in mushairas and discover new poets, to pick up the latest Urdu magazines. Words, words everywhere, his uncle said, chewing his paan. Wajid's father rolled his eyes at his brother's interest in literature, in chess, in pleasure. Wajid understood the irritation; it was when he was with Afzal that Wajid found himself somehow a little less pleased with his life in England. It was his uncle's pride when he spoke of a communist editor he'd met in the teahouse, or the latest racy Urdu novel, or the lecture he'd heard at a Nationalist gathering that did it—Lahore was alive with change, it was where a nation was coming into being.

The summer before Sandhurst, he returned home. He sat at the edge of the table in the teahouse as Afzal and his friends roared at a dirty Punjabi joke he didn't understand. A play on words, a pun, except Wajid didn't understand what the play was; their language had become foreign to him now. The men talked endlessly, quoting Tagore, Ghalib, Allahabadi. They argued, they agreed, they admired one another's recitations, and the men who'd shown such love to their language, to India, to so many Indias in their poetry, an India the British would never know. Wajid thought of the words in which he'd been immersed: Keats, Wordsworth, Shakespeare. He had come to love them over time. But it wasn't like this—this pleasure that came from loving something that was yours. And there were other words, too, forever stuck in his head: Edward Lawrence's *Ripping six* as a cricket ball hurtled over the boundary and *You know they'll never make a darkie headboy.* His Latin master's *vinco, vincis, vincit.* The charwoman's *Make sure you wash before you eat, duck, I know how you lot like to eat with your hands.*

At Eton it had been the same—he sat at the edge of the table. He watched the white boys on the field, boisterous, looking around as they laughed, as if to say, Look at us, the whole world is ours. His father, England-returned too, must have sensed his loneliness when he said to him at the end of one summer holiday: *Be better than them, be so much better, they come to you.* Wajid had left Lahore shamed that his father had realized he was failing: at making friends, at becoming the kind of saab the English would respect. He returned to Eton, to his one friend: Thomas George, whom he didn't much like and whom no one else much liked either, for his snotty insistence that cricket was a bore, that the wall game was brutish— yes, sometimes, but how truly wonderful was the surprise of a six after endless demure clips of the ball, or the thrill when a boy who'd been at the bottom of the pile scraped his face along the wall and pushed through, victorious. Only after several visits to Thomas's house did he realize he'd been invited because Thomas's mother was troubled at the thought of Wajid's heathenism and, in particular, what she'd incorrectly assumed to be his vegetarianism. He just found the boiled meat served in the refectory hard to stomach. He politely accepted the pamphlets she gave him on Christian thought and enthusiastically ate the stringy chicken she served, which seemed to go some way toward alleviating the pressure she felt to bring him into the fold; she had at least saved him from one kind of horror. *Be so much better that you never have to go to Thomas George's house again,* he thought.

He was. He proved himself better at everything: academics, athletics, theater, debating. Mindful of sounding like them, talking like them, so that even though he was better, they would not fear him; they would still think he was one of them. And in the end, they did come to him. In their way.

Afzal laughed again; this time he was the one telling a joke, and Wajid realized as the men turned to look at him that he was the butt of the gag. Laugh along, laugh along, his father always said, and he did. "I will show you things in the walled city you won't believe. We will hear only the best ghazals. It's all there. The best music, the best dance, the best women," his chacha said, and Wajid's face colored as the older men clapped him on the back. "We will take you there and make an Indian of you yet," Afzal added, as if the project of Wajid's life, to become an Englishman, had been an exercise in pointlessness. "Just don't tell your father, because when you come back from the walled city, you'll be Indian-returned," and the men laughed again.

⟡

THEY HAD DRIVEN in Afzal Chacha's own tonga. He'd been to the inner city before, of course, but not at night, not to Shahi Mohalla. It was dark when they arrived, but up ahead he saw diyas burning, he heard the sound of the harmonium, the notes stretching as its chambers inflated, the pounding of the tabla. The fragrance of the flowers was thick outside the kotha, where the flower sellers waited. Inside, Afzal Chacha seemed to know everyone—the naika in charge, the musicians, the gathered men, Hindu, Sikh, and Muslim alike; the world of Lahore was much larger than he had imagined, and that in itself was thrilling.

The *best women*, Afzal had said, not the most beautiful. As it turned out, the women were not beautiful in the way of starlets in the pictures, or the expensively dressed women he'd glimpsed at Claridge's when he'd been invited out for tea by Edward Lawrence and his family; the white women, whose unattainability made even a wide nose or buck teeth somehow more desirable than they might otherwise be. Don't look at them, he said to himself. They cannot know. But of course they did. He stayed up wondering—could Lawrence's cousin Serena think of him as a man? Did she see him in that way, did his skin repel her? So brown; perhaps to her, so dirty. His desire shamed him because he had no say. He could not ask—he could only hope that they might give, and they never would. The ordinary girls from Windsor sometimes did, girls who would give an arm and a leg for an Eton boy. Even a darkie would do for that sort of girl. You could have her, Edward Lawrence said to him, nodding at the new barmaid in the Pig and Goat, as if she were his to bestow. She was pretty and dark-haired and had a loud, boyish laugh. Not with a barge pole, he'd said. Such high standards, Lawrence quipped. What I need is an Indian princess, Wajid said. Nothing less, Lawrence. Not that I expect you to understand, his tone as pitying as he could muster. By which he meant, You'll be lucky if you end up with a dentist's daughter from Harrow. But me, I'll have a Scheherazade, draped in chiffon, her mysterious eyes just visible above her yashmak, carrying around a lantern, summoning genies to grant my wishes—actually, come to think of it, Lawrence, maybe I'll have a fucking harem with a thousand women in it. And still he knew—even if Lawrence thought such nonsense might be true, which he did—Lawrence would still consider himself the luckier of the two of them.

But now the women in Claridge's receded before the dark-skinned woman who came out to sing for them in the kotha to which Afzal had brought him. Everything the tawaif did suggested she knew more than he did, more than any of the men in the room did, and she did not care if they knew it. She did not look at Afzal, at him, or at anyone else, but focused all her attention on one particular man who sat at the back of the room. Now and then the man threw coins at her as she sang, and the other men said wah or clapped and threw coins too, but she looked only at him, glancing away coquettishly after holding his gaze awhile. He had never seen such a public display of desire here; he had never seen an Indian woman make visible her own desires.

Eventually she danced, and Wajid was startled by the pace, the force of her feet as they hit the floor, the stark precision of her movements. It suggested tremendous control, born of practice and discipline, and if he had learned anything, it was that discipline was a rare quality. He decided right then that he would go back and would keep going back until the woman looked at him the way she looked at that man.

"You're not in love, are you? With the mighty Firdous?" his chacha said, noticing how quiet he was on the way home. "Love in Shahi Mohalla does not come cheap." He laughed, and Wajid did too, but this feeling, this desire, was no laughing matter.

He returned again and again. And eventually—as he listened to the ghazals she sang, the nazms she recited—he came to understand the language in the teahouse that felt so distant before. Here he didn't need to know every word, here this woman made him *feel* what the poetry meant when she sang, when she danced, when she looked out into the audience of men. Here to see Firdous again? the naika said each time he returned. Tip, he must tip, and so he tipped and tipped, giving the impression there would be no end to the coins that came from his pockets. You want her, the naika said to him eventually. What do I do? he asked. It will take time, she said. It took months; he borrowed money, he played at wooing her, for Firdous and all the women like her in the Mohalla insisted they must be won.

"I've heard about what's going on," Afzal Chacha said to him. "It was a terrible mistake to take you there. Your father will kill me if you squander any more money on this. You are not, Wajid, an aristocrat, whatever your mother tries to tell you." But for Wajid it was more urgent than ever that Firdous become his; after Sandhurst, his mother would marry him off, and he knew that all pleasure would vanish from his life. His happiness would be eked out around the performance of duties to family, to in-laws, to boring traditions, to children not yet born. Surely, before that, he was owed the pleasure of the company of a woman like Firdous?

Twenty-Eight

As soon as Mehru said Firdous's name, she knew, even over the telephone. Rozina was at a party at a private residence, some new building in a dull, still half-built Islamabad, as a guest of General Ghazi Ashraf, when Aunty Kulsoom whispered that an urgent phone call had come in for her. She had been staring at the general's mouth, open ever so slightly as he listened to the other generals talking of the war. He was leaving soon for East Pakistan and seemed more alert than he had been the first time they'd met—hunching low in his seat as if ready to spring up at any moment. Apparently, the officers there had created a disastrous situation, and the big guns were being called in. She thought of Faraz, who'd written to Amma from Dacca. Was he still there? Had he returned? It made her pay attention to their conversation, for a change, so she was startled when Aunty Kulsoom tapped her on the shoulder. She followed her out of the lounge, wondering if she should apologize, but she reminded herself that she had said the number was to be used only in case of emergency, and, registering that this must be an emergency, she slowed down, a flutter of dread in her stomach.

As she put down the receiver, she willed Aunty Kulsoom to speak, to tut, to sigh—to indicate the great inconvenience, the awkwardness of the discussion she would have to have with the general to explain Rozina's sudden departure. A cavalier response might give her permission to scream, to yell, which was exactly what she felt like doing. Her amma was dead. But Aunty Kulsoom held her, got her a glass of whiskey, asked the general to get his driver to take her to the airport. Rozina was troubled by her kindness, by everyone's kindness, as if they knew more than she did about the nature of what lay ahead—that things would become so much worse than they were in this moment of the telling, as if they knew that she was quietly nursing the fiction that some terrible error had occurred that could be rectified as soon as she got home.

⟡

MINA WAS ON THE TERRACE when she arrived some hours later. She was staring down at the body, which had been left on a charpoy in the courtyard down below, covered with a sheet. From up here, its outlines looked about the size of a child. Mina fell on her, sobbing, and told her the story: Firdous had felt unwell and went to lie down. Mina didn't check on her until much later, and when she wouldn't wake up, called for a doctor, but it was already too late. I should have checked, I don't know why I didn't, how could I have done this, she said, resisting all comfort, all reassurance—that this was God's will, that it had been peaceful, that it was Firdous's time. How could I, how could I, she cried, again and again.

Then Mina and Mehru with the older women in the Mohalla washed the body, their hands tender on Firdous's withered frame. Rozina was afraid to touch her mother's skin, to find it cold with her amma's absence. She sat with her back to them, looking up at the black flags on the terraces smacking the air. When they wrapped Firdous in a white shroud and laid her on the charpoy, the women withdrew; everyone did. She couldn't stand to see Firdous so alone, so she sat on the charpoy next to her. As children, Rozina and Mehru used to sneak out to the shamshan ghat by the river where the Hindus burned their dead. They watched with fascination as the flames licked at the bodies; they had not been afraid of dying then, but of the dead, and so Rozina told Mehru ghost stories for many nights after, stories that made her squeal. Where can I go to find your ghost, Amma? she thought now. What is it I still want to say? She knew there were things she ought not to say, things she ought never to have said, but it was the things she'd never said that churned, that made her feverish with regret. How could I not have said more, spoken more of love, of thanks; how could I, how could I, she thought again and again. She laid her hand on Firdous's face: Sorry, she meant, you did your best, I am more grateful than you knew. Please know it, feel it. When they carried her mother away for burial she tried to see it as Firdous, so pious, would have: as a release, a return to God, to her own mother, not as a life ended with little comfort, after much suffering.

It felt like hours before the men returned from the burial. Rozina sat with the women in the courtyard, her head pounding from crying, her whole face aching and red; yearning to leave, to go home, then remembering again and again that this was home, that there was nowhere else to go. As the courtyard emptied, Rozina told Mina it was time to go upstairs; she could hear the lanes outside getting busier, the night's work in the Mohalla beginning. Mina shook her head, refusing to go in. "I can't, I can't."

"We have to go up now. Come on. It will be busy out here soon."

Mina closed her eyes. "I can't go up to that room. With all her things, her bed. Her smell. I can't go in there if I know she is never going to come inside again."

"It's our home and we have to go in now." Rozina just wanted the day to be over, to begin again.

"I'm not going anywhere," Mina said.

"Fine," Rozina yelled. "Sit outside with these motherfuckers, with the harami pimps. Think what Amma would say if she saw you now, sitting outside with the dalals. What would she say, what would she say if she were here?"

It was then that Mina began to wail, as if she had finally realized Firdous was gone, that she would never speak again, never return again. Her body heaved, her nose streamed, she gasped for breath, and only Abdul Rahim could comfort her, was loud enough to be heard over the noise that came from somewhere deep within her.

Rozina left the courtyard and stepped into the lane outside the house. Groups of men were moving through the streets now, talking, laughing. One clicked his tongue at her as he passed, another called out. But when they heard Mina, they stopped, all of them—the tabla player next door, the men gambling in the music shop, the revelers, everyone stopped to listen to the girl as she shrieked and sobbed. There is no end to what God will take from you, Rozina thought, as the people of the Mohalla waited for Mina to give up, to submit to the vastness of her loss—so that they might return to whatever it was they had been doing before.

Twenty-Nine

On the road from Pak Motors to the airport in Tejgaon, Faraz passed a line of abandoned cars. The doors of the cars were open, the boots gaping like mouths. He stopped and got out to look at them. He couldn't understand if the cars had been abandoned by their owners or if they had been commandeered by soldiers and dumped here. Like the cars, Dacca had been abandoned. Those left in the city would not leave it, or could not. They hid, he guessed. The cantonment, meanwhile, bustled with vehicles, with men, with uniforms. Jeeps ran the roads, ferried the generals to the mess, to the Dacca Club in Shahbagh, to the Chinese restaurant in Dhanmondi; a parade through Dacca's ghostly streets, the bright flowers of the city's krishnachura trees quivering as the tires of jeeps and trucks pounded the streets, the officers reassuring themselves: We are here to stay.

Faraz had been checking on the men he'd posted along all critical roadblocks en route to the airport. Right now the IG, DIG, and all other senior police officials had gathered at the airport to receive new arrivals from West Pakistan, whom they'd shortly be accompanying back to the cantonment. Everything seemed secure; they should pass through here soon.

These new guests were, it appeared, an influx of generals, fresh from GHQ. No one in the department had said anything about these new developments, but they understood that even after all the shelling, even after days of fires burning through Old Dacca, they were not winning. Still the IG and the senior staff had to be there in a show of unity; the East Pakistan Police Force, whatever might be left of it, stands with its soldiers. Still on security detail, Faraz had to trail his senior officers, pretending the same.

The sound of a plane above. He thought of the arriving officers and struggled to imagine where they were coming from, cities untouched by the noise, the shock of war. He'd had no contact with Mussarat since the phone lines had been cut. They were fine, he reassured himself, and in some ways it was a relief that he didn't have to speak to her. What would he say? He couldn't tell her he'd heard on the radio that the army had attacked the police academy, that he could no longer believe Shamsuddin was alive, that he'd thought of Shamsuddin's brother-in-law, Amjad, and his friends from Dacca University when he heard the army had cleared the student hostels of rebellious elements, that for all he knew, they might be among the dead too. He could not tell her what he'd seen at Ramna Kali Mandir a few weeks earlier, that he had scarcely slept since.

He had tried to tuck it all into a corner of his mind, busying himself with his duties, but images from the mandir flashed at him unexpectedly, startling him, presenting him each time with more detail, not less. He'd been sent to the temple because a report had come in that a foreign journalist was taking pictures there, but when he arrived, constables in tow, they found only a solitary calf wandering, lost. There was no temple, no ashram anymore, just an expanse of white sky where the steeple had been. It had been shelled to nothing. The calf tripped its way through the rubble, past the handful of huts that still stood. The constables covered their mouths, hung back. Only Faraz followed the calf, who led him to a pyre. He could not count the number of dead in the tangle of blackened corpses, but he recognized the progress of the murderers—careful at first, then perhaps tiring or rushed, sloppier, the men, women, the children they'd shot and meant to burn abandoned halfway to the pyre, the stench of their bloated corpses unbearable now.

One of the constables came running toward him, handkerchief to his face. An old woman back there from the ashram was saying they took some of the girls; she wanted to know if they could bring her daughter back. Took them where? Faraz said. Where would they take them, what for, he thought, but only for the briefest moment. Will you speak to her? the constable asked. No. Never, he thought. Tell her we'll come back, he lied. Tell her to leave here, to get away from here. The other constable shouted at the approaching calf. She won't leave, the man said, agitated, not without her daughter. Get in the car, Faraz yelled, both of you, and he didn't care that his cowardice was plain, he wasn't even shamed by it or by the thought that hadn't left him since: How the hell can I get out of here? He couldn't tell Mussarat what he'd seen, couldn't tell anyone, not ever, and he couldn't explain that although he was safe, safer than any of the Bengalis in Dacca, from that moment he had been able to think only of his own fear.

In the distance, he could see vehicles approaching. He checked his watch. The caravan, a line of jeeps and staff cars, was on time. He walked the edge of the road, where the trees were as dark as they were tall. He reached out and touched the bark of a tree. He wondered how much the men arriving knew of what was happening here. Were the new brass here with new ideas? Would it be more of the same? Or worse? He marveled at how he'd pretended to himself that none of what he'd seen or heard was real. He had carried on with his job, acquiescing to what he knew was happening in Dacca with his silence. No, he'd told his senior officers, there were no journalists there. There was— he began, but was stopped. That's all we need for now. They knew what was there; it was why they wanted to make sure no one else saw it. And he'd said nothing more. *That's the job*, he tried to remind himself, and whenever the memories flickered, each one more foul, more vivid than the last, when he thought he just couldn't go along with any more of it, he remembered what Wajid, a master of self-preservation, would say: *Needs must, needs must.*

⸎

IT WAS THE SSP who told him that one of new generals, a certain Ghazi Ashraf, had asked to see him in the mess that night. The SSP did not look happy when he asked Faraz how he knew the general. He didn't, Faraz said. He had no contacts in the army other than Mussarat's father, retired now. Perhaps the man was a former CO of his father-in-law's, he ventured. His father-in-law had likely asked the man to check on him. He knew the SSP suspected him of lobbying someone to get him out and took it as a betrayal, even though everyone who had any connections was doing the same. "It'll all be over soon, you know. Before the rains, the generals are saying," he said, with a note of reproach. "We'll be home before long." But they both knew no one believed that.

When he arrived at the officers' mess, Faraz was told to wait for General Ashraf inside. Security detail meant he went wherever the generals went: He was familiar with the glow of tea lights at the mess, the movement of waiters at the Intercontinental, the generals talking over one another, braying at their ADCs. But he preferred the darkness outside, the dank air, the company of the other lackeys.

A bearer led him through the lounge—a whir of khaki uniforms, then a small meeting room beyond. The bearer was young, a teenager, judging by the softness of the hair on his upper lip, and he looked weary when he asked Faraz if he'd like a drink. When Faraz told him no, the young man sighed, relieved, and left him alone. Faraz stood by the door. He'd thought this might be a courtesy call, a favor his father-in-law or Mussarat might have asked of the general somehow. But now the whole setup seemed to confirm his worst fears—why a private room, if not to deliver bad news? Had someone died? Had they not wanted to send him a wire? He considered whether he should take a seat. Would he need it? He began to panic. If he was to survive this, then he had to know that at home everything was as it should be: safe, unchanged, Nazia and Mussarat as they had been when he'd last seen them.

The door opened, and the general came in. Faraz stood to attention and saluted. The longer they were around soldiers, the more compelled they felt to imitate them. The man stared at him a moment—he was stout but still fit, his eyes small, fat pouches under them. His whole face seemed puffy, and he dabbed at it with a handkerchief. Two deep lines from the sides of his nose to the corners of his mouth gave him the appearance of a man disappointed, or at best irritated.

"Inspector."

"Sir."

"Guarding the door, are you?" he said. "Take a seat."

"I'm fine, sir."

"If I intend to sit, then you will do the same." The man's tone was surprisingly brittle. "Never let anyone have the advantage over you in any location," he added, as if by way of explanation.

Faraz sat. It did not seem that bad news was forthcoming, but what, then? Would he be expected to entertain a friend of his father-in-law for the evening? The general said nothing but pulled up a chair for himself, his eyes on Faraz. Most of the generals were chatty in the mess, in social mode, effective at feigning some interest in your family, using it as an excuse to talk more about themselves or to offer advice, but this man looked as if he were never off duty.

"You must be wondering why I wanted to see you."

Faraz tried to maintain a neutral expression. "I wondered if you might know my father-in-law, sir. Captain Arshad. Retired."

"Never heard of him. I don't have much to do with men at that rank, as you can imagine."

Faraz stayed silent.

"I'm here because of your father." The man blinked slowly. It was the only thing about him that moved. "The chief secretary," he said. "He asked me to check in on you."

Faraz sat as still as he could, but he could not match the man's perfect stillness. "That's very kind of you, sir."

"You seem surprised."

Faraz said nothing.

"I understand your wife went to see him, that she asked him to get you out of here. He asked me to look into it."

Faraz looked up at the fan, which was spinning slowly. As desperate as he was to get out, he had told Mussarat not to do this. He knew she would have asked Wajid to keep it quiet, but with Wajid, what would be the point of helping if he couldn't take credit or the opportunity to humiliate?

The general was continuing. "I thought you should know the lengths your father went to. He asked me to see what I could do. I'm going to speak to the IG police, so that you can leave with me in a few days. It shouldn't be a problem." He looked at Faraz with an expression Faraz couldn't quite read—it wasn't irritation, exactly, or hostility, but something close. His mouth moved as if he were chewing something.

"Your father and I served together, do you know that?" Faraz shook his head. "You were just a little boy. We were in the desert, in a POW camp, when he told me he had a son. That he had a son to go back to."

And then he saw the look cross the man's face again, and he knew now what it was: distaste. This general had known Wajid a long time, through difficult times, and he knew something of Faraz's origins. If Wajid had entrusted him with this much, what else might he have confided?

"Thank you, sir. But I am fine here. I am happy to be serving. I couldn't leave the IG and the SSP at a time like this."

"He said you might say that. I wasn't convinced. Most of the men here would give an arm and a leg to get out, wouldn't they? And, well, there's a type. A type that falls apart in a situation like this. Just ask your father." Faraz kept his eyes forward. "And in a situation like this, with these Bingos, well, we can't afford that, we cannot falter." He paused, as if taking stock of Faraz's reaction. "It's not all their fault, of course. The Hindus have encouraged them. Though, honestly, I don't know how many of them really are Muslim. Just look at their women with their"—he gestured to his forehead—"like Hindu women. The quicker we get rid of the treacherous element among them, the better for everyone, them included. Then we get things back to how they were." He looked at Faraz again. "What do you think? You've been here awhile. Give me the insider's view."

Faraz thought of the soldiers he'd seen telling men to lift their lungis to prove they were Muslim, to prove they were like them. He thought of bodies stacked on a pyre.

"I don't think things can ever go back to how they were, sir."

The general looked displeased for a moment, then his expression softened. "Yes, maybe you're right. After the war, the Second World War, it was the same; we needed a new order. That's what we made. A new world, a new nation. We gave everything for it. What we can't do is lose all that now, lose face in front of the whole world, our honor. Not after how we fought for it. For freedom."

Faraz squinted, trying to make sense of the word. *Freedom.* The strangeness of it in the general's mouth.

"You've known the chief secretary a long time, sir," Faraz said.

"Your father?" It seemed to please the man each time he said it. "Yes. We saw through some difficult times together. You have to lean on one another in battle. Just as you are discovering here." It was hard to imagine Wajid in the company of this man, his practiced stillness next to Wajid's theatrical charm.

"You've stayed in contact all these years, sir, with the chief secretary?"

"Well, knowing your father has been an adventure." A clipped response.

"How's that, sir?"

A pursing of the lips; the generals asked the questions, not the underlings, and Faraz had asked one already.

"You're quite the interrogator. But that's a question you might better ask him." He leaned forward. "So, are you sure?" He looked at Faraz, his eyes narrowed, waiting, daring him to reveal his cowardice: Let me tell Wajid how you wept, how you cried for home.

"I'm sorry to have wasted your time, sir."

The general nodded; he seemed pleased. "Not a waste. I'm glad to have met you. And for this insightful chat." His tone was acerbic now. "You don't have a message for him? For Chief Secretary saab?"

Faraz shook his head. He couldn't imagine any reason to send an emissary like this, other than to make absolutely sure he did not return home.

"Well, I'm surprised to hear that. But I owe it to Wajid to tell you the offer still stands. I will be here for two days more, and if you change your mind, you can come and find me."

"Sir."

Faraz waited to be dismissed, but the man didn't move. He settled back in his chair, his eyes still on Faraz. Then he grinned. "A man like you, Inspector, of your background, you would likely know how a man might enjoy himself here in Dacca."

"I don't know Dacca that well," he said, his acerbic tone matching the general's.

"Sir."

"Sir," Faraz repeated, corrected.

"I suppose that'll be all, then," he said, his lips thin.

Outside the mess, the night was cool. Faraz could feel that the clouds were fat with rain, and the promise of a new season made him feel that choosing to stay might not be disastrous.

The next morning, after a meeting with the newly arrived generals, a Bengali colonel shot himself in the mess bathroom with his service pistol. No one knew what had been said that made the colonel despair—something about *showing the Bengali bastards, their women*, he heard later—but as Faraz and his constables were called in to help the orderlies pick up the man's brains and dump his limp body somewhere, he understood that, even if he left, he would never escape the blood they had let, in which they were all now steeped.

Thirty

Firdous looked down shyly after reciting the couplet, as always. Wajid knew this was intended to charm; it was a flirtation. But it was not half as compelling as knowing that it was all a performance; that was what intrigued him.

Firdous's refinement had turned out to be beyond what he had imagined. Her knowledge of verse was extraordinary, her conversation lively, her coquettish manner seductive. But it was only after he had given her several pieces of jewelry that he got an inkling of what she was. It was the furtiveness with which she slipped them into her choli that struck him. She who seemed so sure in everything in this gesture revealed a vulnerability. As soon as it was safely tucked away, she smiled, and the curtain came down again, a glassiness to her expression. It had frightened him for a moment, and then he realized: Of course this was a performance, of course this was work, it was her professionalism that was so impressive. How skilled she was at getting into character! What an art!

Still, he looked eagerly for those moments when she slipped up, when he saw more than she intended him to. Not because he loved her or wanted to know her or anything ridiculous like that, and not because, God forbid, he thought she might love him. It was just that he rather admired her. He was on his way to becoming a soldier and he had learned that a man had to detach himself to do this job well. Since experience had taught him that most men could not, he assumed no woman was capable of it, either. But then there was Firdous. He thought that if they could be frank with each other, she was the kind of woman he could talk to. But that would require trusting him, and she was too smart to do that. She played the part—the refined tawaif the men here came expecting to meet. She slipped up only rarely; once he'd overheard her yelling at her daughter, although she never called her that. My sister, she said, though it was clear the girl was hers. She called on God, on Ali for help, frustrated, unable to stop herself from complaining about the child—who was obstinate and disrespectful, who refused to listen. And then, as if she realized she had said too much, she stopped abruptly and smiled. My poor mother, she said. Poor mothers everywhere. You want children before you understand you will be enslaved to them, everything about your life forever tied up in someone else's life and happiness. It is a curse if you think about it.

He had no idea what she meant. It seemed to him he had brought only delight to his own family; he had not thought of what else his parents were other than his parents, of what they might want, only of what they wanted for him. He laughed, realizing only then how little he thought about them at all.

The other time, of course, was when she told him that she was going to have his child. She was angry when he said, Well, what do you usually do, this must be an occupational hazard, no? She talked frankly for the first time in two years to him. It was what he thought he had been waiting for, but it wasn't what he wanted to hear. She could not go to the dai, she said, she was too far along. He had been alarmed, unsure what this might mean. But then he thought it didn't really have to mean anything, did it? She was a whore. He could leave whenever he wanted. He could help her or not help her. What could she do? Tell me what you need, he said magnanimously, as if she could ask and he could give her anything. What do you think I need? she said, furious now. I can't work for a year. I need money.

He did the right thing for a while, for as long as he thought he should. Kept seeing her, kept giving her money. As her belly grew, he had her move on top of him, enjoying the weight of her, his hands around her stomach. But it seemed to him as if these changes in her body were consuming her, making it hard for her to keep up her usual performance. She cried sometimes now, she talked about her daughter, forgetting to pretend she was her sister. He was grateful to her in those moments—it was the most honest relationship he had ever had. But it was also wearying; he had come for pleasure, for experience, not to *know* her.

It was a year before he went back and saw the baby. He'd said he'd be back in a month—a trip to England, more training. He wasn't sure why he did go back in the end. He supposed he rather missed her, in his way. Perhaps he was, in truth, curious, too. She was cool with him. She showed him the baby, who looked to him much like all babies. He's just like you, she said. He has your nose, your smile, but Wajid wasn't sure. He believed that the boy was his, because Firdous, while a performer, was not a con artist, and she knew she stood little to gain from lying to him. I'm calling him Faraz, she said. And Wajid wanted to laugh, because it was a name that was filled with aspirations that the boy could never meet, a Kanjar boy. But he rather liked her optimism. That was Firdous; wanting more than the world told her she could have, having faith that God would somehow deliver it. Good name, he'd said, certain now that he would not see her again. Good name.

Thirty-One

RAWALPINDI, 1st DECEMBER 1971

Rozina did like riding in staff cars—the newly opened box of tissues in a holder next to her, the rose-scented perfume of some general's begum that clung to the seats, the sense that people outside the car thought someone important was sitting behind its dark windows. The general's ADC, who sat in front with the driver, was young and handsome, even though his eyes were small and his nose much too wide. He smiled easily and often, turning around in his seat to talk to her, asking her about the flight, the weather in Lahore. She asked a few questions about the situation in East Pakistan—now and again she still thought of Faraz, sometimes imagining when she listened to the radio that word of him might interrupt the news report. Although, truthfully, as more and more time passed without Amma, she wasn't sure how she would feel about news of him, or what it might mean to hear from him. With Mina entirely her responsibility now, with the constant strain of their situation, there was little time to dwell on ghostly memories.

"You think the Indians are behind the latest troubles, ADC saab?"

"Wherever there's trouble, there they are," the ADC said, answering her without really answering her, checking his watch. She was surprised; she thought they would still want to talk about it, the army chaps, to rage at the Indians planning to come in and fight for the Bengalis. In Lahore, the war seemed remote, and everyone thought they were winning, ridding the place of the Hindus. "It will all be over soon," she said, "and then we can celebrate the new year." He let out a bored sigh, and she made a note to sound more lively in her delivery with the general.

The staff car didn't take her to the hotel or the private house where she usually met him but to a residence in the cantonment. The house she spied behind the gates was a sprawling bungalow, the white plaster striking in the darkness. The ADC turned to her as they stopped at the guardhouse. "The general thought you might like to meet with some of his friends first." She smiled. It was going to be a long night. She would have to spend the evening on the general's arm, and then the night as well. But the general was fast becoming a regular, and it was important she build on this; she needed to extract some kind of promise of an exclusive arrangement from him. Something that would give her a little security.

"I believe Begum Kulsoom is also here and hoping to see you," the ADC said.

"Wonderful!" she said, wishing she had sounded more sincere even as she said it. There could be no chinks in her performance if Aunty Kulsoom was in attendance; the woman was always looking to find fault. Mistakes gave her a reason for withholding pay or paying late. This was no surprise— all brokers were the same—but Aunty Kulsoom had a way of making her feel as if she had let them both down, so that instead of calling her a sister-fucker, as she would any other pimp, she found herself saying, You're so right, I can do better, thank you for your guidance. It was a deference she knew well, the pitifulness of those women of the Mohalla, who knew their place, who knew their safety was in the hands of others. Rozina had thought herself apart from those women for so long, but here she was, just as pathetic, an ingratiating mess.

She smiled at the ADC as he opened the door for her. He smiled

back—he had to be ten years younger than her—and she thought for a
moment she wouldn't have minded a drink with such a handsome man. She
did not usually allow herself to think such things, to want such things. But
to sit with a man, to flirt a little, to exchange soft glances, to laugh, to make
a man laugh, especially a man who had the confidence of youth, no sense
yet of how life would limit him—well, that might be a really wonderful
thing.

"Thank you," she said. The drivers and aides waited by the cars as the
ADC led her inside. They would smoke and lick their dry lips as they
waited for the VIPs inside to be done, and she felt at one with them, just as
bored, just as desperate to clock off while bound, as they all were, to performing the deference the people they served expected of them.

Aunty Kulsoom sat in a corner of the huge living room, which was divided into a number of seating areas, each with its cream-colored sofas and
soft chairs embroidered with gold or pastel-colored threads and topped
with an abundance of plump cushions. The impression—soft, white, and
billowy—was of walking into an enormous bubble bath. Intimate groups
were scattered through the room, as if numerous parties were happening in
parallel. But it was Aunty Kulsoom's party in the corner that seemed the
most important, for there sat a slew of generals, deep in conversation. Were
it not for her presence, the dark maroon of her sari just visible amid the
khaki, you might think this was a war cabinet meeting, until a roar of
laughter from the generals made it obvious the war wasn't on anyone's mind
here.

Aunty Kulsoom sat back, smoking, and a fat, mustachioed general
leaned in, said something in her ear. She waved at Rozina but did not
beckon her over, which meant Rozina should occupy herself till Aunty was
ready for her. She recognized numerous faces from the papers and from
television; the men, for the most part aging and heavy, were all accompa-
nied by well-maintained younger women; some might be wives but most,
she guessed, like her, were not. Their bushy-browed president—another

general, so many generals—was here somewhere, too, she guessed, indisposed, no doubt. Once she'd seen him at a party like this—sitting on a lounger by the pool, a girl in his lap, his smile sloppy and drunken—she found it hard to reconcile him with the gruff, stern figure she saw on television.

The corner opposite was vacant but for one large man squeezed into a wingback chair. She could be comfortably invisible there until she was needed. She sank into a big sofa, enjoying its deep embrace. A bearer came to ask what she'd like to drink: A 7UP, she said, and the man in the wingback chair looked up at her. "Madam Heer!" he exclaimed. It took her a moment to recognize him as the fat councillor who had represented Shahi Mohalla some years ago. His face had been everywhere at the time—posters always plastered all over the walled city to mark some occasion or other, even when there weren't elections, as if he worried they might forget him otherwise. She smiled, willing his name to come back to her. He stood. "Please don't get up, Madam Heer," he said as he sat down next to her. "What a delight to see you after all these years. My wife, my daughters, we were all such fans of yours."

"We haven't seen you in so long!" Rozina said. Salim—Salim something, wasn't it? "Are you still working in the walled city?"

"Oh, no, I'm a member of the National Assembly now," he said.

"Wah! An MNA, Salim Saab," she said. "That's quite something."

"Thank you," he said. He didn't sound as proud as he might have. "I was voted in during the last election cycle. But of course without a National Assembly actually meeting, there hasn't been much for a member to do."

She nodded sympathetically. "Hopefully, things will be in order by the new year, once the war is over," she said.

He shrugged. "We might be half an assembly by then, half a nation." But then he waved his words away. "Not that that is anything for you to worry over, Madam Heer. Ladies should not be troubled by this . . . drama." They sat in silence a moment.

"So you don't go to the walled city anymore?" she said.

"Oh, no. Not for some time." He waved his fingers. "Burned fingers!" he joked. She smiled. The waiter came back with her drink. "Mushtaq Saab?" the waiter said. That was it: Salim Mushtaq!

"The trouble with Heera Mandi is that there are good things there . . . as you know. Drink and food . . . the best music, dance, and other things, of course, which means people go back . . . but really the place is not what it was. The best artists left during Ayub's time. To think that I used to take out-of-town guests there!"

He was right, she supposed. The place had started to look more and more run-down, some of the function rooms had closed, and how many of the great masters were teaching girls to dance the kind of rigorous kathak she had been taught? Amma would have been distressed to see their craft diminished so.

"Of course," he said, "the other thing is that when a place starts to take a downturn, you get a lower class of people going there—it won't be the nawabs, not the top-notch Lahoris. It'll be the gangsters or the men who might as well be gangsters." He nodded toward the generals.

She laughed. "Mushtaq Saab!"

"Maybe I've had too much to drink," he said, sounding suddenly low. "But I've seen things, Madam Heer."

"You're supposed to see things in the Mohalla. That's why people go," she said.

"Not those things." He took a swig of his drink. She'd entertained enough drunken men to know that the best way to get a man to tell her more was not to probe but to wait. "I couldn't go back after that." He stared at the group in the far corner, the men sitting with Aunty Kulsoom. "I'd put it all out of my head, but I got here tonight and I saw him after all this time and it all came back." The man, big and bloated as he was, sagged as he spoke. Who, she wanted to ask, who did you see? What did he do?

Aunty Kulsoom stood, and Rozina saw her surveying the room. When she clocked Rozina, she waved again. Next to her stood General Ghazi Ashraf. Salim Mushtaq stared at the general, looking distressed. And then

Rozina knew: That's who he meant. What had he done? She thought of how he liked to put his hand over her mouth when he lay on top of her. You're not his type, really, Aunty Kulsoom had said, but I've convinced him he's better off with someone more experienced.

"I suppose I'll be seeing him all the time now," Salim Mushtaq said. "They say he's the favorite of the moment. Really going places." Rozina saw the general fix his eyes on Salim Mushtaq; he didn't look anxious, as Salim Mushtaq did. He looked blank, as if he had no memory of the man at all.

"I need another drink," Salim Mushtaq said, rising as the general came toward them. Mushtaq bowed his head in salutation, and Aunty Kulsoom introduced them as though they were meeting for the first time—what a great honor, Mushtaq said before he excused himself, taking, Rozina saw, a big swallow of his drink before he left. General Ghazi Ashraf looked at her and smiled, showing no teeth. "Always a pleasure to see you, Madam Heer," he said. She smiled back.

A few hours later, in his room, as they lay naked in his bed, she asked him if he'd met Salim Mushtaq before. The general raised an eyebrow, shrugged. No recollection. He smiled. I think I'd remember him, he added, and they tittered at the man's inordinate size, something warming in their shared, mild disgust.

It was much later, the following evening, when it happened, and she would struggle to remember what had set it off. She would remember standing by the drinks table, the general on the phone a few feet away. She would remember that she mixed his drink incorrectly. Perhaps that was what did it. When he pointed it out, the whiskey and water instead of whiskey and ice, she had laughed. How silly of me, she meant, but he went very still, his eyes fixed on her. She smiled. Let me make it again, she said. For the briefest moment, when he put the phone down, she thought he looked more relaxed, but later, when she sat doubled up in the bathroom, she would remember that right before the violence there was always a pause, an instant in which the body readied itself, both yours and his, for what you both knew would come, and her body had been prepared—in the time he put the phone down, as he limbered up, she had already raised her hands to her face to protect her most valuable asset, and he had known she would do just this, so in that gap he'd made the decision to hit her in the stomach, hard enough, she felt, to crack her in two.

❧

ROZINA LAY ON HER SIDE, too exhausted to move. There was a lizard on the far wall, its pale yellow skin a distant smear from where she lay. She waited, but the lizard knew it was being watched and would not move. She contemplated throwing something at the wall and then wondered briefly at how easily she could entertain this cruelty.

The phone rang, thin, persistent. "Don't answer it," she said. Mina stared at her. She had been issuing the same instruction for weeks. They waited for it to stop. Then Mina bustled about their room, cleaning, tidying things away. Rozina had imagined working twelve hours a day as a maid might have Mina craving slovenliness, relishing the chaos of their home, cluttered still with the artifacts of Rozina's old life with Najam—ashtrays and knickknacks and whiskey glasses they had no use for, and then Rozina's dirty clothes, her jars of creams and makeup left open on the sill, and of course her endless half-drunk cups of tea. But it seemed Mina was now never not working; every moment she wasn't working outside the house, she was occupied with emptying and organizing and lining things up in their home. Rozina remembered her servant, Salima, whenever she saw Mina's industriousness. Salima had done her job; Mina, with her incessant, frenzied activity, seemed to be doing something else altogether.

When the phone rang again and Rozina instructed Mina to ignore it a second time, Mina angrily clattered the dishes she was putting away. "You will break those like that," Rozina said. The girl's face was a knot of discontent—just a few months of work at the house on Durand Road, of walking back and forth in the heat and dust, had aged her. She could pass for a woman in her twenties, and this made Rozina feel dismal.

"What's going on?" Mina said. "Why won't you pick up the phone?"

Rozina turned her back. "I don't feel like it. It'll only be Kulsoom, and I want a break. Can't I just have a break?"

"I don't want you to have a break," Mina said, her breath heaving. "I just want you to stop."

Rozina held her breath. The words hung in the air—unlucky words, Amma would have said, a curse that could leave them penniless, a wish that was never to be spoken aloud, in case it put other words in a woman's heart, words like: *I don't want to do this anymore, I hate it*, words that might make a woman think she could choose when there were no choices, not for women inside the Mohalla or even outside it. A kanjari's family could not risk saying such things, but Mina had just said them, Mina who had more to lose than anyone, who would go hungry if Rozina did stop.

"It's not so bad, it's fine," she said. "I'm so lucky. All the important suitors I've had all my life. The money they've paid. How many women here can say the same?" This was what Firdous would have said, but the words felt hollow, and as Rozina said them, she felt hollow, exhausted. Too tired to get up, to dress, to eat, content to keep her eyes on the wall, hour after hour, waiting for the lizard to twitch, to scurry somewhere.

"If that's true, then what's happened to you?"

Rozina shook her head: Nothing, nothing. Mina turned and started emptying the daal she'd cooked into a dish, smacking the pot hard. Rozina watched her daughter's back move, the muscles of her neck tight and strained. She closed her eyes. She could not tell her, she reminded herself; she could not tell anyone.

After that first night he'd hit her, he'd asked for her all the more regularly, and he got rougher—his hands pushing her thighs apart, her head held down. Her complaints to Aunty Kulsoom came to nothing. With the war over, with Bhutto in power, what do you expect? Kulsoom said. All the generals are nervous; they all need comfort right now. Be patient with him. He struck her as a man who needed no comforting, with a distaste for those who did. When she finally just said no to Kulsoom, she would not go anymore, she was done with the general, the woman had shrugged: Fine, up to you. Rozina understood Aunty Kulsoom could not offend the general by bringing her along to places where he would be, and he was everywhere now, so there were fewer options. There are others, Heer, of course there are, she said when Rozina pressed her for work, lower-level types. But you know, she sighed, *maybe it's time.*

Rozina understood she was aging, that a natural decline in her clientele was to be expected, and she had also chosen to limit it. Still it could not be *time*, not yet, maybe not ever, because she had no other means. And so she'd found herself dropped to the second tier, to a party in a faded-looking house in Gulberg, not far from where she had once lived with Najam. A handful of younger women were there, too, wearing more makeup than they needed, and then there were the men, professionals certainly, but no one important, no one recognizable, no one who could get anything done without having to ask someone of real importance.

One of them asked her to dance—something she hadn't had to do in public for years. She laughed it off; he badgered. This was going to happen more and more, more degrading requests the further she fell, tier by tier. One day she might even be working in Tibbi, alongside the ancient, homeless whores who just barely fed themselves. No one would remember the artist she had been, the huge sums she had made, the bold, larger-than-life posters of her that brought fans to the cinema. This was what it was to slide down the ladder toward obscurity—toward poverty.

Fearful that her reluctance would get back to Aunty Kulsoom, that even this work would dry up, she stood. The men began to sing a song from one of her old films, the last film she'd made with Bobby. They were drunk, excited to have a real movie star before them, the kind they'd paid money to see in their youth. The younger women laughed and clapped along, looking relieved that they weren't being asked to perform, too, or not yet. Rozina slipped out of her high heels, moved to the middle of the room, aware that she was heavier, clumsier than she'd been the last time she stood to dance, but her feet stamped the ground with the precision her dance master had drummed into her as a girl. Her posture was rigid, her arms sliding through the air, flicking outward and back in, fingers locked as she turned again and again. Master saab, who sat in front of her, had rapped her legs with a ruler when she failed to elongate her arms, and the snap of the wood against skin came back to her. She extended her arms, surprised by her grace. She marveled for a moment at her body's memory, that after all these years she still knew what to do, how to do it. Did it remember everything? she thought. Did it remember all the things she had trained her mind to forget? Was that why she paced their rooms in the Mohalla, always anxious even when there seemed nothing to fear, certain that some unnamed terror lay in wait for her? Was that why, a few hours from now, after she'd gone upstairs with the man who'd paid for her company—a middle-aged dermatologist visiting from abroad—after she'd done what was expected, she would wake in the night next to him, her skin prickling, aflame, for no reason she could explain?

They applauded, the shabby crowd in the shabby house, and she smiled, suppressing the urge to run from the room, from this body of which she would never be free.

The phone rang again. Mina, kneading dough, looked up. Rozina looked at the phone but didn't pick up, ashamed that she could no longer bear to. Mina wiped her nose on her shoulder, her hands not stopping. How good she'd gotten at kneading the atta, Rozina thought. She had not appreciated all the work that went into looking after a home, looking after *her*, until she saw Mina doing it.

"You're afraid," Mina said to Rozina. Rozina brought the phone to her chest as if to deny it, appalled at how it was spilling from her, after all this time, seeping from her as though she could no longer contain it. Yes, Rozina wanted to say, I am. I am afraid I don't have it in me to do what must be done anymore. There was no one to turn to, no kindly shoulder to lean on, no Bobby, no one. She wanted Amma, to cry to Amma. Firdous would have known what to do, her hardhearted mother had always done whatever had to be done, however brutal, had even found pride in it, so certain that God had fated it for her. Mina stared, unblinking. Amma would never have admitted fear, never to Rozina; a mother's job was to be certain in all things, to show her children that fear was as illusory as their nightmares—it's nothing, just a bad dream, they said—it was a mother's job to show her children she could do anything required to protect them. But Rozina was no one's mother, not really, and so she sobbed and let her daughter come to her and hold her with hands that were sticky with dough and say the things she had always longed for her mother to say to her: *You don't have to do it, you don't have to do it ever again, we'll find another way.*

Thirty-Two

He had dreamed, as he sometimes did, that someone had died, though he wasn't sure who—that was the puzzle he labored over in his sleep—who, what, when, where—and in the first moments of waking, he felt the same frantic urgency he'd felt while dreaming, until he remembered: everyone, of course. Everyone had died, and this truth was easier than thinking of any particular person. He turned on his side, body clenched. *Everyone*, he told himself again, trying to keep Shamsuddin's name, his face, at bay, but of course it never worked. Shamsuddin, killed only six weeks after Faraz saw him in Ramna Park, insisted on being remembered, insisted that Faraz remember that he was a part of that blank, nameless everyone. Faraz lay listening to the other men in the barracks, some of whom were dreaming their own nightmares, from what he could make out, waiting for them to rise, for the commotion of their movement: charpoys creaking, cold hands rubbing against each other, the guttural clearing of throats before they filed outside to be counted—these predictable details making it possible to get through the leaden, tiresome hours of the day when at least he had a reprieve from dreams, and then to the night, and then to the night after that.

"Not sleeping so well, Inspector saab?"

Faraz shook his head and turned to Gul in the bed next to him. "You?" he said. Zafar, a colonel, sat up in his bed a little distance away and Gul stared at him. The colonel was tall, his beard thinning, balding in places, revealing his yellowing skin; he had been Gul's CO. "Who needs sleep, Inspector saab," Gul said, cupping his hands and blowing into them; he smiled, eyes bloodshot.

Outside the barracks, after the guards had counted them, the first of five counts of the day, they lined up for the toilets, then, during these winter months, for an icy wash and a shave. There were several barracks in the compound, which had previously been a training camp for Indian paramilitary forces. Faraz had ended up here as an aide to some SSP who had been temporarily placed with the junior army officers. The SSP was moved, but Faraz was stuck waiting for room to open up in one of the civilian barracks.

A man gave the call for the azhan outside the barracks as they returned from washing; a group of officers gathered five times a day in the area dedicated for prayer, with indefatigable commitment. When they weren't praying, they exercised and played volleyball, walked along the wire fence, or read newspapers in slivers of Gwalior's wintry sunshine. It was at night, after the final count, that time took on a different character, turning into something breathless, frantic. They'd begun digging a tunnel under the barracks, working in shifts to make as much progress as they could in the hours before the morning count. Faraz wished he'd been on rotation last night; digging left no time to think, to feel. But Zafar was the one who decided who did what, and despite the fact that they needed as much help as possible, he seemed determined to keep him at arm's length; after all, Faraz wasn't really one of theirs.

It was only after his breakfast of tea and a puri, after rereading his letters from Mussarat, that he felt he'd put the unease prompted by the dream to one side. A group of officers sat outside the barracks, smoking, shuffling cards for a game of bridge. When they'd first left Dacca after surrendering to the Indians, he'd sat alongside the senior officers from the cantonment in the train, men whom he used to protect as part of his service; furious crowds had gathered at the train station and the Indian soldiers held them back; protecting them was their job now. At Narayanganj, where they caught the steamer to Khulna, crowds had again gathered, and then at every train station from Khulna to Gwalior—raging, gawking, jeering. The officers mostly sat silent or turned to one another or even to their Indian guards and joked, putting on a performance of being quite untroubled. Faraz had looked into the crowds, though—after months watching soldiers roll bodies down toward the docks, it seemed right that they should listen to these insults, that they were animals, that they were beasts. Over the many days it took to transport the tens of thousands of POWs to India, he was separated from most of the officers he knew and placed with men who had served all over East Pakistan. He didn't know most of them—he didn't know what they had done just as they didn't know what he had done, but they didn't speak of those things now; here they behaved as if none of that mattered, as if none of it had happened, their forgetting an exhausting, collective project binding them to one another.

Gul laid out a chessboard on the veranda and gestured to him. He knew little about Gul, really, even after all these months—a misshapen nose from a break playing hockey, a wife and children in Faisalabad. He had served in Comilla with Zafar and some of the other men here, and he had been a patient chess teacher; their quiet games had been one of the few comforts outside of Mussarat's letters and Billa's packages of cigarettes. This game will teach you strategy, foresight, surprise, Gul had said when convincing him to learn—good for a man in your line of work. Faraz had thought himself possessed of such qualities already, but as he played and lost again and again, he realized he'd never truly stopped to imagine every iteration of every play as he should have; what would he have seen if he'd only known how to do that? What, he wondered each time Gul trapped his king, had he been missing all this time?

Zafar stood; prayers were over. He headed back inside the barracks, glancing at their game. "Play over prayer, as usual."

Gul paused, his pawn in the air. "What's amazing is that he manages to pray at all," he said.

Faraz waited, sensing there was more. Gul put the piece back down where it had been. "In Comilla, he called me in one day. 'Get rid of it,' he said, showed me someone they'd killed. A teenager." Gul swallowed. "Nothing unusual about that, really, we all did plenty of it." He looked up at Faraz. "But he wasn't shot, this kid. They'd done it with their hands, there were these marks on the boy. All over. Slow, it would have been—torture. We couldn't just dump him, everyone would see. So we put him in a barrel, loaded it with stones, and threw it in the water. I did it, followed the order. But now I play, Inspector saab," he said, "because I don't know what to pray."

Faraz looked out into the camp; beyond the sentry towers and flood-lights, the barbed-wire fence, there were streets and houses and people, trees and flowers, living things. He could not see how they could move through it all again, how they could ever pretend well enough that all this life wasn't rimmed with the death they'd made. "Your turn," he said.

❖

IT WAS FOUR A.M. when they woke him to take his turn to dig, and sleepy though he was, he clambered into the hole under the heating stove, now five feet deep; a marvel, given they'd dug it out with empty milk tins and spoons and their hands, over many weeks. The ground, at first, had given way eas-ily, wanting, it seemed to Faraz, to let them inside it, but it had grown colder and harder the deeper they went, and now the task—to complete a tunnel forty feet long—seemed insurmountable. All night they rotated bodies in and out, their order for now to widen the tunnel at its base, to create a chamber before they began extending the length. Zafar kept watch at the edge of the opening, ready to cover it should a guard come in.

Faraz bent as much as he could and began scraping at the dirt, slowly picking, chipping. He thought of the dirt ahead of them, dirt they'd have to remove slowly and carefully over weeks. Then he thought of the darkness, of not being able to breathe down here.

"What is it?" Zafar hissed. Faraz shook his head, nothing. "Put a little backbone into it," Zafar said. Faraz glanced up—the whites of the man's eyes. "You'd think you didn't want to get out at all, Inspector."

The dirt smelled bad, rotten. He did want to get out, he wanted to get home to his wife, his child, to move in the world again, but perhaps also he didn't. Or perhaps it was the colonel that he wanted to keep here. The dirt trickled onto his feet, settling between his toes. The innocent had a right to escape, but none of them were innocent. He'd told himself he hadn't done much, but that had, in fact, been his crime. And then there were the crimes he'd committed that had nothing to do with what he'd seen in Dacca, the innocents he'd sent to places far worse than this camp, because he'd been ordered to do so. There'd been plenty of them over the years. He remembered the boy, Khwaja, weeping. How did a man who really had done nothing manage to get through each day without losing his mind? Some days they felt forgotten here, but they knew Bhutto and Indira Gandhi were in talks, their families were clamoring for their return; sometimes they heard messages addressed to them on Radio Pakistan, messages to keep their spirits up. Who remembered the men, the boys he'd put away?

Zafar slapped the ground with his hand, which meant the man at the window had seen or heard something. Faraz stilled, breathing heavily. Guards walked the camp perimeter every two hours, with a kind of languid ease. They checked and counted, but the prisoners were comfortable, their interactions far from hostile. Still, no one knew what they would do if they caught men trying to escape. What kind of punishment would await them then?

The colonel tapped the ground again to indicate Faraz could resume digging. "Come on," Zafar said, "you've gotten nowhere and it's almost time for fajr," he said. Fajr. *Prayer over play.* He marveled that Zafar and the others prayed with such ferocious pride, that they planned escapes, that shame didn't stop them from standing before God or make them wonder if they deserved freedom at all. Faraz held up the spoon he'd been digging with. He bent its head backward. "Sisterfucker, what are you doing?" Zafar said.

"Something's wrong with the ground here. You won't get farther."

"Who says?" Zafar said.

Faraz hauled himself out of the hole, panting.

"Get back down there, your time isn't up," Zafar said, but Faraz brushed past him. He was sitting on his cot, trying to rub his hands and feet clean, when he felt someone behind him. Before he could turn, he felt a hand gripping his arm, yanking him up, trying to drag him off the bed. Gul sat up at the noise, and others did, too, all of them whispering loudly at Zafar to stop, to let go, to quiet down.

"Guard," the man at the window said, perhaps lied, and finally Zafar released Faraz, pushed him away, took a step back. "Sisterfucker," he said, "you can rot here."

Faraz lay down, his mouth dry. He tasted dirt, something metallic. Gul was looking at him but said nothing. Poor move, he was doubtless thinking. A thoughtless strategy, making an enemy of a man like Zafar, a man who could endure the slowest, most painful version of your death if he needed to. Faraz thought of the chessboard, the line of foot soldiers protecting the figures behind them. He would never get better at the game, not really, but he had learned that for a man in his position, on the front line, the moves were limited, and the only possible victory was in abandoning the field altogether. For that, strategy was not necessary—only courage. He wished he possessed more of it, enough to face sleep, enough to face the dreams that lay in wait for him.

PART THREE

*I discovered my Lord
in the breaking of my plans.*

ALI IBN ABI TALIB

Thirty-Three

Ghazi is trying to sleep, when he remembers crawling along the bank of the canal by the shisham tree near his father's house. He inches through the tall grass, scanning the ground. He is searching for the nest of a kala teetar. Kasim squats beside him, the shadows of the grass swaying across his face. They know it is here somewhere. Their plan is to steal a chick, to raise it as a fighting bird. To become rich, richer than they already are. They think it is a great plan, certainly superior to the plan their parents have for them, which is to live and die here, overseeing their lands: endless acres of golden wheat. Ghazi hates the fields; the noisy silence, with its clicks and rattles. It hisses at him, the silence.

It is just when Kasim says he's had enough, it's time to go home, that Ghazi spies it, wedged into a depression close to the edge of the bank. He stretches his hand to reach the nest, but the teetar parents, who have been hunting for food, return, dive at him, and he knocks it down into the canal. He hears nothing as it hits the water, although he expects something: the crack of the nest coming apart, small beaks squawking, a splash. At least that. Ghazi is surprised at the quiet, the serenity of the drowning. Above them the teetars swirl, round and round, screeching for their babies as if they were human. It is the last thing he hears as he falls asleep, or perhaps it is the first thing he dreams when he sleeps, he can't be sure.

⌁

WHEN HE WAKES, he remembers that the war is thousands of miles away. It seems even farther here in Thall, where the sky looks as if it might swallow the fort, his home these last few months. He sees that his bearer has left his kit on a hanger by the doorway. Ghazi imagines the bearer, a man with sad, drooping eyes, watching him as he sleeps. He recoils at the thought. Does he sleep with his mouth open, like a fish? Does he drool? He wonders how easy it might be for an enemy to enter, to kill him as he slumbers. He will reprimand the bearer or, better yet, get rid of him and employ a new one before they leave the garrison. Or else he must sleep more lightly, or less, or not at all. He rises, eager to get outside. It is not yet light, but he is less vulnerable in the hills, he thinks. He dresses, steps into the cold.

He walks the perimeter wall, beyond which looms the mountain that shadows all of Thall. He hears the wind blowing across the Kurram, the river churns with it. They should feel safe behind the fort's ancient walls, but they don't. He likes that. He thinks of Kasim, who will not rise till eleven, will drink his tea on the veranda before being taken to the fields by the overseer, where he will glance at his workers and wonder what is for lunch. Ghazi is relieved to be here. He doesn't know what the day will be like, what any day will be like ever again. He has heard that soon he will be shipped out, that he will arrive at the war, which he imagines as a place you reach, like a railway station. He has seen maps, photographs of aircraft carriers on the Channel, newsreels of Churchill, but he has no idea what war will look like. His commanding officers talk about digging in, tank support; they pore over maps of cities he hasn't heard of. They talk about divisions moving out across the world, from every corner of the globe, nations upon nations of men, this is how vast we are, how powerful, they say, but still he imagines it as a lonely thing; he can see only himself in it. He wonders if the Germans are as sickly-looking, as pale, as his commanding officers, who speak of the Germans with distaste, but also pity. The British officers are confident. They've done this before. Last time, it took staying power; that's all. Jerry might have torn through Europe, their panzers might have trampled borders at pace, but the Germans can't beat staying power. *Resolve.* The Hun has no resolve, the officers nod at one another, and then they start another game of billiards in the mess.

"Up before everyone," Wajid says. He holds a smoke between his teeth. It glows, the paper crinkles. He offers Ghazi one but Ghazi refuses; he doesn't like to take things from anyone. Wajid is the more recent arrival of the two, although it feels to Ghazi as if it is Wajid who has always been there. Pleasant chap, everyone says, *you almost forget,* the British officers say amongst themselves. His eyes are wide and heavily lashed, making him seem more handsome than he is. Ghazi touches his own nose: too long. His teeth are small and square and sharp and so he tries not to smile. Wajid hums, something English. In a moment, he will quote Shelley or some such, he's a bore. From the darkness, a howl. An animal he can't identify. They both stop to listen. A jackal maybe, a fox.

"Something's chasing the birds and grouse. We should do the same." Wajid gestures toward the hills. "There don't seem to be any tribesmen to hunt here." Wajid's right. Their position here is about little more than making their presence felt, the objective to intimidate the tribesmen, but as it turns out, no one's here. The impenetrable, rocky hills are far more likely to beat them than the tribesmen, with their rusty homemade rifles. Wajid smiles, and Ghazi sees that Wajid is relieved, that he dreads the thought of combat. He is the kind of man who will fall apart when they get there, Ghazi thinks, as he watches Wajid head for the mess, where he will jape and joke; he is a deep well of fear.

Later, Ghazi stands to one side in the mess, he watches because he doesn't know what to say. The CO, Captain Macguire, tells them all the story of a Welsh coal miner he met in the Great War. He tells this story night after night. Then he sings a snatch of something. Ghazi has no idea what the story or the song means, what he is supposed to understand from this telling, but the officers laugh. Every night they laugh as if they were hearing it for the first time. He knows he has failed to make an impression; he decides he does not care. But he is embarrassed when the officers look past him for someone else, anyone else to talk to. He cannot find things to say even when he concentrates. He stands by the bar but no one asks him to stay for a last drink, they do not notice when he leaves. He is shamed. Then he seethes.

⊹

THE WAR MUST WAIT. The unit has to move deeper into the mountains, into Waziristan. Operations put all of them in close quarters with one another, even the white officers can't escape contact with the sepoys. They leave the fort by lorry and end up—where? It has a name, this place, but they don't know why. There is nothing here, just the mountains that overshadow their camp. They have only one another here. Wajid laughs nervously at everything now, now that they are no longer held within the walls of the fort. Ghazi hears him from the other side of the camp, always that thin laugh, made thinner by the mountain air.

When Macguire sends the two of them out with a troop, it is Wajid who is to take the lead; Ghazi is to act as a supporting officer. Ghazi's unhappiness is a hard, cold thing: He is certain Wajid is not capable, he guesses that Wajid knows it, too. They must get from the camp to a location several miles away at night. They are to recce the route on foot, ascertain the safety of the planned position on a hill pass before the regiment moves its ancient, rusting armored vehicles. Somewhere out there are tribesmen, rebels, the intelligence officers insist, they just can't see them. Wajid salutes, he has an excellent salute, but his breath is shallow. It's the elevation, he says, that's all.

Ghazi goes over the night charts again and again; he feels his senses sharpen, as if through sheer will he is bringing new parts of himself to life. By the time they set off, he feels he can see in the dark, can feel the breath of everything around him, the men, the snakes, the hills. The hills wear the darkness lightly, as if they might toss it off at any moment; he can see

Wajid's pale face as they lead the company north. Ghazi wonders if he looks as frightened as Wajid does. They inch forward. Out here, the charts don't seem like any kind of guide at all. This place cannot be mapped; the terrain shifts and turns in the darkness. Ghazi nods up at the stars, to tell Wajid to use them, but Wajid just squints at them like a child trying to make sense of a puzzle that's just too hard. The men behind them are growing nervous now, he's taking too long to direct them. Hurry up, Ghazi says, which way? He is on edge now, too. Something feels wrong, something is painful about not being able to move, to run from the darkness that seems set to consume them. The sound of shuffling, of scratching. The men freeze. A goat. A lost goat bleats. They must be near a village, an encampment; they are not where they are supposed to be.

"Get rid of it," Ghazi says to the havildar.

Shoo, says the havildar, and shoo say a few of the other men. But the goat keeps scratching.

"Get rid of it," Ghazi says again. He throws a small stone in the direction of the scratching, and the men flinch as if it is meant for them.

"Never fear," Wajid says. "Where there's life, there's still fight, boys." This is how Wajid cajoles the men, even on drill. Sometimes he dithers, flounders, asks their opinion. Ghazi is waiting for it now, for Wajid to turn to the havildar and say: What do you say, shall we try east, old chap? Does that look like Cassiopeia to you? As if the man would know.

Ghazi is just readying himself to take over, when there is a crack in the sky, then the thump of a rifle firing. The men freeze. Ghazi pulls Wajid down. The sound of the blast tells them that the bullet was aimed at them. Ghazi is unprepared for the fear, for the way his body is quivering, for the way everything he can't see has become louder, larger in the darkness. He wants to scream, to charge at something. To kill before he is killed. "Get down," he tells the troop. The men drop, and he feels their collective awareness that they are slow, that they are late, that if they were in Europe, somewhere in Belgium or France, they would be dead by now, that many of them will die like this soon. "It's fine, you're fine," he comforts. His tenderness surprises him. He knows he will save their lives. Again and again. They will live because of him. He will die to save them if he must. Wajid laughs a little, as if embarrassed by it all, by his terror, by how much he needed to hear this, by how much he needs Ghazi.

Ghazi shushes him, smacks the ground with his hand. He feels the men focus; they look to Ghazi now instead. It came from there, from the northeast, we'll head toward it, he says. The men hesitate, then the havildar nods. They are resigned. To this, to his leadership, to the death that following him promises because it is, at the same time, their only chance to survive.

They reach an encampment. They find more goats, a few mud shacks. Their approach is careful, creeping, although there seems little to ambush. The four or five old men sitting by their mules and goats outside the huts do not look surprised when they are surrounded. They say nothing when Ghazi demands to see their weapons, but hold them out for inspection. They shrug when Ghazi accuses them of firing their rifles. So what? There's no law against using our guns here, there's no law here at all, they say. Ghazi feels Wajid pulling at his sleeve, like a child. They are off course now, they have led a troop into hostile territory with no clear objective, and they have no communication with their commanding officers. Ghazi feels Wajid's nerves, his panic. But the truth is he feels at ease here, as if he now understands what his life is supposed to be, what war will be.

"Who's in there?" Ghazi says, gesturing at a mud hut with a closed door. Our women, the old men say. Women. The very sound of the word bothers him, takes him by surprise. He has forgotten women these last few months. When did he last see a woman? Wajid's sister. In Rawalpindi, as they boarded the train for Thall; she'd come to see him off. A sari, he remembers. Red, like a bride's. Hair thick and wavy. He had looked away. He was embarrassed for the man, his own sister, dressed like that, on view for the whole regiment. He looked away, but he remembers now: long arms, skin. Skin. Ghazi bangs on the door. You cannot go in, the old men say. They are thin and frail, but they are angry now, offended. They come to the door and stand before it.

"I think we should go," Wajid says.

"Not till we've checked there are no fighters in there." Ghazi nods at the havildar, and he and a few sepoys push past the old men. The old men shout, they curse. The soldiers pause before the door, priming their rifles. Then they shove it open.

Inside are three women. They cover their faces with their hands, horrified by the violation. The soldiers step back, unsure what to do.

"Come out of there," Wajid says to the soldiers. "Come out, come out."

The soldiers trip over their feet trying to leave. The old men are yelling, they are reaching for their rifles, they are ready to kill. Ghazi is not afraid when they raise their rifles; he is filled with rage, rage that a gun was fired at him, that they are off route, that these men, who are nothing, continue to threaten them. He barges past the men and into the shack. Their guns are on him. The tribesmen are yelling and Wajid is pleading with them. Ghazi squats down before one of the women and stares at her. The woman, middle-aged, her face lined, weathered, stares back at him. Don't look at her, don't look at her, one of the men screams. Ghazi thinks about smashing her face in, he thinks how easy it would be, how much these men deserve it. He feels his body thrum when he thinks of his hand making contact with her skin. The buzzing in his body gets louder. The only escape from it is to get out.

When at last he leaves the hut, the havildar and the sepoys have the old men on the ground. They will be beaten, taught a lesson. Wajid follows him, babbling; they will be in trouble, and Wajid doesn't like to be in trouble. He talks and talks, but Ghazi doesn't hear anything; he hears only the wind sweeping across the hills.

Thirty-Four

The dermatologist—from London, Rozina discovered—asked for her every time he visited Lahore. He no longer called Aunty Kulsoom to arrange a meeting, but called her himself. In fact, Aunty Kulsoom never called anymore, not since that night at Faletti's when Rozina drank too much; she couldn't recall what she'd said but she did remember being surprised at how loud she'd sounded, and how intently her companion seemed to be looking at her as she talked and talked. Aunty Kulsoom had her own driver take Rozina home that night, walked her out to the car, helped her inside, reached for her hand and squeezed it. Drunk and tired as she was, Rozina knew that Aunty had never looked at her so kindly, and she longed to put her arms around her, to call her Amma. I miss my amma, she wanted to say. Perhaps she had said that. But then Aunty Kulsoom was gone, and Kulsoom's driver took her home, and Aunty never again returned her calls. Suraya, who lived on the other side of their courtyard, mentioned her, though, loudly enough that Rozina could hear: Aunty Kulsoom called to ask about my niece, she wants to meet my daughter, she's sending a car, big people are flying in from Dubai to meet us. "Bitch," Rozina called out the window sometimes, not entirely sure if she meant Suraya or Aunty Kulsoom. Both. All of them. Everyone.

Not long after the night at Faletti's, Nasir had told her about a bit part in a film. She lobbied the producer hard and he eventually cast her—miscast her—as an elderly mother, a favor to Nasir probably. She wore a wig, a dupatta over her head as she watched a much younger woman, a rising star from the Mohalla, practice a dance routine on set. She felt a strange freedom in the little attention any of them paid her, but also desperation when her two days on set were up. Don't you have anything else, she'd begged the producer. I'll call you, he'd said as he breezed past her.

Every month since, things had grown harder. On the nights she couldn't sleep, frequent now, Rozina had taken to smoking a little charas, which was at least cheaper than booze, and sometimes it helped her pass the days as well, waiting for Mina to come home. They lived on Mina's earnings and on whatever Irfan could spare beyond his own household, money he earned from odd jobs in the Mohalla, selling cheap plastic goods, security work. Izzat Raheem had said his door was open, but Irfan wouldn't have anything to do with him, despite Mehru's urging. Better to live on scraps, their bellies rumbling, than to go to Izzat, the two young people told their mothers. Irfan wouldn't even intercede with him on Rozina's behalf, to tell him she was available for private mujras, any kind. "I don't want anything to do with Izzat," Irfan said. "And I won't be your broker, Rozina Baji."

"Better that than I become Mina's," she said, and his eyes flashed with a fury that surprised her. "I know you won't do that, Rozina Baji," he said, "when she's made her decision clear." She wasn't sure if he was saying that he trusted her to respect Mina's choice or was warning her that he would step in if she did not. Eventually, she approached Zaki, a new pimp who'd set up shop by the butcher's. I heard you used to be in the films, he said, squinting at her to indicate he'd never seen her himself. I could maybe get you a stage show, he said. A stage show meant lewd comedy, dance, but not the classical dance she'd been trained in; rather, something vulgar in front of a crowd who leered, called out, heckled. She smoked to get through it. You're too stiff, Zaki complained afterward, you don't look like you're enjoying it, they can tell. Sisterfucker, ma di kus, she yelled.

What about makeup, for the films? Mina suggested. And so Rozina loitered outside the studios, asking the makeup people who had once made her up if she could help. Occasionally they sent her on errands, tipped her as they did the kids on set, embarrassed for her, embarrassed to be put in this position. She wondered how long before she'd be looking for a room in Tibbi with the other washed-up kanjaris. When the phone rang, it was only ever the dermatologist. She smiled as she spoke to him. "How have you been? Lahore has been so dull without you," she said, trying to convey tenderness, coyness in her voice, the kind they all liked. She couldn't lose this, so she tried not to think of his clumsy hands, the sour smell of his breath.

He took her to a new Chinese restaurant in Gulberg, and perhaps because she had smoked a little before coming out, the glow of the lights cast a soft sheen on everything: the waiters, the tablecloths, the silverware. Even the dermatologist. "What do you think?" he said. He had deep lines at the corners of his eyes that made him look older, glummer than he was. "Wonderful!" she said, and he looked at her. Too much. She was overdoing it. She chided herself: Smoking made for imprecision, which was no good at all, but it was becoming harder to get through the work, and the not-working, without it.

When a little while later he said, "You don't seem surprised to see me again so soon," she smiled, trying to mask the truth that she never thought of him at all between visits. He looked bashful. "You must know the reason I keep coming back."

Firdous had trained her to look for moments like these, to work for them, to contrive them, but now that one was upon her, she was unprepared. He twitched anxiously. She knew what was coming. He was about to say he wanted an exclusive agreement. He thought there were still others. She tried her best to look demure, not expectant, not desperate to feed her daughter, herself. She couldn't believe this was being given to her without her even trying. It was perfect—he didn't live here; he'd be gone most of the time. Thank God, she thought, thank God. She looked down at her lap, waiting. But it wasn't a regular arrangement he had in mind or the kind of temporary marriages women in the Mohalla were offered. He said instead: I can't live without you, Heer. I want to marry you. I want you to come back with me. To England. She looked up at him, his heavy jowls, his large, worried eyes, as if seeing him for the first time. What? she said. What?

※

BOBBY LIT CIGARETTES, first one for her and then one for himself. She had not been able to bring herself to tell Mina about the dermatologist—Hanif, she reminded herself. He had a name. Without Amma, Bobby was the only person she trusted to advise her on something so momentous. It had been difficult to call him, but she had kept her tone businesslike, formal even, though she heard in his voice delight, relief. She had done her best not to recall the details of the evening she'd last seen him, that night at Punjab Club years ago. She concentrated on his wrongdoing, his betrayal; it was easier to keep her distance that way, but again and again stupid thoughts interrupted her sensible intentions: how only Bobby had really known her, how he'd been her friend, that he had once loved her.

He had suggested they meet at the zoo, and they had arrived early, the air cool, but warm wherever the sun fell. They walked through the zoo, not talking very much. She told him about Amma and he condoled, about Faraz's letters, about Mina, but they didn't talk in the free, luxuriant way they used to, although she longed for it. How she'd missed him, she wanted to say, to compliment him on his neatly trimmed hair, to say that she worried she was too heavy, that she'd heard a song on the radio from that film they had made. But she restrained herself, and she suspected he was being careful, too.

They walked past the aviary, and he stopped at each cage to look closely at each bird, pointing out ones he recognized, noting a colorful plume, a strange cry. But she was watching the people more than the animals; the families on a day out, moving in packs, trying not to lose a child or leave an elderly aunt behind, a sense of occasion as they stopped to unpack their picnics in the garden at a decadently early hour. Such an ordinary excursion, but such pleasure they seemed to take in having realized it. She wondered, foolishly, if anyone was looking at her and Bobby, if anyone glanced at them and thought they were a couple, their children somewhere up ahead, standing up on the railings peering at the lion or the elephant, calling Mama, Papa, come see this. When he walked ahead of her, she glanced at the skin beneath his hairline and imagined her fingers grazing it, and felt a shudder so intense, all the way down to her pelvis, that she stopped to look at the birds, embarrassed by her desire, how tightly her body held it. How shocking it felt to yearn, to want like this still. But it was *marriage* that every woman was supposed to want, that she had wanted, and having finally been granted her wish, she knew she must never feel anything like this again, not even the hope of it. Bobby turned back to her and she blushed, fearful she had given herself away, and then he took her hand, right there in the middle of the zoo, for all the picnickers to see.

"I'm sorry," he said. "I'm sorry for what I did, Rozina. For years I've wanted to say that to you. I've thought so much of it." She swallowed. "I took something I shouldn't have. I didn't want to be like the rest of them—but I was, in the end."

She felt the knot that was her heart come undone. He had asked, and she got to decide for a change. "I forgive you," she said, and although they could not embrace here, she squeezed his hand, her skin thrumming with his touch. And then she told him why she'd asked him to meet her.

Bobby stopped walking. "You can't go," he said, and her chest was tight. Was this why she'd called him, because this was what she wanted, for him to stop her? She hadn't dared to say it out loud to herself, but she had hoped it. "Not without doing due diligence. You can't go so far and get stuck there if he isn't . . . okay. I'll find out what I can. I know people," he said.

She swallowed, feeling foolish.

"What about Mina?" Bobby said.

"He said she could come, he would find a way. But she won't leave Irfan." Rozina had realized that there was no way to separate them; now she wondered if she should have recognized the value of their commitment to each other earlier. Inside or outside the Mohalla, love was always shadowed by money, so for Mina to have chosen whom to love—to love only for its own sake—that was something, wasn't it? "I thought I could sell up, give them something to set themselves up outside Lahore. I can get work there and send money home."

Bobby squinted at her. The truth was, she had no idea if she could get work, if this man would let her work, let her keep her money if she did. But Bobby didn't seem to doubt her plan, instead he looked mournful. Behind him, brightly colored budgerigars cheeped. "I haven't seen you in so long. Now you'll go and I don't know when I'll see you. Maybe you'll never come back."

She felt something in her swell. She willed him to say it: *Don't go.* To give her a reason to stay, to say there was another way. To be the one to offer her security—a future—her friend, not this stranger. She felt breathless with her readiness to declare her deepest longing to him. How much sooner could she have done this, how much sooner could she have dared to want something for herself?

"Things will be busy here, though for me, too, thankfully, which will help," he said. "I'm finally getting married, too. My editor's sister. She's a widow. I'll get a permanent position at the magazine. No more of this fillum-shillum."

"What?" she said out loud, though she had not meant to.

"I know," he said. "Who would have guessed it?" His smile was gentle, a little shy.

She knew she was supposed to congratulate him, to say this was wonderful news, but she couldn't. She was gripped by a terrible fear—that tears were about to fall, that she could not stop them.

"She's a nice person. A little quiet." She couldn't stand to hear it, not for another moment, and she began to walk, desperate to get away from him, from what she'd felt, from her own stupidity. Angry because men better than him, with more money, had wanted her, when he did not. How could he not, how could he not?

"What is it, Rozina? What happened?" he said, running to catch up to her. "You're crying."

Shamed, she was so shamed. "You're marrying your editor's sister for a job," she said. His face fell and she regretted her words, but also she didn't. A failed artist making a marriage not so different from the kind she was considering in her state of desperation, a decision that meant leaving Mina, her home, everything that she was. And yet he would still have options; he would have all the things she barely allowed herself to imagine for herself, ordinary things she was embarrassed to admit she wanted: children, elderly aunts you arranged to take to the zoo on picnics. "I'm sorry. Congratulations," she said, and then she dashed between the dawdling families, the children hanging on the cages, mothers wiping their children's mouths clean, thinking of how Bobby would be back here one day, with his children, his wife.

It wasn't until she stood on the Mall looking for a rickshaw, blowing her nose, her face blotchy, ugly with grief, that he caught up with her. It was then that he leaned toward her and said the words in her ear, words she realized she had been longing to hear all her life.

❧

IT TOOK MONTHS, many more months than she had thought it would, to leave, and she was glad. In that time, the dermatologist—Hanif—visited her often, and with each visit she performed her love for him so sincerely that she started to believe she might feel something for him. And yet she dreaded the prospect of leaving. On his last trip, they had officially married and signed the nikah nama document that proved it. Rozina was touched by how deeply moved he seemed—he was a middle-aged bachelor who'd resigned himself to a life alone, and Rozina had rejuvenated his quiet world. He was no Najam; this meant something to him, just as much as, astonishingly, her history did not, and so even though the nikah nama didn't feel real to her, she felt the weight of this paper, of Hanif's feelings for her. She looked at it again and again, her fingertips tracing Bobby's name, a witness to the marriage, her heart strangled with grief.

She traveled to Islamabad with Hanif for their visa interview, and they spent days at Hanif's cousin's place, waiting for an appointment at the British embassy. Now, as she stood on the visa line, clutching a sheaf of official documents, she looked down at the certificate, rehearsing the answers to the questions she knew she could expect to be asked about her new husband. She went over them again. Hanif Khan, lives Cricklewood, works at Guy's Hospital. Birth date: 20th February 1938. Pisces. Favorite food: biryani. Family: mother in Lahore, a sister in Karachi, three bedrooms in the Lahore house, where she had been living as his new bride. You will remember, won't you, Hanif had said when they went over the answers. She looked at him blankly; she had been learning lines half her life.

She had covered her hair and gone without makeup today, fearful of being recognized in the visa line. But she needn't have worried; when she glimpsed herself in her compact, she looked nothing like Heer. She'd lost weight in the past few weeks, but her jowls were thicker now, and months of poor sleep showed in the circles under her eyes. Faint brown spots from the sun marked the tops of her cheekbones. She was surprised. She knew she had been aging, of course she had—a little more foundation, a little more of everything had been necessary for some time—but she had always been so certain of her beauty. It was so much a part of who she was that she had never imagined she might not always possess it in the same way. But here she was, and she couldn't recognize herself in this face that, while perfectly symmetrical, seemed stripped of energy. Was this what aging was? Not the lines, not the muscles turning flaccid or the skin drying out. It was the way in which the defeats of your life showed themselves; the evidence of your surrender in the listlessness of your eyes. She realized she didn't care as much as she thought she would, and this, too, was a surprise. Really, when she looked at her life, what had her beauty ever brought her? Mina had said she wished no one would look at her. Perhaps Rozina, too, was finally ready for that; perhaps it would be an immense relief.

The queue zigzagged toward a line of booths. She was struck by the pale faces of the men at the booths, the hard, still way that they stared at the documents handed to them, the quick glances at whoever was before them, a dismay as they clocked the endless line stretching out of the building.

Don't worry, Bobby had said, as long as it all looks in order, which it does, they'll call you in for the interview. So she had thought instead of his mouth against hers, the gentle tips of his fingers on her thighs, how she had quivered with pleasure—how when she looked at him, the steeliness she had always felt inside, that she had felt since that elderly judge first laid his wrinkled hand on her thirteen-year-old back, shifted, just a fraction—so that she opened to a man, so that she could choose to open to a man, for no other reason than because she wanted to. They did not speak of her return, of his marriage, of hers; of a future. They knew there wasn't one. They lay in a tangle because then they did not have to talk or think of anything but where they were. Remember, he'd said when she was leaving for Islamabad, you're a new bride. You're hopeful, he said, his hands directing the scene just as he used to. I can do hopeful, she said.

A visa officer signaled her over. He was bald, his blond mustache untrimmed and a small piece of tissue stuck to a spot on his neck where he had cut himself shaving. She breathed out slowly, as she did before a performance; she wasn't nervous and she wasn't hopeful; she was devastated. She handed him her passport and clutched the other papers to her chest. She thought of the new character she must become, her new role. This is a fresh start, Bobby said; whatever you find there, it will be better than what you are leaving.

"You just got married?" the officer said, flicking through her papers. She handed him the nikah nama, and she reached for the memory of their entwined bodies, hers and Bobby's, of their mouths pressed hard, their mouths pressed soft. The officer glanced up at her, and like a hopeful new bride, she smiled.

Thirty-Five

It was early when the train stopped at Attari. Inside the carriages, the POWs didn't dare speak or even look at one another, fearing that the smallest error might somehow halt their progress home. The windows had been blacked out so that they could not see the landscape outside, which heightened the fear that none of this was real, that perhaps they were headed nowhere. He had no watch, but when he stepped out of the train, the darkness was edged with early-morning light. They were taken out in columns, a motley crew of soldiers dressed in striped pajamas and civilians wearing whatever they had managed to salvage and hold on to these last two years. They were given tea and something to eat, but he knew he couldn't get anything down; he held the hot tea to his cold cheek as he waited for a spot on a lorry that would take them to Wagah, at the border.

When the soldiers banged on the truck to tell them they'd made it to Wagah, he was, at first, afraid to look up, but when he did, he saw the place was a crush of POWs, soldiers, camera crews, men with clipboards. It seemed impossible to think that in a matter of steps he would be in Pakistan again. There was no difference in the landscape—on both sides of the border, it was dusty, with dark, leafy trees skirting the skyline, nothing beyond the different uniforms of the soldiers on each side to indicate where one country stopped and another began. He wasn't sure what borders meant anymore, anyway. Dacca had been part of his country, but when he got there, it hadn't felt so. Now it wasn't Pakistan at all, but a brand-new country: Bangladesh. He'd seen the army in action, listened to the whispered stories of massacres, of camps where women were chained to the walls, of white bones on riverbanks, and with nothing but time to return to the stories in his mind again and again, he had wondered: What did it mean to be a country when your army killed its own people? Did the people not belong to the country, or did the army not belong to it? Shamsuddin had called them occupiers; he had no other explanation. Now, just yards away, was his country—he would be free soon; that freedom was surely how you knew a country was yours, that you were home, wasn't it? But how to wrestle himself free from all that he was bringing back with him, would he ever be free of all that?

He was jostled by officials doing their best to manage the process, the mass of people and paper. He felt the flash of a camera, and he covered his face; they were a spectacle, a curiosity, but also suspect. They had looked at one another in the camp suspiciously—trying to work out who had been where, who might have done what, and who might now turn and work for the Indians. Now, at home, the same suspicions would follow them. A POW he recognized nodded at him, but he didn't look happy, even here, so close to freedom. No one did. Pakistan was not the same; neither, he supposed, were they.

At the border crossing, the pace picked up. Names were checked off lists, hands were held out, he shook them. Those faces so afraid to show any emotion seemed to break open, their eyes at last coming to life—searching the crowds, squinting at the camera flashes, at the calls from journalists. He crossed over, moving slowly; he had no idea what to do next. They had been told that families would be informed of their return, their names announced on the radio, but he didn't know if anyone would come. He walked toward tents—another camp, more waiting. Others pushed past him, walking with the determination of people ready to start over, to unmake the past or at least to pretend it never happened. He wished he could do the same.

Almost a day after his arrival at the border, sitting on a camp bed, he felt a hand on his shoulder, and he turned slowly. Billa looked different, his skin darker, the lines at the corners of his eyes deeper, but it felt the same as it always had to have Billa's wide arms around him, to hear Billa say again and again, brother, my brother; the closest feeling he'd ever had to home.

⌘

MUSSARAT WAS STANDING in the front garden when he and Billa got to her parents' house in the cantonment. "I didn't tell her," Billa said, "in case you didn't come. I thought the disappointment would be too hard." He patted Faraz on the back: Go on, I'm right behind you. The walls of the house were a pale yellow, so it looked like she was standing in front of a column of sunlight. In the small driveway a girl was riding a blue tricycle. He froze; he had spent so long thinking about this moment, he had not expected it to seem so ordinary. Mussarat held a cup to her lips and sipped. The little girl—Nazia, he reminded himself—rode up and down the driveway, singing. She was taller than he remembered, leaner; he remembered her soft, chubby arms, her dimpled elbows. She looked less like him than he remembered. Now he spied his mother-in-law's pointed chin, Mussarat's wide nose. Had they always been there? Or is this what happened, your children surprising you with all that you did not know about them, about who they might become? It didn't matter, he thought—she is mine.

"Look who I found," Billa called out.

"Faraz?" Mussarat said. She froze, and then she ran to him, yelping, calling his name again and again, turning back to the house, calling for her parents to come. She squeezed his arms, held his hands, turned them over as if to check for marks, and then looked at his face, as if doing the same. Behind her the servants came out, then his mother-in-law, then it seemed there were neighbors, strangers from the colony who all came out to welcome him, to cheer his return. He stood, unsure of what to do or to say. He should be jubilant, noisy as they were, but as he held Mussarat's hands and she knotted her fingers in his, all he could think was that she had never touched him like this in public. Nazia didn't come near but watched from her bike. From the neighboring houses, children poked their heads out, waved, called. He felt his face turning red. He wanted to run, to get away, and Mussarat must have sensed it because she put her arm around him as if to steady him, as if to say she would hold him up.

It was hours before people left, the neighbors, his father-in-law's relatives and friends who drove over on hearing the news that he was home. His mother-in-law supervised as the servants brought pots of steaming tea and laddoos for all the guests. His in-laws told him they had been waiting for weeks, that officials said it would be any day now that more POWs would be released, that they must wait for the announcements of the names on the radio. But nothing. Thousands of names they'd heard, but not his. He looked over at Billa. Wajid? he meant. You knew because Wajid told you. Wajid would have found out or perhaps even managed to get him out earlier and then told Billa. Billa shrugged: Does it matter? You're home. Somehow the surprise seemed to have made it all the more miraculous for them. The guests, many of them strangers, held him as if they knew him, told him they had prayed for him, for all of them, their chatter and celebration loud. He was grateful for their warmth, he had never been more grateful—he had not known how much he needed this kindness, that until now it hadn't occurred to him anyone would much care if he returned—but he had also never felt less deserving. Mussarat held his hand throughout, staying by him, speaking for him whenever someone asked him about the Indians, the camp, the Bengalis' treachery, the repatriation, this new country Bangladesh, because he didn't know what to say. What could a person say after what had happened? Did anyone want to know, to hear what *had* happened?

When they finally left, it was evening, and in so many hours Nazia had not come near him.

He walked out into the garden, which was small but well tended. There were new trees, and the lawn was lush and green. Swept up in the celebration of his return, he'd forgotten how foul, how filthy, he was from the travel, the camp. He felt it now. He took off his shoes. In the camp, he had spent a long time wondering what he would do when he got home. What is the first thing, the men liked to ask one another. Food, sex. And it was true, in prison you recognized the appetites you were denied; you longed for those things above all because after a time you got used to not having them, your longing declining, and in that decline you recognized you were not the man you were before. You feared you would never be that man again. What had he thought of? The same, yes, of course, but also this: the outline of the trees in the evening, the cool grass against his feet, an open door, and walking through it and back in again as he pleased.

He heard the veranda door swing open behind him. It was Mussarat. "Bilal Bhai's just calling home to tell them he'll be here another few nights." Nazia came out and stood behind her mother. "Go on." Mussarat pushed her forward. "Sit with your baba." Nazia resisted; she didn't want to go to him, she did not know anymore who he was. Mussarat gently prodded her again.

"That's okay," he said, "that's okay." He sat down on the veranda steps. He spotted her dolls, a small pram, a play tea set.

"Why don't you make me some tea," he said. "No one has made me a cup of tea in many months, Nazia." She tentatively handed him a plastic teacup, and he pretended to sip from it. He told her it was the best he had ever tasted, and she smiled. He played patiently and Nazia seemed to enjoy the game, though when Mussarat made a move to go inside, she said, Don't go. He tried to quell the sadness he felt, the sadness for the loss of familiarity, the everyday. He had been ordinary to her, boring, easy to be with.

"What's that?" he said. He pointed to a corner of the veranda. "It's a tent," she said. It was a small tent put together with three rods, light but awkward for her to carry, so he picked it up and put it in the middle of the lawn. "It's a hideout," he said. He crawled inside, and a moment later she came in, too, holding her dolls. "Did Nana make this for you?" She shook her head. Atif Uncle, she told him. He knew the name but he could not recall. A cousin of Mussarat's, perhaps.

Mussarat poked her head in the doorway. "Can I come in?" she said.

And there in that huddle, with Nazia between them, he felt relief, for the first time in months, maybe years. "What happened to my tea?" he said, mock indignant, and Nazia went to fetch more cups. She came in and out, each time bringing more things with her. The longer he played, the more animated and expansive he became, the more she relaxed. How little it took for a child to love you, really, he thought. What little effort this is, to make slurping noises, silly faces, rude sounds. How easily she laughs, how ready she is to smile, to want to be friends. A half hour later, she brought a book and sat on his lap as if she had always done this, as she always had.

"My baba is away," she said. "He lives in a small room like this because he is very brave."

"This is your baba, silly," Mussarat said. And the girl looked confused, then nodded. And then she asked again—the same baba as the one in the camp? The very same, he said. I am here now.

"Nazia said Atif made this tent." Mussarat's face went still, catching him by surprise. But he recognized the look, the look of a person caught out, and he remembered now. Atif. Not a cousin but the engineer from all those years ago. He had gone out of his way to steal Mussarat from that boy, and while he was away, the boy, now a man, had returned. He wanted to feel furious, but he knew she had only made a reasonable calculation: If Faraz died there, or didn't return, she would be alone, and what good would she be to Nazia then? No man meant no income, no future for either of them. Her parents, who had fed him laddoos a few hours earlier, would have looked the other way while the man came by. A woman in Mussarat's situation needed some kind of insurance policy. And of course, she had loved him once. Faraz looked at the point above where the three rods of the tent met over their heads. The man had played with his daughter. He had made her things she loved. And perhaps this man loved his Nazia, too, enough to build something for her when she had no father to do it. He wanted people to love his daughter; she deserved all the love there was to be had.

"It's looking shabby now," Mussarat said. "We should get rid of it." An apology, a statement of regret, a commitment to the restoration of their old life. She reached out and smoothed the fabric of the tent. She would return to him. It was her duty, and Mussarat was a woman who embraced duty. She would not say it, but he knew she believed life to be like this: We are all prisoners of something. It was why she had agreed to marry him in the first place.

Nazia pulled his collar: "Read," she commanded, holding open her book. And she poured him another cup of tea, and one for her mother, and one for her doll, and they sat there as night fell outside, drinking from empty cups.

Thirty-Six

THALL, NORTH-WEST FRONTIER PROVINCE, JUNE 1940

It is not your job to think, Macguire says at the review of the operation. Ghazi had not been afraid of the review, even though he knew they'd get a rocket for going off course, certainly not afraid in the way he'd been the previous night, when his fear had given him the strange and sudden sense of being alive. It is not your job to lead, to use your mind, Macguire says. It is your job to follow the orders I give. Know your place, he means. Sir, Wajid salutes. So does Ghazi. He sits in silence in the mess tent afterward, sulky, petulant. Even on operations, they are not to speak of warfare in the mess—only of cricket, whiskey, England, and so the British officers talk—of nothing, as usual, and the native officers listen to it all, as usual. No appetite, Second Lieutenant? one of the British officers says as Ghazi pokes at his rations, thin, boiled to nothing as always; whatever it is, always boiled to a tasteless mash.

"I don't know how we're expected to survive on this," Ghazi says, surprising himself by speaking up, but he's in a foul temper after last night, after this morning's scolding—he feels as if he has been carrying the night on his back, as if he can't shake it off. "No doubt you prefer the slop they serve on Sundays." Ghazi stares at him. Curry, they get curry on Sundays.

The only day in the week they understand who they are again, that they feel it in their mouths, their bodies.

Ghazi pushes his plate into the officer's plate. What the bloody hell, the officer says. But Ghazi does it again, harder. The man's breakfast falls into his lap and he jumps up. They stand, as other officers admonish them in clipped, hushed voices. Sit down before Macguire sees, sit down. He catches Wajid's eye, his pleading expression before he turns away, wanting nothing more to do with Ghazi, no more trouble, not in the field, not in the mess. Another officer comes between Ghazi and the red-faced man, joshing, cajoling until the British officer calms down, laughs, even. Ghazi's temple throbs. He has to join in; it is churlish to not join in if the white man is ready to forgive. He tries to smile as he sits back down, but he isn't sure what it looks like on his face, it feels like something cold running through his body.

⬦

A MONTH LATER, he is back home on leave in Muzaffargarh, the operation behind him. Macguire might call it a failure, but he knows now what he is capable of: What else, he wonders, might he do? But he must wait for time to pass till he can get back to the regiment, till it's time to leave for Europe. Ghazi realizes he can no longer stand the place. He can't stand the sluggish way time moves here. He can't stand the fact that he is farther than ever from the war. He can't stand the fields, full of life, but pointlessly so. He longs for drill. The precision and repetition on the parade ground that help contain his body, order his mind. Being here is terrible for him. He watches Kasim, who is fatter than before, more lumbering than ever, survey his workers, his fields with the speed of a half-wit. Kasim. Kasim, who has no praise for him as usual, nothing to say when he ought to be thanking him, really. When he ought to be saying thank you for going out into the darkness that is the white man's land to save all of India. Instead, over dinner, he dominates the conversation. Sometimes he reads out sections from the newspaper reporting that the training of troops is a mess, their equipment inferior to that of the Germans, their officers inept as the Germans spread out across the world like an infection. As always, Ghazi says nothing. Sometimes he grins to show he doesn't care, that Kasim is an idiot. What are they fighting for? Kasim says one evening. Ghazi knows the answer is freedom, but he says nothing because he isn't stupid; to say he is fighting for freedom while denied his own would make him look like a half-wit. This is what Kasim wants. I can't grow enough grain to feed this war, Kasim says, but maybe we can feed it enough men, God knows we can afford to lose them. So many useless men.

Ghazi laughs. The truth is, he wants to say, it is you who are useless, a coward. Kasim, fat and rich and bloated, counting his bundles of wheat, counting his workers, his money. Ghazi intends to live, not just to live off what they've been given.

He goes for a walk. He has days and days left here. It is unbearable. He tries to think of the war, to bring up a picture of it before his eyes. He thinks it will focus him, but in the noisy silence here, he feels blank; he can't think of anything.

What is Wajid doing now, he wonders, right now, while he is on leave, forgotten? He pictures him in the officers' mess, loitering by the billiards table so that when the white officers get up for a game they will have to include him. Dropping names of places Ghazi's never seen—London, Windsor. Moving about the table in that easy way of his, Macguire patting him on the back, talking to him as if he might be more than a native—a *man*. Ghazi tramples through the fields, their fields once, really now Kasim's fields. He has nothing here anymore, he has only the regiment, the war. The war is his. He tries to feel it inside him, this sense he has of it. Like the roar of a horse. He will kill men: Germans, Italians. It is astonishing to think they die, too, that white men die, too. That he will kill them. The thought is troubling, confusing. Impossible. Perhaps, also, thrilling. He starts to jog; the noise of the fields that's always there follows him. He has to get out, he has to leave, but he cannot. There is no end to the land. To India. He feels as if he is lost on patrol.

He looks up; the stars are coming out. He will need to follow them to find his way back, he thinks, but then he hears a noise. The tinkling of bangles, behind him. He turns and he sees a girl, no more than nine or ten. One of the fieldworkers' children. Whose? He is panting. He didn't realize how fast he'd been walking. His skin is damp, tingling. He stares at her, wonders what she is doing here. He doesn't move. He feels the want. It is quick, surprising. It is everywhere, in his legs, his body, his breath.

Her eyes dart. This way, that way. Caught, caught, but then she runs. And he is furious. But when he begins to run after her, he feels everything sharpen, the shapes of the trees, the feel of the ground underfoot. He hears the sound of the water in the canal, louder than ever. He catches her quickly. She's down on the ground. He's confused for a moment, but then he's not. Everything's clear. He just hadn't realized what it was before, what he wanted, but now he does. He is on top of her. It is harder than expected, awkward. Her pelvis is narrow. She is too small, but she's light and she doesn't thrash around or move at all. That helps. He's aware of the smell of soil, of grass, of how he has to do everything, move her thin legs apart, cup her mouth with his hand, how exhausting it all is. It is not pleasant but it is necessary, and it drives away whatever it is that has been plaguing him since he left home, since signing up, since always. It's over, and he's calm. Relieved. He's forgotten everything for a moment.

And then he hears something, a crack, a whimper, the wind, he isn't sure. He pulls off her. Is that blood? He glances at her; he can't make anything of her face at first. Then her eyes, small and black, come into focus; her mouth is closed, lips sewn shut. He does up his trousers. He prods her, no movement. He leans over her. The eyes move. "Get up," he hisses. "Go now." He wonders for a moment what happened, how it happened. Walk, he thinks. Don't look back, but he does. She's sitting there, legs splayed wide, looking around mutely. He has the impulse to throw something at her, to get her to move, but he forces himself to turn around and keep walking, although he wouldn't mind sitting down, wouldn't mind a nap now, actually.

He walks and walks, and the longer he walks, the stronger and clearer he feels. Perhaps he can cut his leave short, perhaps he can get back to the unit early. He thinks of cleaning his rifle, he thinks of loading and discharging his gun; how natural, how easy the sequence is. He thinks about Macguire, about Wajid. He thinks he must make more of an effort—he can never be Wajid but he must do better, smile, laugh at the jokes more. From now on, he must conserve his courage for when he needs it. He is not afraid of dying, he thinks, but there should be a good fight. He is certain he could win a good fight. Bangles, he thinks. His trousers are wet, the smell of iron. That sound again, the wind whimpering. He looks down at the blood. But he is not afraid, he thinks, as he wipes himself clean, not of war or of anything. He is bigger than all of it.

Thirty-Seven

There was something dour about the faces of the buildings as he made his way through Heera Mandi Chowk, fewer music shops, more shuttered function rooms than he remembered from that first visit with George—George—but still the kothas loomed, still the streets narrowed and bent, forcing him to take turns he did not intend. He had moved furtively before, fearfully, but now he wanted to race. She hadn't written, hadn't given him any kind of signal that she had been waiting for his return, but he had known that if he got out of the camp, if he survived, he would come back here.

He found the lane, but he slowed as he approached the end; he could see there was no longer a music shop at the end of it, no security guard outside. He entered the doorway of the new business. In place of the instruments were rows and rows of khusas, delicate, handmade shoes in leather, cloth, embroidered with gold thread, glowing strangely in the murk and dust. A clerk asked if he needed help. "What happened to the music shop?" he asked. The young man shrugged. Before my time, he meant. "I'm looking for the women who live upstairs. Firdous Begum. Her family."

"There's no Firdous upstairs," he said. "There's a tailor on the first floor, Jalal Saab, and the old musician at the top."

"Can I go up?" Faraz asked. "Someone might be able to tell me where they are." The man shrugged again, an okay this time, and led Faraz to a door on the side of the building. "You army?" he said as he opened it. "Police," Faraz said, though who knew when or if that would be true again.

Behind the elderly tailor who opened the door was a little cottage industry. Three young men sat on the floor, working sewing machines, and four young girls in a circle crouched over handwork in another corner. Faraz couldn't help but feel the lumbering weight of his own disappointment. Jalal Saab, the tailor, explained in his hoarse, phlegmatic voice that he'd bought the place from the actress Heer. He had heard that her mother, the famous tawaif Firdous Begum, had lived there once, but she had died years ago. Faraz crossed his arms as the man spoke, his eyes fixed on the apprentices and the steady, rhythmic stuttering of the needles of their machines.

He took the steps downstairs two at a time, not quite seeing where his feet would land in the darkness. Of course he had entertained the possibility that she might be gone, or have moved, or even be dead. But he had never stopped to consider what he would do then. In the camp, survival demanded he ask no questions, answer no questions.

He stepped back out into the sunlight and paused, winded. Disappointment felt almost like his natural state, he'd lived with it all his life; but this disappointment was unexpectedly cavernous, opening a ditch right through him. Did she get my letters? he wanted to ask someone, anyone. Did she know I wanted to find her? Did she think of me, wonder about me? How could he mourn someone he could hardly remember? How could he long for her forevermore with no hope of ever finding her?

"Did you get what you needed, saab?" It was the man in the khusa shop. What had he needed? So many things, such an endless list of things. He'd needed her to ask his forgiveness. To know she was sorry for what she'd done, that she'd wished for his return. Some days he had thought of making her suffer, of telling her she'd abandoned him, done what he would never, could never do to his own child. But now that he was certain he would never find her, see her, feel her hands in his again, he knew that he would have forgiven her. That it would have been a relief to say it wasn't too late, to say: I am yours. I am still yours.

"Did you find out where they are?" the man pressed. Faraz shook his head. "How did you say you knew them, this family?" the man asked kindly, as he rubbed his hands together in the morning chill.

"I never knew them," Faraz said, which felt right then like the truest words he'd ever spoken.

Thirty-Eight

Wajid had been back for almost a year before he called on the boy. At first, he hadn't really wanted to see him at all. His mother had not told him much about taking the child to Jhelum, where she'd left him with one of his second cousins. She'd mentioned that Firdous had resisted at first. Luckily, these people were a pragmatic sort, so the promise of a considerable sum to help her and her daughter, and the guarantee of a better life for the boy, eventually brought the woman around. Wajid's mother had smiled at her triumph. I didn't tell your father, of course, she said; he would have insisted on leaving him there. But when you were gone, when I thought you might never return, I had to bring him. It was like I was bringing you home, all that might be left of you. She cried as she said this, and not for the first time since his return, he wondered what indeed was left of him.

Everything felt different—home was not what it had once been. Or perhaps he wasn't what he had been; he was thinner, fitter, but his temper was changed. He had no patience for the small pleasures his parents cherished: tea on the veranda, a game of bridge, gossip about their neighbors. His father tried to engage him in discussing the news. They were on the edge of something. There was no longer just talk of independence, it would happen. At one time, Wajid would have been thrilled, involved, engrossed. He would have attended the rallies at Mochi Gate, arguing with his father about Jinnah's plans, Hindu conspiracies, but now he could muster no interest. All he thought was that he wasn't sure what Partition would mean. The end? The beginning? Everything he'd known already seemed changed; now it was set to disappear altogether. His silence, he knew, troubled his parents, but he didn't know how to tell them that while he went through the motions of his day, dressing and eating and exercising as he waited for his next posting, he felt as if he were operating at some kind of remove. It was like finding himself at the bottom of a swimming pool, looking up at the light hitting the surface above.

He hadn't wanted to see anyone since his return. But when his mother called him into the living room one afternoon, he found Ghazi Ashraf there. Ambushed, Second Lieutenant! Ghazi exclaimed. He had escaped, of course, as he'd said he would. Wajid had heard all about it, also that he'd fought again in Libya before being shipped out to France, back into the fray. He had thought Ghazi stupid to subject himself to so much more suffering, but Ghazi seemed in better shape than he was. He looked muscular, sinewy. The opening of his shirt revealed the tip of a scar, and he'd lost a couple of teeth at the side of his mouth. The gap made Wajid think of an empty, cavernous hole, that somewhere inside it was Ghazi. This struck him as unbearable. "I am marrying," Ghazi said. "I'd like you to come."

"Of course," Wajid said, bewildered by how easily Ghazi had returned to normal life. He was talking about his wedding, about good postings for a family man and how to get them; he seemed to be imagining a future, while Wajid saw nothing ahead of him. Seeing Ghazi like this made him all the more anxious. The war had become dreamlike and unreal in the months since its end, but with Ghazi here he was reminded it had been real even if he did not speak of it, even though he knew he would never speak of it. He also remembered who he had been before the war, and, seeing Ghazi, who seemed more himself, actually, a much better version of himself—tolerable, at moments almost charming—Wajid missed who he himself had once been. Ghazi had been improved by war, Wajid had not; he wished never to see the man again.

"What happened to your boy?" Ghazi asked as Wajid walked him out.

"He's in good hands." He'd half hoped Ghazi wouldn't bring all that up, half wanted to forget that Ghazi had saved his life, and even made sure the boy was saved, too.

"Well, do come to the wedding. After that we'll be posted," Ghazi said. "Of course, the way things are going, who knows what will happen? I mean, what would you say to a Pakistan Army posting one day?"

A new army for a new country; yes, everything was about to change. And then Wajid wondered: What would happen to the boy? How chaotic might the making of a nation be for a boy without a real family? Would these relatives hold on to him? Protect him? Sell him?

"And then who knows when we will meet again," Ghazi said.

"'We'll meet again, don't know where, don't know when,'" Wajid sang, hating himself for performing joviality for Ghazi, of all people. "But we will. After all, I am forever bound to you, old man," he said, acknowledging his debt. Ghazi had smiled, pleased by this. And that was when Wajid knew that he had to go see his son.

⁂

THE BOY HIS COUSIN BABAR pointed out to him, standing on the edge of a group of children gathered around something in the field, seemed different from the other children, although Wajid could not say how. Perhaps this was how all parents saw their offspring—as singular, more interesting than all the others. His boy, he could already see, was not part of any gang. Wajid walked toward him, still unsure if he would speak to him. The thought engendered a kind of dread. But he wanted a look at him. He wanted to see that the boy was being fed, that the money his mother was sending was being put to good use, to know that he was safe.

The boy was thin but strong-looking. There was something stiff about his face, his jaw wide, his eyes arresting, a shade lighter than they ought to be. That will always be a problem, Wajid thought. And he was handsome—more handsome than his father, Wajid realized, taken aback at this thought, at once irritated by it and somewhat proud. What Wajid had lacked in looks he made up for with charm, with exuberance, an expressive face. The boy seemed intent on showing nothing in his face. He seemed to be cultivating a stillness, a face that said: You will not read me. Wajid thought of the lessons his mother had taught him. Lessons he'd thought of as gifts, of a sort. Look up, sit straight, be pleasant, onward, upward. Only now he was finding it hard to follow them. He had of course taught the boy nothing. And the boy was learning—what? He had no idea, but it had to be better than what he would have learned in the Mohalla.

As he got closer to the group of children, he saw they were digging up something in the dirt. He leaned over: A dead mongoose emerged, its body crawling with fat white maggots. The children recoiled, yelped—some laughed, their laughter edged with nervousness. But his son did not. He bent down and watched and then, perhaps out of some kind of respect for the creature, began to cover it up. "Let me help," Wajid said as the other children stepped back, covering their mouths. He bent down and scraped at the dirt with his hands. The boy's lips moved silently as he worked, and Wajid wondered if he was praying for the dead mongoose. When they were done, he walked away, aware that the boy was looking at him, curious. He didn't want to talk, to say more. But the feel of the soil on his hands, the boy moving next to him, had soothed him. When he left, he said to Babar: I will come again soon, unsure why he'd said it when there was no need to ever return here.

On the way home, he was overwhelmed by the urge to stop the car. He got out and sat by the side of the road. He watched the crows peck at the dry ground, women balancing pails of water on their heads, children leading buffalo to watering holes. There was nothing tying him to this place, to this boy. He didn't have to do anything more for him. And yet the impulse to bequeath him something pressed on Wajid, as if in doing so he might be freed of him. But the boy, fed and housed, didn't look as if he wanted for anything. He had more than most other Mohalla boys: a chance at living an honorable life. Though he wouldn't really escape the Mohalla without a father's name, the one thing Wajid could never give him. He'd always be the bastard offspring of some Heera Mandi kanjari. But giving him a name— any name—would at least mark a new start for him. And it would make the child his. He blushed in surprise that he should want such a thing, but after everything that had happened—after so much death—it seemed contemptible to discard a life you'd made. He wanted to lay claim to it in some way, even if he never laid eyes on him again. Firdous used to call on Ali for help, his name always on her breath. Ali: Sher-e-Khuda. Yes, that was a name that would please her, and he liked to think she would be pleased by all that his family had done for the child. *Faraz Ali.* He felt as if he were giving the boy a future, and this made him feel, for the first time in a long time, the possibilities of his own. It was a parting gift that would liberate them both. He looked down at his hands, at the black soil lodged in the fine ridges and loops of the pads of his fingertips, traced the pattern with his thumbs. Crows cawed, circling the sky above. Perhaps he'd come back once more—see Faraz Ali one last time. What would be the harm in that?

Thirty-Nine

It hadn't been difficult to find the house. It was in a newly built colony in the cantonment, an air of cleanliness about the place, despite the dust of new construction. There had been a pair of guards at the entrance to the colony but there were no guards outside the house, no grand drive, no pillars. So this was what life looked like after Bhutto booted you out of office: tidy but small. Much too small for a man like Wajid.

The servant who answered the door asked him to wait on the veranda; he must have sensed this wasn't a guest who should necessarily be invited inside. Faraz paced as he waited. The garden was more dust than lawn, though the plants in the pots on the veranda had been watered. Reduced circumstances certainly, but Wajid was weathering this new life. Then suddenly Wajid was there, extending his hand, smiling but quizzical. Why are you here? said the look on his face. He indicated a seat, a creaking wicker chair, and had tea brought in, biscuits. He scolded the servant for forgetting the sugar. He seemed too big for the veranda cluttered with potted plants, his chair a squeeze for a man of his stature.

"I can't say I don't miss the old place, the office, my staff, but it's nice to have more time for golf, for the family," he said, acknowledging Faraz's assessment. "And, well, sometimes a little less profile offers a man freedom."

Faraz leaned forward. From what or whom, he wondered, would Wajid want freedom?

"What I mean," said his father, as if in answer, "is we are at their whim—and there comes a point for every man where he can no longer be at the whim of a master he has not even chosen." His voice rose, as if intent on convincing himself of this. But the truth was that Wajid had always been happy to serve any master—he liked having a master. He shrugged, smiled. It would be unsporting for a man of his background to make a drama of what had happened to him, to reveal any hint of bitterness about his fall from grace; such is life, why dwell on it. What was it he used to say? Onward, upward. Wajid smiled again; let's move on from all that.

"My main concern of late was making sure you were safe. In the position I held, one does meet an awful lot of people who are obliged to help you, even when you no longer occupy it. They kept me up to date. I wanted to make sure that you were treated all right. Fed, looked after over there."

"We were fed," Faraz said. "It was fine." He had lost a little weight, but not much. There were many reasons captivity had been terrible, but ill treatment by their captors had not been one of them. What had been terrible were the things he could not now share: the boredom, the interminable sense of being stuck in time even as you felt the seasons change, the never-ending pettiness of camp life, every squabble with another man underlining the smallness of your own pathetic mind. And then, of course, the things they knew of one another, and the things they didn't know.

"People will ask you about it, but really they won't want to know," Wajid said. And for the first time in a long time, Faraz had the sense of Wajid reaching for him; his father wanted him to know he understood when others would not. And he wanted to ask Wajid, just as he had wanted to ask the men in the camp: Do they fade away—the things you did, watched, allowed—or do you just bury them and spend the rest of your life worrying that you might inadvertently trip over them? How do you do it? How do you forget? Bodies on a pyre, dead girls. But he knew what Wajid would say: Forget what?

"I learned to play chess," Faraz said instead, dismissively. Wajid looked put out for the faintest moment, but then he smiled; that's the spirit. "I learned there is nothing worse than boredom, than being stuck in a room with the same men for two years."

"Yes, yes," Wajid said. Then Faraz stopped, because he didn't want to speak of the other things he'd learned. "Yes, yes," Wajid said again, as if he had in fact spoken; it is best not to speak of those things. And then he added, "They say the army gave up. That they are cowards. Is it true?"

Faraz looked at him. "It's true they are cowards. We are a nation of cowards."

"Now we are half a nation."

"No. We are ourselves, whatever that might be. And they, they are free."

Wajid sat back in his chair—his eyes narrowed. He didn't like what he had heard, and Faraz remembered what it was like to have displeased him.

"A General Ashraf came to see me in Dacca. He said you sent him."

"I wanted to get you out of there if I could."

"You sent me there in the first place."

Wajid threw him a quizzical expression: Did I? "I didn't intend for you to be stuck in the middle of an all-out war, naturally."

"My mother died while I was away," Faraz said. It was a relief to say it out loud. He knew no one else who had known her. He had been mourning alone, unable to stem the anguish he felt at this loss—of a stranger, a memory. The secrecy of his grief another kind of loneliness.

"I am sorry to hear that," Wajid said, his voice neutral.

Faraz stared at him. How carefully Wajid had orchestrated his sense of shame, his sense that he should obliterate her from his memory. Why had Faraz let him? What had it all been for?

"Your mother was . . ." Wajid stopped. Faraz put his teacup down. "She was a legendary artist in her time."

Faraz knew he ought to leave but he didn't. This was what he had come for, to hear someone speak of her as real, not just a longing he'd nursed since childhood. But how easy it was for him to say it now—an artist in death when he'd shown only contempt for her in life. He stared at the floor of the veranda, the fragments of colored stones flecked through it.

"A great loss," Wajid said with finality, putting her life, Faraz's loss, to one side. Onward, upward. Always.

When Faraz looked up, Wajid was leaning forward, ready to stand, signaling it was time for Faraz to leave.

"He knew, the general, about me," Faraz said. "I was surprised you told him."

Wajid looked distracted. "He's a very old friend."

Faraz glanced at the drawn curtains, wondering if the family were home. Wajid crossed his arms, then put his hands in his pockets; he didn't seem to know what to do with himself. "He said you served together, were captured together."

Wajid nodded, a little impatiently.

"You trusted him enough to share—"

And Wajid's expression of discomfiture was so fleeting that Faraz couldn't be entirely sure he'd glimpsed it before his father continued, with a smile, "Of course. An extraordinary soldier. And a fine . . . man. Rumor is he'll make governor any day now."

"That night in '68—"

And now Wajid stood. "Not that again. That was settled years ago. They got the man who did it."

"Khwaja, his name was Khwaja. He wasn't much more than a boy. He died in prison, an innocent man." Khwaja had succumbed to a drug overdose waiting for a trial date.

Wajid looked disconcerted, though only for a moment. "Mistakes happen, of course, but I believe he was arrested on good authority. I wouldn't waste your tears."

"We both know it wasn't him." Faraz stared up at him. "You're not chief secretary anymore. Anyone who questions you won't have their hands tied by that now."

"Is this why you came? To threaten me?"

It wasn't. He hadn't intended this, not really—remorse, that's what he'd hoped for, some feeling for an innocent man they'd trapped in their mess, perhaps he'd even hoped that they would feel it together. "I can't bear to think it might have been you," he said.

Wajid scoffed. "How very good of you."

"Who would you go to such lengths to protect? Why?"

For a second, Wajid looked mournful. "He's—they're—on the up now, and they can make sure things are made very difficult for you and your family."

Faraz waited.

"There was an accident, a mistake," Wajid said. "Lives have been lost. Ruining the life of another man isn't going to help anyone."

The screen door swung open then, and a young man stepped out. It took Faraz a moment to recognize him. Fasih. Chota Saab.

"Abbo, is everything all right?" The young man squinted at him. His hair was longer now, fashionably so, like a Westerner's.

"Fine," said Wajid. "Excuse us, will you, son?" Faraz felt a prick of something at the word, a slight he was meant to notice.

The young man stared at Faraz as if trying to place him. "Oh, yes," he said, as if to himself, smiling a little. "The Faiz fan."

"Fasih. I asked you to leave," Wajid said. Fasih looked taken aback, as if unused to being spoken to so sharply. He stepped back inside, and the door banged shut.

"Look," said Wajid. "You could go talk to the SP. You could tell him everything, what I asked you to do. All of it. But there are only so many ways to say this: She was a kanjari. No one cares." A flash of resentment at being compelled to say it out loud. He leaned toward Faraz. "I understand it must have been upsetting to discover that your mother had passed away." Faraz felt tears prick his eyes at the mention of her from Wajid's mouth. "Perhaps you were hoping for some kind of reunion. I can understand you might be disappointed."

"You said—"

"I only ever said what I thought was in your best interest." Wajid shrugged. "Perhaps I was wrong." How easily he said it, as if it were all nothing. His son not having a mother, a lifetime spent teaching him to hate her, to hate himself. These were just things one said. And dead girls, they were just things that sometimes happened; accidents, mistakes. "You decide what you want to do."

But Faraz knew what Wajid already knew. There was nothing he could do but live with it, because even now, no one would want to go near it. He just didn't have Wajid's stamina to endure it all so easily.

"I think that the best thing you can do now is look forward. You're home. Free. That's enough." Faraz noticed for the first time that he couldn't hear the sounds of the street at all here, no rickshaws or hawkers, as if nothing lay beyond the colony's walls, certainly nothing that mattered.

"There are coconut trees in Dacca," he said. "The air is brackish. And it's quite beautiful." He took a long look at Wajid, the deep frown lines, the tight smile. That's enough, Wajid had said. Behind the screen windows, he spotted the shadow of Chota Saab. How long had he mourned not having a family—parents. It seemed to him that he had been mourning their loss all his life.

He stood, ready to leave.

He nodded: Yes, that's enough.

Forty

Faraz's inquiries after Heer in the Mohalla told him only that his sister had left Lahore and traveled to either London or New York—no one knew where for sure, but the rumor was that she had married. Without her new name, he'd been stalled. He visited the film studios and offices where everyone knew her name, but few remembered working with her. That was a lifetime ago, they said, she'd had some good parts, but she never made it big. A minor actress, really. There might be some stills, maybe even reels boxed up in one of the studio basements, he was told, but no one knew where to look. One studio had burned down, another now housed their Steenbecks, and one contained a multitude—twenty-five years' worth—of unlabeled, dusty cans. He'd need releases to access them, but who knew where those producers were now, if they weren't already dead. One young producer he talked to, feeling sorry for him perhaps, invited him to sit in on some filming; he hovered at the back of the set and marveled at the work she must have done: standing under hot lights for hours, dancing for take after take. He admired the way the actress, a lone woman skimpily dressed on a set busy with men, commanded the technicians, charmed them, laughed with them, at them. She was powerful here, and comfortable with her power. A professional, and they treated her as such. It was what so many dreamed of, this life; he hoped it had made her happy. When his search ran dry, he began wandering the city's bookshops. He finally found what he was looking for, in the back of a narrow shop in Anarkali that sold English classics and faded pre-Partition maps. In a handful of old filmi magazines from the early sixties were advertisements for her films. Heer's films. His sister's films. The bookseller hadn't even charged him for them; Faraz was doing him a favor by taking them. In a few, just her name was written on the poster, in wide, gauche lettering, but in others there were illustrations of her. One was in color, her features so exaggerated by the artist that she seemed unreal: lips plumped and unnaturally pink, eyes green and wide, as if she'd been caught off guard. He wondered if the fragments he still possessed, memories that flashed dimly, were even of her. He brought his hand up to his own face, to his own eyes, a shade lighter than usual, more memorable than was good for a police officer.

He stared at the picture, trying to find something of his own face in hers, perhaps even Nazia's. But the rendering was so idealized that it could have been of any woman, any of the actresses of that era. It was all he had. He kept the magazines in the gap between the wall and the bookshelf in the bedroom, and ridiculous as it seemed, just glancing at the gap there made him feel that something important to him was within reach.

⸎

"WILL YOU TAKE NAZIA OUT? Amma's too busy to watch her, and she's not letting me get anything done," Mussarat said, her hair up, her oldest suit on, the one she kept aside for cleaning.

He took the girl outside. He was still stuck waiting for security clearance from Intelligence, who were mired in assessments for thousands of POWs before they could be released back into public service. Stranded, with no salary, they were living with his in-laws. He read, he watched Nazia, he tried to maintain a stable mood.

He followed Nazia out into the colony. She weaved from one side of the road to the other in a curly series of loops. At the camp, he had vowed never to tire of looking at the world; he would appreciate every small thing anew—every tree, every car, every man on a bicycle—but the promise had proved hard to keep. The novelty faded faster than he'd expected, and he found himself getting caught up in the ways of before, agitated by bureaucratic bungling, irritated with the news, trapped in thoughts that swirled and carried him to places from which he struggled to return. Unless Nazia was with him.

"Look, Baba," she said, still not wholly comfortable with the word. She pointed at a column of ants. The world was a never-ending performance to her, one curiosity after another presenting itself. He wondered about Rozina, what she would make of his daughter, whether she would love her, whether she, too, had a child.

"Let's go back inside," he said, suddenly impatient, feeling his mood turn.

⌖

IT WAS SEVERAL DAYS before he noticed. His eyes had fallen on the space between the shelf and the wall time and again, but he hadn't noticed till the sun hit the bookshelf at an angle that the gap was empty. He felt panic as he tried to move the shelf, his voice high as he called to Mussarat. "I had things here," he said as she came in, putting on her dupatta.

"What is it? What are you looking for?"

"There were some magazines here." She shook her head. There were, he insisted.

"I found some old papers, maybe they were magazines, bits of newspapers. I threw them." He ran to the kitchen, where the bucket was filled with food scraps and the plastic bags in which their meat arrived, flies buzzing around it. She came in after him. "What is it? Were they yours? I just thought they were old papers. From the people here before, they were so old." Faraz started to poke at the bucket. "Faraz, stop, they're not there."

He looked at her.

"That was two days ago I cleared them, they went with the rubbish. What were they?"

Faraz swiped the plastic toddler things by the sink to the floor before he got hold of himself. He gripped the counter, panting. Sorry. He held his hands up to her, her expression distraught. Sorry, he said again, they didn't break. He picked them up off the floor. And then he left.

⬦

WHEN HE CAME HOME, it was late. She was watching television, her parents already in bed. He had spent the afternoon in Anarkali trying to find more magazines, anything at all, but there'd been nothing. And now he feared that he had not stored the detail of the illustrations in his mind well enough to remember, and they, too, would disappear in the way of so many of his memories.

"I'm sorry," Mussarat said. "I didn't know you were keeping them." He waved it away. "They just looked like old bits of newspaper. What was in them?"

He was so tired, it just came out. "My sister. They were pictures of my sister."

She squinted at him. "What? What do you mean, sister?"

Sister. The sound of the word, said out loud, struck him; he thought of all the connotations it held: family, connection, blood, memory.

"My sister was an actress." She laughed, astonished, sure he was joking, but he said it again. "Her name is Heer. Those were pictures I had found of her from magazines. They're the only ones I had."

Mussarat folded her arms and drew her neck in, her face a frown. He was serious, and she didn't like it. She stared at him, looking at him as if seeing him for the first time. "I don't understand what you're saying," she said. "What do you mean? Who are you?"

"My mother was a kanjari from Heera Mandi. And so is my sister. I was taken from them as a child." She stared at him. "I don't remember them," he said, unable to explain how this was perhaps the most agonizing loss of all.

She was still for a moment, then she left the room. He sat on the bed. For the first time, it had felt easier to say it than to say anything else; it had felt necessary to say it. He waited for her to come back in, to tell him to pack his bags, to leave her parents' house. She would abandon him. He had always known, hadn't he, that no one would stay, could stay with him? Now that it was done, there was even a certain comfort in no longer having to fear it. From the other room, he heard her turn off the television. He heard her open Nazia's door to check on her, pictured her standing over the bed a long while, looking at their daughter.

She came back in and stood in the doorway. "Who took you from your mother? Who would do that? Who did that to you? To her?" She sounded appalled, as if a wrong done to any mother was shared by all mothers, by her. He put his head in his hands and wept, his body shaking as he knew it had when he'd been brought to live at Billa's house. And she sat down and put her arms around him just as Billa's parents had done, trying to quiet an agony they could only guess at. "Who are you?" she said again, looking at him, curious. "Tell me."

After he told her, he felt freer, lighter, and ready for her to go, resigned to it. But she didn't. She sighed, she looked at him, relieved. As if things made sense now, as if he made sense. She took a breath, readying herself to speak, her eyes focused, clear. "I'm sorry," she said, "that when you were away—" But he stopped her. No, she said. I must tell you, she said, and she did. And they sat before each other, all their wrongs between them, and Faraz wondered if this might be something akin to what love was, in that whatever was said, no one left the room.

Forty-One

S he often dreamed of Bobby. Even now. On those days, like today, she sat down to write Mina an aerogram. She sat at the kitchen table in their three-up, two-down and poured herself a cup of tea from the pot before she began. It was always a relief to know that the letter would take weeks to get to Mina, by which time Rozina would forget what she had written. And so within the blue leaves she wrote everything she felt, things a person should not say to her daughter, things she might have said to Bobby, things she should really keep to herself.

She wrote that the food she ate, food she had cooked herself, didn't taste the same here, that her mouth ached from speaking English, that the impatience of the white woman with the thin lips at the cash-and-carry when she fumbled with her change pleased her so much that she took even longer to pay, that these small acts in which she expressed her contempt for those who were so contemptuous of her were the ones that made her feel like herself. She wrote that sometimes hating people felt wonderful, or at least better than the boredom, the sadness of being in this gray, colorless place. She wrote of the sparrowlike old white women who dyed their hair blue, of the men at the pub who drank as if to ease some great suffering and then got into brawls outside after closing time, but also about her neighbor, Sandra. Sandra was different. She said hello to all the neighbors—the Blacks, the old men who stood outside the mosque on Fridays after Jumma—and she bent down to look in the prams of all the Asian mums to ooh and aah at the babies. Sandra chattered without minding that Rozina couldn't always answer or understand her questions. "Don't worry, darling, the English don't understand me when I talk, either," she said in her thick brogue. She gossiped about the women at the hairdressers where she worked, and occasionally invited Rozina to the caff for a cuppa (never to the pub, out of respect, naturally, she said, though I'd love to get a sly half in you, I reckon there'd be some good craic around here after that) and then tearfully told her about her son, Danny, a plasterer, who was always getting fired for his quick temper. Sandra said, I feel like I did a terrible job with Danny, not for want of trying. I did try to be a good mam, but you don't know what you're doing half the time, do you? Rozina told her about Mina, and there in the safety of Cricklewood, she felt a great closeness to Sandra, a great closeness to all mothers—the ones gripping the hands of their toddlers on the high street, the ones dragging bored teenagers around the supermarket. In those moments, she felt a gratitude for the gray streets, the cold, white skies of England. It was true that she was nothing here, but she could also be anything, and at last, she could say she was a mother. You don't stop worrying, Rozina said. Yes, yes, Sandra said, exactly, and patted her arm as they drank their tea. When Rozina wrote to Mina about Sandra, she said she realized that she hadn't had a real friend since she left the Mohalla. She'd had Bobby, but not a woman friend, a person who might say: *I know just what you mean*; who said: *It gets better*, or, when they had to: *It's not your fault, let it go*. These were the things only a sister would say, a best friend, a woman friend. Do you have a friend, Mina, she asked in her letters, do you have someone you can really talk to? Because I never want you to be as lonely as I have been.

Today, as she dunked a digestive into her tea, she thought about all the different kinds of loneliness she had felt; who knew it could have so many hues, so many iterations? There were the losses—like Firdous, Mina, and Faraz—the world she'd left behind in the Mohalla, the lonely burden of knowing she alone was responsible for the feeding of her family. The lonely shame of being a kanjari in Najam's sneering colony. And then there was the loneliness here, where she drifted through the days, years passing without note, waiting to return home, unsure of what to do about the uncomfortable truth that with each year here the desire to go home provoked as much anxiety as the thought of never returning. What if it wasn't the same? What if she went back and could no longer stand it? What if she missed the loneliness of being here? After all, hadn't this loneliness, like all the others that preceded it, become part of who she was? If she could not go back and she could not stay, what could she do but wait till she knew, till something or someone decided it for her? And what was waiting but more loneliness? She laid her hand on her arm and felt the weight of it; she thought of skin on skin, the warmth of a body, and wondered if this—the absence of a hand on your hand, a mouth on your mouth—was the worst loneliness of all? And then she wrote that sometimes she wished she loved the man beside her in her bed, that she missed loving Bobby, that she thought Bobby would have loved *Morecambe & Wise*. She didn't get all the jokes, but Bobby would have raised his glass to the two entertainers as they skipped off the stage. There was a relief in saying all these things, and as she folded the aerogram, sealing it, her words seemed safe within its panels, like a well-hidden secret.

Mina, busy with her children, hardly ever wrote back, and when she did, the letters were often more like notes written to herself, disordered, cursory: Sajid is walking, I must get milk, the spinach needs planting, Mehru sends her love. She always began: Thank you for your letter, so Rozina knew that her words had been read, and that Mina had decided this was the best way to comfort her. And she was comforted, because Mina said the things Firdous would have: All continues and it always will, and: This is just as God intended. This was how Firdous had coped with her losses, and how she'd prepared Mina for the ones she would know, because what was loss but the condition of a woman's life? At those moments, it seemed right that Firdous had been Mina's mother; Rozina would have protected her, not prepared her.

Twice a year, on Bari Eid and Choti Eid, they spoke on the phone. Dressed up in her holiday outfit and waiting by the phone, Rozina liked to picture Mina getting a ride to the main market to put in an international call. They never spoke for more than a minute, just: How are you, how are you, such a bad line, I can't hear you. How are the children? And the weather? What is the weather like there? It's cold, Rozina said. Always cold. And then it would be over. Then she would call Hanif and tell him all about it, her narrative longer than the call itself. Wonderful, wonderful, Rozina, he said to her, and her heart expanded because, yes, it had been just that. Then she'd take her tea outside to the patio and sit there drinking it, thinking of all the questions she had meant to ask: Did you get the money, the extra I sent for Eid? Are you getting any rest? Did you spend it all on the kids, because it was also meant for you? And she wondered why they wasted their call time exchanging news about the weather, but the truth was she had wanted to know, because when she could picture the sunlight on Mina's skin, the sweat glistening on the sides of her face, cooling her, she felt she knew exactly what Mina was feeling. And when a minute was all you had, you wanted to feel it.

She was due to go in to work at Hanif's practice at noon, so she could post the aerogram on the way. She got up. Another year, he had said, and they might make a trip home; for now, all their money was going into the practice he was trying to establish in Harley Street. She was careful with the housekeeping money, but it took such a long time to save for anything. She wanted to see Mina's children. She didn't think of them as her grand-children, not really. Firdous would have claimed them as hers, as she had Mina, and because Rozina knew she owed everything that mattered to her mother, she gave her this, too.

She put on all the layers she needed for the walk to the Tube station. It would be stuffy on the train, but the walk was long and she was always cold.

On top of her shalwar kameez went the cardigan, then the big gray coat Hanif had given her for her birthday, and finally the scarf and gloves. Now you fit right in, Hanif had said when he gave her the coat—you're as dismal as London. She locked up the narrow semi and began the walk up the winding lane to the high street. Hanif had not been keen for her to work; none of the other doctors' wives did, though some of the Asian women worked in the factories or at the newsagents. She had pressed him, arguing that it would improve her English, that she would make money to send home without taking from his pay. She tried the makeup counters in the department stores first, but none of them offered her a job. Then she tried selling makeup door to door, as an Avon lady, but her feet ached and the bags were heavy, and still she sold next to nothing. When one day a white man opened a door and told her to fuck off back home, Paki, she stared at him, puzzled. When he said it again, she did what she would have done anywhere, what Firdous had taught her to do; she put her hands on her hips and called him a sisterfucker. He stepped out and she thought he was going to hit her; she braced herself for it. But he didn't: He spat on her.

Enough, Hanif said then, work for me, my receptionist is terrible. My English isn't good enough, she said. Maybe, he said, but you'll never roll your eyes at mine, or ask me what that smell is on my clothes. And you can browse Oxford Street at lunchtime, you can invite the other ladies—the wives, he meant—to lunch at John Lewis. She did like to browse, to shop, even, but she never invited any of the other wives to join her. As polite as they were in front of Hanif, she knew exactly what the other doctors' wives thought and said about her.

At the station, she always thought of Bobby. He would have been fascinated by the Tube, the very idea of traveling underground, the network of lines, of journeys you might make, the way you emerged somewhere completely different in a matter of minutes. She thought of him every time. She was grateful, though, that later, when it was colder still, she would come back home with Hanif, his gentle talk of his day a comfort to her. He was a reserved man, private, with only a handful of friends. His mother, back in

Pakistan, seemed satisfied that her middle-aged son had finally found a wife, and not a white woman. On the phone she spoke warmly to Rozina, telling her how grateful she was that Hanif was no longer alone in that cold land. Though Rozina guessed that, with her, sometimes he did still feel alone. But he never pressed her for more than she gave. He understood she was fond of him, and that was enough. He left her alone when he sensed she needed it, tolerated her distance, her occasional impatience. When she re-emerged, he took her to Ambala on Drummond Street, to pick up the samosas she liked, grateful that she had returned to him. Then she cooked and they ate their dinner in front of the telly, laughing with their mouths full as they watched *Some Mothers Do 'Ave 'Em*. It was, she felt—as she walked toward Harley Street—the most loving kind of loveless marriage she could have hoped for.

Forty-Two

It was a Sunday when Fasih—Chota Saab—came to visit him. He wore a starched white shalwar kameez; and the sight of him in their courtyard must have alarmed Mussarat, because when she came to call Faraz from the bedroom where he sat in his shalwar and vest, reading, she looked flustered and flapped around the room, looking for a clean kurta for him. Who is it, why the fuss? he said. Because, she said, stopping to look at him, it's your—father's—son. He dressed, trying not to look troubled in front of her as she stood over him and straightened his clothes, touched the back of his head as she did with Nazia on the first day of school, or with his youngest, Jamil, at doctor's appointments, whenever she sensed the children's anxiety.

She had seated Fasih in the small drawing room they rarely used, the curtains drawn. Faraz knew as soon as the man stood that Wajid had died. He had been waiting for the news—he had heard that Wajid had had a stroke some months before—but he had expected, when it happened, to read of it in the paper.

Fasih held out his hand, and Faraz took it. He was struck by the sharp bones of the young man's face. "Sir," he said.

"Please." Fasih waved the courtesy aside. "I'm not sure if you remember me, but I am Wajid Sultan's son. We met some time ago."

They sat but Fasih struggled to continue. Faraz wanted to spare the man, to tell him he knew what he'd come to say, but the young man seemed determined to get through it as if he knew he needed the practice, that he would be required to tell the story again and again. Last night, he said. It was quick—peaceful. It was still shocking to hear it, to think of a man so large and loud in his memory as gone. Faraz searched himself for sadness, for some feeling of any kind, but all he felt was strange, slightly off-kilter.

"I should be at home, really," Fasih said. "As you can imagine, there are crowds and crowds of people coming." He sounded overwhelmed but also proud. "I suppose it could have waited, but my father asked me to do something a while ago, and I thought I would come now and get it done."

"I'm so sorry, sir," said Faraz. "Your father was a very accomplished man. He will be mourned by many."

"How did you know him?" Fasih said, unexpectedly.

They locked eyes. Brother, Faraz thought, trying to attach what he understood of the word to this stranger. "He took an interest in my career. I appreciated the many things he did to help me advance professionally."

Fasih looked dissatisfied but also too worn-out to press him, perhaps nervous, too—what might he find if he prodded? Did he really want to know now? Ever? He sat back in his chair and closed his eyes.

"Is there anything I can do to help, sir?"

Fasih opened his eyes. "Please don't call me that," he said.

Mussarat came in with a tray and two glasses of lemonade. Fasih took the sweaty glass and thanked her, but made no move to drink. Mussarat disappeared into the next room and they sat in silence, the sound of the children at play drifting in from the courtyard.

"Perhaps I shouldn't have come today," said Fasih. "I don't feel so . . ."

"I can see you home."

Fasih waved the offer away and put an envelope down on the table. He gestured to it. "Last year, when my father had his first stroke, he told me that when the time came he wanted me to give you that." Faraz stared at the envelope, a strange dread coming over him. "I looked. I suppose I wasn't supposed to, but I did. They're photographs. I don't know what they mean. Well, that's not true. I just don't know why he wanted you to have them." Fasih stared, waited.

Faraz sat still. He would say nothing; he knew Wajid would have wanted that, and it was the least he could do for him now. "Thank you for bringing this, especially today."

Fasih sat forward as if he were about to say something, then hesitated before he spoke. "I saw my father every day of my life, but I never felt I knew him as well as I might. I kept thinking I would get to know him better, really know him one day, but now . . . maybe that was never going to happen. What can any of us really know of our parents?" Fasih paused. "He did mean well, I know that. He always meant well."

Faraz glanced at the window, listening for the sounds of his children outside. "May I organize a car for you?" he said.

"My driver's outside." Fasih stood, held his hand out again. "The burial is happening at Mominpura shortly." Faraz did not answer, but when he looked down, he saw that they hadn't let go of each other's hands. "Your voice," Fasih said, and he squeezed Faraz's hand. "Your voice." And then he left the room before Faraz could say any more or follow him out.

In the envelope were two photographs. A picture of Wajid from his army days, lined up alongside a group of polished young men in uniforms that looked too big on them all, as if they were children playing at being soldiers. On the back was written *Troop Commanders, the 11th, Cairo, 1942.* The other photo was smaller and folded in quarters, and when he opened it up, he saw it was a woman, a line like a gash across her face where the photo had been folded. He could just make out her dark eyes and dark lips, the long, thick plait that hung down in front. On the back in a wobbly hand was written:

> *Please find my son. Ask Afzal.*
> *Your loving son, Wajid.*

Faraz sat down, winded. He waited, afraid for a moment before he turned the photo back over to look at her. He stared at the picture, scanning every contour of her face, searching for the shape of his own in it, feeling as if his life, which had so often possessed the illusory, fragmented quality of a dream, had in this moment been verified, been made real by this unexpected gift.

Forty-Three

The last time Faraz had sat on a bus had been when he left Jhelum for his first posting. He'd had no idea of what he was heading toward then, and this journey was not much different. He imagined Nazia, who had hardly been beyond Lahore, would want to hear about his trip, so he tried to make note of striking details along the dusty GT Road: the way fields of pretty yellow mustard and bright green sugarcane gave way to fallow land, which seemed at once to miss water and to want nothing to do with it. It was easy to forget, looking at these stretches of lifeless, empty land, that crops would grow here again, but, he reminded himself, they would.

The bus stopped by a small bazaar outside a large town to give travelers a chance to urinate, to buy a cup of tea. He walked around the handful of shops, taking in the dusty packets of cigarettes in the pharmacy, the ancient makeup samples, with the keen eyes of a tourist. He considered buying some kind of gift to take with him, but it seemed ridiculous to do so, almost as ridiculous as his turning up would be. He could explain that on one of his visits to the Mohalla, he'd heard that Irfan and his mother were living somewhere near Gujranwala, that an acquaintance at the station had gotten an address from Izzat Raheem's people. But how to explain *why* he'd come? He got back on the bus.

It had taken almost a year to identify and trace every soldier in the picture Wajid had left him, but as soon as he identified Ghazi Ashraf, the pieces fell into place. Wajid had trusted this man with the secret of Faraz's birth, and this man had trusted Wajid with his secrets in return. The general was on the up, Wajid had said, and his rise had continued. Faraz had watched him being sworn in as governor of the province on television. He was certain of what he believed, but the evidence he had wasn't the kind that could reopen an investigation or convince a judge. Whatever it was that had bound the two men, Wajid hadn't wanted to break it, even in death. But Faraz hadn't been able to rest, to sleep, with the governor's face confronting him every time he turned on the television or opened a newspaper. And so in the end he surprised himself by calling Fasih and asking him for a favor.

⟡

"THEY TOLD ME THE MEETING was with Wajid Sultan's son," Ghazi said. "I thought they meant Fasih." He smiled at Faraz as they stood in the opulent grandeur of his office in Governor House, dark wood paneling on the walls, a heavy, ornate desk between them. "A DSP now. Your father would have been quite pleased . . . exceeding all expectations, I'm sure."

"I wanted to give you this, sir," Faraz said, remembering Inspector Karim's advice: *Be unfailingly polite around the accused if you are unable to beat him.* "My father gave this to me," he said, showing Ghazi a copy of the old photograph. "I thought you might like it."

"Ah, the Eleventh. This takes me back. Quite a lot of trouble to go to for an old photo. You might have mailed it."

"I wanted to give it to you myself, my father would have wanted that." Ghazi looked at him curiously. He thanked Faraz and wished him well. And Faraz left, knowing that the governor would look into the matter, and that in time he would understand what had come to pass: that Wajid had

323

sent his own son to investigate—or rather, *not* to investigate—the murder of little Sonia Begum, but that finally he had as good as confessed all.

He didn't dwell on whether there would be repercussions for him. And he didn't plan to tell Irfan. What was the point, when no justice could come of it? How would the truth help them now? But he wanted to know, to see for himself that life for the family had gone on.

❖

THE SETTLEMENT WAS a few kilometers from Ferozewala village, and there was no easy way to get from Ferozewala to the settlement, especially at that hour, but the bus driver sent word to the main bazaar. It was always good to do a favor for any kind of official, especially one from Lahore, and they had picked up quickly that Faraz was some kind of official. Eventually a farmer with a small Suzuki volunteered.

How do you know them, saab? he'd asked. Relatives of my wife, Faraz had lied. I don't know them well. Neither do we, the farmer said, speaking for all the locals. It seemed the boy was still somewhat suspect. Faraz feared a visit from him might make him more so.

❖

IT WAS LATE by the time the Suzuki buzzed into the hamlet of perhaps only fifteen or so homes. Faraz could smell onions frying and hear the subdued play of tired children. The farmer pointed out the home. He said he had someone to see here and could take Faraz back to the main market in Ferozewala on his return, unless he intended to stay the night. No, Faraz said, he would not be here for long.

The house was small and a little apart from the main cluster of homes; perhaps they knew no other way to live than at the edge of a community. When Faraz approached, he could hear sounds behind the mud walls; a radio playing, a child singing along with it. Then children fighting, a woman intervening. She spoke firmly, and soon the play began again. He heard a man talking to a woman. He could not make out the words, but the woman laughed. The woman called the children to eat, and someone turned up the radio. He wasn't sure what to do—he had thought he would knock on the door, but he could not stand to interrupt them. He could not stand to go there and say: Remember, remember the terrible morning we met, remember that night your sister was killed, remember your years of suffering. He had come for himself, to reassure himself that the boy was all right. He had not been the one to deliver the boy from his fate but he had wanted to know he had been delivered. And now he knew. The boy lived. The boy had survived; he had found a way to endure.

He turned and headed back to the Suzuki. Behind him, he heard the door open. He turned to look. A man stepped out. He took out a cigarette and lit it. He was lean and strong. He caught sight of Faraz and waved instinctively.

"Irfan," Faraz said hesitantly. He felt foolish for coming, foolish for thinking of leaving without seeing anyone, foolish for calling the boy's name. The man took a step toward him, then stopped. "It's me," Faraz said. "Faraz. Inspector Faraz Ali." The old title felt foreign in his mouth after all this time. The man froze, and Faraz felt regret wash over him at the horror that he was revisiting on this boy, this man. But then the man was running toward him, and calling, "Mina, Mina," behind him, loudly, desperately. He took Faraz's hand. "Mina!" he called again, back at the house. He stared at Faraz, breathless. "It's you," he puffed. "It's you."

❖

INSIDE THE HOUSE, the three of them crowded around him: Irfan, Mina, and Mehru, who laid out the story in fragments as Faraz struggled to follow. Firdous. Rozina. Mina.

"Mina," Mehru said, "this is Mina." He looked at the young woman, trying to place her. Two different-colored eyes. The girl he'd met with Irfan years ago. "Rozina," Mina said, touching her chest, "I am Rozina's . . . Heer's . . ." She stopped for a moment, as if considering her words. "I'm her daughter."

He had a sense of things rushing toward him, moving too fast for him to understand. They gave him a seat and tea, and Mina smiled at him. "Are you all right, saab?" Irfan said again and again. He didn't know what to say, what to ask. He looked at the children in the doorway; how was it possible he had found a niece, grand-nephews and -nieces, in just a moment?

Mussarat had asked him once: What if you found them, what if? He had told her that he wanted nothing more, but he was afraid, too. Afraid that they would feel nothing for one another, that they would not recognize anything in one another, that they would not want to see him again, that he would not. That won't happen, Mussarat had said. That's not how such things end, she said. But he knew things ended any which way they wanted. Wasn't what tied you to your family more than blood? Wasn't it history, the memories you shared, the ways in which you'd seen one another change over the years? If there was nothing they shared other than blood, mightn't they find they didn't feel like anything to one another at all? He thought of Wajid then; Wajid, who had seen something of his life. How little it seemed Wajid had felt for him even then.

He stared at Mina, disconsolate that she looked so little like him, feeling more acutely his mother's absence in this. How to make something of this? How to make up for all the time lost, all that time of not knowing one another? How not to waste more of it, as he sat there with nothing to say? She looked uneasy, too. "This is your nana," Mina said to the children. One of them, a girl with eyes just a shade lighter than usual, took a step forward. He looked at all of them; he had expected it might be strange, but not that they would feel like strangers. He was sure now that this was a mistake, that he would never see them again, that he could not do this, that this young woman felt it, too. It overcame him, a terrible wave of grief, like discovering all over again that Firdous was dead. She sat there, the young woman, squinting at him, fiddling with the end of her dupatta, and he wanted to leave, to forget it all.

"I just remembered, I remembered what Amma told me," Mina said suddenly, and she got up. A moment later, she came and sat by him, a plate with an orange in her hands. "Amma said you used to love dipping the pieces in salt and chilis when you were little, just like Fatimah over here." The little girl with the light-colored eyes laughed shyly at being singled out.

"She said that?" he said.

Mina handed him the plate. Go on, she nodded, straightforward, without sentiment, as the little girl joined him to share the pieces her mother had sliced. And just then, as he tasted the sharp tang of the orange, he remembered, for the briefest moment, all the things he thought he'd forgotten: feathers, rooftops, his mother's scent, marigolds, chipped nail polish, and hands reaching for him, ready to save him, ready to do anything for him.

Forty-Four

LAHORE, 7TH NOVEMBER 1968

Sonia watches the spider as it waits perfectly still in its web. Patience. The spider is the master of patience. It soothes her, its calm, its patience. Her foot itches but she decides not to scratch it. Be patient. Like the spider. She concentrates on keeping her body still, and this is hard because she always wants to move. She feels it all the time, like a tremble from deep within that only quiets when she runs, when she leaps across the roofs of the Mohalla. Sometimes it makes her want to yell, to scream, always there is the urge to move. When she does, whatever it is inside her, the thing that makes her want to move, stills. Sometimes the stillness comes when she isn't even thinking about it, like now, when she sees something that interests her: the edge of a leaf, here where there are no trees, the way a cockroach's antennae twitch, the waiting spider. It is this that interests her, a whole world underneath their world that hardly anyone else seems to notice. It has its laws, its ways of working. Its creatures fight and climb and hide from one another, as in her own world. She wishes she were smaller, that she could be part of it. She senses that there is more to see, more to know. She always senses that there is more to know. You have to go to school to learn those things. Mina has been to school, but when she asks her questions, Mina looks bored, and Sonia thinks that maybe even the kids who have been to school don't know much more than she does. When she asks Mina: Why does the sky change color? Or: How does medicine heal you? How should I know? Mina says, irritated. If you didn't learn that at school, what did you learn? Sonia asks. The six times tables, Mina says. The sevens, the eights. What good is that to you? Sonia asks. Mina shrugs: I don't know, no one knows, why do you think I stopped going? All it's good for is making sure the pimps don't steal from you.

So Sonia waits—that is her life, to wait for the day she will start work. She used to wait outside in the Mohalla with the other kids, she used to sit in the courtyard singing songs, playing seven tiles or carrom. But this last year, since she turned eleven, her mother has said she shouldn't be wandering the Mohalla. She is too old for that sort of thing now, for childish games. And what will the boys in the Mohalla think? A girl of her age now, a girl growing as she is, wandering the Mohalla, would rightly be considered fair game; she is not to waste herself on some useless Mohalla boy. It's fine for a girl like Mina, stupid as she is for wanting Irfan, it's her choice to make, her mother says. Thanks to her sister, Mina will never have to work. But she says this more with pity than with envy, as if Mina has lost an opportunity to have any kind of power over her own life. Sonia doesn't tell her mother that she has overheard Mina and Irfan talk about leaving the Mohalla, about going somewhere where no one knows them, about buying land and growing crops, learning to live off the land. Ridiculous, her mother would say if she knew. This is what we do, we have to work with what God has given us. She says nothing when her mother says she needs to spend more time on her dancing, her singing, if she wants to get anywhere in life.

So Sonia doesn't wander anymore; she perches on the balcony watching the Mohalla down below. Sometimes when the Mohalla and her mother are asleep in the early morning, she sneaks downstairs and sits on the steps outside with the cats. The neighborhood cats love her. They circle her, they nuzzle against her, and she lets them, even though her mother has told her they are dirty, that doing so makes her dirty. They know who she is, not by how well she dances or sings, or how pretty she is, or what price her nath will draw, but through the kindness she shows them; around them, she feels the power of her own gentleness, she feels certain of who she is. But these last few days, as her mother and the other women have been getting her ready, she is less sure; they pluck her eyebrows and pull her hair from her body with a sugar mixture. She must sit still as they apply cream bleach to her mustache and pastes on her skin to make her more fair. They are determined to make her into something else, something new. Every now and then, as the day draws closer, she says to her mother: What will it feel like? Her mother says they will give her a medicine so that she won't feel anything, it will be like a dream. She will wake and it will be done. She won't even remember. None of the other women will tell her more, so she asks Mina. Mina says, I don't know what it will be like for you because the man will be old, but it will hurt. All the girls say it hurts. But then it will be done. Sonia wishes she had not asked, because she is no idiot; she knows it will never be done. They show her the new clothes she will wear, they tell her what a beautiful bride she will be for this one night. They tell her she is so precious and special that this man is paying a fortune for her. But she is still afraid.

When Irfan comes to sit with her on the roof, bringing her food because she will not eat, she tells him her plan: I am going to run away. He does not say, You can't or Amma will kill you, or There is too much money at stake. He says, Where could you go? How could we get you out? She doesn't know, she has never even left the Mohalla. That's not true, he says. You have, he says. When? When? She cannot remember, and she is sure she would remember. He tells her the story, and she pictures it and decides his memory must be hers, and so she believes it—a day they left to join the crowds on the Mall, to see a grand motorcade, the rose petals the crowd threw, getting lost, getting found. Yes, I remember a little, she says, as he tells her she reached up to catch the petals when he hoisted her to his hip, that there were petals in her hair. When she says it, she pictures it and it almost feels like a real memory. When we go, he says, Mina and I, we will take you with us, if you want. When will that be? I don't know, he says. But I promise, Sonia. Could you really leave this place? she says. He does not hesitate. Yes, a thousand times, yes. We will be free then of all this, of this chutiya life. What do you say? he says. She looks out across the rooftops. Her life is here in the Mohalla. It is the world she sees from the rooftops and the one she sees when she sits with the cats. Now there will be a new world. She leans over the balcony and looks down. She spots a spider spinning its way up toward them. Look, she tells Irfan, look. He watches with her.

"Spiders," she says, "they eat their webs, I've seen it."

He looks at her. "You notice things," he says; he seems to appreciate this about her, the things she teaches herself, the things she likes to tell him. The way he looks at her makes her feel marvelous, it makes her brave. Yes, she says to him. I say yes. A thousand times, yes. He leaves but she keeps sitting, watching the spider. The web is its home, she thinks, to carry your home everywhere, for your home to live within you, can you imagine that?

ACKNOWLEDGMENTS

This book has been helped along on its journey by many hands, and I am forever indebted to the tremendous talents and skills of the following people.

Deepest thanks to my wonderful agent, Ayesha Pande, who believed in this project when it was just a slip of a story. To my brilliant editors, Rebecca Saletan and Carole Welch; their wisdom and insights have improved this book beyond all my hopes. To Rebecca Saletan for caring for every word in these pages. I'm also very grateful to the teams at Riverhead and Sceptre for working so hard and with such dedication to get this book out into the world.

Thanks to the Faiz Foundation for allowing me to use excerpts from the work of one of Pakistan's greatest poets in this book. Gratitude to Tahira Habib Jalib for granting me permission to also include the words of the brilliant revolutionary poet Habib Jalib. And special thanks to my mother for her renditions of all the Urdu verse in the book; I was beyond lucky to have easy access to such a renowned translator.

My mother (who has read more drafts of this than anyone should read of anything) is also among my generous first readers, who include as well Amanda Schiff and Ash Davidson.

I would not have embarked on this project had it not been for the Iowa Writers' Workshop, which changed the course of my life—or rather, created a course for my life. I thank Lan Samantha Chang, Connie Brothers, Deb West, and Jan Zenisek for giving me a home in their community. I also thank my teachers: ZZ Packer, Julie Orringer, Ethan Canin, Charles D'Ambrosio, and especially Kevin Brockmeier, for his enormous generosity and support all these years. Charles D'Ambrosio helped me find my way with this project in its earliest days, and his crime-writing seminar was life-changing. The friends I made in the program enriched my life with their brilliance and kindness: Ash Davidson, Shabnam Nadiya, Christa Fraser, Andres Carlstein, Hannah Kim, Jill Logan, Debbie Kennedy, and Tom Corcoran.

Thanks also to the Stanford Creative Writing Program, where I completed the first draft of this book. Immense gratitude to the faculty there: Daniel Mason, Adam Johnson, Chang-rae Lee, and Elizabeth Tallent. Particular thanks to Adam Johnson for a crucial, insightful read of an early section, and to Elizabeth Tallent for her mentorship and wisdom. I would still be halfway through a first draft were it not for her insights into a writer's purpose and her guidance on trusting the process. I thank all the Stegner Fellows and especially my smart, thoughtful cohort: Chris Drangle, Ben Hoffman, Onyinye Ihezukwu, and Callan Wink. Huge thanks also to Jennifer Cornish for helping me build a writing routine that saw me over the finish line. Thanks also to Jenn, Onyi, Ben, and Ruchika Tomar for generous support, laughs, and being good company through it all.

A Rona Jaffe Foundation Writers' Award allowed me to come a step closer to completing the book, and I am indebted to the foundation for the encouragement that kept me going.

To the amazing women in my life: Hameeda Chaudhry-Hill, Brigitte Chaudhry (Aunty B), Sevi Lawson, Shireen Jayyusi, Sonya Nathoo, Sara Khan, Aarti Waghela, Bianca Lawson, Laura Watson, Christina Pagel, Christabel Cooper, and Natasha Tariq. It doesn't matter what I make or do, you always show up to support; I treasure you all.

Deep gratitude to all my family in Pakistan and special thanks to my Lahori family and the Durand Road gang, who instilled a love of the city in me. I wish I could have shared this book with Jimmy Chachoo, Lado Khala (Babbar Sher always), and Ayesha Baji, each of whom knew Lahore so well.

Love and tremendous gratitude to the entire Naseer family for their endless prayers and love. Thank you for nurturing and caring for my boys with such boundless love, for supporting my work with incredible enthusiasm and faith over many years. I do believe your duas made this all come true; I am so very lucky to be a part of your family.

To my beloved family. My brothers—the best in the world—I thank for their total belief and support. To Ali for our discussions, for sharing books and research, and for reading the draft with the utmost care. To Omar and Erica for providing me with a place to write when it was most needed, and for sending me to London to work when I felt I was never going to finish the book. And to my parents, whom I cherish. Ammi and Aboo: Where to begin? Thank you for *everything*—for the endless love and support and for cheering on every proposition no matter how ridiculous. Your strength, optimism, and generosity have made all I've ever tried to do possible; I love you beyond words.

Finally, deepest gratitude to my husband, Omar Naseer. Thank you for allowing yourself to be dragged all around the country in the cause of this project; for lending your intelligence, vast knowledge, and best ideas to this book's pages; for being the first person to say I should write a book, creating time and space so that I could, and then staying by my side through all the hard parts. Your love made every word possible, just as it makes everything else worthwhile. I thank God each day for you, Issa, and Mustafa—the dearest blessings in my life.